Dedication

In loving memory of my fathers
Denny Hickey and Bernie O'Brien,
and to the woman who adored them,
Kay Johns Hickey O'Brien,
my "rocks," Sussan, John, Kevin and Chris O'Brien
and to the one who turned my head—Julie.

In prosperity our friends know us;
In adversity we know our friends.
C. Collins, *Aphorisms*

Prologue

5:35 PM
February 26, 1995
West Lafayette, IN

The silence was deafening. It pounded Mike Redding's eardrums, making it difficult for him to think. He had never heard Liberty Arena this quiet. None of his twelve players, his four assistant coaches or the team managers and trainers had made a sound since the show had gone to commercial. Besides Mike Redding, there were twenty-one people sitting in silence on folding chairs at center court watching the big-screen television.

Mike would not permit anyone else to be with his team as they learned their fate, not the media, not the program's most loyal boosters, not the university's president, not even the school's athletic director. Just the immediate basketball family was present. The season had started the previous September when these people made a commitment to Mike Redding and themselves. Mike saw no reason to include others in what they had begun six months before. Since it was his team, his family, only this group watched the NCAA Tournament Selection Show in Liberty Arena.

After nearly two minutes of mindless commercials, Mike was finding it difficult to hold onto the remote. The palm of his right hand, the hand that gripped the remote, was drenched in sweat. Forty-two eyes along with Mike's stared intently at the television screen. When the tournament selection show had disappeared and a montage of images promoting Chevrolet trucks replaced it, Mike had hit the mute button on the remote and the tremendous silence ensued. Now, two minutes after CBS's "Road To The Final Four" logo had left the big screen, the incredible silence was almost unbearable.

When Pat O'Brien's smiling, mustached face reappeared on the television set, Mike hit the mute button again. The sportscaster's crisp, distinctly melodic voice instantaneously filled the cavernous arena, resonating softly from the wood floor up into the rafters high above. At that moment Pat O'Brien was the most important person in Mike Redding's and his players' lives. They stared at the sportscaster, not daring to take their eyes off him for one second. Some of the players prayed inwardly to God, while one or two of them prayed to Pat O'Brien. He possessed the information they craved, the information all of college basketball craved.

Even though his team had already earned a berth in the NCAA tournament, Mike and his players wanted to know—just as every college fan in the country wanted to know—what region his team would play in, what seed they would be and what teams stood in their way of a third consecutive trip to the Final Four tournament. When the NCAA selection committee held its annual tournament selection show and announced the four regional pairings, the regular college basketball season was put to bed and the post-season tournament—the season which determines the national champion—began.

Mike held his breath as Pat O'Brien repeated the names of the top two seeds in the West Region. He desperately wanted a number one seed. It didn't matter to him what regional bracket they were placed in. If his team received a top seed their chances of reaching the Final Four would be significantly improved, because the number one seed would play the bracket's lower caliber teams first.

A huge bulletin board suddenly flashed onto the large screen. The revelation could not have come any sooner. A micro-moment before the tacit tension and ear-splitting silence could drive Mike Redding mad, the name of the team he coached, UNI, appeared on the bulletin board in the slot of the Midwest Region's number one seed.

The noise from the group surrounding him was deafening. It was so loud Mike found it difficult to analyze his team's draw. He tried to focus his thoughts, but the raucous sounds made it nearly impossible to concentrate. Ecstatic shouts of joy pounded his eardrums. He had never heard so few people make so much noise in Liberty Arena. The arduous journey to the NCAA title could not have started any better for Mike Redding and his players.

Chapter One

11:33 PM
March 2, 1995
Washington, D.C.

"I don't take crap from anyone and I'm not gonna start now," the squat, barrel-chested man yelled at the bartender. "I could have this hole-in-the-wall closed by noon tomorrow."

The source of his irritation, a peroxide-blond waitress, eyed him icily as she filled another bowl of pretzels for the table of Georgetown University Law students.

"You couldn't close a door behind your fat ass, let alone close this bar," the waitress replied. "It's been here over thirty years and it'll be here thirty more."

"Was the service this lousy thirty years ago or are you the worst goddamned waitress ever?" he shouted, his face contorted into a half-jeering scowl.

The majority of the patrons scattered throughout Old Glory paid little attention to the irate drunkard, partly because they didn't know how important he was, but mainly because they were used to his obnoxious and slurred tirades. Only the four law students knew the loud, slovenly-dressed patron named Al was actually Allan Clancy, distinguished third term congressman from Indiana. They came to the rundown bar not only to take study breaks from constitutional law and property rights, but also to watch Congressman Clancy's drunken outbursts.

Clancy had been coming to Old Glory every Tuesday and Thursday night for three years. He missed only when Congress was not in session because of the holidays, or when he was campaigning back in Southern Indiana. Everyone inside the loop in Washington knew Clancy had three passions in life: rum, young Hispanic hookers and the environment. He attacked all three with amazing energy and herculean strength. As good as Allan Clancy was at drinking and whoring around, he was without peer when it came to cleaning up the environment. He'd started a neighborhood recycling program when he was fourteen years old, a good ten years before most people knew paper, glass, and cans could be used repeatedly. In high school he'd created a committee that taught schools, businesses and homeowners how to recycle and turned people on to products that were environmentally friendly. During college he held fund-raisers in shopping malls, wrote articles in newspapers, talked on radio stations and got civic leaders involved in his crusade to clean up Indiana University's campus and the city of Bloomington.

In time, Bloomington Mayor William Jennings became aware of the corporate entities lining up to support Allan and the youth working with him. In a shrewd political move, Jennings jumped on Allan Clancy's green bandwagon. He gave the young activist a key to the city, proclaimed June 15, 1976 "Allan Clancy Day" and awarded him a $10,000 municipal fellowship bond to start a waste management company. Allan attended college classes at Indiana University during the day and managed his fledgling business at night. Jennings' decision was a huge success. When Allan finished college and entered law school at Indiana University in Indianapolis, Green Leaf Inc. was netting Allan a profit of $200,000 a year, most of Bloomington's and part of Indianapolis's urban communities had undergone breathtaking environmental revitalizations and Mayor Jennings' popularity was at an all-time high.

All that abruptly changed in 1986 when Allan Clancy, just three years out of law school and with a net worth over one million dollars, announced his desire to run for Bloomington's Eighth District Congressional seat. Just three weeks earlier, Mayor Jennings had stood on the steps of Market Square Arena after watching the high school basketball Final Four along with 17,000 other Hoosiers, and declared his candidacy for that same Eighth District seat. Even with Jennings slinging mud and denouncing Clancy as a traitor, the race was over before it began. Hoosiers love underdogs and rags-to-riches stories, so Allan Clancy was Indiana's newest favorite son. He won in a landslide and headed to Washington eager to take his environmental message nationwide.

Allan Clancy became the brightest young star on Capitol Hill. America loved its handsome, charismatic young congressman who fought powerful oil companies and huge automakers. He sponsored countless bills to clean up cities and protect children, and many of those bills became laws. His cause was noble, his methods were ingenious, and his name was golden. That's why the power brokers in Washington had always looked the other way when it came to his outrageous drinking and womanizing.

Allan Clancy's star had recently dimmed, however. There were few places to take the environmental movement now. After years of crusading on Earth's behalf, Clancy had taken the green movement about as far as it could go. The cause didn't excite people anymore. New topics had captured the public's attention and Clancy himself was losing his appeal. Capitol Hill buzzed with rumors that he had lost millions of dollars in risky business ventures. Sensing the elite leaders of Washington's inner circles were falling out of love with the controversial congressman, the national press had recently started hammering him.

The hard life of drinking had begun to catch up with him, too. The movie star looks had faded, the boyish charm had been replaced by cold cynicism, even the golden name had lost its magnificent sheen. With little money in his campaign war chest and public sentiment swiftly turning against the heavy drinking, tree hugging legislator, Clancy's once brilliant political star was now nearly extinguished. So, Congressman Allan Clancy frequented Old Glory Tuesday and Thursday nights. There he could escape the red-hot glare of the media's spotlight and drink himself happy again.

"The service in this bar is a joke. I can go to the license branch and get waited on faster. I'm tired of this shit. You can bet your sorry ass I won't be in here again," Clancy told the bartender.

The law students strained to keep from laughing as Congressman Clancy shuffled past the out-of-order jukebox. They had heard him issue this same threat numerous times in the last six months. They knew the congressman would be back next Tuesday; his routine was always the same. He usually arrived at Old Glory around 9:00 or 9:15 with three or four drinks under his belt. He drank rum and coke until almost midnight and then he stumbled out the door and walked to Georgetown to find a companion for the night.

Jeremiah Forsey, a second-year student at Georgetown, shifted his feet under the table. He averted his eyes from Congressman Clancy by peeling the label off his beer bottle.

"Hey, guys," he said quietly. "Should I . . .."

"What? What were you gonna say, Jer?" his friend Brett asked.

"Never mind," Jeremiah said a bit too quickly. "It's all good."

"You sure?" Brett asked. "You've been quiet all night, man. What's up?"

"Just drop it, okay?" Jeremiah replied harshly. And then realizing he was calling attention to himself, he added with less edge, "I can't even remember—another brain fart."

Tension hung in the air until one of the law students broke the silence with a joke about Dan Quayle. Jeremiah didn't hear one word of the joke; he was miles away. He wanted to tell his buddies about his encounter with the reporter the day before, but he was afraid they would be critical of his actions. They came to Old Glory to watch Congressman Clancy, not follow him around. But Jeremiah had been so curious about where the congressman went after leaving Old Glory; he couldn't resist the temptation to tail him. The duality of the congressman's personality fascinated Jeremiah, and he found the dark side particularly intriguing. Jeremiah loved juicy gossip, so uncovering dirt on a famous politician was like winning the lottery.

He wondered what Americans would think of their "Environmental Congressman" if they knew he spent Tuesday and Thursday evenings polluting his body with rum and teenage Hispanic prostitutes.

Jeremiah had told no one about following Congressman Clancy to the tiny apartment on M Street—until the day before when the reporter approached him. At first Jeremiah tried to play dumb and act as if he didn't know anything, but when the reporter offered him a thousand dollars for information about where the congressman went after leaving the bar, he couldn't say no.

"If you don't tell me, someone else will. You might as well be the one to get the money," the reporter had told Jeremiah.

As he sat with his friends and watched Clancy struggle to put his trench coat on, Jeremiah did not feel so good about his decision. Something about the reporter bothered him. Why was he willing to pay so much for the information? Jeremiah had never heard of him, and he knew most reporters didn't have an extra thousand dollars lying around to pay informants. The mysterious reporter troubled him, yet Jeremiah forced the concerns out of his head. The semester was almost over. Soon he would be going home for the summer and he would take an extra thousand dollars with him.

Grunting like a cow giving birth, Congressman Clancy pushed open the heavy front door of Old Glory. Stopping in the doorway, he turned to face the bar, and gave the finger to the bleached-blond waitress who stood beside the bartender.

"That finger's all you'll get up tonight," she yelled at him.

"Kiss my Hoosier ass, you ugly, yellow-haired bitch."

Satisfied with his show of contempt, the congressman stepped out the door into the damp, cold Washington night. He crossed the intersection and headed toward Wisconsin, where he was invisible against the backdrop of townhouses and apartment buildings. Even when he was drunk, his mind was razor sharp. He could make the seven minute walk to M Street with his eyes closed and half-asleep.

Directly ahead of the congressman a vagrant sat on the sidewalk curb. Next to him was a grocery cart filled with his belongings. The homeless man paid no attention to Clancy when he approached. Pulling his wallet out, Allan Clancy flipped through a wad of ones and fives before removing his last four twenties. He handed the bills to the man.

"Can you read?" Clancy asked. Both the amount of the hand-out and the question surprised the vagrant.

"Yeah, I can read . . . and spell. So what?"

"Get a hot meal," Clancy said, ignoring the man's sarcastic tone. "And if you really want to use this money the right way, go to a barber shop and get cleaned up. Maybe buy yourself a new shirt and shoes. You can read and think for yourself; you're too smart to be living on the street. The work might suck, but you can make decent money at McDonald's or other places. At least you wouldn't be dependent on anyone else. I hope you get back on your feet, pal."

"Like you care," the vagrant replied, turning his back on Clancy.

As Allan Clancy walked south on Wisconsin, the misty rain soothed his head and neck. He was excited. Edgar had promised him a freebie because he had complained a lot recently. Clancy liked new girls, especially young ones, because he craved variety. The last one had been too old. Edgar had said she was twenty-four, but Clancy knew she was closer to thirty-five. She had been great in bed, but he liked a hooker to have an innocent, schoolgirl look.

Still, something incredible had happened that night with the older prostitute, and it would change his life for good. Clancy frowned as he thought of his beneficent fortune. He hated himself for what he was doing, but he had no choice. The end definitely justified the means. He rationalized his decision by thinking of all the people who would benefit in the long run. He simply had to maintain his seat in Congress regardless of what it took or who he hurt. Tomorrow's meeting was the price he had to pay. Despite the shame and remorse he felt, he knew it was a small price. A very small price indeed, because after the meeting all his problems would be solved and his life would be perfect again. Tomorrow would be the beginning of something great, and all because of that hooker.

Turning west on M Street, Congressman Clancy reached into his coat pocket to make sure he had the index card with the name and information. Whenever he was with a professional, he liked to make it more intimate by greeting her by name and knowing things about her. He loved to make each one feel special, and being attentive and personal always made for more intimacy and eroticism. As he pulled the card from his pocket and read the name on it for the third time that evening, the south wall of Castle Dry Cleaners came to life behind him. The moment he placed the index card in his pocket, a pair of strong, wiry hands grabbed the congressman's shoulders and shoved him face-first into the brick wall.

Before he could open his mouth to shout, the cold, sharp point of a letter opener ripped open the back of his neck two inches above the spinal cord. The attacker placed a second hand on the weapon and shifted his weight behind it. Two powerful hands pushed hard on the letter opener until it cut cleanly through Allan Clancy's throat, its tip becoming embedded in the brick wall. By the time the assailant pulled the steel blade out of his neck, the violent convulsions that shook the congressman's body had ceased. So too had his heart beat and brain waves.

A gloved hand reached into the congressman's coat pockets, first on the left side and then on the right. The left side produced nothing, while the right pocket held two index cards. One card had a date marked in huge red letters, while the other contained barely discernible notes scribbled below the names Carmen Jalomo and Gina Catalino. Next, the stalker reached into the congressman's trousers and grabbed his wallet. Inside was a short letter and a round-trip plane ticket to Indianapolis. The assailant removed the letter and ticket and started to put the wallet back. Suddenly, he remembered to take the congressman's money and credit cards.

After looking in each direction to make sure no one was watching, the stalker stood over Allan Clancy's corpse, let down his zipper and undid his pants. Staring intently at Clancy's blood-stained head, he urinated on the congressman's forehead and face. The mixture of soft rain and warm urine caused steam to emanate from the pink, puffy skin. Starting at the congressman's shoulders and working his way down, the assailant spelled out the letters of his own name until he ran out of urine at Clancy's knees. Dark, crimson blood ran like water from a faucet out of the gaping hole in the neck, and when it hit the puddle of bright yellow urine, Clancy's head lay in a halo of brilliantly colored body fluids. After pulling his zipper up, the stalker took a step back, gathered his considerable strength and kicked the corpse so hard it nearly turned over. A second more powerful and vindictive kick completely flipped the carcass. Allowing himself the indulgence of admiring his work a final time, the assailant gazed at Allan Clancy's corpse before sprinting up Wisconsin. The Environmental Congressman's soiled body was left face-down in the majestic halo, another piece of litter on the city's grimy sidewalks.

Chapter Two

6:45 AM
March 3, 1995
West Lafayette, IN

David Butler jogged in place and checked his wrist watch to monitor his breathing. He had run five miles, but his pulse was only 125 because he was working at an exertion rate of about sixty percent. He looked up the hilly road in front of him, but didn't see or hear anything.

"Where's the boy scout?" Butler muttered. "He's never late."

Mike Redding was usually so punctual, his friends set their watches by him. The odds of his being late for an appointment or workout were about the same as the odds of March weather in Indiana being predictable: slim to none. David Butler's pulse was falling quickly due to the lack of strenuous activity. His normal resting pulse was sixty beats per minute, and within two minutes he would drop to that level if he didn't start running hard again. He pulled his knees higher to his chest, and pumped his arms faster as he continued to run in place at the corner of State Road 43 and Soldiers Home Road. His steady breathing was visible in the cool spring air. West Lafayette was still cold this time of the year, especially early in the morning. The only noise David Butler heard was the gentle whispering of the Wabash River which ran parallel to State Road 43 into West Lafayette, and had once been a vital watering hole for Tecumseh's warriors during the War of 1812.

David Butler couldn't afford to have a poor workout. Anyone attempting a comeback for the 1996 Summer Olympics had to make each training session count. He decided to give his friend two more minutes before leaving him behind. The thought of the '96 Summer Games stirred old memories of his race seven years before in Seoul, South Korea. Butler remembered the emotion he'd felt lining up for the Olympic Final in the 1,500 meter run. Short, stocky and muscular, David Butler did not fit the mold of a cross country runner. He'd been an oddity standing with the other runners at the start/finish line. In grammar school and high school Butler had been a wrestling prodigy. He was the first Indiana schoolboy wrestler to win four consecutive state titles in four different weight classes. He finished his high school career with 154 wins and no losses. The premier wrestling schools in the country recruited him, but he shocked everyone by choosing the University of Northern Indiana (UNI) over perennial national powers Iowa and Penn State.

After gazing up Soldiers Home Road and seeing no sign of his jogging companion, Butler continued running in place while reminiscing about his college years. Because of their close friendship in high school, he and Mike Redding had enrolled at UNI in August of 1978. Within four months David Butler was the top-ranked wrestler in America in the 147 pound weight class. Two weeks later he lay unconscious in a ditch along I-65 south, the victim of a hit-and-run drunk driver. Even though his rapid recovery had shocked everyone, doctors told him the damage to his clavicle, sternum and rotator cuff would prevent him from participating in competitive sports, especially wrestling. So David Butler vented his anger and frustration on his healthy legs. Since running was the only way he could get an adequate workout, it became his obsession.

Mile after mile he ran the winding, wooded paths beside the Wabash River and up the hills of West Lafayette. He soon became an embarrassment to the UNI cross country team members because his workouts doubled theirs in intensity and length. During his sophomore year he reluctantly joined the track team. Expecting running to be boring and monotonous, David Butler had been surprised by the exhilarating rush he felt when he finished third in his first 5,000 meter race. He found running to be every bit as challenging as wrestling, only now his opponent wasn't another athlete, it was a clock.

David Butler had thrown himself wholeheartedly into running, devoting every spare second to his new passion. Three years later he graduated from UNI with a degree in Athletic Training as an All-American runner. By the time the 1988 Summer Olympics were held, Butler's comeback had inspired sports fans across the country. Still, he was viewed more as a human interest story than an actual threat to win a medal in the 1,500 meters. The Kenyan national team boasted three runners who had accounted for five of the ten fastest 1,500 meter times ever. Standing confidently at the starting line that day in Seoul, David Butler believed something extraordinary was about to happen, and it did. He ran the race of his life: the fastest time by an American, and the third fastest time in history. Butler's effort was good enough for the silver medal behind Kenyan Daniel Ngobyi's world record time. Upon receiving his silver medal he announced his retirement from competitive running. After his incredible Olympic performance only one job appealed to David Butler. He turned down numerous endorsement opportunities and immediately began serving as head athletic trainer for his beloved alma mater, UNI.

David Butler was really impatient now. He peered at his watch for the umpteenth time in the last five minutes and looked up Soldiers Home Road for some indication his running partner might be coming.

No way he lives this down. I'll make sure he never hears the end of it, Butler thought as he turned back to State Road 43 and started jogging south toward State Street.

At the top of Soldiers Home Road, a large four-bedroom, three-bath, brick ranch stood among the conservative homes on the winding old road. Inside the huge master bedroom, Mike Redding hit the snooze button on his alarm clock for the third time that

morning. He had flown out of New York at 12:45 AM the night
before and did not get home until 3:30. Everything about the trip
had been enjoyable, from his guest appearance on David Letterman's
talk show to the Eric Clapton concert at Madison Square Garden.

The highlight of Mike's trip was the ceremony honoring him
as Eastman Kodak's Coach of the Year. Ever since he was a sixth
grader at Saint Lawrence Grade School in Indianapolis, he had
dreamed of winning the award. Other kids idolized players like Jerry
West and Walt Frazier, but not Mike Redding. He yearned to draw
up offensive game plans, diagram defenses, and to formulate strategies to beat the Boston Celtics, New York Knicks and the Los Angeles Lakers. He even practiced his acceptance speech in his base-
ment.

". . . and finally I would just like to thank God for allowing
me to coach the game I love, the greatest game in the world, basketball."

The night before he had stood in a packed room at the Plaza
hotel in front of coaches, sportswriters and TV cameras and spoke
those words for the thousandth time in his life. *Giving that speech felt
even better than I imagined*, he thought. *A lot of coaches say that, I just
hope they mean it like I do.*

Mike smiled as he pictured his childhood friend waiting for
him at the bottom of the hill on State Road 43. He was excited David
was contemplating a return to competitive track and field. They had
been running together the past two months and he was impressed
with Butler's conditioning and strength. Mike Redding had jogged
the nine mile course down Soldiers Home Road and up State Road
43 since his undergraduate days at UNI. He would finish his morning workout with a light breakfast at Leahy's Diner on State Street
before going to class. When Mike Redding returned to coach UNI's
basketball team, he built a house on Soldiers Home Road, started
jogging the old course and began stopping at Leahy's after his workouts. His routine was so structured, area residents knew precisely
where he could be found every Monday, Wednesday, Friday and
Sunday mornings from 6:30 to 8:00.

Yawning and stretching like an old, pampered cat, he easily

filled the entire water bed. At six feet, four inches, his tapered, muscular body was easy on the eyes. His face was serious and authoritative. Creases in his forehead and lines under his eyes showed wisdom and character, maybe a hint of pain, beyond his years. Dark, smoky eyes, a rigid jaw line, short, jet-black hair and a prominent nose served to make his face appear even more formal and solemn. At worst, he was handsome; at best he was unforgettable.

As good as things have been the last few years, high school and college were still the best years of my life, Mike thought rolling over onto his back. He remembered the wild, spontaneous road trips he and David Butler had made to see Allan Clancy and Quentin Conway. Suddenly, a depressing thought made Mike Redding's glory years a distant memory. There had been five of them. He and the others had not heard from that fifth high school buddy for so many years Mike had nearly forgotten him.

"Damn it, don't give up that easily," he chastised himself. "We used to be inseparable. After the tourney's over I'll start looking again. And this time I'll find him."

While David Butler jogged south on State Road 43, he glanced at his watch and checked his breathing. His pulse was 188 and rising. Jogging against the traffic on the left side of the road, he calculated the remaining distance to State Street. He had another two miles to run and he wanted his pulse to go above 200. He gritted his teeth and picked up the pace. Behind him less than sixty yards away, an inconspicuous Ford Taurus wound slowly around the curvy, tree-lined road. The blue sedan seemed to feel its way through the bends in the road, as if it were unsure of its destination. Butler wiped his forehead, which was soaked with perspiration. He was now working at an exertion rate of more than ninety percent. Pumping his legs faster he felt a familiar burning sensation developing in his hamstrings and quads. The Taurus moved forward deliberately, some twenty yards behind on the opposite side of the road. David Butler threw a sidelong look over his right shoulder at the sound of the slow-moving vehicle. An experienced runner, he never wore headphones or a walkman so he could hear his body as well as feel it.

The moment he returned his eyes to the road in front of him, the Taurus lashed out in a powerful explosion of speed and rocketed toward David Butler. Hearing the loud hum of the gunned engine, Butler instinctively wheeled around to face the oncoming projectile. The car was fifteen feet behind him and completely across the yellow dividing line when he made his decision. Expecting the automobile to continue its diagonal course across the left side of the road onto the trail where he ran, Butler lunged off the dirt path back toward State Road 43. Seconds later he realized the driver had anticipated the move and swerved expertly back onto the road to intercept him. As surprised as Butler was by the driver's lightning-quick maneuver, that feeling was trivial compared to the shock he felt when he saw the driver's face just before impact. The sound of steel and plastic crushing human bones punctured the chilly spring morning a moment before David Butler was lifted off the ground and slammed head-first against the hood of the Taurus. By the time the mangled, rag-doll body landed in the thick brush growing alongside State Road 43, the blue Taurus had snaked around the next curve and sped out of sight. David Butler's mutilated corpse lay less than ten feet from where Mike Redding should have been jogging.

Chapter Three

Tiptoeing up the second floor stairs, Ben Rooks thought how strange they must look stealing quietly through the school's corridors with huge trash bags slung over their backs. The leader of the group, Quentin Conway, swaggered with confidence and self-assurance. When they reached the second floor landing, Quentin turned, smiled mischievously at Ben and disappeared with Mike Redding down the long hallway toward the second floor janitor's closet. Ben sneaked onto the third floor alone.

Ben had to admit the plan was ingenious. Since their freshman year the five boys had pulled a prank to get out of school the last class day before final exams. He and Quentin were the masterminds behind the schemes. His pranks were devilishly clever, but Quentin's were daring, bold and flagrantly ostentatious. The ultimate gamesman, he was always searching for a new challenge or thrill. Their freshman year they spray-painted the numbers on the padlocks of the upperclassmen's lockers and super-glued the key holes on all the third floor classrooms. The janitorial staff needed the rest of the day to get the lockers and doors cleaned so finals could be taken. The next year they built a four-foot-high brick wall across the freshman floor hall. The scheme initiated their personal battle with Principal James Tarvin. In an attempt to show students and teachers who was in control of Bishop Charing High School, Principal Tarvin suspended the five boys the last three days of the year, which was exactly what they had hoped for. Junior year Mike and Quentin purchased 3,000 crickets from bait stores and unleashed them after Allan Clancy, David Butler and Ben Rooks had lubricated the school's stairwells with fifteen gallons of motor oil. Principal Tarvin suspected them, but couldn't prove anything.

This year Tarvin had vowed the group of friends would not be able to disrupt school or get suspended the last day of classes. It was his personal mission to prevent another prank from taking place. He had set up an around-the-clock watch-team of teachers, parents, and do-good students to guard the school during the month of May. When he arrived early Friday morning and found the school in perfect condition, he believed he had beaten the boys.

Ben laughed nervously as he peered down the deserted third floor hallway and imagined the look on Tarvin's face in fifteen minutes. *Why am I anxious? My job isn't that hard,* he thought. *I set all this up. That's why I'm a part of this group.* The third floor was empty because the senior class was in the gymnasium preparing for the Spring honors banquet. He knew the reason his friends had sent him to this floor—the chances of him screwing up or getting caught were greatly diminished. Ben bristled with anger at the thought.

This was easily Quentin's boldest scheme. Principal Tarvin expected the prank to be carried out at night; he never dreamed they would do it during school hours. Tarvin was supremely confident his month-long watch team would prevent the boys from pulling off another prank. He could not have been more wrong. Exploiting their unconditional faith in him yet again, Ben had used his connections with the guidance counselor and the business manager to steal locker combinations from the administration office. He also devised a near-perfect strategy from information gleaned during conversations with administrators, teachers and students. The scheme would be so disruptive classes would be called off, yet Tarvin would never be able to prove who was behind it. The five seniors planned no physical damage to the school, so they could not be prohibited from graduating. The only part of the prank Ben didn't like was that Quentin would get all the credit for it, while he had been the one who actually planned it and made it happen. *Nothing new there*, Ben thought ruefully. *I do all the grunt work and one of them gets the glory.*

A sharp pang of jealousy raced through Ben as he thought of his four best friends. One was an all-state athlete, another the school's valedictorian, and they didn't even stand out in the group. The other two were immensely intelligent, incredibly charming, athletically gifted and devastatingly good-looking. They were everything he was not, and Ben marveled that they included him in their circle.

Ben checked his watch and readied himself for the mad dash about to take place. Two boys on both the first and second floors, and Ben Rooks on the third floor synchronized their watches and waited. At precisely 8:25 AM, each boy attacked a locker. They quietly opened the lockers by matching the locker number to the combination on their cheat sheet, pulled a wind-up alarm clock preset for 8:45 from their trash bag, and deposited the clock on the bottom shelf of the locker. By 8:33 the four boys were finished with their fifteen lockers on the first and second floors, while Ben struggled with the lock on his thirteenth locker. Suddenly, Mike and Quentin appeared. After snatching Ben's bag out of his hands, they deftly opened the remaining lockers and placed the alarm clocks inside. Inwardly, Ben Rooks seethed with anger.

As they ran out to the parking lot, Ben silently cursed his friends for assisting him. Once again they had made him look like an inept moron. Ten minutes later Mike was driving north on I-65 when Principal Tarvin's morning announcements were rudely interrupted by thunderous ringing throughout the school. At 8:59 Tarvin conceded defeat when he discovered the padlocks on all seventy-five lockers had been switched to other lockers.

An hour and twenty minutes later the boys reached the home of Mike Redding's grandparents on Lake Freeman, one of the smallest man-made lakes in the Midwest.

They spent the rest of the day water skiing, tubing and lying in the sun. After dinner the five boys walked down to a boat dock that looked out over the lake's dark, shimmering water. Under a moon-lit sky they relived the highlights of the last four years of their lives. Sitting on the dock wrapped in a heavy Navajo quilt, Ben Rooks did not participate in the lively conversation. His high school years were far less memorable than those of his friends, and his future was not nearly as bright as theirs. Unlike the others who knew what fields they would conquer, Ben would have been happy to simply find an industry he could survive in. At the end of the summer the boys would be splitting up, going off to college, and embarking on separate journeys. While his friends faced the unknown full of confidence, passion and optimism, Ben was more unsure of himself than ever before.

Just before midnight Mike Redding toasted the group's friendship, and Quentin Conway issued a challenge to his friends. Within twenty years they must all have a million dollars, be famous in their field of work and succeed big-time—be somebody of note.

Standing on a bridge forty-five feet above the water of Lake Freeman, the five boys prepared to seal the pact by jumping into the lake together. Each boy had unique thoughts running through his head. One visualized a life of politics and public service, while another dreamed of competing athletically at the world-class level. The two boys in the middle, Mike Redding and Quentin Conway, linked hands and envisioned futures of professional achievement, personal fulfillment and tremendous wealth.

At the far end of the group, Ben Rooks was trying to conceal his fear and anxiety. *These challenges are stupid,* he thought. *Why do we have to constantly prove ourselves to each other?* Once again, Ben found himself lacking miserably in comparison to his buddies. Seconds later his trance was broken when Mike grasped his right hand. The next instant he sensed cool air rushing past him and empty space beneath his feet. When the five boys plunged toward the expansive, black abyss, Ben closed his eyes and screamed as the dark, cloudy water rose up to meet them.

Chapter Four

4:10 PM
December 22, 1979
Chicago, IL

The room was so dark he couldn't find the aluminum foil. He groped under his legs and then behind his back. Sitting on the floor, propped up against the wall, the well-dressed stranger examined what appeared to be a hole in the floor board below him. He wasn't sure if it was a hole or just a stain on the wood so he ran his hand over the board. When his index finger caught a jagged edge, he abruptly yanked his hand away. Bringing his hand up close to his face, he checked for the splinter.

The out-of-place stranger had been there for two days and had not eaten at all. He slept when he could, relieved himself twice a day and spent most of his time negotiating and bartering. No one else had to negotiate, but he had to because he wasn't welcome there. The tenants in the apartment didn't like him because his skin was white. But since green, the color of his money, was more important than black or white, he was allowed in. He was in a foul mood because he had to leave soon. Christmas was a few days away and his family expected him to be home for the holidays. He didn't like to waste time looking for aluminum foil, but it was necessary. As he probed his left index finger, the stranger realized his hands were so numb from the cold he could barely feel the splinter, or anything else for that matter. Even though his buzz was fading, he refused to panic. He was an expert at holding onto a buzz.

Squinting across the barren room, the clean-cut stranger saw two other people. A homeless bum lay in the far corner, covered by the Sunday editions of *The Chicago Sun Times* and *The Chicago Tribune*. A funny thought came into his mind as he looked out the doorway into the hall of the apartment building. He knew the circulation totals of both newspapers and read Mike Royko's column a couple times a week. His dad got him started on Royko when he was thirteen. Sifting through the trash in an abandoned apartment building in Cabrini Green, reading Mike Royko with his father seemed like a memory from someone else's life. He heard yelling down the hallway, but didn't bother to look in that direction. Without provocation, the bum in the corner wearing the newspaper mumbled something.

"What do you want, old man?" he asked the bum impatiently.

Bombed out of his mind on drugs and liquor and barely able to sit up, the bum tripped over his slurred words. "Sa, sa, sa, say man. You got, you got some smack?"

"Shut up and leave me alone," the stranger said, annoyed by the interruption.

"Don't freak, man. Don't freak. All I wan . . . , all I wan is some sugar. Gimme a 'lil juice, man. I know you got some horse. I jus wanna take me a ride. Beam me up Scottie and I'll never ask again. Cool?"

"No, it's not cool. Just shut up and leave me alone. I don't want to talk to you or share my dope with you. I'm not here to make friends, you old fuck. I'm here to get away. You and I are nothing alike. You're hooked on this crap. I just do it because it feels good. End of story. I ain't giving you shit, you got that? Now shut up and don't bother me again."

As he turned away from the bum, the stranger caught a glimpse of a young mother of three trading sex for heroin in the next room. "You people are pathetic," he called out to everybody within earshot of him. "Really fuckin' pathetic."

The outsider had convinced himself he didn't have a problem. He didn't have to get high. Drugs were just a way to relax and escape reality. He didn't hurt anybody or owe anyone—he just loved the way he felt when he was high. The stranger pulled his legs up to his chest and put his hands in his pants to keep them warm. Hearing a scrunching noise, he felt under his butt.

"Aahh, there's my good friend Mr. Reynolds," he said to no one in particular.

Grabbing the aluminum wrap from under himself, he stuffed it into the blackened tennis can and grinned wickedly. The tennis can was a long way from the ritzy country club it had come from. The noise down the hallway had grown louder. Aubrey, an enormous black man who was the proprietor of the run-down house, was yelling at the tenants about paying rent to party there. Ignoring the commotion, the stranger reached into a hidden pocket in his expensive parka, removed two plastic zip-lock bags and set them on his lap.

With his thumb and forefinger he extracted hash from the first bag and carefully placed it in a hole that had been cut into the side of the tennis can. The aluminum foil formed a small bowl at the bottom of the can and held the hash in place. As he raised the top of the tennis can to his mouth and slid his frozen thumb over the lighter, angry voices spilled down the hall toward him. Blocking out the disruptive noises, he inhaled generously, held the smoke in his lungs until the burning became intolerable and then slowly exhaled. This procedure was repeated for the next ten minutes. When he had finished the hash, the stranger reached into the other bag and took out a small, white nugget. He placed the heroin in the pipe and lit the white candy, careful not to light the aluminum foil on fire. Once he had set his hand on fire when he had carelessly lit the foil.

By the time the man had smoked the second heroin nugget, he was flying so high he barely recognized Aubrey standing over him. Even with his faculties fried, he sensed something was wrong. Aubrey was screaming and gesturing wildly. Partially illuminated in light from the hall, two people stood in the doorway behind Aubrey. As he put the last piece of heroin in the tennis can, the stranger wondered who they were and why Aubrey was so agitated. A weird feeling came over him; he sensed everyone was watching. A small voice in the back of his head told him there was something unusual about the two people—they weren't smoking anything. He was too stoned to see who they were, but guessed they were women because he was becoming sexually aroused. An odd feeling of deja vu came over him as he sat against the wall and inhaled the last of his drugs. Trapped in a drug-induced fog, the man wondered why he was being so paranoid about Aubrey and the visitors.

As the individuals in the doorway called Aubrey over to them, orgasmic waves of pleasure raced through his nervous system, and he closed his eyes and started to climb toward nirvana. In the distance he heard Aubrey yelling again about paying rent to party in the building. He felt people standing over him, but with the intoxicating rush overwhelming him, he had neither the strength nor the desire to open his eyes. His final conscious thought before passing out was that he should join the conversation Aubrey and the visitors were having or harm would be done to him. The well-dressed stranger awoke one hour later with a flashlight in his face and handcuffs on his wrists. As he was led out of the apartment building, he saw the homeless bum and several other junkies and prostitutes being released by the police. After Miranda Rights were read to him, he was thrown in the back of a police cruiser. Aubrey and the two visitors were nowhere in sight.

Chapter Five

11:48 PM
March 5, 1995
Sky Harbor International Airport
Phoenix, AZ

Diana Fleming was both frightened and excited to finally meet him. "I wish it was under better circumstances," she confided to the junior flight attendant as she poured a glass of ice water. She had been serving the pilot and first officer for over three hours and desperately wanted to wait on the famous man. Now she was about to get her chance at the least opportune time. Diana had been in the cockpit listening to stories about their celebrity passenger when the pilot had been instructed by the air traffic tower to hold their flight pattern at the city's outer marker for an indefinite period of time. In essence, they had been told to circle Phoenix until further notice was given. The job of serving Quentin Conway refreshments had then been dumped in Diana's lap.

"That's just like Sharon to make me wait on him right after he found out," Diana complained.

"What does Sharon have against you?" the young attendant asked curiously.

"I'm not sure, but it must be big. He's probably ticked off the landing's delayed and since he can't yell at the controllers, a flight attendant will make a great scapegoat," Diana said bitterly.

In the past six months there had been a bit of friction between her and Sharon West, but Diana knew this was a blatant attempt by the head flight attendant to make things difficult for her. As Diana dropped extra ice cubes into the glass and prepared a tray of cold cuts, she repeated Captain Roger Hennessey's description of Quentin Conway to the attendant.

"Ninety-five percent of Quentin Conway is pure gold. He's the most generous, big-hearted and affectionate person you'll ever meet. The other five percent is what you need to guard against Captain Hennessey says, and he seems to know. That part of him is relentless. He's so instinctive and aggressive. No one closes a deal as well as he does. Quentin Conway sees right through people. He always finds their weaknesses and is unremorseful in exploiting them. His instincts have made him a billion dollars and earned everyone's respect, yet he never forgets who has helped him or hurt him. No matter how large or small the act is, he always repays people according to how they treated him. And he does it in a big way."

Diana shuddered as she placed a travel size bag of chocolate chip cookies onto the tray.

"He seems like a vindictive monster, repaying those who cross him and seeking retribution, yet everyone speaks glowingly of the countless charities he sponsors and the good deeds he's performed for less fortunate people.

"I don't understand this guy," Diana continued. "He's got two sides that are completely opposite. How can one person have such different personalities? He's supposed to be this wonderful person most of the time, but he can also be the cruelest person anyone's seen. Everything about him is unconventional. He's got a trillion dollars, right? But he acts like a teenager without a care in the world. It doesn't make any sense."

"It makes sense to me," the junior attendant replied. "He's living exactly the way a person with a ton of money should live. He has more fun than anyone else, and he seems completely happy. People are always saying their childhood years were their best years, and this guy is thirty-something, acts like a kid and still feels good about himself. Maybe he knows what the rest of us don't, and he's enjoying life more because of it."

"Wow, that's deep," Diana said impressed with the young attendant's assessment. "You might be right. Maybe he's living life on his own terms and isn't about to apologize for it."

Diana wanted to ask the attendant her feelings about Quentin Conway's dark side, but the question would have to wait. She had put off serving him long enough and he didn't strike her as the type of man who was used to being put on hold.

He seemed to notice her before she approached him. Quentin Conway was reading a thesis paper titled "The Practical Applications of Solar Energy for Fuel" when she came to his seat. She realized he was looking at her calves and waist. Quentin put down the paper and addressed her as if they were old friends. "A doctoral student from Rose-Hulman Institute of Technology recently set a new land-speed record for a solar-powered vehicle and I'm trying to decide whether to offer him a job."

Ignoring his comment, she smiled and came close to him.

"Here is your appetizer, Mr. Conway."

The word appetizer was said with as much contempt in her voice as there was courtesy in her smile. Part of her wanted to believe he was a spoiled, arrogant plutocrat.

Besides being armed with a clever mind and a quick, sarcastic wit, Diana Fleming possessed unbelievable natural beauty that could not be restrained by her conservative Delta Airlines uniform. The tiny, sly smirk that turned up the corners of her mouth should tell him she was not a fan of his.

Quentin seemed to catch the invisible smirk. "If I didn't know better, I'd say you were mocking me with that little smile," he said inquisitively.

Diana's mouth dropped open for a split second. Completely flustered, she scrambled to regain her composure. "Of course not, Mr. Conway. I can't mock someone I don't know."

Her response seemed to amuse Quentin. Diana Fleming was breathtaking. She had an innocent, angelic face highlighted by large, rich brown eyes. A beguiling smile ran the entire width of her face. Her skin was smooth as porcelain, yet lightly covered with golden-blond baby hair that resembled the cotton-soft look of fine cat fur. The face was perfect, flawless, except for the nose. The nose was not unusually large, but appeared to be because the nostrils were so small.

Surrounding this distinctive face was long, thick, honey-colored hair that rolled over her shoulders and fell majestically down her back. The large nose fit the exotic face, its character and strength somehow offsetting the beauty of the face and hair. He leaned towards her casually. She thought he might reach out and touch the baby-fine hair that caressed her cheeks.

"You don't necessarily have to know someone, just things about them to mock them," he said.

"What could I possibly know about you?" Diana asked, feigning her most naive facial expression.

"Well, first of all you know I either have money or am important because I chartered this plane and hired a crew of pilots and attendants who are trying so hard to please me. That's obvious, so I'm sure you got that." His tone was somewhat sarcastic and condescending. Diana was both embarrassed and angry by the way he addressed her, but he either did not see her reaction or was indifferent to it because he continued speaking without pausing.

"You know I like junk food because I specifically asked for it. I'm sure you've noticed I love to drink water, and that I look like someone who tries to stay in shape. I'm tan which means I'm vain enough to want to look good even if it is harmful to me. All of this probably suggests a lifestyle that is healthy yet superficial. This isn't a lot of information, but it's enough to make me look like I'm one huge contradiction. I think it's safe to say it would be rather easy to mock someone with these characteristics. Wouldn't you agree?"

Diana was speechless. Had he read her mind?

"I'm sorry, Mr. Conway. I don't know what to say. I did hear that you were a complicated person with two different sides to your personality. I wasn't sure which side I would get, so I prepared for the worst. It made me feel a little more secure about myself to make fun of you and dismiss you as an eccentric megalomaniac. I certainly didn't mean to show you so little respect and I apologize for that."

When Diana finished apologizing, it was Quentin's turn to be rendered speechless. He looked at her with new found respect. She had apparently shown him that beauty and class can coexist with honesty.

She studied him closely. He sat comfortably on the airplane sofa as if he were at home watching the evening news. Tall, lean and tapered, he possessed the God-given physique of an athlete. His skin was brown from thousands of hours in the sun, but few wrinkles could be found in the milky smooth complexion. There was no excess fat anywhere on his body; the bronzed skin appeared to be stretched tight over a long, sinewy frame. His hair was sandy brown with numerous strands of gray that made him look young and boyish, yet older and distinguished at the same time. A recently grown goatee was also sandy brown; the gray sprinkles had been subtly colored. Although bushier than most goatees, it was wickedly stylish and made his face that much more intriguing. Quentin Conway's face was dangerous. Innocent and friendly, it was the face of a choir-boy. His smile was bright and came often. It lit up the handsome face, yet was in marked contrast to his eyes.

The eyes were the heart and soul of Quentin Conway's face. They were a mirage of different colors: slightly green, partly blue and a shade of soft gray. Mixed with these colors were brown and yellow speckles that highlighted the blackness of the pupil. Drawing even more attention to these mysterious eyes were thick, dark eyebrows that served as a magnet to pull people in. Quentin Conway's eyes spoke volumes about his appearance and his character. He was at once incredibly attractive and soft, menacingly frightening and cold, powerful and sexy, yet dark and ominous. Diana Fleming peered into these hungry eyes and saw a contradiction she did not understand.

"Now that I've managed to be rude and embarrass myself, why don't you give me your version of what Quentin Conway is really like. How'd you start your career?"

As the huge commercial aircraft circled Phoenix's city limits, the fourth wealthiest man in America shared his amazing odyssey with Diana.

"I made money the old-fashioned way. I did old things new

ways. From the time I was six years old, I saved every dollar I got from birthdays, Christmases and graduations. In high school I tried my hand at entrepreneurship by starting a lawn-care business. I went door-to-door to find clients and paid other guys in the neighborhood a small percentage of the profits to cut the grass. After realizing I could make more money by getting people to work for me, I held car washes in church parking lots and worked on my tan while others cleaned the cars. I've never lost it. I'm very proud of my twenty year tan."

Noticing his casual, self-deprecating tone, Diana posed a question she had wanted to ask earlier. "You poke fun at yourself and are so matter of fact about things. Do you care at all what people think of you?"

"Sometimes sure. I'm human like everyone else. But I already know what the people I really care about think of me and that's all that matters. If I feel good about myself and my loved ones do too, I could care less for the most part what others think. I am what I am. I don't want to give you the impression I'm anti-social though. My first big moneymaking idea in college actually stemmed from worrying what others thought about me. I was at Saint Thomas, a tiny, parochial college in Rensselaer."

"Between Lafayette and Merrillville?"

"Exactly. It's roughly ninety miles southeast of Chicago. I was there on a basketball scholarship. I tore my knee up in practice freshman year and had to have reconstructive surgery done to repair blown ligaments and cartilage. I waited a day and a half after the surgery for a continuous passive motion machine to be delivered from a supply company in Chicago. The pain was indescribable and my attitude toward the nurses was worse. There was this one night nurse I liked. She was amazing. I still know her name—Heather. She wouldn't go out with me because she thought I was too arrogant. At the time it crushed me. It worked out great though because I realized doctors didn't like waiting on these machines and supply companies were slow delivering them. I decided right there in my hospital bed to buy two CPM machines and lease them to doctors."

"You decided on the spot that fast?" Diana asked, respect in her voice.

"That fast," Quentin repeated, apparently relishing the effect the story was having on her. "I spent the next five months working every job I could find and exhausted my life savings to buy the machines, which cost $7,000 apiece. Plus I had to get hazard insurance to protect myself from malpractice lawsuits. To this day I can't believe I came up with the money. My friends still don't know how I did it—they're convinced I robbed a bank or liquor store."

Diana saw the playful glint in Quentin's eyes and laughed out loud with him. Obviously he enjoyed telling the story and seemed to be reliving the experiences right before her eyes.

"How I came up with the money wasn't the important thing, what I did with it was. My service helped all three corners of the iron triangle: physicians, insurance carriers and patients. I traveled to local hospitals, strapped the patient's leg in the machine, and came back two or three days later to retrieve it. A typical knee reconstruction required two days' use of a CPM machine after the surgery. Patients were billed $200-$300 for the machine. My compensation was 80% of the bill. Since I delivered the machines faster than the supply companies, my business took off right away. After the first year, I'd made a profit of $21,000, bought a third machine, and hired a courier to deliver and pick up machines. I knew rising health care costs and the increased number of sports injuries would make my CPM machines more profitable so I concentrated on finding another income-generating project.

"My next idea came while listening to a classmate give a presentation on franchises and chain restaurants. I took a two week accelerated real estate class the summer before my junior year. I didn't look to sell any houses, though. I spent all my free time researching buying patterns, studying demographics and learning where new construction homes were being built. Directly north of Indy in Hamilton County, a small, rural town called Carmel was in the infancy stage of expansion. I pored over maps to learn about traffic and accessibility routes, checked the differences in property taxes between Indy and Hamilton County and spent hours driving the countryside surveying the soil and topography. Due to escalating violence in downtown Indianapolis and emerging strip malls, I gambled on people flocking from the city to the suburbs. I was sure not only families would relocate to escape high taxes and excessive crime and pollution—corporations and businesses would too.

"I busted my ass for the next ten months to find the perfect parcel of land and raise the money to buy it. Same as before, I put up my life savings, this time to buy fifty-eight acres of dung-infested farm land. I knew I was either going to be one happy millionaire or an extremely disgruntled fertilizer magnate."

Having picked up momentum the last two minutes, Quentin barely slowed his soliloquy when Diana broke into laughter.

"While my CPM machines were bringing in around $50,000 a year, I hit the books and the kegs as hard as I could. A year and a half later when I graduated, I hadn't sold one house, but my land in Carmel was worth twice what I paid for it. My first twenty months out of school, I sold real estate like a madman. I didn't always know what I was doing, but nobody worked harder than I did."

"And longer," Diana interjected.

"I worked with clients from all over Indiana, but always steered them in one direction. It didn't take long before I was *the* Carmel real estate specialist. It was incredible, Diana. All I did was market myself as the area expert and the phone rang off the hook. As the population in Carmel exploded, so did my income. At this point my combined yearly income from the CPM machines, real estate and other ventures was about $350,000. I forced myself to be patient because the time to sell wasn't right yet. I wasn't trying to get on base. I wanted a home run.

"After two more years of selling over a hundred homes a year, I finally got the call I'd been waiting for. I quit selling real estate that day and began negotiating the sale of my manure patch, as I affectionately called it. Farm houses and corn silos didn't surround it anymore. There was a Walmart and a Sam's Club, a Bank One branch, a golf course and four hundred unit housing addition, and an office complex. Sitting smack dab in the middle of all this big business was my fifty-eight acre pot of gold. Now, I call it my golden manure egg. Putting the transaction together was complicated because of zoning variances and land-use regulations, but when the smoke cleared after nine months of negotiating, a medical manufacturing company from Chicago outbid Subaru-Isuzu. They got fifty-eight acres of prime manure patches, and I had $19.2 million dollars."

The rest of the story practically told itself. Quentin was more of a willing passenger than a conscious storyteller as the rags-to-riches tale flew from his mouth.

From that point on, everything he touched made money. He invested in a fledgling ten-minute oil-change operation and soon McQuik's Oil Lube was making Quentin millions of dollars. He started a home health care agency where physical therapists, occupational therapists and nurses treated homebound patients in their homes. With the emphasis in health care changing from inpatient hospital care to outpatient treatment, his home care agencies were a huge success so he franchised them regionally and then nationally. By age twenty-eight, Quentin had bought sizable blocks of Microsoft stock, and added chain restaurants, office supply warehouses, express car washes and video stores to his portfolio of investments. His net worth was over a billion dollars before he was thirty years old and in 1994, when he turned thirty-five, his vast business empire stretching across twenty-one countries on five continents, was valued at six billion dollars.

Diana sat mesmerized as Quentin finished describing his meteoric rise to fortune and fame. She seemed enthralled by his story, so engrossed she failed to notice the plane had stopped circling the city and had started its descent. There was a knock on the cabin door just as Diana appeared ready to ask him a question.

"Come in," Quentin said, not pleased by the interruption. William Dodd, Quentin's administrative assistant and public relations spokesman, looked past Diana and addressed him hesitantly.

"Quentin, I just found out why we're delayed. It's very important." His voice was strained; a hint of distress showed on his face. From his tone Quentin knew the assistant wanted to speak in private.

Quentin's attention shifted from Diana to him. "You can tell me now. What is it?" he asked.

The solemn look on William Dodd's face scared Diana. With obvious trepidation, the PR man spoke. "The FBI ordered the delay. Allan was found dead in Washington D.C. today. He was murdered sometime last night. This morning Indiana state troopers found David's body beside the Wabash River. At the very least it was a hit and run. The FBI has been assigned to Allan's case and they're also handling David's investigation. They're treating Butler's death as a murder. When we touch down two agents will be waiting for you. They'll guard you twenty-four hours a day. Mike will get the same protection. This could be group-related, Quentin. The deputy director of the FBI believes Mike's in grave danger and you might be, too."

Chapter Six

As he sat in his rocking chair he thought back to the day he learned how to master the headaches. Thinking about that day gave him a slight sexual thrill. He liked to rock because it helped ease the pain of the headaches and made him feel secure. Rocking gave him power over the headaches, and allowed him to control his mind and body. He craved control. He was alone that day as usual, sitting at the breakfast table, when the pain from a migraine headache became unbearable. The pressure on his forehead and temples was so intense he felt his head was trapped in a vise and would soon explode.

Compounding the pain in his temples were the bright white bolts of lightning that shot across his eyes. They appeared only when his eyes were closed, but with the vise tightening its grip on his cranium it was impossible to keep his eyes open, so the lightning bolts came often. While he fought the demons that terrorized his head, the rest of his body writhed in misery. During this agonizing attack, he realized the motion of his body rocking back and forth created a soothing sensation that eased his pain. Once he discovered rocking made the migraines subside, he rocked religiously whenever he could. Not only did it alleviate the pain when the headaches came, it reminded him he could master anything, and that made him feel powerful. Since then he had rocked every day for seven years.

Reaching over to the coffee table beside his rocking chair, he picked up the newspaper and spread it out over his lap. He focused on the headline emblazoned across the front page: *Congressman Allan Clancy Murdered By Unknown Assailant.* He looked at the picture accompanying the article, and rocked faster as the headache moved up his skull and worked its way toward his forehead. Because of his growing discomfort, he was not able to read again the obituary which described Allan Clancy as one of Capitol Hill's most respected and distinguished lawmakers.

"Clancy was no saint," the man yelled. "He drank himself stupid and wasted everything he had. What's so distinguished about that?" As the headache approached its zenith, his forehead swelled, his temples bulged and his eyes burnt with pain.

"He ruined himself and his life. He wanted to die," the man screamed through the torrent of pain and light.

Just when he thought his head would burst open, the familiar soothing sensation created by the rocking motion started to take hold of him. His breathing slowed, the bright lights disappeared, and the vise released its deadly grip on his cranium. For a moment, he felt a tremendous surge of sadness and empathy, and wished Allan Clancy had received a different fate.

There's no time for sympathy, he reminded himself. *I can't pity them. I must stay in control and move on.*

Drawing himself out of the rocking chair, he carried the newspaper across the living room into a sparsely decorated bedroom. In a corner of the spartan room, underneath a huge bulletin board was a brown card table and one folding chair. He pulled out the chair and sat down. Beside the card table was a gray file cabinet. He took a key from his pocket and unlocked the top drawer of the cabinet. After pulling a large brown scrapbook from the drawer, he opened it and set it on the table.

The first picture was a newspaper clipping of an embarrassed teenager accepting a plaque from an older man. The subsequent pages contained photographs, clippings and press releases from newspapers and magazines. The scrapbook was a shrine to one person:

Allan Clancy. Next, he removed a pair of scissors from the bottom drawer of the file cabinet and cut out the article and picture from the front page of the newspaper. Grabbing tape from the file cabinet, he taped the article and picture of the slain congressman to the last page of the scrapbook.

As he rocked methodically in the hard folding chair, he put a pair of latex gloves on his hands and pulled a manila envelope from the file cabinet. Three hours of cutting and shaving magazines provided him an assortment of letters to work with. Every letter he needed had been cut out twice in case he made a mistake, even though he knew he wouldn't make a mistake. He held the envelope upside down. Tiny, multi-colored letters spilled out onto the table. For the next hour he painstakingly pasted the letters onto a sheet of white typing paper. When he finished typing the address on the outside of the envelope he picked up the nondescript white paper and read the message.

This is your warning. More deaths to follow. Take special caution. I feel you're next.

With warmest regards,
Your Shadow

He laughed at the little joke in the letter; an eerie, hollow laugh that bounced off the ceiling and walls and reverberated throughout the room. *That should do the trick,* he thought to himself, confident the letter would instill a sufficient amount of fear and paranoia.

The tension in his head was starting to build again. The events of the last few days had exhausted him, but he didn't want to sleep. Lately, he had been plagued by terrible dreams. The dreams were memories from his past. They troubled him because he couldn't figure out why he was having them. The flashbacks were so unsettling, he dreaded sleeping. He wanted desperately to control them, but so far he had not found a way to do so.

Before he could return to his rocking chair there was one final task he had to complete. After placing a long strip of white masking tape across the middle of the scrapbook, he wrote Allan Clancy's name on it in bold black print. Finally, he opened the top drawer of the file cabinet and put the scrapbook on top of a blue photo album that had David Butler's name written on it. After closing the drawer and locking the cabinet, he set the letter on the table. In the morning it would be mailed to Quentin Conway.

Chapter Seven

He bit so hard on the whistle when he blew it, he tasted silver in his mouth. "No, Byron, that's not the shot we want," he said walking toward the free throw line where nine players gulped down large amounts of air. Tired as they were, they all knew not to bend over while they sucked in oxygen. Their coach did not permit it, and none of the players wanted to incur his wrath. The tenth player stood alone at the top of the key waiting for the coach to address him. As Mike Redding approached his star sophomore, he observed his players' facial expressions and their body language. *They're exhausted,* he thought. *They're sick and tired of practicing because I've been riding them so hard. The best way to get my point across is to do what they least expect.*

Mike Redding practiced his players harder than other coaches did. He was a staunch believer that championships were won through hard work day after day in practice. Most coaches did not work their players strenuously before the NCAA tournament. Some feared injuries in practice while others tried to minimize the wear and tear on players which occurs during the grind of a thirty game season that lasts more than five months. Mike Redding was different from other coaches, though. He worked his players arduously at the end of the year so they would be sharper than their opponents.

This year he practiced his team even harder than usual. UNI had been to the NCAA Final Four tournament two consecutive times, and three of the last four years, but each time had failed to win the national championship. In past years sportswriters and basketball journalists had been unforgiving in their criticism of Mike and his teams. The deaths of Allan Clancy and David Butler only made things worse. The media was going crazy over the story. Two of Mike Redding's life-long friends, one a famous congressman, the other the athletic trainer for UNI's basketball team, viciously murdered days before UNI was to begin its drive toward a national championship. A *People* magazine cover photo of the group was beginning to pop up on newspapers and magazines everywhere. Reputable periodicals sported sensationalistic titles such as: *Hoosier Hysteria In The Heartland, Indiana Icons Murdered, Indiana's Wonder Group Cut In Half,* and by far the most popular, *March Madness Murders.* The story was a godsend for the media, a nightmare for Mike and his players.

The national press had taken over the UNI campus. They camped out daily around the basketball stadium, and followed Mike Redding home at night. Even though he refused to speak to the media, reporters followed him everywhere and recorded every move he made. He tried to suppress the pain and sadness he felt over the loss of his friends so he could prepare his team for the NCAA tournament, but while he had hidden his emotions from the press and the outside world, his players had not escaped unscathed. He had been an unrelenting tyrant all week. His infamous temper seemed to explode every twenty minutes, and the team's morale was beginning to be adversely affected. So as Mike Redding neared his star forward to address the mistake he had just made, he knew his players expected another angry tirade.

"Byron, you know what I'm going to say, don't you?"

Looking straight into his coach's face, the twenty-year-old thoroughbred with awesome ability did not hesitate. "You're going to say we didn't need that shot. We should run time off the clock and then work the ball down low for a better look. I shouldn't have taken the three-pointer. There was too much time left."

Mike was pleased; he couldn't have said it any better. That's why Byron Lewis was so unusual. Not only did he possess unlimited physical talent, he understood the game of basketball. He was the rare player who had the God-given natural ability to be a superstar, yet knew the intricacies of the game well enough to be a coach on the floor. He was as equally talented mentally as he was physically, and Mike had never coached a more competitive player. In an effort to make the most of the situation, Mike turned to the rest of the team and challenged them.

"Byron shoots two free throws. If he makes both, practice is over. If he doesn't, we practice another hour harder than you have been. If you don't want to chance it, we'll scrimmage another thirty minutes and then hit the showers. Let me see some hands. Who wants Byron?"

Nine players on the court and two subs standing on the sideline raised their hands without hesitation. The only player not to raise a hand was Byron Lewis. He didn't need to. Byron knew he'd make the free throws, but he didn't mind practicing longer. He wanted his teammates to decide their own fate. Mike had little doubt Byron would hit the free throws. More importantly, he saw excitement on the faces of his players for the first time in a week. They were grateful for this opportunity to get out of practice early, but they would have to earn it. Their coach gave nothing away. Mike Redding did not know the meaning of a free lunch. He picked Byron Lewis to shoot the free throws and his players were thankful. It was the closest thing to a gift their coach would give them.

As Byron toed the free throw line, the other eleven players gathered beneath the basket. Their job was to make enough noise and activity to disrupt the shooter's concentration. Inwardly, they prayed for Byron to sink the first shot, yet waved their arms and yelled to challenge him. As was customary whenever free throws were shot, the student manager working the scoreboard pressed a button and the public address system came on. In an effort to simulate game-like conditions in practice, Mike played a cassette tape of crowd noise so his team would be able to handle the distraction in a game. As the PA system's speakers blared the piped-in noise throughout the arena, Mike stood off to the side taking in the scene. He had made the right decision. His players had not shown this much enthusiasm in a long time. The point was made, Byron and the other players definitely would not make the same mistake in a game, and a grueling week of practice could end in a tremendously positive way.

"He better bury these," Mike said to one of the coaches standing next to him. "If he doesn't, the team's confidence in him to come through under pressure will be shaken. They could lose faith in him and me because I issued the damn challenge. C'mon Byron. Drop these and we'll get the hell out of here."

Standing at the free throw line, Byron Lewis was oblivious to the noise and activity around him. Mike imagined his mind was blank, except for two thoughts the coach had ingrained in his head: shoot softly and shake hands with the rim. After three rhythm dribbles, he eyed the front of the rim, and then effortlessly uncoiled his six foot eight inch frame. Rising to his tiptoes with his arms and hands stretched toward the basket, he let the ball float off his fingertips, his eyes never straying from the target, while the globe arched high above the rim and dropped gently into the net. The moment the white net caressed the orange leather ball, eleven players on the baseline erupted.

After the ball was thrown back to Byron, the players again waved their arms and screamed as loud as they could. The All-American sophomore repeated the same procedure. Three rhythm dribbles, a moment of intense concentration and then the graceful release. But this time the release was different, something was terribly wrong with it. As he began to uncoil his long, muscular body, Byron dropped his head and closed his eyes. When the ball left his hands it rose in a ridiculously high trajectory toward the top of the backboard, a good three feet above the rim.

Upon releasing the shot Byron turned away from the basket, started walking off the court and shouted "glass." Less than a second later the orange Rawlings rain-drop banked high off the glass backboard and fell cleanly through the net. Eleven disbelieving players stood motionless for a few seconds, then exploded jubilantly in unison before running off the court toward the showers. Watching their reaction delighted Mike. It reminded him that his players were the biggest reason he loved coaching. He felt happy and fulfilled for the first time since he lay in bed savoring the Coach of the Year award five days earlier.

Mike Redding loved the psychological side of coaching. He loved the rush he felt when he was able to get inside a twenty-year-old kid's head, and push him to work harder and be better. He believed the game of basketball was 60% mental, 30% physical and the remaining 10% was purely desire. Any coach could give a player a list of drills to improve his physical ability. Plyometric drills such as jumping on and off boxes or sprinting through sand increased a player's quickness and jumping ability. Running down hills lengthened a player's stride and made him faster. But desire was either burning in a player's stomach, or it wasn't. Desire could not be taught or learned. Either it was there or it wasn't, and no coach could teach it or instill it.

Mike believed good coaches were beaten by great coaches because of the mental part of basketball. The difference between a winning season and a losing season was the 60% of the game he referred to as the mental game. In Mike's opinion only a small portion of this 60% involved knowing the game and understanding it. Many players understood the game and knew how to play it, but very few players were mentally tough. This is what set Mike Redding apart from almost every other college basketball coach in America. His players were mentally tough. They knew what to do in all situations. During an important game and especially at the end of a big game, his players made the right decisions and executed under unbelievable pressure while other teams faltered.

This was the gospel Mike preached to his players: Don't let the opposing team play sharper or execute better. To himself he vowed not to put a team on the floor that was less prepared than their opponent. He was obsessive about execution, particularly during the closing minutes of a game. He tortured his team in practice by putting them in all types of game situations. They learned how to handle the situation in practice so there would be no uncertainty or hesitation in a game.

Mike taught these lessons to his players in a variety of ways. Sometimes he was patient and paternal in his approach; other times he chided and goaded them. Often he praised his players and built up their confidence and self-esteem. But more than anything else, Mike used fear and discipline to teach his players. He crawled into their heads by yelling, cursing and intimidating them. He did whatever it took to get his point across, often embarrassing and humiliating players, berating his assistant coaches and even degrading the athletic training staff. His fans loved him while his critics grudgingly admired him. His methods were accepted by the University of Northern Indiana, other coaches and his players for two reasons. He was rarely wrong, and his teams won. His teams won a lot, and everyone knew it was because of him.

As Mike made the long walk up the players' ramp to the basketball office, he thought it had been a long road to this moment. 1985 had been a turning point. His life changed forever that summer. Mike was an assistant coach at Butler University in Indianapolis at the time. Butler's venerable head coach, Don Sutton, had discovered him at a basketball camp the summer before his sophomore year at UNI.

After Mike graduated from UNI at age twenty-two, he started coaching as a graduate assistant for Butler University's basketball team. In his first year as a graduate assistant, he received a Master's Degree in sports psychology, studied the coaching philosophies of legends like John Wooden, Hank Iba, Adolph Rupp and Phog Allen, and became Butler's recruiting coordinator. It wasn't long before Mike had earned the respect of Don Sutton and inherited the role of Sutton's right-hand man, even though he was only promoted to the job of second assistant at the end of his first year.

College coaches have one assistant they trust more than the other coaches on their staff. Often it starts as a mentor-student relationship and blossoms into a right-hand man relationship. A head coach does not consult his entire coaching staff when he must make the most difficult decisions, he turns to one assistant. The person a head coach trusts to run the team in his absence or make crucial choices on recruiting high school talent is this one coach.

After two years at Butler, Mike Redding was Sutton's right-hand man. Don Sutton was a loyal man, however. When he decided to retire from coaching, he recommended Mark Athmann, his first assistant of eight years, for the head job. When a coach in good standing with a university retires, the search for a new coach usually begins and ends with the person the old coach recommended. Mark Athmann was named Butler's head coach, while Mike rose to the position of first assistant.

Right away, everyone close to the team knew who Butler's real coach was. Mike's brilliance was undeniable. He analyzed and broke down opposing teams' strategies so well it seemed he had played for them. By charting opponent's weaknesses, he found effective ways to exploit them and implemented his findings in Butler's game plans. He came up with creative new drills in practice to improve his own players' flaws and enhance their strengths. Mike pushed the players to work harder with their bodies, and think quicker and clearer with their minds. His work ethic was astounding, and his energy and enthusiasm wildly contagious.

News travels rapidly within the college coaching fraternity, and it didn't take long for word to get out about Mike Redding. As Butler University piled up victories and landed more top high school recruits, Mike's reputation grew. He was known to be creative and innovative in his coaching techniques, but well-versed in old-school coaching philosophies. His cutting-edge ideas made him radical, yet Mike had great respect for history and tradition. Above all, he was a warrior. Throughout college coaching circles the word on Butler's young firebrand was that no one competed harder.

This reputation was the reason Mike was chosen to participate in a high school all star tournament in Cancun, Mexico. A phone call in March of 1985 started his amazing coaching odyssey. When Clay Hobson, the assistant to Denny Crum at the University of Louisville, called to see if he was interested in coaching at the tournament, Mike was ecstatic. The ten days in Cancun turned out to be nothing like Mike expected. The best young assistant coaches from premier programs had been invited to coach eight teams of high school stars from across the United States. The list of head coaches sponsoring their assistants was impressive. Dean Smith of North Carolina, Bobby Knight of Indiana, Georgetown's John Thompson, Lou Carneseca of St. John's University, Jerry Tarkanian of UNLV, Gene Bartow of Alabama-Birmingham and Louisville's Crum.

Mike quickly discovered why he was selected to participate. While the rest of the assistants played golf, lounged around their hotel pools, and went snorkeling at Cozumel with their famous bosses, Mike held daily basketball camps in downtown Cancun. Eight hours a day, six straight days, he taught hundreds of Mexican kids how to dribble a ball, shoot a jump shot and play defense. He ran the camp in the middle of Tulum Avenue, the busiest thoroughfare in downtown Cancun, on makeshift goals in sweltering 105 degree heat.

The trip was the most humbling experience of Mike Redding's life. Each day as he conducted camps and taught English to the Mexican children, he thought of the other seven assistants meeting with top officials of the National Association of Coaches and the NCAA Rules Committee in the Sheraton's air conditioned convention hall. Following meetings that lasted two hours, the assistants joined their head coaches in exploring the beautiful ruins of Chichen Itza, taking in bull fights near Xcaret, swimming with dolphins at Isla Mujeres or fishing in the see-through blue water of the Yucatan Peninsula.

By the middle of the first week, Mike had finished designing his plan to get even, and had started implementing it. The high school stars would arrive on a Thursday morning. The coaches would see them scrimmage Friday and the games would be played Saturday and Sunday. The eight assistant coaches would select five of their team's seven players after seeing them Friday in the three point shootout and the exhibition dunk contest. The key to Mike's plan was to scout the players before Friday's shootout and dunk contest. While the high-profile assistants golfed and went sight-seeing, Mike invited the high school stars to Thursday's camp. Three of the fifty-six players showed up. Their dedication and desire proven, Mike searched for two more players with the qualities he looked for in a basketball player.

On Friday during the three-point shootout, Mike watched a small left-handed guard from Louisiana hit nearly everything he shot in warmups. He finished fifth after tiring toward the end of the contest, but Mike knew the boy could fill it up so he concentrated on finding his last player. He had heard players talking about a defensive wizard named Simon, so he watched the dunk contest to see the big center play. What he saw pleased him. Simon La Grange was a spindly six foot, eleven inch black bean pole from Beaumont, Texas. He had the longest arms of any basketball player Mike had ever seen. Simon La Grange looked terrible dunking a basketball because he was all arms and legs, but he fit perfectly into Mike's plan. Early Saturday morning the eight assistants gathered to pick their teams. Each coach was randomly assigned two players. The remaining five players on their team would be picked by the coaches, one at a time until each coach had seven team members. Mike got every player he wanted except one.

As he prepared for his first game against Carneseca's assistant's team of stars, he realized he did not have any of the top fifteen players in the country on his team. What he did have was a team of hardworking, intelligent stars with very specialized skills. One was an excellent ball handler and passer, another a tremendous penetrator and scorer. He had the outstanding left-handed guard to shoot three pointers, and Simon La Grange, his defensive anchor, shot blocker and rebounder. Mike had players with strong desires to win who were extremely coachable. This was important because, unlike his well-known counterparts, Mike Redding planned on doing a lot of coaching. He had spent the previous three nights analyzing the coaching philosophies of the assistant's superiors to determine what type of players each would select. Mike needed coachable players that were quick learners because he had figured out in advance how he would beat each coaches assistant—before he knew who his team would play.

The first game against Carneseca's assistant was easy. Mike

knew Lou Carneseca liked to pressure the other team's point guard and run a transition game, so he played three guards at all times, executed an intense full-court press and blew Carneseca's assistant away. Mike Redding's team led by nineteen at half-time and won by twenty-seven points. Carneseca's top assistant was complimentary after the game, but angry Mike's players had not stopped pressing late in the contest when the outcome was decided.

The second game later in the afternoon pitted Mike's all stars against Jerry Tarkanian's assistant's stars. This game was worse than the first. Mike knew "Tark the Shark" loved an up tempo game with a lot of three-point shooting. To counterattack this style, Mike played his tallest and most athletic players. While Tarkanian's assistant's all stars bombed away from three-point-range and fought over who would shoot, Mike's players pounded the ball down low and played aggressive half court defense. The strategy was brilliant. The further Tarkanian's assistant fell behind, his team fired more often from three-point-range and fouled Mike's players. The game ended with Tarkanian's aide having only four eligible players because of foul trouble. Tarkanian's assistant suffered through a long afternoon. His talented All-Americans lost by thirty-six points to a team of less heralded stars and an assistant coach from a small college in Indiana.

That night at the coach's banquet the main topic of conversation was the young assistant from Butler who was walloping the more established coaches by absurd margins. Later that evening Mike received a phone call at his hotel from Dean Smith, the legendary coach of North Carolina. Mike was staying at the Plaza del Sol, a poorly maintained, inexpensive hotel in downtown Cancun while Smith and his assistant resided at the plush Marriot Hotel in the touristy hotel zone that overlooked the Gulf of Mexico. Smith congratulated Mike on his success that day and reminded him that the all-star classic was a showcase of high school talent: an exhibition put on for the enjoyment of the fans and players. He asked Mike if he and his players would consider dropping their win-at-all costs mentality the following day when Mike's team played his assistant in the championship game.

The request infuriated Mike. "I value your opinion a great deal Coach Smith, but I think most people would agree winning is a lot more fun than losing. We'll be playing to win tomorrow; it's the only way I know to coach. And with all due respect, if this exhibition was being played just for fun, they wouldn't keep score. Tell your assistant good luck tomorrow," he said and hung up the phone.

The game the following day was a massacre. Mike had been working for six months on a new flex defense called the web. He unveiled it against Smith's assistant's all stars and the result was dramatic. The objective of Mike's web defense was to employ a halfcourt pressing defense that forced the offensive team to feed the ball into the center of the court. The ball handler would then be trapped in the middle of the press, hence the name web. In order for it to be effective, the web defense required quick, athletic players, and a large, mobile center. Simon La Grange was the perfect spider in Mike Redding's web. The defense was so different than anything anyone had seen that the inexperienced high school players wilted under its pressure.

Mike's team raced to a 17-2 lead and increased the margin to 42-10. When the end mercifully came, Mike's stars had won the championship game of the Cancun All-Star Classic by the lopsided score of 106-62. The only thing Dean Smith said after the game was that his assistant head coaching job would be open in one year, and he wanted Mike to fill the position. Ten months later Mike Redding became the first assistant to Dean Smith at the University of North Carolina. Smith's new right-hand man was twenty-six years old.

As Mike exited the tunnel and turned right down the hall toward his office in Liberty Arena, he thought of his years at North Carolina. He had learned so much during his four years under Dean Smith. There wasn't a better program in the country for a young coach to develop the tools of his trade. But when Mike was given the opportunity to coach his alma mater, he couldn't pass it up. At the age of thirty, he returned to UNI as the youngest head coach in Division I basketball.

Mike was brought back to the present by the sound of laughter coming from within his office. When he entered it, Mary Crawford, his long-time secretary and receptionist, sat at her corner desk and stared off into space before erupting into laughter again. Mike knew Quentin must be on the other end because he was the only person who could make Mary Crawford laugh. Quentin usually called Mike once a day. Whenever he called and Mary answered, he always had a dirty joke or funny story for her.

As Mike passed her desk, she said, "One moment Mr. Conway, he'll be right with you," and held up three fingers indicating the call was on line three.

Shutting the door behind him, Mike wondered if old Henry Crawford knew his wife loved Quentin's racy jokes. It dawned on Mike he couldn't remember the last time he had finished practice before Mary had gone home for the day.

"This's Mike," he said into the receiver.

"How's it going, Red? Ya okay?"

Mike knew what Quentin was referring to, but he wasn't sure he wanted to talk in detail about their friends' murders. So far Quentin was the only person he had been able to discuss it with and even that had been difficult. Knowing his friend wouldn't push, Mike avoided the intent of the question.

"Good considering. Practice ended on an up note today. We're as ready this year as ever."

"You better be or they'll hang you if you don't win it this time. Kentucky and Michigan are the only teams as good as you, and Michigan could be outcoached by dear Mrs. Crawford."

Mike smiled at Quentin's sarcastic remark. He rarely talked basketball with his closest friends because most of them didn't know the game. They didn't play competitive basketball past the tenth grade, and like thousands of armchair critics across the country, they thought they knew the game but didn't. Quentin was different, though. He excelled at basketball in high school and college. He did more than read *USA Today* or watch basketball on television—he could play the game. He didn't have the basketball mind Mike possessed, but he had always been the better player of the two. Quentin often teased his best friend about this and Mike had accepted it long ago. Mike often thought his friend would have made a great coach had he chosen to enter the profession. But that wasn't saying much. Everything Quentin Conway did, he did well.

Their discussion of basketball reminded Mike of past conversations with Allan Clancy. Allan was knowledgeable about the game, not as much as Quentin, but he loved to talk basketball for hours. Remembering the endless debates he and Allan shared made Mike sad. He desperately missed those conversations. *Poor Allan, so screwed up and tortured inside. What the hell happened? And worse— David. There'll never be a day I won't miss him*, Mike thought.

Sensing a change in Mike's disposition, Quentin asked, "How ya holding up, Red?"

"Okay. Not great, but not bad. I've been too hard on my players. I'm taking everything out on them. I need to ease up or they'll be burnt out by the start of the tourney. It's almost a blessing this all happened now because I haven't had time to think about Allan and David. If there's such a thing as good timing for shit like this, it'd be now."

"Hang in there, Mike. Allan and David would want you to concentrate on the tournament. They'd tell us to go on with our lives and do the best we can. Things are going to be hard for awhile, but we'll get through it."

"Damn right, we will. We always have," Mike reasoned.

"I hate saying this, Mike, but I think it's gonna get worse before it gets better."

"What the hell does that mean?" Mike asked, no longer wanting to avoid the topic.

"The FBI is keeping it quiet; they don't want the media to find out. I got a death threat today."

A cold, hollow feeling spread from Mike's stomach throughout his body. He couldn't believe what he was hearing. "Christ, Quentin, what'd it say?"

"It said more deaths will follow and that I should watch out. I'm next."

"Does the FBI know what bastard wrote it?" Mike asked angrily.

"They've got no idea. No idea at all."

"Do they have anything?" Mike asked.

"I gave them the letter this morning. They said it's clean. Whoever the person is, he's good. He hasn't made any mistakes. The letter was postmarked in Chicago, but that might not mean a thing. The FBI is being cautious; they're taking the letter seriously. They've assigned two more field agents to me. I have three of my own body-guards, one undercover policeman and four agents."

Mike shuddered. Such an invasion of his privacy would drive him crazy.

"Someone has to be insane, completely fucking insane to kill Allan and David," Mike said. "Does the FBI think the person that killed Allan also killed David and sent you the letter?"

"They're not sure. It's possible, but so far they don't have enough evidence to say whether everything is related. The letter could be from a copy-cat or just be a prank. They're not going to rule out anything at this point. Listen, Mike, Agent McCaskill thinks you're in as much danger as I am. I agree. You're a high-profile target because the tournament is about to begin. With all the traveling the next four weeks, you'll constantly be in public. That kind of visibility and exposure makes you an accessible target. Agent McCaskill . . . ."

As Quentin spoke, Mike sensed what was coming and cut his friend off. "Did the FBI ask you to talk to me, Quentin, or did you volunteer yourself? Ahh, it doesn't fuckin' matter. There's no way in hell I'm going to let two more agents follow me around. I don't care what Agent McCaskill thinks. I'm not putting up with two more suits looking over my shoulder twenty-four-seven."

"Just one, Red. Let them assign one more agent. I know you already have two guarding you, but it's a necessary evil. As soon as the tournament is over you can get rid of them. Even though you hate having them around, it's worth it."

"No, it isn't," Mike shot back. "I don't want anyone baby-sitting me."

"Dammit, Mike, the issue isn't convenience or practical-ity—it's safety! We're talking about your life. You won't do yourself or your team any good if you're in the hospital or six feet under. Let them guard you three to four weeks, and after the tournament is over, they're gone."

Quentin didn't say everything he was thinking. Would that be enough time? So far the FBI had no leads in the case.

Mike was silent for a few seconds. Quentin almost never got upset, so Mike knew the issue was important to him. "Okay, Quentin. I'll let them put one more on me. Only one, you got that. Three agents are enough. They can watch me during the tournament, but afterwards I decide if they stay or go."

"You're doing the right thing, Red."

"Who's doing this Q?" Mike asked exasperated. "Is it a psycho fan of our group, some jealous schitzo, or an ultra-competitive alum of another college? We never should have done that *People* magazine cover."

"I don't know, Mike, but I'm not going to drive myself crazy wondering. Neither should you. I don't need to understand their deaths, just accept them. Hey, with all the shit knocking the fan over last week, I haven't had a chance to talk to you about a strange call I got from Allan two days before he died. He was acting real weird. He seemed excited and sort of stressed. Did you notice anything like that the last few times you two talked?"

Mike was continually amazed at how Quentin knew what people were thinking, and by his ability to put into words precisely what others felt.

"Yeah, the night before he died. That's exactly how he acted. He was hyper, almost giddy. I remember thinking I hadn't seen him so excited in a long time. I was concerned because he was acting like a freakin' nut case."

"What'd you guys talk about?" Quentin asked.

"He said he was calling to talk hoops, but I knew right away it was more than that. I could usually tell when Allan wanted to talk about something, and that night he wanted to. I asked how things were going, and he said fantastic. He had this nervous excitement about him. When I questioned him about it, he said he was excited about what he was doing and things would get even better in the future."

"Any idea what he meant?" Quentin asked curiously.

"It was strange, he was talking in riddles and being evasive. He said things weren't the way they appeared. I asked him to explain, but he told me I'd find out in due time. He used clichés like only time will tell, and you can't judge a book by its cover. I asked why he was being so cryptic and he laughed and told me to be patient. I knew he'd been drinking so I didn't take the conversation seriously. I don't know if he'd just gotten laid, or if his ex-wife wanted him back, but he was good and excited. Maybe he got news a husband of one of the skirts he's screwing wants to donate money to his campaign. That would've put him in a damn fine mood. What was he like when he called you?"

"Same way," Quentin said. "He was jacked about something, but he wouldn't talk about it. He assured me everything was great, just as he did you, but two days later he's dead."

"It's so fucking frustrating," Mike said. "Why'd he call us so excited, but not tell us what's going on?"

"The phone calls and strange behavior were more than just coincidences," Quentin said. "Whatever caused Allan to act that way might be the reason he's dead."

Minutes later when Mike hung up the phone, he swiveled his chair around and ran his eyes up the wall behind his desk. Amid countless UNI team pictures and two diplomas hung a framed cover page from a recent issue of *People* magazine. Mike studied the title of the cover spread, "The Wonder Group: Indiana's Homegrown Hoosier Heroes Go National," and the photos juxtaposed beneath it. One picture showed five high school seniors beaming brightly at their commencement ceremony, while the other photo depicted four thirty-something year old friends hanging over the bow of a world-class yacht. The only difference in the pictures; the trappings of tremendous success, a trace of cynicism in the smiling faces and the absence of the group's fifth member.

"The article barely mentioned Ben is missing," Mike grumbled angrily. "Some wonder group. Two are dead and a third hasn't been heard from in almost twenty years."

The freshly cleaned glass in the picture frame was nearly singed under Mike Redding's searing gaze. Time and understanding were suspended as twenty years of unconditional friendship, ferocious loyalty and intoxicating memories melted into one moment, and one disarmingly disturbing realization. *Quentin is right,* Mike thought. *Whatever Allan was so nervous and excited about probably caused his death.*

Chapter Eight

Walking hurriedly down K Street, Carmen Jalomo took a quick drag on her cigarette and glanced over her shoulder. She had been on the run for five days. Five endless days running from someone and something she did not know. Zigzagging through the maze of pedestrians, she grew more agitated with each step. She felt as if the eyes of every passing person were on her, so she quickened her pace near the intersection of K and Wisconsin. A bookstore two blocks away was her intended destination. There she'd be safe. For the first time since hearing about the murder five days before, Carmen Jalomo believed she might make it out of Washington alive.

Stopping at the traffic light at K and Wisconsin, she turned to a businessman on her left. "Perdona, Señor. Que hora es?"

"What did you say?" he asked annoyed by the question.

Pointing at his watch she said again, "Que hora es?"

"Twenty of three," was the curt response as he brushed past her and started across the intersection.

She realized she must look terrible after five days on the run. She had slept less than two hours a night, eaten sparingly, and bathed only once. The two rules she had followed, the rules that had kept her alive, were trust no one and always stay in a crowded place. Carmen Jalomo's world had been turned upside down in the seven days since she had done the job. She would never forget that night.

The john had shown up late and more than a little drunk. Her pimp Edgar had warned her that the john was a very important man so Carmen should do whatever he wanted. The moment the client saw Carmen, he had been disappointed. He didn't complain much while she simultaneously danced and masturbated over him. When she tied him to the headboard with her fish net stockings, soaked his naked torso with a muscle-relaxing oil, and lowered her pierced pubis onto his, the complaining stopped altogether. Carmen Jalomo held nothing back that night; she satisfied her important guest every way she knew. Two hours later, he lay exhausted yet content next to her. A beat-up old Magnavox television had been on ten minutes when Carmen heard the voice. Staring at the blurry picture, she searched her memory to recall why she knew the man on the screen. After a few moments, she remembered the last time they met.

"That is bad man," she said in broken English.

"What are you talking about?"

"That man on screen. I know him before. He is not good."

Angered by what he believed was stupidity and insolence, the john blew up. "You don't know that man. There's no way in hell you'd know him."

Carmen was upset. Edgar had warned her not to be rude or discourteous with this client, but she couldn't help it. "I know this man before. I know him good. He is crazy one. I would not forget this bad man. I know him and jail."

As the client listened, Carmen Jalomo told her incredible story. Quickly the john's attitude switched from cynicism, to intrigue, and finally, unbridled joy. Leaping from the tiny, twin-sized bed, he half-ran, half-danced across the dirty apartment bedroom. Grabbing his pants off the back of a chair, he removed a shiny gold Rolex. After thanking Carmen Jalomo a third time, he gave her the watch. She didn't see the engraving inside the band until he left. The insignia read: Honorable Allan J. Clancy—Congressman, IN.

Two days later Edgar telephoned her about another job. Carmen was still in a drug-induced haze from the non-stop partying she had done with the huge tip the congressman left. The last thing Edgar told her before hanging up almost knocked her to the ground. Congressman Allan Clancy had been murdered less than two blocks from the apartment he had shared with her on M street. Carmen Jalomo went into hiding immediately. She told no one, not even Edgar, of the knowledge she possessed. The only person she had shared the secret with was dead. She knew her only chance of survival would be to stay underground until her cousin Manny could get her out of Washington. She hoped Edgar and the other girls hadn't talked to anyone. Surely, they knew not to talk to strangers. Carmen was to meet her cousin Manny at 3:00 PM at an adult bookstore on the corner of K and Wisconsin. Manny had arranged for her transit to Mexico with a truck driver. All Carmen had to do in exchange for safe passage across the border was sleep with the trucker. From Tijuana she would make her way home to Mexico City.

Carmen walked faster when she saw the bookstore a half block away. She flicked her cigarette to the pavement, and reached into the shabby brown purse that was slung across her chest. Pulling out a box of Marlboros, she glanced again behind her and over both shoulders.

"Ay, I de la chingada madre!" she cursed when she opened the empty cigarette box. She had pawned a gold bracelet her first day on the run. The $200 she received for it had been spent on alcohol, cigarettes, and a compact 9 millimeter handgun. She wanted to wait until she was in dire need of money before selling the congressman's Rolex. As she neared the bookstore, Carmen clutched the tattered purse tightly to draw strength from the gun inside.

Upon entering the store, Carmen looked in every direction to make sure no one was watching her. She thought she was early, but wasn't sure because the Rolex was buried at the bottom of her purse. She was supposed to be inside the women's restroom at 3:00 PM sharp. Manny would knock on the door four times to let her know he was there. As Carmen moved through the rows of shelves toward the bathroom in the back, she didn't notice a man holding a *Penthouse* observing her. After slipping into the restroom, she checked behind her to make sure she wasn't followed. Now safely out of public view, Carmen leaned against the bathroom sink to slow her racing heart. For the first time in nearly a week she relaxed.

In the middle of the store the man holding the *Penthouse* studied the positions of the store's customers while inadvertently putting the magazine back in the wrong rack. Confident no one was watching, he pulled a walkman from his coat pocket, placed the headphones on his head, and covered his hands with a pair of thin, black gloves. The music from the walkman enhanced his concentration and eased the pain in his head. After checking the store's patrons one last time, he turned and in nonchalant fashion, moved toward the bathroom. As he walked he removed a three-foot long nylon cord from his jacket pocket, and pulled it taut between his hands.

Pausing momentarily at the bathroom door, he closed his eyes and savored the fleeting thrill of the chase. The hunt was over. It was now time for the kill. As Steppenwolf's "Born To Be Wild" blasted in his headphones, the stalker burst through the restroom door just as Carmen Jalomo lifted her wet face up from the sink. Before she could turn to defend herself, the nylon cord was wrapped around her neck, flush against her larynx. The stalker watched amused as her facial expressions in the mirror changed from shock to terror, and ultimately, after the cord had crushed her windpipe, no expression.

Released from the death grip, the lifeless body crumpled to the sticky tile floor. Layers of her skin rolled over other layers causing Carmen Jalomo's plump, saggy body to resemble a bag of Idaho's finest spuds. Peering down at the dead hooker, the stalker flirted with the idea of masturbating on her, but decided it would take too long. After shutting the bathroom door behind himself, he walked casually through the bookstore toward the front, careful not to make eye contact with anyone. Less than a minute after he had stood over the dead whore's body, he opened the tinted front door and walked out. Manny Jalomo was a half block away, but infinitely too late.

Special Agent Frank McCaskill leaned back in his chair and rubbed his blood-shot eyes. He had been poring over volumes of information on the Clancy-Butler murders for over a week. The data the FBI had accumulated in the eight days following the two murders was staggering. Deputy Director L.C. Bailey originally assigned a total of seventy five agents to the investigation. The death threat sent to Quentin Conway confirmed McCaskill's hunch the murders were linked, so Bailey subsequently assigned forty more agents to the case. The FBI had much to either gain or lose in its handling of the high-profile case; Deputy Director Bailey was taking no chances. Frank McCaskill was the Bureau's top investigative agent. Bailey had put him in charge and allocated a record amount of money and manpower for the investigation. All the FBI's resources were at Frank McCaskill's disposal.

While he waited for Special Agent Bill Cooper to arrive at his office, McCaskill opened a massive brown logbook and resumed reading. The log was as thick as a phone book and contained information extracted from the two crime scenes. The first field agents to reach the sites had secured the areas so forensic experts could search for blood samples, skin tissue, hair follicles, clothing fibers and any other residue left behind. After they scoured both sites extensively, they had very little to show for it, either on the sidewalk in Washington or on State Road 43 in Lafayette. Suddenly, McCaskill's concentration was broken by a knock on the door. Without waiting for a response, Bill Cooper strutted into the office like a regal peacock.

"We need to talk, McCaskill. I can't believe what I just heard. Mason told me you're sticking to your lone gun theory."

"I haven't ruled it out, if that's what you mean," McCaskill replied.

"How many times have we been over this? It had to be more than one guy. Do you have anything new or are you basing this grand theory on instinct and your belly?"

McCaskill couldn't ignore the insult. He had heard far too many from Bill Cooper during the past week. "We can do this one of two ways, Cooper. You can lose the attitude and work with me and the rest of the Bureau to make this case go away."

After a lengthy silence in which McCaskill simply stared at him, Bill Cooper asked in a less confident voice, "What's two?"

"Other than being reassigned, there is no two. Stop freelancing and cut the grandstanding and we won't have a problem. Keep it up and I'll start a power play for Bailey's and the director's support. We both know you'll lose. I don't know what you've got against me, but you better set it aside. This is a monster case and it'll take everything we've got. The last thing the director needs is the media getting wind of dissension and in-fighting among the ranks. I won't have it—you got that. It ends now."

Shaken by McCaskill's emotionless chastising, Cooper nodded his head in agreement. "Good. Now let's get back to business," McCaskill said. "I'm not a hundred percent convinced, but I do think the murders were committed by one person. The lone signature on the death threat to Conway isn't the reason. Both crimes were done efficiently and with great precision. No evidence and zero witnesses at either crime scene smells like one person to me. Everything was too clean and systematic for multiple killers. Multiple killers are sloppy and make mistakes. You know the drill, Cooper. Multiple killers increase the chance of error and leave more debris behind. These murders were works of art—Rembrandts. It's improbable one person committed flawless murders in two places so it's even more unlikely multiples did it and left nothing."

"I'll give you that," said Cooper. "A lack of evidence points to one guy and your nose is usually right when you smell a theory. But don't lose sight of the big picture. Your argument is that perfect homicides mean one guy. Times of death make it virtually impossible. Preliminary DNA testing and tissue samples are against you. With all the rain, blood and piss Clancy was swimming in, times were hard to come by, but forensics narrowed the window from midnight to 1:30 AM. Butler's expiration date was between 7:00 AM and 7:05. This means a lone killer ripped a hole in Clancy's neck in Washington, ditched the weapon and cleaned up, caught a plane to Lafayette, Indiana, picked up a car and then waited for Butler to jog by. All this in five to seven hours. And the important thing to remember is that in all the rushing around, at this helter-skelter pace, the guy doesn't make one mistake or drop any clues. It's possible, but I just can't see it, Frank. That kind of killer doesn't exist. No one could pull it off. He'd have to be Superman to get all that done and not make a mistake. It had to be more than one person."

Frank McCaskill took in everything Bill Cooper said. Cooper's argument was compelling. Extremely compelling. If not for the motives of the crimes, McCaskill would believe Clancy and Butler were killed by a group or organization.

"Times of death make my theory hard to swallow, I'll give you that. But there's a problem with the multiple person theory," McCaskill said. "There's no motive to either murder, let alone motive tying them together."

"What are you saying, Frank? A lack of motive means one killer or that the murders aren't connected in any way?"

McCaskill knew it was a loaded question so he took his time before answering. "The murders are connected. Clancy and Butler were killed for the same reason. You've had ten field agents working under you for a week to find political or financial motives and so far . . ."

Cooper cut McCaskill off in mid-sentence. "Dammit, Frank, if you're implying my men aren't doing the job right—"

"I'm not implying anything, so just relax. What I'm saying is that it's been extremely difficult to find motive and you've been digging everywhere. For a congressman, Allan Clancy had remarkably few enemies—none of whom had ties to Butler. Clancy wasn't hated by many people. He was a harmless drunk activist. Butler wasn't hated by anyone. What I'm saying is we can't establish motive for Clancy's murder and even if we could, it wouldn't fit Butler's. So if they weren't killed for money or politics, it had to be personal."

"I don't buy personal," Cooper said, emphatically shaking his head no. "It was money or power, or both. The man was a United States congressman. He and Butler were famous and they had a ton of connections. Some group, corporation or organization wanted them dead, and we just haven't found the link yet. Once we find the common thread between Clancy and Butler, we'll have the motive and the bastards that did it."

"That's what I wanted to talk to you about," McCaskill said. "Randolph's report is done. His men pieced together every relevant fact they could find about Clancy, Butler, Conway and Redding. It didn't take long for the shrinks down in the dungeon to come up with psychological profiles for them, but there's so little evidence they couldn't begin to do a composite of a killer. The profiles turned up something interesting. Clancy and Butler had nothing in common other than being teenage buddies. Randolph found no common interests or associations that might provide motive. Psychologically they were worlds apart. Aside from being great friends in high school, they had no mutual interests. They had nothing in common except a highly personal, twenty-year friendship, so it's unlikely a Fortune 500 or PAC hired the gun.

"Randolph still has three agents working on the background check. They're looking for more info on the fifth friend that Conway and Redding told us about. The guy's name is Ben Rooks. He's a soft suspect at this point. We know he did time in the mid 80s for a drug-related crime. He was close friends with our four musketeers, but we can't find any current data on him. Besides tracking this fifth friend, Randolph's men will continue to look for links between Clancy and Butler. In my opinion, the lack of evidence and motive point in one direction: they were killed for personal reasons. And I'd bet the source of those reasons is buried deep in their twenty-year past."

"Your theory looks better with Randolph's report in, but it still doesn't fly for me," replied Cooper. "High school friends from Podunk, Texas, kill each other for personal reasons. We're not in Kansas, though—Dorothy and Toto aren't in body bags. This is D.C. and the corpses are a rich congressman and an Olympic champion. The whole thing smells of big money, politics and a paid hit. It was too clean to be an amateur and choreographed too well for a crime of passion. I've got eight agents working around the clock reviewing all current and future environmental legislation in the House and Senate. My guess is money was the prize and the green movement was the ball game. Clancy's support of a major environmental bill could cost someone billions of dollars. Take him out of the picture and, presto, there's no more opposition and no legislation. What we have to do is find the link between Clancy, a piece of environmental legislation and David Butler. Then we'll know who ordered the murders."

"Regardless of who did it, let's make sure we get them and we do it soon," McCaskill said. "Bailey wants us to pursue both angles. You work the leads off your theory, and I'll work mine. Let's get together twice a day for fifteen minutes to go over each other's findings."

Lowering his eyes, McCaskill turned his attention back to the crime scene log on his desk. Ten minutes with Bill Cooper took more out of him than one hour in the FBI's weight training facility. Realizing the meeting was over, Cooper stood and walked out of McCaskill's office as quickly as he had entered.

Finding it difficult to concentrate on the file in front of him, McCaskill set it aside and compared his theory against Bill Cooper's. McCaskill knew Deputy Director Bailey agreed with him about the number of assailants, but it didn't matter. The Federal Bureau of Investigation was known to be the most thorough, meticulous and professional law enforcement agency in the country. Regardless of Deputy Director Bailey's personal opinions, all scenarios would be analyzed, each possibility would be considered and every individual related to the case would be investigated. No matter how remote or unlikely a lead was, it would be given ample attention. That was the Bureau's way.

McCaskill spun his chair around and studied the picture on the wall of the burly college student. Twenty-five years had passed since Frank McCaskill had been an All-American fullback at the University of Pittsburgh. The years had been good to him. The closely cropped black hair in the picture was thinner now, but remained dark and military short. There were circles under the large blue eyes, but they were more a result of working too many sixteen-hour days than from age. Thick, dark eyebrows and olive-colored skin gave away his mother's Mediterranean heritage. Other than ten extra pounds spread evenly across his immense upper torso, Frank

McCaskill's chiseled, two hundred and thirty pound body was as hard at forty-seven as it was when he was blasting through defensive linemen in college. No one close to him had been surprised when, upon completion of an illustrious four year college football career, he chose the University of Virginia Law School over the National Football League.

After graduating Summa Cum Laude from Virginia, McCaskill took his law degree up the road to Quantico, Virginia, the national headquarters of the FBI. The Bureau requires its recruits to have a speciality. Frank McCaskill had two: an undergraduate degree in clinical psychology and a master's degree in jurisprudence. His area of expertise became serial murders and pre-meditated multiple killings. With twenty-two years of service under his belt, he could either retire early in three years or wait for Deputy Director Bailey to step down and fill his position. Frank McCaskill was a lethal weapon. Few federal agents were as physically skilled in the field, and none were as sharp mentally and analytically. McCaskill could have made millions as a trial lawyer or NFL fullback, but he never considered working for anyone other than the FBI. From the age of thirteen when his father was randomly murdered in a bank robbery in Hershey, Pennsylvania, Frank McCaskill's sole ambition was to protect innocent lives as a law enforcement agent.

McCaskill closed the thick log. He couldn't focus on the file's contents because his thoughts continually drifted to the phone call. He had analyzed the anonymous phone call too many times to count, yet still didn't know what to think of it. The call had come into the FBI's Washington office two days ago, and McCaskill hadn't stopped thinking about it since. The caller had asked for him by name. When told it was not customary procedure for calls to be passed directly to Special Agents, the caller threatened to hang up without disclosing the information he knew about the Clancy murder. The switchboard operator immediately notified McCaskill, who took the call.

The caller's raspy voice had been hard to understand; clearly it was disguised. He wanted to give the FBI some information concerning Congressman Clancy's murder, but would wait until later to give the rest. McCaskill had objected to this, but the caller insisted it be done his way. The informant told him Allan Clancy and Mike Redding were the intended victims, not Clancy and David Butler. Butler had been mistakenly killed because he was running where Mike Redding normally jogged. He believed Redding was still a target of the murderer. Ending the conversation with a bombshell, the informant hinted he might have a physical description of Clancy's killer, but was not ready to talk about it.

Floored by the caller's last statement, McCaskill had pressed the anonymous caller for information. Why couldn't he reveal more? How did he have a description of the killer? When did he plan on describing the killer? Why had he specifically chosen McCaskill to talk to? The only question the informant answered was why he had to wait before giving a description. He had been researching the deaths of Allan Clancy and David Butler, and wanted to be sure the information he provided was accurate. He was also concerned about his safety, especially if he talked to law enforcement officials. Before hanging up, the informant promised McCaskill he would call again in four or five days.

McCaskill could not stop thinking about the conversation. The caller had been extremely nervous and tense. That was not unusual, but everything else about the call was. As the days passed and no motive was found for either murder, McCaskill started to take the anonymous phone call more seriously. He wasn't sure what researching Clancy and Butler's deaths meant, and he wondered if the informant really knew what the killer looked like.

The call had been traced to a pay phone on the southeast side of Washington. McCaskill did not discuss his growing interest in the call with other agents because most of them, particularly Bill Cooper, thought it was either a prank or a hoax. The FBI had received over 20,000 calls, almost all of them anonymous, yet no useful information had come from them. McCaskill was not ready to disregard the call. Something about the man's attitude and demeanor made him believe the call wasn't a prank.

After glancing at the clock on his desk, Frank McCaskill turned off his computer and raised his weary body from behind his desk. He didn't want to be late for an afternoon meeting with the Deputy Director. As he switched off his office light, McCaskill said a silent prayer that the call wasn't a hoax. He had no solid leads to pursue and the NCAA tournament started in five days. If the murders were connected to the high school gang and the first round tournament site turned into a shooting gallery, the other two friends, and maybe the third, could be in grave danger. Despite the potential danger, Mike Redding planned on coaching his team and Quentin Conway insisted on attending the games to support his friend. McCaskill didn't want to think about how hard it would be to protect the coach and his friend. They would be incredibly accessible targets; the killer would have prior knowledge of their whereabouts and they couldn't be shielded from the public.

Sitting in the rear of the bus with his head buried in a newspaper, he tried to blend in so no one would notice him. When the bus reached his destination in ten minutes, his ordeal would be over. Jeremiah Forsey was scared. He had every right to be. The previous seven days had been the longest week of his life. The week started well when he was paid $1,000 for providing a *Washington Post* reporter information concerning Congressman Clancy. Two days later he was horrified to hear the congressman had been murdered a block away from the apartment he had told the reporter about. Jeremiah went into a state of shock upon hearing about the congressman's death. His mind was bombarded by a variety of terrifying questions. Was it just coincidence or was the reporter involved in the congressman's murder? Were news accounts suggesting a connection between Clancy's and David Butler's murders accurate? Had the information Jeremiah leaked contributed to Clancy's death? Was the reporter simply a pawn or was he the actual killer? If the reporter was the murderer, was Jeremiah in danger?

After aimlessly wandering around his Georgetown apartment for two days, Jeremiah had gone to the Georgetown University Library and began researching the lives of Allan Clancy and David Butler. Curious as to whether there was a connection between their deaths, he read every magazine and newspaper article available. By the end of the ten hour day, an interesting picture had emerged. Although they had been friends since they were teenagers, the two men were quite different and seemed to have very little in common.

Midway through his second day of research, Jeremiah Forsey was convinced the men were not killed for money or power. In fact, he believed Mike Redding, not David Butler, was the killer's intended victim. So Jeremiah turned his attention to Mike Redding. He researched the coach's background to find a reason someone would want him dead. As far as Jeremiah could discern, no organization, company or political entity would benefit from Allan Clancy and Mike Redding's deaths. Finally, when his research reached an impasse, Jeremiah could no longer put off what he feared most.

The next day he called *The Washington Post's* circulation office. When connected with a receptionist, he asked for Bill Rodman, the reporter he had given the information to. Jeremiah nearly dropped the phone when the receptionist told him no one by that name worked at the newspaper. He then requested to be switched to the editor in charge of political reporting. After once again inquiring about the journalist and describing him physically, Jeremiah was told by the editor-in-chief that the *Post* had never employed a reporter named Bill Rodman or anyone using that alias.

Jeremiah spent the next three days holed up in his apartment, not sure what he should do. He knew he had spoken to Clancy's killer, or at the very least someone involved in the murder. Part of him felt an obligation to go to the FBI. For the past week the major news story had been the lack of evidence in the FBI's investigation of the Clancy-Butler murders. But Jeremiah worried about providing the FBI a description. It could become public knowledge that there was an informant. Considering the incredible media attention given to the story and the amount of information being leaked to the press, Jeremiah knew it was a distinct possibility. And if it did become public knowledge, the people responsible for Clancy's murder would know he was the informant. That was enough to scare him from going straight to the FBI.

As the old city bus barreled through a crowded intersection on its way to Georgetown University's law building, Jeremiah shuddered at the thought of his face splashed across the front of newspapers throughout the country. *How the hell had he gotten himself into this?* Knowing the answer, he cursed his own greed and naiveté. He had absolutely no desire to play law student-turned-sleuth like the character Darby Shaw in the book *The Pelican Brief.* He didn't want to live his life a hunted animal on the run. All he cared about was obtaining his law degree and returning to Alabama to set up a small law practice in Birmingham. After his girlfriend came home from serving overseas in the Peace Corps, they would be married and could begin having little Crimson Tide players. This was the life Jeremiah Forsey desired, not one of constant fear and paranoia.

Jeremiah had decided to tell no one of his encounter with the reporter when he heard a news flash that Quentin Conway received a death threat. The news anchorman said the FBI and Capitol Hill police were investigating a possible connection between the threat and Congressman Clancy and David Butler's murders. The next twenty-four hours were a nightmare for Jeremiah as he oscillated back and forth between calling the FBI and maintaining his silence. Eventually, upon realizing he was afraid to go out in public and was already living in fear, he made his decision.

As he sat motionless on the back of the metro bus, Jeremiah wondered if he was doing the right thing. The previous day he had called Georgetown's Dean of Academic Affairs and set up an appointment. He was nervous about the meeting. He hadn't slept much since finding out about the congressman's murder, and being out in public frightened him. A meeting with the Dean of Academic Affairs was enough to scare any Georgetown Law student anyway. Dean Belding was as cold and stern a man as Jeremiah Forsey had met. His physical appearance was as intimidating as his demeanor. Easily 6'5", he was lean almost to the point of being gaunt, and possessed a full head of silver hair. The only thing colder than his usual blank facial expression was his nasty disposition. Theodore

Jefferson Belding was known to smile on two occasions: when he had convicted a criminal for committing a crime against the District of Columbia and when a guilty defendant received the stiffest sentence on the books.

Belding had become the Dean of Georgetown Law School after serving seventeen years as Washington, D.C.'s District Attorney. In that time he amassed one of the highest kill ratios, a DA's record of guilty verdicts, in the nation. He was extremely bitter when the new mayor of D.C. asked him to retire. Choosing early retirement over an inevitable political pink slip, Belding picked the academic atmosphere as his next job because few employers wanted a high-priced, sixty-three-year-old retired attorney on their payroll.

Jeremiah checked his watch for the third time in five minutes. He was growing more anxious as he neared the campus. The bus would reach the law school in three or four minutes. Once there, he would face Dean Belding. Jeremiah had selected Belding as a confidant for two reasons. Washington's entire legal community was familiar with Belding's fanatical belief in justice. No one believed in justice with greater conviction and fervor than Theodore Belding. Secondly, although certainly not a law student's friend, Belding was an ideal confidant because of his unconditional loyalty. Whether it be an individual person or a collective cause, once Theodore Belding joined a fight, no one in Washington was as fiercely loyal.

After the dingy gray bus pulled up to the curb and stopped in front of the massive stone building, Jeremiah Forsey pulled his worn Massimo cap down over his eyes and jumped onto the sidewalk. He wore a cream-colored Eddie Bauer turtleneck under an oversized Nautica windbreaker. His boyish face was well hidden under the old cap and seven days of thick stubble. Bounding up the concrete steps three at a time, he quickly made his way through the large glass doors into a long hallway. Moving rapidly down the hall, he carried a brown suede backpack on his shoulders and hunched over to avoid oncoming eyes. He walked to the far end of the hallway, and turned left toward a marble stairwell landing. Upon reaching the stairwell, he cautiously shot a look back down the hallway. Seeing nothing alarming behind him, he headed up the spiral staircase to the second floor. With the fear beginning to subside and his breathing slowing, he felt secure for the first time since he had left his apartment.

Theodore Belding's office was the third office on the left, just past the Alumni and Registrar's offices. The empty hall was so quiet Jeremiah heard soft music coming from the alumni office as he passed the open door. Nearing the registrar's office, he started to walk faster until he heard a voice that stopped him in mid stride. Not only did the man's voice startle him, the question he asked sent shock waves of terror ricocheting through Jeremiah's head. Instinctively, Jeremiah threw himself against the wall. It was an involuntary reaction; he had momentarily lost the ability to reason. Jeremiah tried to think rationally. He had to confirm his suspicions. Hugging the wall tightly, he inched his way toward the door of the registrar's office. His heart pounded so fast in his chest, he thought everyone inside the office would hear it beating.

Peeking his head out past the wall, he looked through the upper portion of the door that was clear glass. Standing at the front desk with his back to the door was Bill Rodman, the reporter from the *Post*. Upon recognizing the fake reporter, Jeremiah instantly yanked his head back and pressed himself flat against the wall. Pinned against the wall and paralyzed with fear, he was beset with horrible thoughts. When the man spoke again, Jeremiah closed his eyes in an effort to shut out the voice and make him go away.

"Thank you for the class schedule and address," the man said graciously. "My firm would like to set up an interview with Jeremiah as soon as possible and you've been a big help. Have yourself a nice . . . ."

Not waiting to hear anything else, Jeremiah took one step backward, bolted off the wall and headed down the hall toward the stairwell. By his calculations he had two options—either hide in the tiny alumni office or try to make it to the stairs before he was spotted. Jeremiah made his decision in a split second. Running past the alumni office door, he leapt toward the staircase and ran down the steps four at a time. He hit the floor at the bottom of the stairs in full stride and sprinted up the long hallway as if he were late for a final exam. Ninety feet later he veered to his right and darted out a custodial entrance. Using every side street and back alley he could find, he ran over a mile before jumping into the back seat of a taxi cab.

As the cab drove further away from the university, Jeremiah planned his next move. The killer knew who he was—Jeremiah had to leave Washington. He would go home to Alabama, but he had no idea where he would stay. Jeremiah didn't want to endanger his family. If the killer could find him that easily, locating his family wouldn't be a problem. There were many things he wanted to do before going underground, but he knew they wouldn't get done. Now that Jeremiah Forsey knew who the killer was, only one thing was certain. He would go into hiding immediately and nothing would bring him out.

Two hours later Dean Belding picked up his phone and punched in a private number. The phone rang once before being answered.

"The Forsey kid didn't show," Belding said.

"Why not. What happened?"

"No idea. He seemed anxious to talk yesterday. He hasn't contacted my office so I don't have a clue as to why he skipped the meeting," replied Belding.

"Do you think he knows anything?"

"Oh, yeah. He knows something. I'm not sure how much, but he wouldn't request a meeting with me if he was in the dark. He might not know exactly what happened, but he hung out at the same bar as Clancy so my guess is he's privy to a lot."

"But do you think this kid's the one?"

"Ninety percent sure," Belding said. "The fact that he bugged out today tells me he's your man. I'd go after him."

"We're being pulled in twenty directions. I've got to be smart about time and personnel. Tell me one thing—from an old friend to another—is it worth our time and trouble?"

"It's worth it," Belding solemnly advised. "I know your plate is full, but take my word on this. If you don't find him soon, there'll be one less law student in the world."

Chapter Nine

Alone in the trainer's room with his head cradled between his hands, Mike Redding did not appear to be college basketball's most successful coach. His elbows rested on his muscular thighs and bore the weight of his neck and sagging head. Mike Redding was by nature a conservative and superstitious person. Tonight he was experiencing unfamiliar emotions. Feeling the perspiration accumulating under his armpits and in his palms, he could not remember a time in his adult life when he was this nervous. He was used to the butterflies and anxious energy that came before every big game, but this was different. This year the NCAA tournament was different.

In the past Mike's teams were picked to do well in the tournament, but this year UNI was the consensus favorite to win the national championship. Most analysts considered UNI the best team in college basketball. Anything less than an NCAA title would constitute a disappointing season. The deaths of Allan Clancy and David Butler only increased the pressure. The NCAA tournament had been shoved in the background while Mike Redding's story took center stage. The media hype incensed Mike. It angered him that his personal dilemma threatened to overshadow the three week tournament known around the country as March Madness.

Mike Redding didn't want to fail in such a public forum. The entire nation was watching his team's quest for the national title.

Not since O.J. Simpson drove down the Los Angeles freeway on live television had a sports story captivated so many Americans' attention. CBS, the network airing the tournament games, was salivating at the prospect of garnering the highest television ratings ever for a sporting event. For Mike, Nielsen ratings were the last thing on his mind. Now that his friends were dead, the only thing that mattered to him was basketball.

As he leaned back on the wooden bench and stretched his long legs, Mike became aware of the sound of muffled noise in the player's tunnel. Seconds later the locker room door swung open and George Horrigan, UNI's Athletic Director, walked into the room. Behind him a mass of humanity resembling a rock star's entourage entered the small confines of the training room. Standing in the midst of five bodyguards and four FBI agents was Quentin Conway. Smiling broadly, Quentin rushed across the room to embrace his friend. He was so excited to see Mike Redding, his face looked like that of an eight-year-old-boy on Christmas morning.

"How's the best coach in America?"

As Mike was about to respond, he noticed the woman next to Quentin. "Good. Hanging tough. We're all set to go," Mike said trying to pry his eyes off her.

He had never seen such an attractive woman before. She wore a slightly faded pair of Donna Karan jeans and a long-sleeved white blouse. The blouse hung just below her shoulders, high enough to be modest, but low enough to expose a tiny opal and diamond pendant that rested on her smooth brown skin. Slung carelessly over her shoulder was a black leather jacket. In direct contrast to the shiny black leather, golden blond hair fell halfway down her back.

Realizing he did not hear Quentin's last comment, Mike asked, "What'd you say, Q?"

"I was talking to Diana. I need to make some introductions. Mike, I want you to meet Diana Fleming. She's a fan of yours."

Mike tried to conceal a smile. He hoped his face didn't show that Quentin's innocent remark pleased him.

"Diana, I'd like to introduce you to my oldest, best and ugliest friend Mike Redding."

"It's a pleasure to meet you, Diana," Mike said in his most pleasant tone, ignoring Quentin's barb.

"Nice meeting you. I hope you play well tonight. I know coaches say the first game of the tournament is dangerous because they aren't sure how their teams will play."

"We should be ready," Mike said. "I don't think there's anything else we could do to prepare. At this point of the season it's a matter of executing and carrying out the game plan. The team that makes the fewest mistakes usually wins."

Diana Fleming seemed to be knowledgeable about basketball and was definitely friendly and personable. Mike wondered why she was with Quentin. He didn't know the girl at all, but for some reason she didn't seem like Quentin's type. She appeared to be level-headed and down to earth; Quentin usually dated flashy, glamorous beauties. Women were basically a hobby to Quentin, a pleasurable diversion from making money and acquiring new toys. Mike wasn't sure why, but Diana Fleming struck him as a woman who would see past Quentin's exciting, fanciful lifestyle and realize dating him led nowhere.

"You've seen my office," Mike said casting his eyes around the locker room. "What pays your bills?"

"I'm a flight attendant with Delta, based out of Chicago. I fly fifteen days a month. That's the best part of the job. It lets me pursue my real passion."

"Which is?"

"Designing clothes. My dream is to be a fashion designer. Flying gives me the time and income to design."

Mike Redding was interested. She appeared to be extremely independent and ambitious. He wasn't sure why she was with Quentin, but at least she wasn't a brainless gold digger like many of the women his friend dated.

"Are you a hoops fan, Diana, or are you here to impress Quentin?" Mike asked the question in a joking manner, but purposely put her on the spot to find out how much she liked Quentin.

"Fanatic is more like it," she replied. "I've been nuts about basketball since I was ten. My two brothers were all-state in North

Carolina, but they committed the ultimate sin. One turned down a scholarship to Carolina, the other NC State, to stay home and help my father run our tobacco farm. I developed my hoops addiction through them as every little sister should. Contrary to what Hoosier hysterics and blue-grass hicks think, Tar Heel country is *the* hot bed of high school and college basketball. And, no, I'm not here to please Quentin. I came to watch Byron Lewis, and because first round games are usually very exciting due to upsets." Diana smiled sweetly at Mike after deflecting the pointed question.

"We've got a live one here," Quentin said, trying not to crack up. "Damn, Diana, you need to work on being more candid. I'm not sure Mike can take so much love and encouragement."

Feeling her point had been made, Diana glanced at Mike before replying. "Well, Quentin, I don't think he has a lot to worry about tonight. A number one seed has never lost to a sixteenth seed since the sixty-four team tournament started."

Quentin laughed louder and said to Mike, "She's been reading USA Today again."

Mike wasn't laughing. He was upset with himself for being distracted before a game. He and Diana Fleming were verbally sparring when he should have been preparing himself for the game.

"I've gotta go to work. There're a few last minute adjustments I want to make," Mike said suddenly.

"Listen, Mike, I know you'll be absorbed in the game, but try to stay on the bench as much as possible. The more you stand and move around, the easier target you become."

"Don't start Q. I don't give a shit what kind of target I am. I'm not gonna change how I coach because of some crazy lunatic."

"I know you won't and I don't want you to. Just do as much coaching from the bench as possible, especially if it's a blowout, okay?" Quentin had phoned UNI's assistant coach earlier in the day and told him to keep Mike seated on the bench as much as possible. Mike would be livid if he found out about the phone call, so his reaction now was hardly a surprise.

"Jesus Christ, Quentin. I'm trying to win a game here. If I can't get up and move around, I can't coach. And that's what I'm paid to do—coach and win games. I'll try to stay seated; it just depends on how we play. No promises, Q, I'll do what I can if it gets out of hand."

"Good enough," Quentin said. "You're wearing your bullet-proof vest, right?"

"It's heavy as shit and annoying as hell," Mike said tapping his finger against the bulge under his dress shirt. "I'm not thrilled about wearing it, but I guess it's worth the hassle."

"Trust me, Red. It is. It'll keep you safe and sound so you can repeat as national champs next year."

Mike frowned at Quentin's prediction. "To hell with next year. I'll be happy with a win tonight. I've gotta get going so I'll talk at you later. Thanks for coming by. Pleasure meeting you, Diana," he said staring into her eyes.

"Luck, Red," Quentin said.

"You, too," Diana replied softly.

As Mike walked through the trainer's room toward the coach's office, two thoughts stood out in his mind. He hoped the bullet-proof vest was only a necessary inconvenience and he wondered why he was disappointed Diana Fleming was dating his best friend.

Quentin told Diana the outcome of the game pleased him for several reasons. He was happy for UNI's players and thrilled for Mike. The last week had been extremely difficult for his friend. Even though he tried not to show it, Mike was devastated by the events of the last two weeks. He was taking David Butler's death especially hard. Since Butler was UNI's athletic trainer as well as one of Mike's closest friends, everything Mike did reminded him of his friend. The one place Mike Redding was able to escape the pain and grief was the basketball court. When the ball was thrown up, he blocked out all distractions and focused on coaching. In no other setting did Mike feel so comfortable. The basketball court had become his solitary place of refuge, a psychological and emotional safe haven where misery and despair could not intercede.

The final score of 92-69 did not reflect how well Mike's team played. UNI led by thirty-six points early in the second half when Mike pulled his starters. Detroit Mercy had a solid team, but simply could not compete with the Big Ten Conference Champions. Detroit had eased into the tournament by winning the Midwestern Collegiate Conference's post-season tournament. They were the MCC's best team, but were no match for UNI's experience and talent. As in past tournaments, the number one seed was an untouchable. There would be no first round upset of the top seed in the Midwest Region.

After briefly visiting Mike down on the court to offer congratulations, Quentin and his bodyguards quickly climbed the stadium steps to the main concourse level where Diana waited. Grabbing her around the waist, he pulled her body close to his as they headed toward the elevator leading to the parking garage below the arena. Not wanting the FBI agents around them to hear his question, Quentin whispered in her ear.

"Let's lose the agents and bodyguards and get out of Knoxville. How does a night on the town in Nashville sound?"

"What? You aren't serious," Diana said incredulously. "You can't change plans and ditch the FBI. They have four agents guarding you for a reason. They're supposed to be protecting you."

"I'm a big boy, Diana. I'll be fine. Think about it. If the FBI is watching me and they can't find me, there's no way the bad guys will. It's just one night."

"I don't know, Quentin. It seems too risky. We couldn't lose them anyway. Your bodyguards, yeah, but not the agents."

"Sure we could," Quentin said, a devilish grin spreading across his face. "The only question is if you want to. How 'bout it, Diana," Quentin asked, breaking into the jingle-like refrain of The Clash's hit song, "Should we stay or should we go?"

Diana thought for a moment. Spending an evening in Nashville did sound more appealing than staying in Knoxville or flying back to Chicago. She didn't know Quentin well enough to travel overnight with him, but they weren't physically involved and he had been a complete gentleman, so she wasn't worried about his taking advantage of the situation.

"Let's go for it," Diana said, not giving herself time to change her mind.

Immediately, Quentin called Tony Kirby over. Tony Kirby had worked for Quentin seven years. He started as a bodyguard, but his intelligence and loyalty impressed Quentin so much, he soon became a supervisor of security personnel. Following five more years of devoted service he was now the Director of Security for QuinWay Inc., the parent company that owned all Quentin Conway's businesses. Speaking under his breath so no one could hear him, Quentin described his plan to Tony Kirby and gave him specific instructions to carry out. As Quentin, Diana and their entourage of bodyguards approached the stadium's restrooms, Quentin took two $100 bills out of his pocket and grasped Diana's hand as if to hold it. Leaning down to hug her, he whispered the plan in her ear. When they released their hold on each other and headed for separate bathrooms, Diana palmed the hundred dollar bills and Tony Kirby barked orders to Quentin's bodyguards. Three of the bodyguards went into the men's restroom while another waited for Diana at the exit of the women's restroom. Tony Kirby remained outside the bathrooms with FBI agents Dan Albers and Tim McCallom.

Once inside the restroom, Quentin began offering UNI fans money for their hats, tee shirts, and signs. After paying a man $150 for a brown suede jacket, Quentin took off his v-neck sweater and gave it to a bodyguard. Next, he bought a homemade sign from a young boy for $10. Finally, he purchased a UNI baseball hat from a student who was over six feet four inches and 240 pounds. As he checked his disguise in the mirror, he told his bodyguards to give him a two minute head start before informing the agents what he had done.

Pulling the hat down over his brow and carrying the sign in front of his face, Quentin pushed his way past the incoming traffic as he slipped out the restroom entrance. The six foot four UNI student walked on the inside of Quentin, effectively shielding him from the agents who searched for him in the massive stream of fans pouring out the restroom exit. Quentin jogged all the way to the ground floor elevator at the south end of the arena. Thirty seconds later he felt a tug on his right arm. He laughed uncontrollably when he saw Diana Fleming. Her black leather jacket had been replaced by an oversized Detroit Mercy cheerleader's warm-up. A navy blue baseball cap rested on top of her head. The luxurious blond hair had been rolled into a bun and was hidden under the cap. Completing the disguise was a pair of blue and gold pom poms that engulfed her tiny hands.

"Oh my God. How'd you get a cheerleader's uniform?" Quentin managed to ask between howls of laughter.

"Hey, don't laugh," Diana said pretending to be hurt. "I always wanted to be a cheerleader. This look fits me. I only had to ask one girl. She was a senior and since tonight was their last game, she didn't mind giving up the uni."

"She gave it to you for free?" Quentin asked surprised.

"Nope. I gave her the whole $200. I figured she needed it more than King Midas."

"She'll be the life of the party tonight," Quentin joked. "Remind me to never let you negotiate for me again."

Clasping her hand, Quentin led Diana out the door and down to the street that ran parallel to the arena. From the sidewalk curb they hailed a taxi, talked the cabbie into servicing the unusual fare and piled in the back. As Quentin and Diana settled in for the long trip to Nashville, Tony Kirby listened in silence as Agents Albers and McCallom berated him. They would be severely reprimanded for losing track of Quentin, so they vented their frustration on the only people possible—the bodyguards. After chastising Tony Kirby another thirty seconds, the agents left to report Quentin's disappearance to Special Agent McCaskill.

Removing a hand-held phone from his pocket, Tony Kirby dialed the number of Quentin's limousine which was parked in a private garage beneath the arena. Hardmon Simmons, Quentin's long-time chauffeur, had been playing solitaire for over three hours when FBI agent Eric Howard arrived at the limousine as the game ended. They passed the time by playing a variety of card games while waiting for word Quentin was coming down. Their game of liar's poker was interrupted when the limousine's phone began ringing.

"Hardmon Simmons. May I help you?"

"Hard, it's Tony. Quentin and Ms. Fleming aren't coming down. I'll tell you why later. It's a helluva story. Take the limo back to the hotel, vacuum it out and wipe 'er down. When you finish, you're free the rest of the night."

"Okay, Tony. I'll see you first thing in the morning," the driver replied.

"Naa, sleep in. Quentin won't need you until at least noon."

"Works for me. Thanks Tony. See ya tomorrow."

After hanging up the phone, the chauffeur began cleaning up the playing cards strewn across the dashboard and front seat. "What's going on?" Agent Howard asked.

"Change in plans. They're not coming down. All I have to do is get this puppy back to the hotel, clean her up and I'm done for the night."

"How about a lift to the west parking lot on your way out?" Howard asked. "I left paperwork in my rental and I don't feel like footing it over there."

"No problema. I'll have you there before you can count to three."

The moment Hardmon Simmons put the key in the ignition and turned it, Quentin Conway's black stretch limousine lurched forward violently, was lifted high off the ground, and exploded into a ball of brilliant orange flames.

Chapter Ten

Hunched over the small card table, he peered intently at his work. He felt it was much better than the first. He had spent a total of eight hours working on this second letter. For five straight hours he worked diligently, stopping only to take a twenty-minute break. After using the bathroom and snacking on grapes and bananas, he returned to the card table feeling refreshed and sharp. The next three hours flew by as he immersed himself in his work. He cut up magazines, measured angles, pasted letters and then burnt the left-over paper shavings. He could not afford to make a mistake at this stage of the game. While rocking in the folding chair, he was aware of a knot of tension forming in the base of his skull. He wanted to finish reviewing the letter before the pain from the next headache became unbearable, but he refused to rush himself. The letter had to be flawless.

"Damn, my hands are good. I must have been a famous surgeon in a previous life," he said praising himself. "As far back as I can remember, I've always been a great cut-up."

His body swayed back and forth in the folding chair as he laughed at his inane joke. When his laughter died away, he rocked faster to combat the pain cresting in his skull. Forcing himself to concentrate harder, he proofread his work. He had purposely left an obscure clue in both letters. Even if the FBI found the clue, they wouldn't be able to track him down. He made sure that if his identity became known, no one would be able to locate him.

This second letter was longer than the first. The length of this letter and the fact that it could be compared to the previous one made his job more difficult. When he finished examining the typing paper for errors, he scanned up the page and read the letter out loud.

> *Mike Redding*
> *A game far more important than basketball is at*
> *stake…life. Quentin Conway was lucky. He won his*
> *first round game. Here is your warning. Be prepared because*
> *warm-ups are over. You're next.*
> *Your Shadow*

The pressure in his head was building toward a nightmarish crescendo, so he rocked faster. He couldn't believe Quentin had escaped death two days before. Quentin and Mike had always seemed different. Mike was incredibly successful at a few specific things because of his work ethic, competitive spirit and inner drive while Quentin was known to excel at everything he tried because of ability, talent and unbelievable good luck. Escaping the car explosion could only be explained as another example of Quentin's charmed life. Things just went his way.

As he placed the letter in the addressed envelope, intuition told him Mike would not be as fortunate as Quentin. He sealed the envelope with tape and removed the latex gloves from his hands. Rocking as hard as he could, he feared the folding chair might topple over at any moment.

"If only they knew how smart I am," he cried out through the blitzkrieg of white lights and intolerable pain. "Don't they understand I'm doing this for their own good?"

By now the headache had reached its apex. Screaming the whole way, he ran to his recliner in the next room and rocked for fifteen minutes. After the headache subsided, he watched the evening news to see if there was any new information about the bombing. He was extremely tired, but wanted to stay awake to avoid the terrible flashbacks that haunted him when he slept. The same flashback had dominated his dreams every night for ten days. Without provocation, his thoughts returned to the second letter.

"Wonder twin powers activate," he said under his breath. "Form of: a fly on the wall of that Fibbie McCaskill's office when the mail is delivered. Shape of: the biggest, baddest, best son of a bitch there ever was." Closing his eyes and rocking gently to keep the demons at bay, he whispered to himself. "I hope he finds the clue. I hope he finds the clue. When he sees the letters pasted to the envelope, he'll know exactly what it is. I hope he finds the clue."

"I'll never be ready on time," she muttered after looking at herself in the full length mirror. The jeans she wore were the third pair she had tried on. "C'mon, Diana, get a hold of yourself. It's not that big a deal."

She wondered why she was going to so much trouble to look good for Quentin Conway. Before she could finish the thought, the answer came to her. The person she was trying to impress was Mike Redding. But even if he did notice her, Diana believed the possibility of his taking an interest in her was slim to none. Diana couldn't help but feel she would never get a chance to get close to Mike Redding because of the tragic and unusual situation he was in. She was troubled by this thought but resigned to the fact that there was little she could do. So she did what she could. Namely, look her very best in an effort to gain his attention.

Diana was extremely nervous about the game, partly because of her interest in Mike, but more so because of the bombing two nights before. The FBI had intensified the security around Quentin and was taking every precaution possible, but still she was scared to be near him. The last time she saw him they almost died. Diana had said numerous prayers of thanks that she had opted to go to Nashville instead of staying in Knoxville. After thirty-six hours of soul-searching indecision, she decided to go to the second-round game. In the end it was the FBI's special security arrangements that eased Diana's worries and convinced her to go.

Even after the explosion, Quentin had told her the idea of missing Mike's next game had never entered his mind. Diana wished she could be as trusting and secure as Quentin. Despite her wariness, she would not have attended the game if she thought the FBI couldn't protect them. Besides, if Quentin Conway felt safe going to the game—that was good enough for Diana. She either had great faith in the FBI's ability, or Quentin's confidence was beginning to rub off on her. Regardless of where her confidence lay, deep inside Diana knew she was risking harm to herself not for Quentin, but for Mike.

As she ran a brush through her hair, Diana wondered if Mike was the type of man that would pursue his friend's date. Because of her physical appearance, Diana had grown accustomed to men going to extraordinary lengths to win her over. She sensed something different, something more sincere than physical attraction from Mike. She remembered the smile on his face when Quentin said she was a fan of his, and he seemed genuinely interested when he asked about her livelihood. She wasn't certain, but Diana felt she and Mike had connected the night they met. Even though she enjoyed spending time with Quentin, Diana didn't want their relationship to develop past the friendship stage. That wasn't the case with Mike Redding, though. She was intrigued by his fiery personality and astute mind. He fascinated her. She was definitely interested in getting closer to him.

She set the hair brush on the bureau, then checked the time. Quentin would be there within five minutes. She ran around the hotel bed to the closet. Grabbing a pair of jeans she had tried on earlier, Diana changed outfits for the fourth time. She thought it ironic she was going to so much trouble for Mike when he had done nothing for her. Quentin, on the other hand, had gone out of his way for her on many occasions. As she tried on the first pair of jeans again, Diana recounted Quentin's generous acts of the last two weeks.

He had taken her to a Broadway play in New York and treated her to a shopping spree. After dining at Oprah Winfrey's restaurant and meeting the talk show queen, Diana had been Quentin's guest at the exclusive Chicago premiere of Tom Hanks' latest movie. For this second round game Quentin had flown her from Chicago to Knoxville in his jet and offered to cover her hotel room. Although Quentin was only being thoughtful, Diana adamantly refused. She didn't believe in accepting too much from men. She would have felt like a kept woman if he had paid her hotel bill, and she never wanted to be dependent upon anyone.

Although she was apprehensive about being out in public with Quentin, Diana was excited about the second-round game. She had never been to an NCAA tournament game until two days ago. Diana sensed the excitement and intensity increased with each additional round. She was also anxious to see Mike. Diana had been thrilled when Quentin called a day earlier and informed her he had asked Mike for two tickets. She hoped Mike had wondered who would use the second ticket. Cringing at the thought, she scolded herself.

"You sap. Quit being so flighty. You're acting like a high school freshman with a crush on the prom king." As she admonished herself, the sound of the phone ringing cut her off. Diana ran around the bed to the nightstand and picked up the receiver.

"Hello," she said, expecting to hear Quentin's deep, scratchy voice. Instead, an imitation of an elderly woman's voice made her break into spontaneous laughter. "Thanks. I'll be down in a sec." She was already used to Quentin's playful manner and practical jokes.

Diana hung up the phone and hurried back to the full length mirror. She eyed herself critically, from the blond hair on her head to the black flats on her feet. She was pleased with what she saw. Conscious of the time, she rummaged through the junk in the bottom of her Louis Vuitton purse. After applying Clinique's Raspberry Ice lipstick, she stole one last look in the mirror. Nodding in approval, she threw a checkered blazer over her shoulders as she rushed out the door. The intentionally poorly dressed, scruffy man watching on a hidden surveillance camera in the next room wrote down the time when she passed his door on her way to the elevator.

Chapter Eleven

A casual observer might have guessed the town was under martial law. An individual watching the activity around Linwood Square might even believe the FBI had moved their headquarters from Quantico, Virginia, to Knoxville, Tennessee. The residents of the city were less than thrilled by the arrival of an army of agents in their beloved Volunteer state. Knoxville is a friendly, laid back, medium-size southern city. Locals address each other with warm smiles and greetings such as "Ya'll fixin' to have a good day?" Blue jeans, flannel and rugby shirts are customary attire in Knoxville, and many contracts are still bound with a handshake and a man's word. Few people are in a hurry in Knoxville; the two speeds at which locals move are slow and extra slow. So when the FBI descended like horseflies on the city for the second round game, the agents did not blend into the pine-clad hills.

Linwood Square, a commercial business complex of hotels, retail stores and office buildings on the city's north side had been converted into a quasi-FBI fortress. The flagship of Linwood Square, the Westin Hotel, served as the command center for Frank McCaskill and the hundred and fifty agents working under him. The FBI had taken over the top three floors of the Westin after reimbursing expelled guests who now stayed in hotels a hundred miles outside of Knoxville. With scores of navy suits and black wingtips running around at a breakneck pace, Knoxville looked more like a generic version of Wall Street than the home of "Rocky Top." Adding to the mayhem caused by the presence of the FBI personnel and equipment, more than three thousand press members from across the U.S. had come to record everything Mike Redding and Quentin Conway did. Knoxville was also, of course, swarming with college basketball fans who had converged on the city to witness the NCAA's first and second round games. Because of their single-minded devotion to a school and coach, college fans are the most fervent basketball fans in the world. The presence of twenty thousand crazed basketball loyalists intensified the chaotic and surreal electricity that gripped Knoxville.

Amid the buzz of activity in the Presidential Suite on the Westin's top floor, Frank McCaskill went over his two conversations with the anonymous informant. He had listened to audio tapes of the conversations so many times he knew them by heart. McCaskill was obsessed with the phone calls. Not only were they the FBI's strongest leads, he believed the person who made the calls knew the killer personally or had inadvertently stumbled upon the killer's identity. Either way, intuition and twenty plus years in law enforcement told him the informant was the key to solving the case.

McCaskill checked his watch. Quentin Conway was due to arrive in twenty minutes. Opening a manila file folder marked Jeremiah Forsey, he glanced through the biographical sheet to make sure there was nothing he had overlooked. The previous night McCaskill discussed the anonymous calls with Deputy Director Bailey. He told Bailey about the telephone call from his friend Theodore Belding of Georgetown Law School and the aborted meeting with Jeremiah Forsey. Bailey agreed the law student fit the description of their informant, especially since he was reputed to be an experienced researcher. McCaskill knew Jeremiah Forsey was a law student who hung out at the same bar as Allan Clancy. Certainly he must be the anonymous informant. Field agents in Washington, Chicago and Alabama were searching for him, as Frank McCaskill sat in the FBI war room atop the Westin reviewing Jeremiah Forsey's file. McCaskill's train of thought was broken when a tall, muscular man walked up to him and thrust out his hand.

"Alec Taylor at your disposal." McCaskill stood up to greet the towering giant. At six foot six and two hundred fifty-five pounds, Alec Taylor was quite a physical specimen. His streaked blond hair was considered long by FBI standards. The massive shoulders, V-shaped chest, tree-like thighs and bronzed skin gave him the appearance of a body builder or buff surfer, not the youngest special agent in the FBI. Alec Taylor could afford to wear his hair long and maintain his deep tan because he was the bureau's fastest rising-star. Two years earlier when he was already someone of note at the bureau, his stock soared during a highly publicized special investigation. While checking out a remote lead, he single-handedly identified and collared a Philadelphia school teacher responsible for the serial murders of five teenagers. With Alec Taylor standing in the FBI's war room, McCaskill's investigative team was instantly much stronger.

"Good to have you on the team, Alec. I'm glad you were able to get here before Mr. Conway arrived. Why don't we review some files and then I'll bring you up to speed on tonight's security arrangements."

McCaskill spent the next fifteen minutes briefing Alec Taylor and going over the planned entrance and exit routes for the game that evening. McCaskill's job would not have been as difficult if Quentin Conway didn't insist on attending the games. Quentin's absence would not only have made it easier for the FBI to protect him, it would also buy five days preparation time until the third round began. And McCaskill and the FBI needed as much time as possible. Mike Redding's team was a heavy favorite to win the Midwest regional and move on to the semifinals in Auburn Hills, Michigan. When asked by McCaskill to skip UNI's second round game, Quentin had sternly replied it was Mike's decision to coach and his decision to support him by attending the game. McCaskill knew there was no point in debating the issue. He admired Mike's and Quentin's resolve and determination, even though his job was complicated by their decisions. In his typical no nonsense manner, Frank

McCaskill accepted the challenging hand dealt to him and prepared to do his best.

As they reviewed Jeremiah Forsey's file, McCaskill was impressed by Alec Taylor's extensive knowledge of the case. The young agent had been assigned to it less than twelve hours, but had read numerous case logs during his flight from Dallas and was already familiar with the key aspects of the investigation. Their discussion was interrupted when Quentin Conway and Diana Fleming were ushered into the Presidential Suite.

"Good evening Mr. Conway, Ms. Fleming. Thank you for rearranging your plans to meet with us. This is special agent Alec Taylor of our Dallas office. He'll be working with me the duration of the investigation."

Quentin shook the agent's hand, while Diana simply nodded hello. She felt uncomfortable being there, but had agreed to attend the meeting since she was accompanying Quentin to the game.

"I asked you both to come in so we could go over tonight's plans." McCaskill gestured for Quentin and Diana to sit down. "We're going to bring you in the arena's west entrance, Mr. Conway. You'll have four agents along with your personal bodyguards in the limousine. This particular limousine is normally used for diplomats and foreign delegates. It's bullet-proof, flame resistant, and strong enough to withstand an explosion that would topple a two-story building. The limousine will be escorted by six marked Tennessee cruisers, each of which will carry two additional agents and two state troopers. After leaving the hotel, the motorcade will not stop until we reach the parking garage. The entire underground parking area has been sealed off the past two days.

"At precisely 6:50, as you are exiting the limousine, two identical entourages will exit limousines and enter the north and south entrances. All three groups will have the same number of agents and state troopers. The only difference among the three entourages will be that you and Ms. Fleming are in one of them. The agents and troopers in the other groups will be protecting decoys that resemble you. We have altered their physical appearance with wigs, makeup and body suits. Other than their voices, they could pass as your twins even to people who know you. None of the agents or state troopers will know if they are guarding you or the decoys. They have all been instructed to carry out their duties as if they are guarding you. This precautionary measure is done to obtain optimum security and protection."

McCaskill did not add confidentiality or secrecy even though they were legitimate concerns. The fatal car bombing that killed agent Eric Howard and Quentin Conway's chauffeur two days before had raised questions within the Bureau's ranks. It was unlikely, but nevertheless possible, that a mole had infiltrated the hierarchy of the FBI.

"You will be seated in the box seats directly behind the visiting team's bench. The other entourages will sit in box seats at the north and south ends of the arena. The agents, policemen and bodyguards will stay with you and your decoys throughout the game. The three entourages will exit the arena from the same entrances they entered. Do you have any questions?"

"Yes," Quentin said immediately. "How will you get me to the locker room to see Mike before and after the game?"

McCaskill had prepared for every eventuality Quentin Conway would throw at him, especially this one. "All three entourages will be led to the base of the players' tunnel when you arrive at the arena. The decoy groups will wait in the tunnel while you go inside the locker room. The team will be warming up on the court so you and Mike will be alone. The same procedure will take place after the game. Wherever you go, the decoy entourages will too. As you requested, Mr. Kirby will not leave your side. We've already briefed him on tonight's schedule. He'll be next to you at all times, while the rest of your bodyguards will be positioned behind our agents."

As Quentin gave McCaskill his approval of the security arrangements, Diana let out a nervous laugh. The visual image of FBI agents and state troopers huddled in the player's tunnel amused her. She couldn't believe the amount of trouble the FBI had gone to in an effort to accommodate Quentin. Suddenly, she was struck by the realization of what was happening. For the first time since she met him two weeks before, Diana understood how powerful Quentin was. He was the target of a sadistic killer and an FBI agent had died protecting him, yet he was allowed to attend the second round game and visit Mike before and after it was played. He was even able to dictate where his personal bodyguard would be positioned. Diana guessed only a few elite private citizens wielded enough power and clout to tell the FBI what to do. Quentin Conway was one of them.

Standing in the midst of laptops and PCs, whirring fax machines and over-worked federal agents, Diana listened as Quentin drilled Special Agent McCaskill with questions. She was scared. She wondered if a basketball game was this important. Wasn't something terribly wrong when decoy groups and escape routes were needed to attend a sporting event?

Diana had decided to tell Quentin she had changed her mind about going to the game when she thought of something he had told her. She had asked him why it was so important he see Mike prior to and after every game. Quentin told her Mike couldn't coach without it. Seeing his best friend calmed Mike and reassured him. It also let him know Quentin had made it to the game safely. After the game Mike wanted to see Quentin because they were as close as family. Mike's parents had been at all of his games from the time he started coaching at age nineteen. They sat in seats behind his bench so he could spot them. After games his parents stopped by the locker room to congratulate him or cheer him up.

Following his father's death from a heart attack when Mike was twenty-four, his mother became despondent and never left her house except to go to his games. Three and a half years later she died and Mike was left with no family. Quentin sensed Mike's incredible loneliness following his parents' deaths, especially at basketball games. Their ritual started innocently when Quentin dropped in to see Mike before a big game in 1988. After the game Quentin again visited the locker room to congratulate Mike on the victory. During a telephone conversation a few days later, Mike asked Quentin if he would come by and see him before the next game. Seven years and two hundred games later, Quentin had visited Mike before and after every game. He was Mike's family. Mike knew that for Quentin, the thought of missing a game or failing to visit his friend in the locker room was intolerable.

Mike needed him at his games; he depended on Quentin's presence. Unknown to everybody but his three closest friends, Mike had suffered a nervous breakdown when his father died and his mother refused to leave her home. For a full year, until he was twenty five, Mike met twice a week with a psychologist in an effort to work through the breakdown. While his professional life in coaching was becoming wildly successful and fulfilling, his personal and social lives were pathetically unsatisfying.

Feeling that guilt should be assigned somewhere or to some-one—it always was on the basketball court—he questioned why he had not been more committed to changing his father's eating and exercise habits and blamed himself for his mother's refusal to go on with her life. Unable to help his mother deal with the sudden, tragic death, Mike did the one thing he did best. He shouldered all the responsibility and worked even harder to help his mother move on with her life. She became the focal point of his existence. He lived to make her happy and comfortable, all the while ignoring his own basic needs for companionship and affection.

As his mother became more dependent on him emotionally and financially, he closed off everything else. Only basketball and his group of friends from high school did not suffer the ill effects of his self-crucifixion. Relationships with other friends and women became hopelessly unattainable. Both the conscious anger he felt concerning his father's death and the subconscious bitterness he experienced from being forced to care for his mother suddenly mani-fested itself in a raging temper that roared out of control at a moment's notice. Almost overnight, his cool, even-keel disposition was re-placed by an edgy, volatile demeanor that erupted without warning.

Damaged most by his personal self-castigation was his rela-tionship with himself. Off the basketball court Mike struggled to find contentment. His self-image was poor due to a misguided belief that his family had disintegrated because of his neglect and lack of commitment. The harder he tried to please his ailing mother, the worse he felt about himself. Any progress he made with his analyst was offset by his negative view of himself and the deteriorating relationships around him. He tried to make himself happy through external means instead of looking inward to find happiness and satisfaction.

When his mother passed away shortly after he had accepted the assistant coaching job at North Carolina, Mike's personal life spiraled out of control. He became obsessive about basketball. The only thing that gave him enjoyment was coaching basketball and interacting with his three buddies. At the time in his life when he should have been settling down with a wife and starting a family, he withdrew from dating. The women he did come in contact with found his temper and vulgar language offensive.

His inability to see his parents' deaths for what they really were made it impossible for him to like himself or receive satisfaction from anything outside of basketball. He unintentionally coped with the sadness and grief by venting his anger on everyone around him and then relished the ascetic punishment of making up for what he had done. He hated himself for letting his parents die, so he welcomed the scornful reactions his rude and obnoxious behavior brought as penance for his sins.

Finally, with the help of a new psychologist, a Catholic ministries peer group, each of whom were going through a similar healing process, and hundreds of hours of intense prayer, Mike lifted the guilt of his parents' deaths from his shoulders and stopped blaming himself. The results were dramatic. Once he stopped feeling responsible, his self-image improved, he rediscovered his smile and laugh and he was able to find enjoyment in hobbies other than basketball. With the return of his self-esteem, his confidence grew and he felt good about himself and did not have to depend on other people and superficial things to be happy.

Unfortunately, scars of the painful experience still plagued him long after he stopped beating himself up over the deaths. The violent temper and vulgar language were remnants of the struggle he went through while coping with the demise of his family. Even worse was his reluctance to become emotionally involved with people.

Not able to get close to anyone, particularly women, for fear he might lose them, Mike shied away from new relationships, especially those that looked promising.

As he became more successful and famous from coaching, he retreated deeper into an emotional shell. Not knowing the ordeal he had been through caused him to be closed off, women mistook his psychological fear of dating and committing for arrogance or indifference. The self-fulfilling prophecy had become an unbreakable cycle that imprisoned Mike's emotions. The more he cared about a woman, the more anxious he became about losing her, so he pulled away to protect himself. Inevitably, the woman involved misread his actions and distanced herself from the coach. Unbeknownst to himself, Mike had created a negative pattern of behavior that left his personal and social lives in disarray. The thing that scared him most, the very experience he was desperately trying to avoid—that of losing a dear friend or loved one—he encouraged and brought on. He had locked himself into a behavioral pattern that threatened to prevent him from having new meaningful relationships and most importantly, impeded his ability to commit to and be a part of a relationship with a woman he might love.

Intense professional pressure served to magnify the problem. During the last week Mike Redding's temper had been unmanageable. His behavior could be described as insolent and standoffish at best. His friends' murders were having the same effect on him as his parents' deaths had. The self blame, the feelings of helplessness and the fear of losing loved ones had resurfaced and once again tormented him. So too had the irrational, impudent outbursts. Now, for the second time, Mike was experiencing severe psychological and emotional crisis.

Quentin had not told Diana about Mike's bout with depression after his parents' deaths, the formidable fight to stop blaming himself or his inability to open up emotionally in new relationships. What he did tell her was that if he didn't see Mike before and after his games, his friend would feel the way he did following his parents' passing. Without knowing what Mike had been through, Diana had understood by the look on his face and the tone of his voice that

Mike had at some time been plunged into an emotional hell-hole and that Quentin would do anything to ensure his best friend would never visit it again.

After recalling Quentin's explanation, Diana realized there was much more at stake than a basketball game. Initially, she wondered if Quentin had some type of death wish. Now she believed the opposite. He had a life wish. He wanted to live every day to the fullest, as if it was the last day of his life. Diana realized Quentin understood better than anyone that he could not stop living because of terroristic threats. To give up what he held closest to his heart would be another type of death, obviously more transient than the cessation of life, but nevertheless just as destructive to the heart and soul. Diana sensed he refused to allow the killer to murder him emotionally and psychologically. The only way Quentin could beat terroristic intimidation was to stand up to it and continue to live with a free will.

As she listened to Quentin and Agent McCaskill finish a discussion about alternate departure routes, Diana once again began to feel secure about attending the game. When she heard McCaskill address her, Diana returned her attention to the conversation in front of her.

"Thank you for dressing casual, Ms. Fleming. Here are the clothes you'll be wearing this evening."

Diana's heart sank into her stomach as she thought of the time she had spent picking out an outfit. Frank McCaskill saw the look on her face.

"Sorry about the inconvenience, Ms. Fleming. We had to choose an outfit in advance so the decoys would look identical to you and Mr. Conway. I'm sure these clothes wouldn't be your first choice, but I hope they're satisfactory."

Diana sighed as she examined the UNI sweatshirt and jeans Alec Taylor held. "Well, at least I'll be comfortable," she said, faking optimism as Quentin inspected the shirt and Levi's picked out for him.

"You can change in the master bathroom, Miss Fleming. Agent Taylor will show you the way. While you're getting ready, I need to go over some additional details with Mr. Conway. Feel free to take your time. We'll be a while." Even though she could tell the statement was an order, not a request, Diana didn't mind. She wanted time to herself so she was happy to oblige.

McCaskill waited until Alec Taylor returned from the bathroom before speaking again. "Mr. Conway, what we are about to discuss is confidential. Only six people including agent Taylor and myself have knowledge concerning all aspects of this investigation. Ordinarily, we wouldn't discuss confidential or sensitive information with an individual we're protecting. This is a unique case, though. We believe you and Mr. Redding are targets of the person responsible for Congressman Clancy's and David Butler's deaths. Pardon me for referring to you as targets, but unfortunately, that's an accurate way to describe the situation. I'm sharing this information with you because it's important we're on the same page. Communication between us is vital. May I ask you a few more questions?"

"That's fine," Quentin replied.

"I've already spoken to Mr. Redding about this. I felt duty-bound to notify him before the game so he could make a decision whether or not to coach. Obviously, he decided to coach. We've found no motive that would link yours and Mr. Redding's deaths to the previous murders. The only common thread among you four is a lifelong friendship. It is an extremely vague common denominator, but so far as we can tell, it's the only thing you all share. We haven't ruled out any motives yet, but we are focusing our attention on your group's friendship. I believe the killer wants you and Mr. Redding dead for personal reasons. After analyzing every possible motive, only one is plausible. Someone close to your group killed Congressman Clancy and David Butler and is attempting to do the same to you and Mr. Redding."

Quentin sat on the sofa and didn't say a word. Before McCaskill spoke again he hesitated a moment, thinking for the twentieth time how he should phrase his next statement. Finally, he went with his gut instinct. McCaskill reasoned a man of Quentin Conway's character and stature would want to hear the truth straight out.

"There's enough evidence to bring in your old friend Ben Rooks for questioning . We believe he killed Clancy and Butler and tried to kill you." McCaskill waited for a response, but none came. No emotion, no change in expression, not even a tiny movement of the mouth.

"The problem is we can't locate him. Mr. Rooks first became a suspect when we discovered he was part of your high school group. Red flags went up when we couldn't locate him or find data on him after 1991. You and Mr. Redding stated in your interviews last week that you each lost touch with Ben Rooks during your sophomore year of college. Your attempts to contact him were unsuccessful because he was incarcerated at the Indiana State Penitentiary in Michigan City.

"Our field agents in Chicago dug up some interesting information. He was arrested on December 22, 1979, during a routine drug bust at a housing project on Chicago's south side. An anonymous caller tipped off the police. Mr. Rooks was arrested for possession of narcotics, possession of drug paraphernalia and consumption of a controlled substance. He had only one prior arrest on his record, a juvenile offense, but was sentenced to three years in jail." When McCaskill stopped at the bottom of the page he was reading from, Alec Taylor handed him a notepad with tiny notes scribbled on it. McCaskill continued speaking while he glanced down at the notepad.

"The arrest and incarceration were unusual. After three weeks at a medium security correctional facility in Joliet, Illinois, he was transferred to maximum security at Michigan City, Indiana. A petty offender like Rooks had no business doing hard time with rapists and murderers in the state pen. Before he was transferred to Michigan City, he was examined by the resident psychologist at Joliet. Dr. Charles Moorman described Ben Rooks as a manic-depressive with a severe inferiority complex. In Moorman's opinion the inferiority complex originated from his parents' divorce and the group of friends he ran with in high school. His analysis was that in college Rooks turned to drugs as a way to escape. The drugs were used to compensate for his poor self-esteem and image."

McCaskill paused for a moment to see if Quentin had any comments. When he offered no opinions or questions, McCaskill continued where he left off. "During a three hour interview with Dr. Moorman, Rooks became bitter and showed intense animosity toward you, Mr. Redding, Allan Clancy and David Butler. He claimed the four of you were responsible for his low self-esteem, which in turn led to his drug use. His view was he had allowed himself to be the whipping boy of a group of immature jocks and it cost him the best four years of his life. According to Dr. Moorman, the inferiority complex prevented Rooks from dealing with reality. He thought so little of himself he couldn't hold himself responsible for his actions. In his mind he was an innocent victim. He blamed all his problems on his group of high school friends.

"Dr. Moorman concluded his report by outlining how dangerous an individual can be if he doesn't feel accountable for his actions." McCaskill was silent for a second. When he found what he was searching for on the notepad, he resumed speaking. "This is a quote from the doctor's report. 'The inability to shoulder responsibility coupled with severe depression makes a person extremely irrational and inherently dangerous to himself and those around him.' Dr. Moorman suggested a person with Ben Rooks' fragile psychological makeup would be better served by a year of rehabilitation in a mental institution than by incarceration in a state penitentiary. For what appears to have been political pressure to toughen criminal sentencing, Ben Rooks was sent to Michigan City to do hard time despite Dr. Moorman's warnings.

"Unfortunately, the doctor's diagnosis was accurate. Rooks was repeatedly beaten and raped his first six months in the state pen. He attempted two escapes during that period and received longer sentences each time he was caught. Desperate to end the beatings, he intentionally fought with prison guards so he would be removed from the general population and placed in solitary confinement. He spent weeks at a time in solitary confinement. As soon as he was released back into the common population, he broke more rules and wound up in solitary again. As the years went by, he grew stronger physically but more imbalanced mentally. His addiction to heroin also got worse. After a few years at Michigan City, Rooks was a different man. He had built up his body through weight lifting and had read everything he could get his hands on. He was a control freak. Prison life is very regimented and he became extremely structured. The other inmates were scared of him because he spent much of his time devising elaborate plans to gain revenge on guards and prisoners."

McCaskill studied Quentin. The agent had been talking for five minutes, yet Quentin offered no response, so McCaskill kept going. "Rooks was released in 1986, seven years after his arrest. The parole board described him as a classic example of a petty criminal hardened by the penal system. Instead of rehabilitating him, the state pen did the opposite. It enhanced his flaws and buried his redeeming qualities. After being released from Michigan City, Rooks did something strange even by his standards. He got a job at a paint factory in Chicago and stayed out of trouble. From 1986 to 1991 he was a model citizen. We couldn't find a parking ticket or jaywalking violation during that time."

For the first time in five minutes Quentin spoke. "There's more, isn't there?"

"Yes. He disappeared in the summer of 1991. Since then there is absolutely no record of his existence. No tax returns, credit information, medical treatment or death certificate. Nothing. We talked to the manager at the paint factory and the employees working there when Rooks did. All of them said he was a good guy who worked incredibly hard. Almost every person we interviewed described him as quiet and reclusive. The manager and an employee who used the locker next to his provided valuable information. They said the inside of Rooks' locker was covered with pictures and newspaper clippings of you and your three friends. The employee noticed the pictures accidentally. The manager saw them while checking the locker for drugs. He had seen marks on Rooks' arm and suspected drugs. According to the manager, the marks decreased over time, but never completely went away. As the marks diminished, Rooks suffered from violent migraine headaches. During this period he turned in his three week notice and left the factory. He hasn't been seen or heard from since."

Before McCaskill could go on, Quentin interrupted him. "You believe Ben worked on a new identity from 1986 to 1991 and then went into hiding to develop a plan to kill me and my friends because he blames us for his drug addiction and prison stint."

Hearing the theory worded that way made it sound improbable. But remembering the thousands of man hours the Bureau had put into the investigation, McCaskill replied, "Do you think it's farfetched, Mr. Conway?"

Something seemed to be bugging Quentin; he'd obviously been working on it, a subconscious thought or idea in the back of his mind. Choosing his words carefully, he addressed McCaskill's question. "No. He's the only person with motive to want all of us dead. He has no alibi for the two murders or the limo bombing and emotionally and psychologically he's a loose cannon. Hell, he'd have to be the primary suspect. It is hard to imagine though."

Alec Taylor nodded his head in agreement before speaking. "Everything points to him. There's no evidence incriminating anyone else—not that we're going to stop looking, but he's clearly our prime suspect. The death threat you received confirmed Agent McCaskill's hunch. The letter expressed a bit of concern for you, yet threatened your life. He referred to Congressman Clancy in a familiar tone as if he knew him personally. Rooks had a severe inferiority complex when he entered the state pen and a god complex when he got out. The crime scene reflects these traits. The killer's full of himself, but he's also insecure. Urinating on Congressman Clancy's body after the murder is a good example. He was flaunting his skill, yet had to feed his ego by denigrating the victim. It all fits Rooks' psychological portrait—the MO, the brazen, gangster slayings in public—he's trying to prove he's better than his old friends. He's followed your career all these years and now he's trying to one-up you."

"That wouldn't be too hard. I haven't exactly kept a low profile," Quentin replied ruefully.

"It's a game to Rooks. He's boasting how good he is. The

death threat shows his confidence. The letter was postmarked in Chicago where Rooks resided after getting out of prison. That's hardly incriminating, but the name on the letter is. The death threat you received was signed 'Your Shadow.' Looking through some old souvenirs and papers of David Butler's, we discovered Ben Rooks nickname in high school was . . ."

"Shadow," Quentin blurted before Alec Taylor could finish the statement.

Quentin's sudden response confused Frank McCaskill. He knew from reading the files Quentin possessed a nearly photographic memory. Unbeknownst to Quentin and Mike, at the beginning of the case the FBI had investigated them and every other person close to Allan Clancy and David Butler. McCaskill investigated Mike, while Bill Cooper researched Quentin. As expected nothing turned up in the background checks. Neither Quentin or Mike had motive to kill Clancy and Butler, and both men had ironclad alibis. McCaskill learned a lot about Quentin Conway by reading Cooper's research. He was even more impressed with Quentin's accomplishments after reading his file. Since one of the talents mentioned on the profile sheet was a magnificent memory, McCaskill wondered why Quentin remembered the nickname now, but didn't recognize it when he first received the death threat.

"Mr. Conway, did you recognize the name Shadow when you first received the letter and didn't say anything, or did you recall Ben Rooks' nickname a second ago?"

"Just a second ago when Agent Taylor referred to David's old souvenirs. I haven't heard the nickname since high school, but even then I never called Ben by that name. Only Allan and Mike did."

"Do you remember where the nickname came from?" asked McCaskill.

"Sure. Ben used to kid around and say he was the best defensive soccer player in the state. He told us we couldn't score on him because he played better defense than a shadow. Allan thought it was hilarious and gave him the nickname. From there it just sort of stuck. I didn't like the name, though, so I never used it. I hate to agree with you, but it's hard not to. Everything points to Ben. It's just difficult to believe the Ben Rooks I knew in high school could be capable of murdering Allan and David."

"This isn't the same individual. Extended periods of drug use and prison changed him. He's very capable," Alec Taylor replied. "Don't forget Ben Rooks is the person with the best reason for wanting you all dead. Eighty percent of the time in murder cases the one with the most motivation is the killer."

"But how could he do it?" Quentin queried, knowing the truth but wanting to hear the answer.

"Rooks is a psychopath," Taylor said, anger creeping into his voice. "Rules of society don't factor into his decision-making process. He's completely uninhibited; normal societal restraints aren't recognized or considered. He has no conscience, so he'll do whatever he wants without regard to laws or the sanctity of human life."

As Alec Taylor discussed Ben Rooks' psychotic tendencies, McCaskill wondered if Quentin's memory was being triggered and if images were flooding his mind. McCaskill himself could see in his mind's eye the five friends standing on a bridge high above Lake Freeman. From the Bureau's exhaustive research, he knew about the challenge Quentin had issued his friends; each must accomplish three goals within twenty years. Allan Clancy, David Butler, Mike Redding and Quentin Conway were all independently wealthy, famous in their professions and huge successes. Frank McCaskill's pulse skipped two beats as he pondered the results of Quentin's challenge; only Ben Rooks had failed to accomplish the three goals. And now two of the groups members were dead. McCaskill knew he had to protect Mike Redding and Quentin Conway from what appeared to be their old friend's deviant new challenge.

Chapter Twelve

The drive from the Westin Hotel to Thompkins-Bowles Arena usually took twenty minutes. Even with the throng of reporters, fans, and curious onlookers slowing it down, the motorcade made the trip in eight minutes. As soon as the limousine came to a standstill in the parking garage below the arena, six FBI agents opened the car door and formed a semi-circle for Quentin and Diana to walk through. Nine feet away an open elevator waited for them. A minute after the limousine had stopped, the entourage was in the elevator heading up to the ground floor. As Quentin and Diana stepped out of the elevator at the main concourse level, two identical entourages set off media firestorms at the arena's north and south entrances.

While FBI agents and state troopers guarded the decoys at the base of the player's tunnel, Quentin and Diana were rushed down the ramp to the UNI locker room. Alec Taylor had called ahead from the parking garage, so Mike anxiously awaited Quentin's arrival. When the locker room door swung open, a battalion of agents and troopers entered first. Moments later, the army of flesh parted, and Quentin walked across the crowded room. Without saying a word, he grabbed Mike and hugged him. It was an awkward moment for the FBI agents and state troopers, but not for the two friends. They hadn't seen each other since the previous game two days before. Failing to notice Diana, Mike turned and walked into the coach's office. Quentin followed behind and shut the door once he was inside. When Mike faced Quentin, Diana could see the toll the last two days had taken. Although he was clean shaven and wore an expensive suit, Mike looked haggard. Even worse, Diana sensed uncertainty, possibly even fear in the coach's eyes.

"You ready, brother?" Quentin asked.

"How the hell would I know? I'm so damn confused I'm apt to brush my ass with my Oral B and wipe my teeth with toilet paper. This's been the toughest damned game of my life to get up for. I've had second thoughts about coaching ever since your limo was blown up. Christ, Quentin, you could have been in it. I keep wondering if I'm putting my players and coaches in jeopardy by staying on the fuckin' bench. I can't let anything happen to them. They're my responsibility."

"Nothing's going to happen to them, Mike."

"How can I be sure? Three days ago I was confident of that. Now, I'm not sure of anything. Every person in the stadium knows we'll beat the crap out of Minnesota whether I coach or not. Is this game worth sacrificing everything? Is the whole damn tournament worth it? I don't have a wife or kids yet, Quentin. I can't stop thinking about not getting the chance to have a family of my own."

Realizing he was so worked up his voice could be heard outside the office in the locker room area, Mike took a deep breath and tried to calm down. "You probably think I'm out of my freakin' mind. I feel like I've lost control of everything, Q. I don't know if coaching's worth risking my life and missing out on a family. I've always said basketball is life, but now I'm not sure. I want to coach, but I don't know if that's the right thing. I refuse to risk everything simply because I was too proud or too stupid to step down."

Leaning toward his friend, Quentin placed his arms on Mike's shoulders and looked into his face. "Mike, the issue isn't if basketball and coaching are worth dying for. Looked at that way, nothing is worth dying for. The issue is what's worth *living* for. This is about pursuing your dreams and not letting anything stop you from reaching them. Do you want to live the rest of your life with regret, always wondering what could have been? Think about what'll happen if you don't coach. You won't be living—that's worse than death. Are you willing to give up what you love, and let Ben prevent you from realizing your greatest dream? I know you want to coach. It's what you do. Remember the picture hanging over your fireplace? 'Many things in life will catch your eye, but only a few will capture your heart—pursue those.' Basketball and coaching are the things that have captured your heart, Mike. You only get one chance at living. Is a psycho friend from our past going to make us compromise ourselves and give up our dreams? I won't do it, Mike— I can't. I've got to go for broke. I can't live any other way, and I know you can't either."

"What a kick in my ass," Mike said as Quentin's words sank in. "I'm second guessing myself way too much. I've been so worried something might happen tonight I've barely concentrated on the game. I won't be held hostage by someone else's delusions of grandeur. This is my year to win it all. I can taste it, Q. You're looking at the coach of the next national champs."

"That's more like it," Quentin said. "The tiger is back."

"Things have been fucked up lately. It's like all this crap isn't happening to me, or I'm living someone else's life. The one thing not royally screwed up is you and me. This's the toughest thing I've been through, and you're there, man. I appreciate you watching my back, Q. You know, coming to the games, visiting me and sticking by. It means a lot. You're the only person I have now, brother."

"You're my man too. But I'd articulate it a lot better with less profanity," joked Quentin as the two friends hugged again. Unlike the first time, when they broke from this embrace, Mike was smiling.

"You set, Red? You're about to coach in front of the largest basketball audience ever. Isn't this your dream?"

"Hell yeah," Mike replied. "But if we get bounced, I'll be the coach who goated in front of the largest audience ever."

Quentin laughed. "Don't worry, half the people watching don't know anything about basketball, so they'll never know!"

"Oh, that's great," Mike replied sarcastically. "Fans of 'Cops' and 'Rescue 911' don't give a rat's ass who wins. They're watching to see if I can be resuscitated when I'm turned into Swiss cheese."

Quentin didn't laugh at the dry remark because he had something serious on his mind. "What do you think about Ben? Does knowing he's the murderer make it harder to deal with?"

"A helluva lot harder. Allan's and David's deaths seem even more pointless. The idea that someone from our group is killing us blows my mind. It's un-fucking-comprehensible."

"If you think about it, Red, he wasn't really one of us."

"That's for damn sure," Mike said growing angry. "I can't believe I actually considered stepping aside because of that little prick." An ominous expression flashed across Mike Redding's face. Dark clouds rolled down his brows and into his eyes signifying the storm had arrived. The infamous temper was about to be unleashed. "It's a good thing I'm not giving interviews, because if I was talking to those stupid media leeches, I'd give them two killer quotes. We're gonna stomp all over Minnesota's sorry asses and if Ben Rooks is in the building tonight, I'll rip his fuckin' head off and piss down his throat."

Diana Fleming was disappointed. As she sat in the box seats with Quentin waiting for the game to start, she couldn't take her mind off Mike. He had barely noticed her in the locker room and it bothered her. She had juggled her flight schedule, given up valuable vacation time and been subjected to near-harassing conditions by the FBI so she could attend the game. For all the trouble Diana had endured, she had seen Mike less then thirty seconds. Diana hoped UNI won easily so she and Quentin could spend time with Mike after the game. If UNI won, they would not play for five days, so Mike would probably relax and unwind with Quentin. Diana needed to see Mike Redding again. She hadn't stopped thinking about him for two days. Seeing him was the only way she would be able to sort out her feelings.

Scheduled tip-off time was 8:30 PM UNI and Minnesota had

originally been slated to play the 6:00 PM game, but CBS and the NCAA agreed to switch the Kansas-Marquette game to 6:00 so UNI could play during prime time. Saturday evenings had traditionally been one of CBS's poorest nights for ratings, but that was about to change. Network analysts expected the game to be the most-watched sporting event ever, surpassing all Super Bowls, World Series and Dream Team basketball games. This second round NCAA tournament game had one element those games lacked: live human drama involving the possible murder of one of the game's key participants. An hour and a half before tip-off, Eyewitness News 13 of Indianapolis went on the air to break a story about an FBI press conference that would be held within two days. The purpose of the press conference was to give an update on the investigation, and according to an anonymous source, announce a primary suspect. The news raced through the packed stadium like a bolt of electricity and made the capacity crowd buzz like a live-wire of energy and excitement.

The crowd in Thompkins-Bowles Arena did not look like an ordinary college basketball crowd. The seats behind both baskets which were usually reserved for students and fans had been transformed into a press section for the thousands of journalists, photographers and media types. Every major press entity in North America, from CNN to *Playboy*, was covering the game. Tabloid television shows and newspapers that glorify sex, greed, and violence were also highly visible presences in Knoxville. The fans themselves behaved in bizarre, dramatic ways. Many stored spring water and food from the concession stand in their pockets in case of an explosion or fire. Home-made survival kits were plentiful.

A recent Gallup Poll surveyed the number of Americans following the murder investigation and basketball tournament. Ninety-one percent of the eight thousand people polled were following the story. The investigation was by far the main topic discussed on radio and television talk shows. Across the nation people debated the effectiveness of the FBI's investigation and whether or not Mike Redding should continue to coach this team in the tournament. The story fascinated Americans because at least one of the elements involved was of interest to individuals of all backgrounds. Since the drama's key figures were rich and famous, TV tabloid shows were having a field day reporting the story as a true-life soap opera. No story since Watergate had been so explosive that the reporter breaking the case would instantly become a household name. Mike Redding's worst fear had become reality. The NCAA tournament, a three week display of the purest, most unpredictable and passionate basketball in the world, had been turned into an over-hyped social drama by politicians and the media.

While his coaching staff gave the team last minute instructions in UNI's locker room, Mike walked up the player's tunnel with eight agents and two personal bodyguards surrounding him. When they reached court level, the UNI fans rose to their feet and began showering Mike with thunderous applause. The Minnesota fans along with the remaining Kansas and Marquette supporters also clapped in polite respect.

After the entourage had made its way to the scorer's table at midcourt, Mike asked the public address announcer if he could speak to the crowd. Sitting amid a protective cocoon of agents and state troopers, Diana Fleming sensed what he was about to do and held her breath in nervous anticipation. Mike's unexpected entrance had sent numerous television cameramen scrambling to broadcast the activity. Minutes later when the crowd finally quieted down, Mike addressed the 17,000 fans in attendance while millions of viewers watched at home.

"I want to talk about why we're here. People at home have their own reasons for watching, but I want to remind all of you in the arena why we're here. The first reason is so two teams can compete to determine who's better. The second is so you fans can support your team and enjoy an entertaining contest of teamwork and skill. That's it. There're no other reasons. We're not trying to promote ourselves, make money or do anything else. The players, coaches, officials and everyone involved with the game are here for those two reasons, so there shouldn't be any other reasons *you're* here."

Without notice, Mike Redding's voice changed from a reserved, diplomatic tone to a louder, more assertive, impassioned tone. "Many extraneous events the last two weeks have impacted my life and this team. Let's keep them outside this building. I want to make something clear to everyone watching this game. We're here to play basketball. For the last nine months these teams have been running, lifting weights and practicing so they could reach this point. We're here to see which team performs better. Let's not lose sight of that because of events going on elsewhere. This isn't my team, either. It's not Mike Redding's team playing Minnesota. This is UNI's team. It belongs to the students, faculty, alumni, employees and all the people who support the university. These teams are competing against each other because we cherish and respect the game of basketball. I'd like you all to do the same. If not for the game, please do it for the players. They deserve it. Thank you."

The applause was deafening two minutes after Mike Redding stopped speaking. As soon as the last note of the national anthem was sung, the noise picked up again. Following the introductions of the starting lineups and coaches, the UNI fans were surprised a second time when Mike's players peeled off their warmups, revealing new uniforms. Mike wanted to take the focus off himself and the investigation and put it back on basketball, and he thought his players would be excited by the change. Quentin had loved the idea and urged Mike to do it; as his starting five walked out to center court for the opening tip-off, Mike could tell by the crowd's reaction and the expressions on his players' faces that the new uniforms were a hit.

The first five minutes went exactly as Mike had planned. UNI controlled the tempo with a tenacious, man-to-man pressing defense. At the ten-minute mark of the first half, UNI had kept Minnesota's potent offense off-balance and established a 22-14 lead. As usual, Byron Lewis was sensational. He got going quickly, accounting for eight points, five rebounds and two steals in the first ten minutes. When the action stopped for a TV time-out, UNI's sideline huddle resembled a military field meeting. Mike didn't like to waste time during time-outs; his huddles were extremely organized and business-like. As he talked to the five players in the game about defensive maneuvering, offensive spacing and soft areas in Minnesota's zone defense, his assistant coaches conferred with the scorer's table on the number of time-outs UNI had left and how many fouls their players had been whistled for, while student managers handed dry towels and Gatorade to the players.

The noise in the arena made it impossible for Mike to be heard without yelling. To help overcome this problem five chairs from the bench had been carried onto the court. The seven subs not in the game stood around the chairs to shield their coach and the starters from the noise. Mike yelled instructions while a trainer rubbed Byron Lewis' calves to prevent cramping in his muscles and a student manager adjusted tape on another player's pinky and ring fingers.

While he knelt in the middle of the huddle and screamed over the noise of the cheerleaders and crowd, Mike watched the new trainer work on Byron's legs. The coach felt light-headed and queasy. David Butler should have been in the huddle tending to Byron's cramps. He had always done that. More than any time since he first found out about his friend's murder, Mike felt an acute sense of loss as he watched the trainer work on Byron. They had been so close— nothing would ever replace that. In an awkward moment of pain and sadness, Mike forgot his train of thought in mid-sentence, still kneeling in front of his players. Not able to regain his thought pattern or his composure, he sheepishly asked them to play harder.

Perhaps sensing his vulnerability, and motivated by the embarrassing lapse, the team tore out of the huddle on their way back onto the court. When play resumed UNI attacked Minnesota's perimeter offense and forced their guards into one turnover after another. During the next ten minutes Minnesota's miscues were converted into breakaway dunks, uncontested three-point shots, and easy lay-ups. Only the half-time buzzer could halt the onslaught. By then UNI had reeled off a 27-12 run which sent them to the locker room with a commanding 49-26 lead. Minnesota got no closer than twenty points the rest of the way. At the ten-minute mark of the second half, Byron Lewis took a seat on the bench, as did Mike Redding. With its star player resting on the sidelines and an assistant coach finishing the game, UNI coasted to an easy 87-66 win over the Midwest region's eighth seeded team.

As UNI was putting the finishing touches on their second round win in Knoxville, a beige four-door Toyota Camry rolled to a stop in a secluded area of Guntersville Lake in Guntersville, Alabama. The driver of the car turned off the Camry's headlights and opened the sun roof to let in the cool spring air. After taking a large swig from a bottle of Jose Cuervo, he gazed through the open roof at the millions of tiny stars that illuminated the sky. The tranquil beauty of the peaceful lake and the magnificent splendor of the celestial bodies calmed his nerves.

"Everything will be hunky-dory," he said softly.

When the horn sounded signaling UNI's win over Minnesota, he turned off the car radio and pulled the keys out of the ignition. His thoughts drifted to his mother and all the things she had done for him. Without her love and support he would be lost. Next, he thought of his girlfriend. She was beautiful, sweet and southern: an incredible girl with a heart of gold. One day she would make a wonderful wife. As he pictured her radiant smile, he pulled an envelope out of his pocket and set it on the dashboard.

The last person he thought of was Congressman Allan Clancy. Remembering the loud, raunchy outbursts, he silently cursed the congressman for being such an entertaining drunk. Then he cursed his own susceptibility to curiosity, temptation and greed. After reciting the Lord's prayer and a Hail Mary, Jeremiah Forsey took one final gulp of tequila and picked up the revolver he had been cradling in his lap. Leaning his head back so he could see the luminous stars in the immense southern sky, Jeremiah took a deep breath, opened his mouth and blew out the back of his head.

Quentin was in the middle of telling Diana a story when Mike and his bodyguards walked into the room. Instead of going to the NCAA's hospitality room with his players and the media after the game, Mike wanted to unwind with Quentin in a private spot. The NCAA moderators and tournament organizers had been more than willing to accommodate Mike's request, because his presence brought publicity and money to the tournament and the city of Knoxville. While waiting in the empty press room for Mike to finish his post-game talk with his players, Quentin and Diana drank Rolling Rock beer and snacked on buffalo wings, nachos and mozzarella sticks. They had been in the vacant room for thirty minutes when the entourage walked in.

While Mike made his way over to Quentin's and Diana's table, the agents guarding him sat down next to Quentin's bodyguards. These agents were drinking water, eating nothing and trying to keep their eyes off Diana Fleming. After the game Diana had changed back into her own clothes. Her original outfit of jeans, a cream tunic and a checkered blazer was simple yet stunning. Mike noticed her long before he got to the table. He hoped it wasn't obvious how attracted he was to her.

"Congrats, Red. Great job," Quentin said while high-fiving his friend. Mike found a seat next to Quentin and Diana faced them from the other side of the table.

"Thanks, Q. I hope I didn't keep you waiting too long. Hey, Diana, it's good to see you."

"Likewise," Diana answered sweetly. "What a game. You must be happy with their performance."

"I am. We could've won by forty and Minnesota is a solid team."

As Mike settled in, a tournament moderator entered the room with a fresh tray of cold cuts, wings, nachos and salsa. He carried it across the room and set it down on the table in front of Mike. The food had already been tested by a poison specialist, so Mike wasted no time digging in. Diana was excited. She enjoyed being with Quentin, but it was different when she was around Mike. She felt alive when he was near. It was more than physical attraction. She was drawn to him for reasons she herself did not understand.

As Mike feasted on the appetizers, Diana studied him. He was tall and lanky, a shade over six foot four and one hundred ninety-five pounds. He wore his dark black hair stylishly short. His pressed white shirt, silk Lagerfeld tie and charcoal Brooks Brothers suit would have made a Madison Avenue advertising exec proud. Despite the expensive name-brand clothes, there was nothing flashy about Mike Redding. His dark features and athletic body made him naturally good-looking. As usual, he appeared to be so involved in what he was doing he wasn't aware of his strong physical presence.

Although he was extremely attractive physically, it was Mike's personality and disposition that intrigued Diana. Although she had been warned of Quentin Conway's dual personalities, Mike Redding had turned out to be the one with contradictory qualities. This night-and-day demeanor fascinated Diana. She liked everything she had read, heard and seen about him except for the destructive temper and vulgar language. She didn't understand how a man of his vast intelligence, who possessed such tremendous compassion, could be so violent and crude when set off. She found Mike the walking contradiction, not Quentin. To Diana's surprise, she was more attracted to his demanding, take-charge, fiery personality than Quentin's laid back, easy-going disposition.

She knew why, though. Diana felt there was another side to his personality, a side buried deep beneath the rigid, volcanic exterior. Although she couldn't put her finger on it or even come close to knowing where to look, Diana sensed frailty and weakness in Mike. To her the temper tantrums and foul language seemed to be masking greater problems. It was what lay underneath the surface of his personality—an indiscernible vulnerability, a child-like plea for attention and help through wholly irrational and unacceptable behavior, that drew her to him.

Certainly Quentin had everything in the world going for him and was attractive in all the ways women find men desirable. The problem with him was that he had no flaws—at least none that she had seen. She wasn't a business adversary, so his ruthless side didn't concern her. Like most women, Diana found a man without flaws completely undesirable. This was Mike's magnetic appeal. As cold and demanding as he was on the outside, he was even more weak and susceptible on the inside. He was flawed, piteously flawed, and although Diana didn't know for sure why he was, she intended to find out. And then she would fix it.

"You're playing as well as anyone in the country," Quentin said between bites of wings. "How do you think the team will hold up the next two weeks if Ben isn't found?"

"They'll be okay. They're using the attention and hype to motivate themselves. Byron in particular has elevated his play. He's at a level few college players have reached. Alcindor, Walton, Bird, Magic, Sampson, Jordan and maybe Glenn Robinson, but not too many others were this good. He sees how hard this is for me, so he's determined to win the title. He and Butler were damn close; David used to tell him he was overrated. He gave Byron more shit because he thought he was gonna be one of the best college players in the last fifteen years. They had tremendous respect for each other. Byron jokingly told David he was a trainer because he couldn't handle real classes in college. But when it came to exercise programs, conditioning drills, anything related to his body, Byron swore by David. He wouldn't listen to anyone else. The morning I told the team about Butler's death, Byron had his worst practice at UNI. We're such a closely knit group, the players feel like a family member has died. The sense of loss is difficult, but they're rallying around me. I've never said this, Q, but I know we're gonna win it."

"You been watching the Psychic Friends Network?" Quentin asked, surprised by the bold statement.

"Yeah, Dionne Warwick told me we'd win it. I can't explain it, but this year is different. In all my years of coaching, I can't remember a feeling like this. As the stakes get bigger and the pressure increases, this team plays better. If we win our next two and go to the Final Four again, we'll be cutting down some nets."

"How do the next two games look?" Diana asked.

"Tough," Mike replied. "Marquette is well-coached and disciplined. They blew through their conference tournament and carried a lot of momentum into the NCAA's. Just ask Kansas—Marquette stuck it to 'em tonight. Marquette's dangerous because they got hot at the right time, but they don't have the talent or depth to play with us forty minutes. The first half will be close, but they'll tire in the second half. I like Kentucky over Duke in the other game. Both those teams worry me. Our bracket's a bitch. We got royally shit on by the selection committee. I still can't believe they put Duke, Kentucky and us in the same region. Duke and Kentucky have the players, benches, and experience to win it all. Not to mention outstanding coaching."

Smiling at Mike's last comment, Diana stood up, stretched her arms and legs and sat back down. Those teams were well-coached, but so was UNI. She couldn't help noticing that during the five minutes Mike had been there, he had cursed only a few times. It was probably a record of restraint for Mike. Diana had no idea what was causing it, but she liked the change.

"Who would you rather play, Kentucky or Duke?" she asked.

"Duke. They don't have Kentucky's inside-out game and they play eight guys. Kentucky goes ten deep. I'd say besides us, Kentucky's the team to beat. Their power is awesome. They have so much talent and shoot the three so well, they can bury you in a matter of minutes. Kentucky should get by Duke and then play us in the Final Eight, which will be the real championship. The Final Four will be anti-climatic."

Diana was enthralled by Mike's remark. "I know you'd never say that publicly for fear of giving another team bulletin board material to motivate them. Do most coaches think one way yet say the opposite?"

Mike stared at her a moment. He found her curiosity and genuine interest appealing. And she looked incredible, even better than he remembered. *What was her relationship to Quentin*, he wondered. He couldn't ask right now but would look forward to finding out.

"Yeah, most of it's lip service. We say what's politically correct. It's hard for a lot of them because of their massive egos. Sometimes we hold back because we don't want to reveal information or strategy that might help an opponent. Other times coaches keep stuff to themselves so they don't get reprimanded or fined by the NCAA. Usually, we make stuff up because reporters and sportswriters ask asinine questions. Have you ever listened to the questions at a press conference, Diana? They're terrible. Not all sportswriters are idiots. Many are knowledgeable and professional. There's just an amazing number of incompetent jackasses covering sports. Many of them resent coaches because of the money and fame. I'll be the first to admit coaching isn't performing daily brain surgery and the perks are unbelievable, but at least the majority of coaches are competent.

"Some sportswriters are frustrated athletes who weren't good enough to play in college or the pros. They either don't know the game well enough, or they vent their frustration on athletes and coaches. These are the ones doing a disservice to their profession and the sports they cover. If I said this publicly, writers everywhere would rip me a new ass, but it's true. Their job is easy. I could do their job a lot better than they could do mine. I promise you all coaches feel that way. Dealing with the media is the one part of my job I could do without. That's the only good thing about this whole ordeal. I haven't had to deal with the press for two weeks."

For the next thirty minutes the conversation revolved around basketball and the NCAA tournament. Diana was fascinated by the behind-the-scenes discussion of college basketball. She hung on Mike's words so closely that her arms and upper torso were sprawled across the table that separated them. Diana asked Mike countless questions about recruiting, how he kept alumni and boosters away from his players, what he thought of other coaches' abilities, and what went through his head when a game was on the line and he had to make a tough decision.

Mike answered the questions candidly. Normally, he didn't talk openly with someone he had just met, but he trusted Diana Fleming and found the discussion extremely enjoyable. Mike admitted how badly he wanted to win a national championship. He acknowledged feeling extra pressure after going to the Final Four so many times without winning it. He believed the pressure was self-imposed, not a result of scrutiny by the media or the university's administration. Try as he might, he couldn't bring himself to tell her how his obsessive desire to win a national championship had taken over his already dismal personal life. As much as he wanted to confide in her and share his true thoughts about his career's impact on his private life, he was afraid to open up to her for fear she would be put off and would not want that kind of presumptive intimacy. The last thing Mike needed after his friends' murders and during his pursuit of the national title was to be hurt by a woman.

After a while the conversation turned to the investigation. Quentin and Mike had briefly discussed the case, but Mike wanted to talk about it at greater length.

"Quentin, I want your opinion. I realize Ben had the motive and opportunity to kill Allan and David, but do you think he's capable of doing it?"

"It's hard to believe, Mike, but the facts are indisputable. A friend on Capitol Hill told me McCaskill is the FBI's best and Taylor's got the talent to be the next McCaskill. They're convinced Ben's the murderer. Do you have doubts?" Quentin asked.

"I wouldn't call it doubt. I just can't imagine Ben killing anyone. It has nothing to do with him being in our high school group. I can't believe he has what it takes to kill. He was constantly screwing things up. Simple tasks were adventures with him. According to McCaskill, prison life changed him. That's understandable, but it's still hard to believe he's capable of committing two perfect murders. Shit, he's the last one of our group I'd guess could pull it off."

"I don't know what to tell ya, Mike. I think your instincts are wrong. But if they're not, someone's got the FBI snowed."

"You barely seem affected by all this, Quentin. Are you even scared?"

"Hell, yeah, I'm scared," Quentin said, surprised by the question. "I'm freakin' out on the inside. I don't enjoy knowing an old friend wants me dead. Every day I wake up scared shitless, but I'm angry as hell, too. I want Ben to pay for what he did. When I get upset about being hunted like an animal or when I'm scared of what could happen, I focus on Allan and David. They'd want me to be strong and keep going. That gets me through it. And besides, nobody is gonna make me change who I am or what I do."

"The uncertainty is killing me," Mike said. "I have no idea what's ahead, I just hope it happens soon. I can't believe the timing of this, during the tournament and all. I know it's a major story, but don't people have lives of their own? Every time I turn on the TV or look at a newspaper or magazine, I see our faces. All I want is a national championship. Instead, I'm trying to keep breathing, so I can see the Final Four. I'm worried about your safety and my players' safety, and the damned press won't stop hounding me. The FBI better find Ben soon, because I can't take this shit much longer."

Realizing he had become hyper and was nearly yelling, Mike took a deep breath and collected himself. He was embarrassed by his adolescent display of emotion. Refusing to lose control of his temper in Diana's presence, he silently counted to three before speaking again.

"Sorry about that. I bet you guys want to know how I really feel, huh? I can't begin to express how frustrating this is for me. Two things Q. Do you think we'll win it all and can McCaskill find Ben before the championship game?"

Quentin's answer surprised Mike and frightened Diana. "You'll be national champs if you're on the bench, but if the FBI doesn't find Ben soon, you might not be coaching—and I won't be watching."

He looked at the alarm clock on the night stand next to his bed. The clock read 3:42 AM. He had lain in bed unable to sleep for over three hours, playing and replaying the mental video of the game earlier that night. Two thoughts stood out in his mind: UNI had won convincingly and Mike Redding was heavily guarded. UNI was playing better than any team in the country. Mike Redding seemed destined to finally win a national title. The security at the game had been intense. Federal agents were all over the arena, but UNI's coach was still vulnerable. Every time he left the bench and stood up on the sidelines he was an easy target for sniper fire.

The man's last thought before dozing off was that sniper fire was a boring, unimaginative way to kill someone. Falling deeper into a restless slumber, he eventually reached REM, the unconscious state of mind where dreaming occurs. In his mind's eye he saw a man shrouded in darkness in a large room. The man seemed out of place—like a stranger who didn't belong. The empty room was so dark the image of the man was barely visible. Although the man looked like an apparition, he was flesh and bones.

The sleeping figure tossed and turned as his subconscious mind processed information in an attempt to figure out why the strange man in the dream seemed so familiar. Suddenly, the slumbering man's subconscious mind recalled the scene from the past and transferred the knowledge to his memory. Startled by the realization, he awoke to find himself sitting bolt upright at the end of his bed. A flood of memories filled his head while perspiration dripped profusely off him and soaked the bed sheets. Upon seeing the time of 5:17, he realized he had blacked out after having the same dream again. This time the dream was more vivid and lasted longer. Although Ben Rooks still didn't know why he was having the dream, the latest episode did reveal one thing. He was the man shrouded in darkness. The dream was a flashback from his arrest sixteen years before.

Chapter Thirteen

McCaskill pulled the second page of the report out of the fax machine and quickly read down it. Before the next page was finished transmitting, he ripped the sheet from the machine and searched for the time of death.

"Nothing," McCaskill said. "His letter doesn't even mention Rooks. ETD was between 6:00 PM and midnight on the 19th. Christ, Taylor. Forsey blew his brains out during the game."

While he listened to McCaskill voice his frustrations, Alec Taylor read a faxed copy of the suicide note. The possibility the death was actually a homicide had already been discounted when both the Bureau's calligraphy and forgery experts reached the same conclusion. The handwriting in the letter belonged to Jeremiah Forsey and it showed no signs of coercion or duress. After studying the angle of the exit wound and the trajectory of the bullet, forensic scientists set the probability of a self-inflicted gun shot wound as the cause of death at 95% to 98%.

When he finished reading the note, Taylor realized the magnitude of the FBI's problem. The only person who could identify Ben Rooks was dead. He had taken his own life because he knew too much. Taylor rubbed his forehead to ease the knots of stress forming in his temples. The timing of events further complicated the situation. That afternoon the FBI was holding their first press conference and the media would have a heyday if they found out the Bureau's main informant had blown himself away. With UNI's next game three days away, the risk for Mike Redding grew daily. The clock was ticking and the FBI was beginning to feel the pressure. Thinking about the extraordinary circumstances surrounding the case made Taylor sick. He wasn't a twenty-year veteran of the Bureau like McCaskill, but he couldn't recall another case this difficult. Not only were the murders performed with incredible skill and precision, but the killer had also removed himself from society years before, leaving no incriminating trail to follow.

Lately, Taylor had heard increased grumbling from the media. Many journalists questioned the Bureau's procedures and editorialized about whether Mike Redding should be allowed to coach during the tournament. Others openly blasted the investigation and the FBI's handling of security arrangements. With UNI advancing steadily through the tournament and the sensational nature of the story growing exponentially, the media did not appear ready to back off the FBI or Mike Redding any time soon. Only two things could bring an end to the biggest story since O.J. Simpson's trial: the arrest or death of the March Madness Murderer or the assassination of Redding. Taylor's thoughts were interrupted by the sound of people entering McCaskill's office.

"Let's get started. I want to brief the director in less than an hour," Deputy Director Bailey said, taking a seat opposite McCaskill's desk. Special Agents Walter Haslett and Gary Dalton entered the office behind the Deputy Director and sat in leather chairs in the corner.

"Whose press conference is it?" asked McCaskill.

"Taylor's. Both the director and I agreed," Bailey replied. "Alec's a better speaker and easier on the eyes. We need to win points with the press. They've had us for lunch and they're ready for dinner. The director wants to use the press conference for PR and to inform the public of our progress."

"I guessed it'd be Alec so I prepared an outline. He's been going over it since yesterday." McCaskill handed a copy to Bailey, who didn't bother reading it. If McCaskill had written the outline, it was good.

"Alec, you've got an appointment to get your hair cut when we're done and a makeup guy will be here an hour before the conference. Your suit's fine, but that tie's too flashy. Find another one. What's next, Frank?"

"Nothing new on Forsey's suicide," McCaskill told Bailey. "The lid's on tight, so the media should be in the dark about the info he gave us. If Forsey talked to someone and they leaked, Taylor will play dumb and bury the question with stats about the number of anonymous calls, etc. If it comes out later we communicated with Forsey, we'll hide behind the confidentiality of sources clause in our charter. It'll be enough to avoid a Senate or House ethics investigation."

"What are the chances this kid talked?"

"Slight to none," replied McCaskill. "He was so scared of Rooks he turned himself into a Pez dispenser. Unless he told someone early on, he wouldn't waste himself after endangering others. I seriously doubt he told anyone."

"Damn Murphy's Law. We can't catch a break," Bailey said, showing his frustration. "It's spilled milk, let's keep moving. We need to talk about the press conference. I want to hear everyone's opinion about naming Rooks before I make my final decision."

Special Agent Walter Haslett spoke first. "I say we finger Rooks. Publicly naming him puts pressure on him. The media attention will be incredible. It'll either scare the shit out of him or cause him to make a mistake."

"I agree," said Gary Dalton. "Let's use the public. We stand a better chance of catching Rooks by naming him than by keeping it under wraps. John Q. Public can do one thing we could never do and that's be everywhere at the same time. If we release Rooks' picture and a bio, millions of people can work for us. We'll generate so many new leads we'll have to add agents to the case. But it will all be worth it in the end. Someone out there knows where he is. If we go public the media will broadcast his name and face to the far side of the moon and half the country will be looking for him."

Alec Taylor couldn't hold his tongue any longer. "I'm against naming him. It won't help the investigation that much, plus we'll have to deal with thousands of false leads. We'd open a can of worms we couldn't contain. The safety issue alone is reason enough not to do it. We can't have people abusing each other because they're scared shitless or they're trying to play top cop. Identifying Rooks will turn the investigation into a wild goose chase. The last known picture of him is seven years old. He looks so different now it wouldn't help. We should announce there's a primary suspect, but not name him. That'll crush a lot of the negative press, yet won't tip off Rooks."

Deputy Director Bailey and the other three agents looked at Frank McCaskill. Taylor, Haslett and Dalton knew McCaskill's vote would be the difference. Bailey trusted the special agent's opinion so much, he would side with McCaskill whichever way he went. While they waited for his input, McCaskill read the notes he had written at 3:00 AM that morning. When he finally spoke, he sounded as persuasive as a star defense attorney giving a closing argument in a murder trial.

"Rooks isn't going to change his plans because of us. He's got his own agenda and he'll stick to it. He won't be pressured into slipping up or making careless mistakes. He can't be scared or intimidated, so we can rule that out. The best-case scenario we could hope for is to apprehend him before he attempts any more murders. The most effective way of accomplishing that is to catch him off-guard. The element of surprise is our most valuable weapon now that Forsey's dead. Rooks has no idea what we know. Let's keep it that way. If Taylor says there's a primary suspect, but many others we're investigating, Rooks won't know what we have. Let's sell that. He'll make mistakes from overconfidence and arrogance before he'll crack and screw up. Just because we're getting heat from the press doesn't mean we should start shopping for a quick fix. We're not desperate enough to enlist the American public to do our job . . .."

McCaskill was interrupted in mid-sentence by the piercing ring of his cellular phone. "This is McCaskill," he barked. After a few moments the expression on his face soured. "What is it?" He remained silent for ninety seconds, his face clouding over the longer he listened. "Fax that report ASAP." From the time he answered the phone to when he hung up, McCaskill now looked tired and worn out.

"Can it get any worse?" McCaskill said to no one in particular. "A psychologist named Phillip Burris from Park State Mental Hospital has been reviewing Rooks' chart. He thinks Rooks might have multiple personalities. According to Dr. Burris, Rooks possesses many of the warning signs: delusions, hallucinations and spontaneous and sporadic change of character. Multiple personality disorder can be caused by a tragedy or traumatic event a person can't deal with. To escape the trauma, the psyche will snap and splinter into a second personality or multiple personalities. Dr. Burris believes the break occurred when Rooks was in prison. He couldn't deal with being beaten and raped so he escaped into a new personality. This second personality manifests itself in an alter ego that is cruel, vicious and remorseless."

"Would multiple personalities cause the dramatic changes he's undergone?" Taylor asked.

"It would explain the transformation in prison and subsequent change back to model citizen after his release. If Rooks has a multiple personality disorder, Dr. Burris said he'd be unbelievably dangerous. The second personality could kill prolifically and the first wouldn't even be aware of it."

Alec Taylor couldn't hide his frustration. "Son of a bitch, I can see that bastard pleading insanity and walking because another personality committed the crimes."

"Let's not get ahead of ourselves," McCaskill cautioned. "We don't know for sure Rooks has split off another personality. Anyway, he's not in custody, so let's work on finding him and protecting Conway and Redding."

While the agents absorbed the new information, the conference room door opened and agent Bill Cooper walked across the room toward McCaskill. Alec Taylor noticed the envelope in Cooper's hand. He knew the contents of the envelope had to be important for Cooper to interrupt the meeting. "Frank, we just received this. I thought you should see it right away," the agent said in an uneven voice.

As soon as McCaskill saw the multi-colored magazine letters on the envelope, he knew it was a letter from Ben Rooks threatening

Redding's life. After a pair of latex gloves were delivered to the conference room, he tore the envelope open along the crease and set the typing paper on the table. McCaskill noticed three differences from the first death threat. The first letter was sent to Quentin Conway's home; this one threatening Mike Redding was mailed to the FBI's headquarters. The previous letter was not as hostile and angry. The last difference was the most important. This second threat was arrogant and condescending, much more egotistical than the first.

As he read the letter a second time, the scowl on McCaskill's face didn't go unnoticed by L.C. Bailey. "What is it, Frank?" the Deputy Director asked.

"Rooks is getting cocky. This letter is longer than the first. He should keep it short to give us less to go on, but he doesn't care. The prick's playing with us. He sent the letter to me to mock our investigation, and I won't put up with that."

Bailey had not seen Frank McCaskill lose his temper in a long time. "Don't let him get to you, Frank. Keep it on a professional level. Remember, he's going after the whole Bureau, not just you."

"No, he isn't," replied McCaskill. "My name is on the envelope. Sure, he's toying with the Bureau, but he's taunting me in particular. He's daring me to catch him before he kills again. Well, let me tell you something L.C. Our informant's dead, we're dealing with a psychopath and Redding and Conway are more vulnerable every day, but we're gonna nail that son of a bitch anyway. I'm gonna nail him myself."

"Frank, I understand how bad you want Rooks," Bailey said in a grave voice. "This is the biggest case you'll ever have, but you can't let it get personal. Remove yourself emotionally so you can stay objective. It's not you against him. It's not a game to see who's better. He's trying to draw you in—don't let him. I want this lunatic too, but we can't lose sight of the big picture. Don't get too involved, okay?"

As he listened to L.C. Bailey, McCaskill flipped the envelope over expecting to see the same Chicago postmark as the first letter. Instead of Chicago, the letter was postmarked Lafayette, Indiana. A split second later McCaskill realized the ramifications of the postmark. Rooks was in Lafayette with Redding. Balling his fist up tightly, he slammed his hand as hard as he could against the solid oak table.

Ignoring the searing pain in his hand, McCaskill began spitting out orders. "Taylor, call the field head in Lafayette and tell 'em Rooks is there. I want the net around Redding expanded and twenty-four hour surveillance started immediately. See me when you're done so we can prep for the press conference. Haslett, coordinate random sweeps with both local and state police. I want all of Lafayette, West Lafayette and the surrounding counties combed thoroughly. Have the lab techs go over every inch of the letter. Dalton, get hold of Banks and Wurstin. I want to talk to Conway before I tell Redding about the letter and that Rooks is in Lafayette."

When McCaskill finished barking out instructions, L.C. Bailey rose from his chair and motioned for him to follow. There was much to do prior to the start of the press conference. Whether Deputy Director Bailey liked it or not, the investigation was personal. Ben Rooks had made sure of that.

Diana Fleming flopped down on the hotel bed. Her shift as flight attendant on the previous night's flight from Miami to Chicago had left her drained. The plane didn't touch down in Chicago until 12:45 AM. By the time the attendants finished sanitizing the aircraft, it was 1:15. Diana didn't get home and fall asleep until 2:00 in the morning. The flight itself had been terrible. A tropical spring storm in the Atlantic wreaked havoc on the air pressure in the skies above Florida and an unruly plane load of passengers compounded the situation—eighty percent of the passengers were attorneys.

During the first thirty minutes of the flight, the rough turbulence unnerved the attorneys, and they dealt with the turbulence the way lawyers normally handle problems. They drank. Diana felt like a mobile bartender as she pushed the heavy drink cart up and down the plane's narrow aisle. As they consumed more liquor, the attorneys became either surly or flirtatious. For the remaining three hours of the flight, Diana and the other attendants catered to the attorneys' whims while fending off their crude advances. When she finally got back to her apartment and lay down to sleep, Diana's back was sore and her feet ached. Her resolve to design clothes was stronger than ever. Three hours and twenty minutes later, the ear-splitting sound of an alarm clock shattered her peaceful slumber. At 6:30 AM she flew out of O'Hare and arrived in Phoenix at 7:12 AM Arizona time, nearly comatose from a lack of sleep.

Lying across a large queen-sized bed in the Radisson Hotel, Diana tried in vain to doze off. She was too nervous to sleep. During the flight from Chicago she had decided to call Mike Redding. She needed to tell him how she felt. Though she preferred the old fashioned way where men initiated the contact, Diana thought there was really nothing wrong with a woman calling a man or asking him out.

Stretching her body across the large bed, Diana closed her eyes and thought of her mother. Betty Lee Fleming would not have approved of her only daughter calling a man, especially one ten years her senior who was best friends with the man already pursuing Diana. Betty Lee Fleming believed it was inappropriate for a woman to be the aggressor in any type of relationship. Diana smiled as she remembered the puritanical advice her mother gave her as they baked pies and home-made bread when Diana was fifteen.

"Always be a lady. Regardless of the situation you're in or the problems that face you, represent yourself and your family as a lady. Dignity and gentility are the greatest assets you possess. When dealing with others, never fail to act as a lady. No one can ever take that away from you."

Diana missed her mother and thought of her daily. Betty Lee Fleming died the day before Diana's sixteenth birthday. Cancer from thirty-five years of smoking ate away at her insides until she was nothing more than a frail wisp of a woman. She died in her own bed planning Diana's surprise birthday party. The party went on as scheduled the following day, and Diana wept unashamedly through it. Finally,

Jack Fleming mercifully called an end to the festivities. After sending her friends home, he took Diana into the room where her mother died. The memory of her father sitting on the bed talking to her was forever burnt into Diana's mind. Holding her tightly in his arms, Jack Fleming reminded Diana she had the strength, intelligence, and talent to do anything and urged her to never settle for less than what she deserved.

As she cried softly on his shoulder over the loss of her mother, he shocked his daughter by telling her a story she had never heard. Since she was a child, Betty Lee had dreamed of writing a book. As the years rushed by, school, marriage and children dominated her life so the dream was pushed further into the background. Aware of her passion, Diana had begged her mother for years to start writing. Unbeknownst to Diana, her mother had done just that. After three and a half years of writing on weekends, early in the morning and during lunch breaks, Betty Lee Fleming finished her first novel.

Only Diana's father knew about the book. He and his wife decided not to tell Diana about it until it was bought for publication. At the same time Betty Lee began mailing manuscripts of her novel to publishers, she began experiencing severe nausea and found a small lump in her lymph node. A subsequent biopsy showed malignant cells in her throat and thyroid. Betty Lee forgot about the book when her doctor informed her she had three months to live. The next twelve weeks were a bitter-sweet saga of incredible happiness and indescribable misery for Diana and her mother. They spent hour upon hour taking long walks, window shopping at flea markets and conversing in their backyard. Diana grew to respect her mother in a new way. She saw a strength and dignity in her dying mother the likes of which she had never before seen in anyone else.

As the weeks passed, Betty Lee's cancer-ravaged body became emaciated, but her spirit and soul flourished. During the final days of the ordeal, Diana had never seen her mother so happy and at peace with herself. Betty Lee Fleming passed away in her sleep a day before Diana's surprise birthday party, unable to give her daughter one last gift of love. As Jack Fleming cradled his grieving sixteen year old daughter against his chest, he stroked her beautiful blond hair and whispered her mother's secret into Diana's ear. Two weeks before, the novel had been purchased by a major publishing house in New York. The book would be printed in a few months and 25,000 copies would appear in bookstores in less than a year. The book's topic: a fictional coming-of-age story about a mother and daughter. Unconditional love was the theme. Diana was stunned by her father's story. She was overjoyed her mother had realized her life-long dream, but devastated she had not lived to see her book in print. Sitting on her mother's bed with her father's arms wrapped around her, Diana vowed to live every day as if there was no tomorrow and to chase her dreams with reckless abandon.

Diana's thoughts returned to her predicament with Mike. Her mother would not be pleased to know her daughter was about to call a man, but she would have trusted Diana's judgment—she always had. Diana couldn't wait any longer to phone him. She needed to know if there was something between them. She was nervous about calling, but was tired of wondering how he felt. Reaching into her purse, Diana pulled out her calling card and a piece of paper with UNI's telephone number on it. After dialing the number and going through UNI's switchboard operator, Diana was connected to Mike's office.

"May I please tell him who's calling?" the secretary asked after she was put through.

Diana hesitated for a moment and then made up her mind. "This is Diana Fleming."

"Thank you. Just one moment while I see if he's available." Before she could respond, Diana was put on hold.

Oh God, I shouldn't have called, Diana thought. *Of course his calls are being screened. He's got ten FBI agents protecting him from a psycho killer.*

As she struggled to block out the annoying elevator music in the earpiece, Diana wished she hadn't given her name so she could just hang up and forget the embarrassing phone call ever took place. Without warning Diana's thoughts were interrupted by a voice on the other end of the line.

"Diana, hi. What's up?"

"Aah, good. Not much I mean. Not much." Startled by the sudden greeting, Diana fought to regain her composure. "Did I get you at a bad time or do you have a few?"

"Sure, I've got time," Mike replied earnestly.

Trying to sound as if she called regularly, Diana casually asked, "How've you been?"

"Very busy, but that's good this time of the year in my line of work." His next comment made her smile. "What a nice surprise, plus your timing's perfect. I need to get away from the game tapes. My brain's turning into one large VCR, so you're my head cleaner. What's up?"

This was the part of the conversation Diana dreaded most; how to tell Mike she wanted to see him when Quentin wasn't present. Diana didn't want to come across as aggressive or pushy, and she certainly didn't want to appear slutty. After a deep breath and a silent prayer, Diana spoke from her heart.

"This is a bit uncomfortable for me. I'm following my instincts so bear with me. I called to see if we could get together and talk. I know things are crazy for you, so there's no hurry. I wanted to have this conversation now so we'd know if there was something to talk about later." And then laughing nervously, she added, "Do you have any idea what I'm talking about?"

"No, not really," Mike replied slowly, afraid to hope for something good only to be disappointed.

Gathering her courage, Diana decided to lay it all out in the open. "Well, let me try this again. I have a great time with Quentin, he's really cool, but he's not the type of person I'd date. You know better than anyone how unique he is, but I'm not interested in anything other than friendship with him. I'm telling you because I look at you differently. I'd like to get to know you better, Mike. I hope I'm not putting you in an awkward position. If I am, sorry. I'm not worried about Quentin because he's not attached to me. Besides, he can get any woman he wants. I thought I should take a chance and tell you how I feel, or I might miss out on a great friendship and maybe more. In a nutshell, Mike, that's what I'm trying to find out. Is there a chance for something more than friendship between us?"

Starting at his lips, a large smile had formed on Mike's mouth and spread across his face. Cupping his hand over the phone's receiver, Mike stood up out of his chair, held the covered phone over his head with both hands and stomped his feet in jubilation. Careful that his voice would not carry, he repeated over and over, "Yes, yes, yes!"

After quickly sitting and calming himself down, especially his breathing, he said, "I'm glad you took a chance and called, Diana. I've thought about calling you, but I didn't know if I should. I usually butcher these conversations anyway. I never know what to say and I always end up making an ass of myself or ruining things before they get started. I'm glad one of us knows what to do. I'd like to go out one evening and have the conversation you're referring to."

A light knock at the door cut Mike off. The door opened and his secretary walked over to his desk. She placed a yellow memo in front of him, turned around and left the office as quickly as she had entered. He immediately read the message.

"Diana, Agent McCaskill is on the other line and it's an emergency. I need to take the call."

Diana was instantly worried, but tried not to show it. "Sure, of course. I hope it's nothing too serious."

"Thanks. Listen, this is about the first good news I've gotten in a month. I'm not sure when, but I promise we'll get together soon." And then in a casual tone, "By the way, I'd like for you to come to the game Thursday if you can."

"Count on it. Please take care of yourself," she said with more than a little concern in her voice.

"Ditto. Thanks again, Diana."

After hitting line two, Mike said, "Sorry, I was on another line. What's going on?"

Frank McCaskill didn't sugarcoat the news. "This morning a letter threatening your life arrived at our Washington office. Ben Rooks wrote it. This letter is longer than the first and it was addressed to me. Rooks mailed it from West Lafayette two days ago and could still be there. We're stepping up the security around the university and your house. Additional agents will be arriving from Chicago in thirty minutes. I don't want to alarm you, Mr. Redding, but every four hours we're going to sweep your house, office and UNI's gym for explosives. We're approaching a critical stage of the investigation. Rooks is growing short on time. The best time for him to try something is during the tournament when you and Mr. Conway are in public. Once the tournament is over, or if your team loses, you can disappear and Rooks won't be able to find you."

Mike was taking in the information, but he was having a hard time digesting it. "You think he'll do something soon. When?" Mike asked, but didn't want to hear McCaskill's answer.

"The next seven to ten days. He almost has to strike while you're coaching. If he waits and you go away indefinitely, we'll have months to find him. He's got the advantage right now because you have games to coach, and he knows ahead of time where you'll be. Once the tournament is over, we've got the upper hand and he loses leverage. Rooks knows what he's doing. He probably planned the attacks to coincide with the tournament, which means he'll make his move soon while your team's playing."

"That piece of shit coward," Mike yelled angrily. "Why is this happening?" After a prolonged pause in which McCaskill heard nothing, Mike spoke again. "It sounds like the best thing for me would be to step down or lose the next game." McCaskill didn't say anything, but that was exactly what he had thought numerous times during the last ten days.

"How did everything get so damn complicated?" Mike asked, dejected. He was talking more to himself than McCaskill. He felt as if his world was falling apart piece by piece. The nightmare had started with Allan Clancy's and David Butler's deaths and had grown progressively worse. Every time Mike believed he had hit rock bottom, something else happened lowering him deeper into his own private hell.

"Why'd the bastard send you the letter? What'd it say?" Mike asked.

"I'm not positive, but I have some ideas. Probably to taunt me and the Bureau. The gist of the letter was you're the next target. We haven't decided if we're going to discuss the second threat during this afternoon's press conference. Right now, we're leaning towards telling the media. I don't think we could keep it quiet for long, and if it did get out, it'd be twice as bad."

"Jesus Christ, that's all I need," Mike said disgusted. "Those shit-for-brains press leeches will never leave me alone."

"We've got to do damage control, Mr. Redding. We want to dictate when news of the threat gets out and how it gets out. If we disclose the threat, we'll be able to manipulate the flow of information, but if it's leaked or the press discovers it, the flood gates will open."

Mike knew McCaskill was right, but he was still irritated the FBI couldn't sit on the letter. It would make his job easier and give his team a better chance of winning. "You win. Tell the press about the letter, but I'm not saying one solitary word to them. You quote me on that, McCaskill. I've got nothing to say to those spineless sons of bitches."

"We'll take care of it with the NCAA. No press conferences or public appearances period. One last thing, Mr. Redding. You're only going out for practices and games. Does the death threat change your position about coaching? You would be much easier to protect if you weren't coaching."

"Hell no, my position hasn't changed. If anything I feel stronger about being on the bench. I'm sorry for making your job difficult, McCaskill, but I'm trying to do *my* job. To be honest, I hope I make your job real fucking difficult because I plan on coaching UNI to the national championship."

After slamming the phone down, Mike leaned back in his chair, exhaled slowly and tried to release two weeks of pent-up tension. Less than five minutes later he regretted blowing up at McCaskill. He considered calling back and apologizing, but decided against it. He rationalized it was part of the job and McCaskill wouldn't take it personally. Mike felt as if he was living someone else's nightmare. Allan and David were dead, he and Quentin were living in constant fear of a sudden violent death, and the media had turned his life into a freak, side-show attraction the whole nation was watching in sound bites. Mike's life had been thrown into utter disarray; he couldn't go to the store to buy milk and bread without being mobbed by reporters or being gunned down by an old high school friend.

All Mike wanted was a shot at the national championship. It was all he had ever wanted. Instead, he was in the biggest fight of his life—a fight for survival. He couldn't win the national championship unless he won the fight to stay alive. A cold, hollow feeling swept over Mike as he thought about the next two weeks. Would UNI win it all? Would he be alive to see it? What about his best friend? Would a championship ring mean anything if Quentin weren't there to share the achievement? And what about his fear of closeness and commitment? Would he ever get over his emotional impotence? Was Diana the woman who could help him have a normal, healthy, loving relationship? Unable to handle the strain any longer, Mike hit the intercom button on his phone and told his secretary he wanted no calls or interruptions for twenty minutes. The dam had finally broken. Putting his head down on his desk, he covered his face with his hands, then closed his eyes and wept.

Alec Taylor walked past the conference table for the fifteenth time in ten minutes. His nervous pacing did not bother Frank McCaskill, who sat at the table reviewing notes for the press conference. Taylor was anxious with good reason: this was the FBI's biggest press conference in the last ten years. All three major television networks, CNN and FOX were broadcasting it live. The press room in the FBI's Washington office held a little over one hundred people, but more than one hundred and fifty media credentials had been passed out and dozens of additional reporters congregated outside. The news conference in this same room announcing the arrest of serial killer Jeffrey Dahmer had been a major media event, but this was larger. Much larger. It would be a three-ring circus and Alec Taylor was the ringleader.

"When's Mr. Bailey gonna be here?" Taylor asked. The press conference was scheduled to start in thirty-five minutes and Deputy Director Bailey had not finished reviewing the statement Taylor would read.

McCaskill didn't look up from his notes. "He'll be here anytime. Sit down and try to relax."

Except for the Director of the FBI, Mrs. Elaine Bailey and Frank McCaskill, everyone called L.C. Bailey Deputy Director or Mr. Bailey. No one else knew his birth name was Leopold Cristabol, but even if they had known, they wouldn't address him that way. As Taylor began scanning the revised press statement, the door to the conference room swung open and L. C. Bailey walked in, followed by two administrative assistants.

"How ya holding up, Frank?" Bailey asked while he took a chair at the head of the table.

"I've been better. It's been one crazy day. Ask me how I am when he's in custody."

"We'll all sleep nightmare-free then," Bailey replied. "You'll live another day, Frank. I need you 'til tonight; then you can rediscover what your wife and house look like."

Bailey nodded at McCaskill and then turned his attention to Alec Taylor. "The statement is strong, Alec. I like what you've added. Listen closely, I want to go over a few things. We're still getting calls from the congressional delegation from Indiana, and now the White House is involved. That little prick Daniels called the director's home this morning at 5:45. He's the biggest son of a bitch, backstabbing press secretary I've seen in thirty years with the Bureau. He told the director he was calling to let him know the President has been following the investigation closely. In a not so subtle way, he reminded the director how politically important this case is. Everyone knows the President couldn't spell green movement, let alone clean-up the environment, but Clancy was the point man for the White House's environmental team. He made the President look good, so now the Great Charlatan of Pennsylvania Avenue has got to act concerned about the environmental movement and outraged by the murders.

"Between us and these walls, the director couldn't give a shit if every congressman and senator from Indiana calls, or if the President himself pays us a visit. Our job is to conduct the most thorough investigation possible. Publicly, of course, we'll play the game. Right now we don't have enough evidence to convict Rooks of loitering. We know he's our man, but we can't make anything stick. He can't be placed at either crime scene, there's no murder weapon and we have no eyewitnesses. Alec, you won't name Rooks. With nothing but circumstantial evidence, there's no way I'll put you in front of those wolves to identify Rooks as our primary suspect."

While Alec Taylor was rapidly scribbling notes, he managed to listen to L.C. Bailey rail against everything under the sun. "Rooks is our man, but I'm not about to appease some chicken shit congressmen who are trying to use this case to get re-elected. We're gonna buckle down, conduct a detailed scientific investigation and ride out the criticism. I want no mention of Rooks' name and no background information given. As for Redding's death threat, release the information we previously discussed. Do not, I repeat, do not disclose that the letter was sent to the Bureau in McCaskill's name. I don't want Rooks winning public support. People are so twisted they'll think the March Madness Murderer is cool, and the press will glorify his actions. We don't need him made into a natural-born hero. Any questions, Alec?"

Still frantically writing notes, Taylor said, "No, sir."

L.C. Bailey stood up out of his chair. He was always a blur of motion, fidgeting constantly and seemingly moving even when he was sitting down. As he walked up and down the room, his mind went over the last minute details. "Anything else, Frank?"

"Yes. Alec, we don't need to tell you how important this news conference is. The press has been kicking our butts from day one. The tone you use and your delivery will be as crucial as the information you give. The *Post* and *Times* are going to pound at you. They'll try to trip you up any possible way. Don't sweat it. Work at your own pace and remember to be professional, cordial and succinct. Don't give them anything extra. Thank them repeatedly for their cooperation and assistance. Let them know how concerned we are with finding the killer and protecting Redding and Conway. Drive those two points home and be emphatic. Maybe even show some emotion there, but stay in control. They're going to ask sensitive questions we don't want you answering, especially after you announce Redding's death threat. Politely reject any loaded questions that are volatile or controversial. Answer ten to twelve questions, thank them and then stop. Be yourself. Don't come across stiff and rehearsed. That's why you were chosen to address the cameras. You might even consider a well-placed smile toward the end of the question/answer session. Remember, you're the best person to carry this off so be yourself."

"Thanks, Frank," Bailey said shaking McCaskill's hand. "Kick some ass, Alec." Just as quickly as L.C. Bailey had entered the conference room, he was gone. Alec Taylor was left with three pages of notes to study in fifteen minutes while McCaskill headed to the bathroom, thankful Taylor had to face the press, not he.

It took Taylor exactly seven minutes to read the FBI's prepared statement. He didn't stumble over a single word, never stopped to clear his throat, and appeared to be completely at ease in front of the battery of microphones and cameras. Most of the female reporters in attendance and a handful of male journalists noticed the rugged attractiveness of the FBI's youngest special agent. His demeanor was so polished, and his physical appearance so mesmerizing, he looked more like an actor in a movie about the FBI than an actual agent at a press conference.

"At this time, I will open the floor to questions," Taylor said after finishing the statement. This was the portion of the press conference that was dangerous. McCaskill had coached Taylor well, but simulated questions in the safe haven of a practice environment were not the same as frying on the hot seat in front of a hundred media vultures and a live national television audience.

"I will answer ten to twelve questions, spending up to a minute on each. When those questions have been answered, copies of the written statement will be distributed by special agent Bill Cooper. At that time the news conference will be over. First question."

The moment Alec Taylor's voice trailed off, pandemonium broke out as thirty reporters yelled and waved. Taylor was tempted to smile as he surveyed the bedlam in front of him. McCaskill wanted the media throng to act up during the question/answer session so the FBI would have a legitimate reason to end the press conference early. It appeared he might get his wish.

"Ladies and gentlemen, please. I can answer only one question at a time. We have to do this in an orderly fashion."

A reporter in the first row from the *Boston Globe* shouted first. "Will Mike Redding continue to coach UNI in the NCAA tournament, and if so, what are the reasons behind his decision?"

"Yes. Mr. Redding will coach UNI's next game. As far as the reasons for his decision, the FBI is not privy to that information and I don't want to speak for Mr. Redding. Next question."

A woman from the *Miami Herald* spoke fastest. "In regard to the primary suspect you're investigating, is this person responsible for Congressman Clancy's and David Butler's murders as well as the threats to Mike Redding and Quentin Conway, or are the murders not related to the death threats?"

Alec Taylor's mental data base considered many responses before choosing the right one. "We believe the primary suspect in the Clancy-Butler investigation is the same individual who has sent threatening letters to Mr. Redding and Mr. Conway. So, yes, we believe the murders and death threats are related."

A *New York Times* reporter called out the next question. "How does the FBI respond to critics who say the case is taking too long to solve, that it's been handled inefficiently, and that Coach Redding and Quentin Conway might die because the FBI can't catch the killer?"

Controlling the anger flaring up inside him, Alec Taylor withstood the urge to engage the sleazy *Times* reporter in a verbal sparring match. "We don't. We're busy conducting an investigation," Taylor said waving his hand as if dismissing the repugnant journalist.

In a spacious, secluded second-floor office once used by J. Edgar Hoover, L.C. Bailey, Frank McCaskill and the Director of the FBI watched the conference on TV and smiled at Alec Taylor's response. "Helluva idea to use Taylor. So far he's been outstanding," Bailey told McCaskill.

Never one to seek attention, McCaskill responded, "You made the call."

Down in the press room, Taylor's answer wiped the smirk off the *Times'* reporter's face. There was no time for Alec Taylor to enjoy the small victory, though. Questions came at him more rapidly. In the front row an attractive woman from *New Yorker* magazine beat the other journalists to the punch. "Newspapers are calling the killer 'The March Madness Murderer.' What does the FBI think of the nickname?"

"You're trying to sell newspapers and magazines, we're trying to protect two men and solve a double homicide. The murders are in no way connected to the NCAA basketball tournament. It's merely coincidence that one of the men being stalked is a prominent coach of a top team. The entire NCAA organization has been outstanding as far as working with us and cooperating with our investigation. But once again, the crimes have nothing to do with the tournament. Go ahead," Taylor said pointing to a *Washington Post* journalist in the second row.

"I assume with Mike Redding coaching, Quentin Conway will continue going to UNI's games. With both men in the same place at the same time, it seems these games would be a likely place for an assassination attempt. What's the FBI doing to protect the thousands of fans who will attend these NCAA tournament games, and why doesn't the FBI instruct Mike Redding not to attend the rest of the games and avoid endangering those fans?"

This was the question McCaskill and Taylor feared most. Through the whispering of a hundred and fifty people and the snapping of camera shutters, Taylor had heard every word the *Post* reporter said. But since he wasn't ready with an answer, he gambled in an attempt to buy time.

To the surprise of every member of the press in the room, Alec Taylor grinned bashfully and flashed his best "aw shucks" smile. "I'm sorry, I couldn't hear the second half of your question. Could you please repeat the last minute or two of it?"

The media members broke into laughter. Fifteen seconds went by before the commotion died down, during which Taylor began working on an answer. Since the *Post* reporter didn't know what part of the question Taylor had not heard, he repeated the entire question.

By this time Alec Taylor had formulated an answer to the loaded question. "You bring up a major concern of ours. Safety is the top priority. Safety for Mr. Redding, his players, Mr. Conway and all the people around them at any given time. We will take extra precautions at the tournament games due to the number of spectators present, measures I obviously can't divulge publicly. To date we have no solid evidence indicating an assassination attempt will be made during a tournament game; therefore, we will not dictate what Mr. Redding and Mr. Conway can or should do. Society can't come to a standstill because of terroristic intimidation and certainly the FBI can't tell free-minded people how to live."

And then showing the genius which had propelled him rapidly up the FBI's hierarchical ladder, Alec Taylor looked directly at the *Post* reporter and said in a sincere voice. "I'm glad you brought this issue to the attention of college basketball fans. They can make an educated decision whether or not to attend UNI's games. The FBI cannot guarantee the fans' safety, but we do pledge to do everything in our power to make the tournament games as safe as possible."

Taylor's skilled handling of the *Post* reporter's question set the tone for the rest of the press conference. He answered five more questions before ending it. Inside the private office on the second floor, McCaskill, Bailey and the director were thrilled with the special agent's performance. With fresh information to sell newspapers and magazines, the media would stay off the FBI for awhile. Undoubtedly, the news conference would affect public opinion in a positive way. The press conference was a huge success, and Alec Taylor was the reason for that success.

As Taylor thanked the assembled media and stepped off the stage in the FBI's press room, the occupant of a dirty motel room in West Lafayette turned off a black and white television set. The March Madness Murderer was anything but worried. Even though the FBI was getting closer, they couldn't begin to fathom what would happen next. The killer's thoughts shifted to the surprise awaiting Mike Redding when he arrived home that evening.

"Won't that be pleasant after a long day at work," he said out loud. "I hope he likes my gift. It was so hard figuring out what to get. I went to a lot of trouble. Oh well, it doesn't fucking matter. Who cares if he doesn't like the gift. It makes me happy and isn't that the point of giving? Yes, sirree. I believe I'm right. It must be a good gift. I feel better already."

Chapter Fourteen

Mike was upset with himself. All morning he had found it hard to concentrate on basketball. He thought practice in the afternoon would get his mind off the death threat, but even practice didn't help. During the first hour of drills he found himself thinking about the news conference. He wondered what the FBI was telling the press, and if Ben Rooks were watching and knew he was the primary suspect. The news conference was at the same time as UNI's practice, but Mike was taping it so he'd be able to watch it when he got home. For the first time in his sixteen-year coaching career, he wished practice would go faster so he could escape from it to do something else.

Focusing his attention on the action in front of him, Mike blew his whistle to stop play. "Reggie, what are you looking at? Keith is wide open on the block. Damnit, that's the second time you've missed him. Give him the ball down there. He'll either get a six-footer or they'll foul him. We have to attack Marquette down low. I want the ball going into the belly of their defense. We need to wear down their big men and pound at their interior D. C'mon now, Reggie. It's not that difficult. Get the ball to Byron and Keith as much as possible. Understand?"

Reggie Avant had the face of a fourteen-year-old paperboy. He looked so young it appeared he might cry if Mike yelled another word at him. But he had been chewed out so many times during his three years at UNI, the tongue-lashing went in one ear and out the other. The message would stick, though. Reggie Avant would not make the same mistake again. After another thirty-five minutes of light scrimmaging, Mike blew his whistle three times to signify the end of practice. Gathering the players around him at the free throw line, he racked his brain in search of a creative way to make them run wind sprints before hitting the showers.

"OK, here it is. You run ten full court suicides before we call it a day." Before Mike could continue, a number of tired groans were heard. "I'll give you a chance to knock that number down. One of you will shoot ten free throws. However many he makes, I'll take off that number of suicides. So, if your designated shooter hits nine, I'll take away nine suicides and you'll only run one."

"What's the catch?" asked Reggie Avant.

Mike grinned. His players knew him well. "There's two. If the person you pick hits less than eight, you'll all run twenty suicides."

None of the players worried about the first condition. They all knew who would shoot for them, and they knew he'd hit nine or ten out of ten.

"Second catch," Mike said. "If Byron shoots for you, the same rules apply except he'll shoot treys instead of free throws. You've got one minute to decide," Mike said turning to walk away. Before he had taken three steps, someone behind him spoke.

"I pick myself," Byron said walking past the free throw line to the top of the key. There had been no consulting of teammates or group decision-making involved. No one was given the chance to voice his opinion; no debate had taken place. Byron Lewis simply wanted the burden of being responsible for the entire team's fate.

In college basketball the three point line extends 19 feet 9 inches from the edge of the rim. Since a shot made behind the line is worth three points, three out of ten is considered average to good shooting, the equivalent of five out of ten made from two point range. Six out of ten shots made from behind the three point arc is excellent shooting while eight or nine out of ten is rarely accomplished. Mike noticed the stoic expressions on his player's faces as

Byron set himself to shoot the first trey. They realized how difficult a task it was to make eight of ten three-pointers.

Despite all he had done during the course of the long year, Byron's teammates suddenly questioned his ability to come through at crunch time. Mike sensed their uncertainty. Many of the players were second-guessing Byron's decision. They would have preferred to have Reggie Avant, a career 88% free throw shooter on the line, but it was too late. Byron fired the first trey much quicker than his doubting teammates would have liked. As one shot after another rose high in the air and fell like a soft drop of rain through the net, the blank expressions on the players' faces changed to relief and then excitement. Ten rainbow shots were launched from behind the three point arc, and nine of them ripped cleanly through the white cords.

After the last ball had been retrieved, Byron turned to Mike and shrugged his shoulders. "I didn't feel like running, coach." After completing one full-court suicide, the players congratulated Byron and headed for the showers. Byron's incredible clutch performance left no doubt in Mike Redding's mind; UNI would win the national championship.

Upon entering his office, Mike was greeted by Stan Turner, a young agent assigned to him the last week and a half.

"Mr. Redding, you had two calls during practice. Mr. Conway called. He said it was nothing urgent. Call him this evening when you get a chance."

"What's the other message?" Mike asked, glad to hear he'd be able to talk to Quentin. His best friend had been working the night before on an important deal so they hadn't talked for twenty-four hours.

"The second call was from one of our agents, Dennis Quigley. He and Agent Myers picked your dogs up from the kennel earlier this afternoon. Special Agent McCaskill didn't want us making any unnecessary stops, so your dogs are at home."

"Cool, thanks a lot." Mike was pleased. He could watch the tape of the press conference, play with his dogs and call Quentin before watching more game film. It would be a good night. The first good night he'd had in a awhile.

The plan was incredibly simple. At first he couldn't figure out how to kill Mike Redding. The FBI had turned the coach's house on Soldiers Home Road into a fortress. Whenever he went out in public, which was hardly ever, Mike Redding was accompanied by at least eight federal agents. There seemed to be no way to get close enough to kill him.

The idea, so simple it was scary, came to him while he was masturbating in the bathtub. He couldn't get close to Mike Redding because the FBI expected him to get close. They anticipated an attack from close range and had effectively negated that threat. Due to the heavy security presence around Redding, there was no viable way to kill him and escape, so someone or something else would have to do it. After that realization hit him, he changed his whole approach. He had been looking at the situation from the wrong perspective. Instead of figuring out how he could get close to Redding, he began analyzing who or what was already close to him. The answer was obvious. Too obvious for the FBI to figure out.

Lying on a rickety cot in a Motel Six in Demotte, Indiana, the March Madness Murderer reflected on his actions of the previous days. His experience with home-made, designer drugs had been useful, but he still had to spend four hours in a library researching drug interactions. He received perverse pleasure telling the reference librarian he was a pharmacy student at UNI and needed to research violent chemical reactions for a semester final. The librarian unknowingly directed him to the information that would enable him to kill Mike Redding. His next stop was Hawthorne & Son's Kennels, where he spent an hour casing the establishment. During the stakeout he mapped out the four-acre property in the form of a scaled-down engineer's survey and pinpointed a window that couldn't be seen from the driveway and adjoining road.

After returning to the motel to alter his appearance—again he wanted no one to remember him—the killer went back to the kennel to take a closer look. While striking up a conversation with an older gentleman, he discovered the man was a friend of the Hawthorne family. An innocent comment about searching for a kennel for his dogs produced a wealth of information. For fifteen minutes the old man extolled the virtues of Hawthorne's kennel and revealed valuable information, including the hours Mr. Hawthorne kept and the type of security system he employed. After a brief conversation with the owner, the March Madness Murderer had memorized the layout of Mr. Hawthorne's office and knew where the dogs were bred, trained and most importantly, housed when their masters were out of town.

During the next hour he visited outpatient hospital clinics, where he took two insurance claim forms with doctors' signatures and stole a prescription notepad. He chose outpatient clinics because they were usually understaffed and the frenetic atmosphere was ideal for what he needed to do. Another hour was spent at the public library in Monticello. From the 1995 *Pharmaceutical Redbook* and *The Physicians Desk Reference*, he learned how to write the prescriptions he needed. After practicing copying the doctors' signatures off and on for several hours, he was ready. He wrote a prescription for Detracil and signed it with the name Dr. Dennis Guye. The second prescription for Cytaturic bore the forged signature of Dr. Lloyd Riley. It took him a half hour to perfect the large looping "R" and flamboyant "Y" in Riley, but it was worth the trouble. It was imperative no one could trace the prescriptions back to him. Finally, using Doctor Guye's signature a second time, he prescribed himself insulin and made a notation to purchase a month's supply of hypodermic syringes.

After driving around Monticello awhile, he stopped at a Revco Drug Store and had the prescription for 10 ccs of Detracil filled. At Osco Drugs in West Lafayette he purchased insulin and syringes. His last stop was at a Walmart in Lafayette where he disposed of the insulin in a trash bin and bought 20 ccs of Cytaturic. He was worried when the pharmacist viewed his fake identification a few extra seconds, but when he provided a second piece of ID the pharmacist asked no more questions and filled the prescription.

When he returned to the motel he cut up all three fake ID's

and burnt them. Even though he purchased the drugs and syringes at three different drug store chains, he had made three fake ID's so the purchases couldn't be tracked to one name. He spent the duration of the evening going over the plan, mentally walking through every aspect of it from start to finish. Like Mike Redding, he was a firm believer that visualization enhanced productivity and created better results. Unlike his old high school buddy, he wasn't using visualization to improve free-throw shooting or stimulate stronger mental attitude. He was using it to kill Mike.

From the moment his alarm went off at 4:00 AM, he moved like a machine. Everything he did had been painstakingly planned and rehearsed over and over. By 4:45 he had made a tiny slit in the protective seal of a new vinyl window and was standing in the main office of Hawthorne & Son's Kennels. He had thirty seconds to deactivate the alarm. He found the security system's control pad and entered a code that rebooted the system. Now in re-booting mode, the alarm defaulted, turned off and waited to be reprogrammed. Mr. Hawthorne arrived each morning at 6:00 AM, so the killer set the timer on his watch and went to work. A *Sports Illustrated* story the year before included pictures of Mike Redding's prized Siberian huskies so he had memorized what the dogs looked like. After twenty minutes of tedious searching, using his flashlight only when he had to, he found the sleeping huskies in adjacent cages. Within five minutes he had entered both cages, injected the venomous drugs into the dogs' necks and returned to the office. After replacing the master set of keys, reactivating the alarm system and slipping out the window, he ran the half-mile back to his car in less than three minutes.

His excursion into the kennel had taken place nearly twelve hours earlier. It had been easy to pull off. The hardest part of his day had been the wait. All day he had to wait for the press conference to begin and UNI's practice to end. As he sat on the motel's rusty bed, he finished analyzing the press conference. Agent Taylor had been impressive. The FBI had definitely won back public support. He wasn't upset, though. He had lost some of his edge over McCaskill and the FBI, but they were still three steps behind.

McCaskill had no idea what he was planning. The FBI would be stunned when Redding was attacked by his own dogs. Then McCaskill and the agents would know beyond a shadow of doubt who was in control.

He had chosen Detracil and Cytaturic for two specific reasons. When interacting with each other, they produce an incredibly violent and destructive effect. The reaction is brief, usually one minute, ninety seconds at the most, but the effect is dramatic. No other drug interaction creates such a short yet potent burst of strength, aggression and hostility. The second reason he selected this particular drug combination was their cycling period. Detracil and Cytaturic required twelve hours of continuous flow through the bloodstream before causing the violent reaction. At 5:30 AM he had unlocked both cages and injected the dogs within thirty seconds of each other, ensuring an almost simultaneous chemical reaction. After coursing through their bloodstreams for twelve hours, the liquid venom would set the dogs on the edge of a cataclysmic explosion. The first person to handle the dogs after 5:30 PM would be tossed into the path of a raging eight-legged hurricane. Mike Redding was due home after practice at 5:45.

Just thinking about the plan excited him. No one on the FBI payroll, not Alec Taylor, not L.C. Bailey, not even Frank McCaskill, could compete with him. He was the best there was at this game of cat and mouse. They'd never catch him. He was too creative, meticulous and patient. He was simply better than they were. Changing positions from one end of the cot to the other, he checked his watch and tried to picture Mike Redding's whereabouts. The agents had arrived at Hawthorne's Kennel at 4:10. A good distance from the kennel and well hidden by his disguise, the March Madness Murderer had watched them pick up the dogs. The large huskies, each weighing over eighty pounds, appeared tired and sluggish as they were loaded into an FBI van. While the dogs were being transported to Mike's home and the drugs were percolating through their veins, Mike was wrapping up practice in UNI's gym.

During the twelve-hour cycling period, the drugs enter the tissue, cells and muscles of the dogs' organs. At the end of twelve hours, the heart would stand ready to explode. Any type of physical contact would trigger the explosion. Within twenty seconds of contact, the heart rate would double, and hormones and adrenaline would race through the dogs, providing them with a brief yet colossal burst of energy and strength. The dogs' hearts would then accelerate so fast they would overheat. Within sixty to ninety seconds the animals' hearts would reach boiling point and shut down. The huskies would be dead as would anyone or anything in their path. The March Madness Murderer smiled, a fat, satisfied smile as he thought of Mike Redding rushing home from practice only to be massacred by his beloved huskies. Just as they do in a perfectly cut jigsaw puzzle, the pieces were falling right into place.

The three Crown Victorias slowly swung off State Road 43 onto Soldiers Home Road. In the back of the second Ford, an impatient Mike Redding had grown belligerent. "Hey, numb nuts, can you drive any slower?" he asked the driver who kept his eyes on the curvy road ahead of him. In accordance with Frank McCaskill's instructions, three cars with dark tinted windows were used whenever Mike was transported so Ben Rooks could not kill him with sniper fire. Each day alternate routes were used to bring him home from practice. But on a day when Mike was in a hurry to get home, Agent Stan Turner had mapped out a particularly long course and was uncharacteristically slow in driving it.

"We have a police escort and we're going thirty miles an hour. What's the point of the damn escort if you're not gonna use it?" Mike chided Stan Turner.

He was furious. Practice had ended on a high note, which was very important to him. Mike believed it was vital to leave the court in a positive frame of mind, whether it was at practice or the end of the first half, so the momentum would carry over while his players were off the court. Things had immediately soured once practice was over, however. UNI's starting point guard, Craig Coryell, came into his office because Mike wanted to talk to him about the shooting slump he was in. The junior guard wasn't shooting poorly; he was barely looking to take open jumpers and appeared tentative and unsure of himself. Mike blew up when Craig Coryell told him he had injured his shoulder diving for a loose ball in UNI's last regular season game. Coryell thought his shoulder might be separated, but didn't tell anyone because he feared sitting out the tournament.

Mike tore into his point guard for being selfish and putting his own interests before the team's. Not only had he hurt the team by playing when he was only 70% healthy; he risked damaging the shoulder worse by avoiding treatment and playing with the injury. After calling UNI's team physician to set up an immediate evaluation, Mike sent Coryell to the athletic trainer for light treatment and therapy. It was still hard for him to accept that David Butler, the best trainer he'd ever seen, was no longer with him. Seven years with David had spoiled Mike. His shoes were too large to fill. When Mike finished briefing the new trainer about Craig Coryell's condition, he was ready to go home, but the FBI wasn't ready to take him. Stan Turner was waiting for the field surveillance team to report the route home had been secured. While Mike stewed in his office for fifteen minutes, the field agents double-checked their work.

As Mike Redding rode in the backseat of the car, the strain of having his privacy invaded twenty-four hours a day, the stress of preparing his team for the Sweet Sixteen and the paranoia of being stalked by a psychotic killer caused him to snap. The internal demons created by his parents' deaths, demons that had recently been resurrected by his friends' murders, had simmered quietly the past two weeks waiting for the right moment to boil over. Unknowingly, Agent Turner had provided the opportune moment.

"Turner, you better do something. If you don't make this slow son of a bitch hurry up, I'm going to stick my foot in his ass and keep shoving until he does eighty. Get me the hell home!"

In his career with the FBI Stan Turner had encountered

scores of men with mercurial, fiery temperaments. None of them compared to Mike Redding. The warnings he received about the UNI coach's famous temper did not prepare Turner for the real thing. Sitting next to him in the close confines of the Crown Victoria's backseat, Stan Turner felt physically intimidated by Mike Redding. For Turner it was a weird sensation; he hadn't felt physically threatened by someone since he was a child in grammar school. If he could have made the driver stop, Stan Turner would have gladly walked to Mike Redding's home rather than sit in the cramped car and incur his wrath. Instead of stopping the vehicle, Turner pulled the hand-held phone from his coat pocket and called the car in front of them.

"Sanders." The agent in the first car answered.

"This is Turner. We need to speed up. Mr. Redding would like to get home as quickly as possible. Do whatever you can to accommodate him and be fast about it."

Minutes later when Agent Turner opened Mike's car door after they had parked inside his oversized three car garage, Mike stepped out of the vehicle in stony silence. He was too angry at himself and embarrassed by his actions to apologize to the agent. Heading toward the utility room adjacent to the kitchen, Mike stopped at the door and glared at Turner. Even though his infantile antics made him feel rotten inside, he wanted someone else to hurt as much as he did, so he couldn't resist firing a final insult at the agent.

"God help your stupid, scrawny ass if you ever keep me waiting again!"

Once inside the kitchen, Mike threw a frozen pizza into the oven and put ravioli lunch buckets in the microwave. Next, he opened an Amstel Lite and walked down the hall to the bathroom. After using the bathroom, he heard agents talking in his den while walking back to the kitchen.

"There's another reason I'm not married," he said as he pulled the steaming hot containers out of the microwave. "Can't have people bothering me and I sure as hell don't want people telling me what to do and when to do it."

He was still pissed at Craig Coryell for hiding his injury and somewhat angry at Stan Turner for delaying him. Most of all, he was angry at himself for blowing up at the agent simply because the trip home hadn't gone the way he wanted.

Long-time staples of his dictatorial coaching style, his desire to control everything around him and always get his way were traits he did not wish to exhibit in his life outside basketball. But since there was so much pain, depression and fear inside him, he invariably released this angst through the only emotion he felt comfortable expressing: anger.

Grabbing a bowl of pretzels, the ravioli and the sausage pizza, he headed into the family room so he could watch the tape of the press conference. While rewinding the tape to the beginning, Mike realized what he had forgotten. "Damn, I haven't seen Oscar and Woody yet. My boys need supper."

The Siberian huskies were named after Oscar Robertson and John Wooden. Robertson, once considered the greatest backcourt player ever, was Mike's favorite player. A high school wonder boy in Indianapolis during the 1950s, he starred at the University of Cincinnati and later for the Milwaukee Bucks in the NBA. Wooden, known as the Wizard of Westwood for the unprecedented ten national titles he won at UCLA, was Mike's favorite coach and would probably always be viewed as college basketball's best. Wooden grew up in tiny Martinsville, Indiana, a short thirty minute drive from the south side of Indianapolis. After an exceptional playing career at Martinsville High and Purdue University, Wooden became a basketball legend with his philosophical approach to coaching and unparalleled results at UCLA. Other than his father who had been a rock-strong, religious man, John Wooden was the person Mike Redding emulated most. Mike didn't know if Robertson and Wooden were his favorite player and coach because they were native Hoosiers, or if his background of being born and raised on Indiana basketball had endeared them to him. Either way, in a state certifiably crazy about basketball, Oscar Robertson and John Wooden were state treasures cherished by every red-blooded hoops fan.

As he waited for the VCR to finish rewinding the tape, Mike thought about Oscar and Woody. He needed to feed them and let them run before night fall, but he was occupied with the tape.

"Turner, get in here," he yelled toward the den, the demons once again flaring out of control.

Seconds later Turner walked into the family room. "My dogs need dinner, but I want to watch the tape of the press conference to see if you guys screwed that up, too."

Mike spit the words at the agent, yet Stan Turner stared blankly at the coach the way one of his players would. On the ride home Mike had buckled from the pressure and stress he was under, but now the bottomless pit of self-loathing he was mired in created by his inability to cope with his friends' deaths got the best of him. Whether he deserved it or not, Turner was the person Mike had chosen to vent his anger and frustration at.

"It's time for you to earn your salary, Turner. I want you to do something for me. I'll go real slow so you can keep up. It's a simple task so you'll need two or three of your buddies to help you. Start by going out in the back yard . . .."

When Mike finished dressing down Stan Turner, the agent left the room in a hurry. Mike immediately regretted treating the agent so poorly. He had asked the agent to do something that wasn't part of his job description. The FBI wasn't there to do housework or walk Mike's dogs; they were there to keep him alive. Mike decided he would apologize to the agent when he returned from the backyard. Better yet, he would put in a good word for Turner with Special Agent McCaskill.

The tape was fully rewound, so Mike hit the play button and turned the volume up. He manually fast-forwarded through most of Bernard Shaw's pre-conference commentary. For thirty minutes Shaw and other analysts talked about the case, the press conference and Mike and Quentin. Mike couldn't believe that much commentary was necessary to set up a twenty-minute news conference.

"This is unbelievable," he said to both himself and Shaw's image on the screen. "Are Americans so stupid we have to be spoon fed our news or are they just playing up the story for ratings?"

Soon Bernard Shaw's face disappeared and was replaced by a montage of sound bites recapping the events of the last three weeks. Mike closed his eyes and fast-forwarded through the pictures of Allan, David, Quentin and him. He didn't want to be reminded of the state in which Allan's and David's bodies were found. Their funerals had been hard enough, but to see the bloody images of them now was too much for him to deal with. Mike had long ago grown accustomed to seeing himself on television, but to hear himself and Quentin described as the March Madness Murderer's next targets was macabre and deeply disturbing. He had never enjoyed the media and the public aspect of coaching, but this whole experience with Allan's and David's deaths had surprised even him. He couldn't believe the stories he had heard about himself and Quentin in the last three weeks.

The National Informer was running a story about his affair with an eighteen-year-old high school senior. Unnamed sources were quoted as saying Mike and the girl were seen holding hands and carrying on like newlyweds during a night on the town. The night on the town was actually part of a fund-raiser sponsored by UNI and Big Sisters of Indiana which benefited high school dropouts and teenage runaways. Mike spent the evening with over thirty high school girls bowling and eating pizza. Someone had snapped a picture of him and a teenage runaway high-fiving while bowling and sold the photo to *The National Informer*. The picture was plastered across the front page of trashy tabloid magazines throughout the country. Even though Mike was known in college basketball circles as one of the coaches who was most generous with his time and money when it came to charities, in two days the issue became the *Informer's* top selling cover of the year. The irony of the story was that Mike had not been on a real date, teenager or otherwise, in over a year because of his obsessive work schedule and intense phobia of getting close to someone he might eventually lose.

Finally, after Mike had manually fast-forwarded through thirty minutes of sensationalistic reporting, Bernard Shaw's face disappeared from the television screen. In his place was a dark podium in the middle of a platform. On the wall behind the podium was the round, blue-and-white seal of the FBI. Seconds later Mike saw Special Agent Taylor walk across the platform and settle in behind the battery of microphones jutting up from the podium. The bustle of noise in the crowded conference room quieted down after a few moments and Taylor looked ready to speak.

The sound Mike heard startled him. It came not from the TV set, but from outside in his backyard. The horrific, inhuman noise temporarily paralyzed him. He was frozen with fear as the sound echoed in his ears. Upon hearing the repulsive noise again and realizing what it was, his face twisted into a hideous mask of confusion, fright and disgust.

After what seemed like hours, but was actually only a few seconds, he jumped out of his recliner and ran through the kitchen toward the garage. In front of him two agents were sprinting into the garage, weapons drawn, ready to terminate the cause of Stan Turner's ungodly suffering. Before he reached the garage Mike knew the source of Turner's pain. Along with the agent's shrieks for help, he had heard another sound that sent currents of terror rocketing down his spine. Never in his life had Mike experienced such a vile, revolting feeling as when he flung open the back door of the garage and saw his dogs eating Stan Turner. The agent lay pinned to the ground beneath Woody, his chest cracked open by the predator's gargantuan front paws. While Oscar ripped Turner's scalp and left ear off his head, Woody sunk his gleaming white teeth into the mushy, red mass of flesh that used to be the agent's right shoulder.

Despite running at a dead sprint, Mike was still seventy five feet from the small fenced-in area where the dogs liquefied Turner, while the agents in front of him were sixty feet away. The closer Mike got, the more repulsed he became. His huskies made noises not of this earth; at that moment he knew the dogs must die. As he neared the gate, Mike heard a sloshing, bubbling noise that sounded like water flowing over a small rock formation. Upon entering the gate, he realized the noise originated from the hole in Turner's shoulder. Woody was hungrily lapping up blood from the wound as quickly as it spewed forth. Every second or two Turner's hideous screaming started up again and his body jerked in agonizing spasms of pain.

Now inside the fenced area, Mike became aware of a putrid odor. The stench of human excrement was so powerful, he felt as if he had run face first into a brick wall. The sudden ferocity of the at-tack had caused Turner to lose voluntary control of his bowels and resulted in the sea of blood and defecation in which he floated.

As the two agents approached the dogs from the side, Oscar opened his jaws and bit hungrily into the side of Turner's face. The swift bite tore off part of Turner's nose and a chunk of skin from his cheek. Mike turned to yell at the agent closest to the dogs. The agent stood ten feet from where Turner was being devoured, gun drawn, eyes focused like lasers, poised to kill the huskies. But with his blood-ied colleague directly in the line of fire, he didn't risk firing a shot that would extinguish Turner's life force along with the predatory canines'. FBI procedure was clear on this matter. An agent must never die by the hand of one of his own.

"Shoot them. Shoot them now," Mike screamed as the agents scrambled behind the dogs to find an unobstructed line of fire.

Out of the corner of his eye Mike saw Woody bury his head deep in Turner's shoulder socket just above the clavicle. The dog's blood-soaked head swiveled back and forth inside the gaping wound as if searching for a better grip. Suddenly, the rabid dog dug into the ground for better footing, arched its head and snout back, and yanked the agent's limp limb from his body. Stan Turner's eyes rolled up into his forehead as he passed out. After fainting from the crude disembowelment and the pain of the primitive amputation, he was delivered to his Maker, bloody as the day he was born.

While Woody lay on the ground sucking his prized fleshy bone, Mike lurched forward and vomited on himself and the lawn. As he finished emptying the acrid bile from his stomach, he saw the crazed, drugged look in Woody's eyes and became enraged. Ges-turing wildly toward the dogs, he yelled louder.

"Kill them, goddamnit. Shoot the damn dogs."

With his colleague deceased and Bureau procedure no longer an issue, the agent restrained himself no more. The first bullet ripped through the back of Woody's head and exited out his throat. The shot killed the dog instantly, but the agent put two more bullets in him to make sure. Oscar had begun to shake violently when the second agent behind him fired a bullet into his back. Immediately, the spastic dog jumped off Turner's lifeless body, and began convulsing in the fluid-filled grass. Seconds later when Oscar seizured, Mike was overcome with grief not only for Stan Turner, but also for his dogs.

"Shoot him again," he pleaded as the dog's nervous system was ravaged by the synthetic adrenaline. "He's in pain, goddamnit. Put him out of his misery."

While Mike cried hysterically, the agent pumped three more bullets into Oscar's drug-infested body. Dropping to his knees in anguish, Mike clutched his head in his hands and sobbed uncontrollably. All three mutilated carcasses lay within fifteen feet of him. Gagging from the smell of fresh blood, feces, entrails and vomit, his innards were also being wrenched inside out by the pain of knowing another person was dead because of him. His parents, his friends, even strangers could not escape the fatal plague that arose from being involved with Mike Redding.

"That's it. Enough," he whispered, his eyes burning from the salt in his tears. "I don't know how you did it, Ben, but you turned my babies into monsters. Too many people have died. You win. I'm done coaching."

Chapter Fifteen

Dodging scissors, thread and fabric strewn across her living room floor as she ran for the phone, Diana was able to pick it up on the fourth ring, one ring before her voice mail would have answered. "Hello."

"Diana, it's Mike. Do you have a few minutes?"

"Oh, my God, Mike. I heard what happened. Are you okay?"

"Yeah. No, I'm not. I mean I'm alive and unhurt, but not okay. I need to be distracted. I can't stand to think or talk about what happened another second. I've spent the last three hours rehashing a nightmare. I'm gonna lose my mind if I don't get those damned images out of my head."

"It's okay, Mike. Slow down—I've got plenty of time. We'll get through this together. Let's talk about something entirely unrelated."

"Like what? Everything I do is related to coaching basketball and that's been stolen from me."

Knowing she had to steer him away from the subjects of basketball and the FBI, Diana racked her brain in an attempt to come up with a diversionary topic. "How 'bout Quentin? He told me a little bit about his career, but there has to be some great stories he left out. How'd he get such a ruthless reputation in business? I know, tell me about his house. I saw pictures of it once in *People* magazine."

"It's unbelievable. He bought the house and ninety acres two years ago for $32.4 million. It's on the far north east side of Phoenix. A director built the home in 1988 and had to sell it after his last two big budget films flopped. It's 30,000 square feet, Quentin bought it so friends, family members and business associates could shack up if need be—it's sort of a retreat house. His parents live there part of the year and spend the other four months in Carmel, Indiana."

"What does it have to make it worth $32 million?" Diana asked, trying to continue the flow Mike was in.

"Everything. It's a Swiss-style brick and stone chateau. Besides having a man-made waterfall and a petting zoo with exotic animals, it has two pools, tennis courts, stables, a twelve-hole golf course and a 6,000 square foot party pavilion. Inside there's an Olympic size pool, basketball and racquetball courts, a four-lane bowling alley and a movie theater that seats forty people. Next to money and sports, movies are Quentin's passion. He collects classics and director's cuts that never make it to theaters. Other than Ted Turner, he's probably got the largest library of movies in the world. The second he saw the theater he wrote an offer to buy the home. By offering $500,000 more than list price, he bought the home an hour later."

Mike appeared to be engrossed in the conversation, but Diana did not let up. "Is Quentin really that ruthless? I don't trust what I read in the papers anymore."

"Yes and no. Mostly he isn't but he can be. Pardon my bluntness, but I've seen him cut people's balls off when they upset him. The majority of the time he crosses the line it's for fun and games. His pranks in high school were legendary—they never hurt anyone—and he breezed through college on savvy and creative schemes. Before one big exam he stole cereal, toast, and cranberry juice from the school's cafeteria. After chewing them into a liquid , he spit the concoction on the wall and leather couch of the Dean of Academic Affairs. He was excused from the exam when he showed the Dean's secretary the vomit. He left for spring break a day earlier than everyone else, and when he got back he had the test answers.

"Another time Quentin was late submitting a twenty-page political science paper. Reports not turned in by midnight Friday automatically meant a failing grade. Quentin finished the paper Saturday night at 10:30. Knowing the professor never worked Saturdays, he climbed a fire escape chute, cut a hole in a window screen and slid his report under the prof's door with Friday's date on it. For good measure, before slipping the paper under the door, he took his shoes off and lightly put four imprints on the cover so it would look like the night security guard had stepped on the report Friday and Saturday night when checking the office. Thirty percent of the class flagged the assignment, but Quentin got the second highest score."

"Give me an example of a prank that crossed the line," Diana said.

"One of his more vengeful schemes happened when he was a sophomore at St. Tom's. He got Father Joseph Barrett, the president of the college, fired. The priest pissed Quentin off by enforcing tougher disciplinary rules and ignoring student requests. His biggest mistake was intentionally embarrassing Quentin and some others during a campus forum. For almost a year Q worked on a plan to pay back the priest.

"He got a job in Father Barrett's office as a courier and earned his trust by stroking his ego and getting involved with a lot of committees on campus. From there he got access to personal information. First, Quentin anonymously sent fabricated stories detailing Father Barrett's drunken, obnoxious behavior to an editor at the school's newspaper. Next, he sent photos of the priest drinking, dancing and socializing with women half his age. Actually, the stuff in the pictures was hardly offensive, Quentin had manipulated the angle, positioning and timing of the photos so well they looked risqué. The article and pictures made the town and college go berserk; Rensselaer's an ultra conservative farming community. Barrett was an idiot. He tried to laugh it off and when people got upset, he denied it and said it was no one's business. When bottles of liquor, sex toys and child porn were found in the president's office, the Board of Trustees made him resign. He'd been president for thirty-one years, Diana. Quentin got him fired in less than twelve months."

"God, that's awful. Why is he like that?"

"I'm not sure. I think it has something to do with his brother dying when they were kids. Nobody knows what happened—not even me, and I'm his best friend. Quentin grew up in Oregon. His family moved to Indy right after his brother died. It's the only thing he doesn't discuss. My guess is the vindictive streak is related to losing his brother. Most of the time he's the most wonderful, considerate and generous person you'd want to know. But don't cross him—"

As he finished the sentence, Mike glanced at the time on the basketball clock that hung over his fireplace in the family room. "Sorry to cut this short, Diana, but I've got to call the master game player right now. I'm bushed and he and I haven't talked in awhile."

"No problem. I'm glad we were able to talk as long as we did."

"Me too. I hated calling under these circumstances, but I didn't want to be alone with my thoughts. It worked too. You got me completely out of my head."

"I've been there too many times myself," Diana said ruefully. "Feel free to call any time you need to be distracted."

"Bet on it. You are quite a lovely distraction," Mike said before hanging up, leaving Diana smiling from ear to ear.

After being on the road the better part of the last week, Quentin relaxed on his wraparound, L-shaped sofa in the spacious great room of his sixteen-bedroom mansion. He was used to sleeping in beds other than his own. He often stayed overnight in his office when he was involved in a transaction with an overseas corporation. During the past week he had worked and slept in the plush master bedroom of his office headquarters while finalizing a licens-

ing agreement with a clothing manufacturer in Tokyo. As he relaxed on the large sofa, Quentin listened to a Fidelity Magellan fund
manager on CNN's *Money Line* summarize the transaction for host
Lou Dobbs. According to the money manager, the intense nego-
tiations had been extremely onerous because of controversial labor
issues. The deal had been vehemently opposed by a number of politicians, civic leaders and union representatives because Quentin
planned on manufacturing the merchandise in Taiwan instead of
in Bakersfield, California. Critics had argued it was ludicrous to send
business abroad when Quentin's corporate counterparts in Japan
wanted the product manufactured in California. The Magellan
manager speculated that Quentin could care less about keeping
money in the continental U.S. or saving jobs in Bakersfield's crum-
bling economy. His pocket book had been his only concern.

After persuading his associates in Tokyo to move their plant
facilities to Taiwan, thereby cutting operations expenses and labor
costs in half, Quentin had defended the decision by pointing to the
bottom line. The analyst guessed that in reality, Quentin Conway
had simply ignored the criticism. It didn't matter to him what his
detractors had thought. He had saved himself tens of millions of
dollars in start-up fees, employee wages and health care costs and
corporate taxes. The new licensing agreement would be one of his
most profitable ventures in recent years. Bakersfield's loss had been
his gain. The spot concluded with the fund manager surmising that
once again, Quentin Conway had won the war. And as usual, he
had won big.

Tired of reclining on the sofa, Quentin checked the time
on his antique grandfather clock. It was 7:30 PM in Phoenix, 9:30
PM in West Lafayette. Waiting for Mike to call was driving him crazy.
Setting a carton of Chinese take-out aside, he got up off the sofa
and walked to the gym in the west wing of the house. After select-
ing a basketball from a rack, he began shooting jump shots. Playing
basketball had always been a tension breaker for Quentin. Since he
was ten years old, the rhythmic motion of shooting a basketball had
been his way of relieving stress so he could think deeply and focus
on a problem. Quentin missed the first two shots he took, but nailed

the next five in a row. He didn't think about what he was doing. He had performed the act of shooting a jump shot so many times it was an unconscious habit.

As with most boys raised in the Hoosier state, the process of shooting a jumper was a semi-sacred ritual for Quentin. When all parts of the body used for a jump shot—feet, calves, legs, torso and shoulders, arms, wrists, hands and fingertips and eyes—were working in conjunction, the ritual was as sweetly satisfying and beautiful to watch as ballroom dancing or horses frolicking in a field. Oddly enough, Quentin became an outstanding shooter at age fourteen when he realized the one part of the body not involved in the jump shot was the brain. As any Indiana school boy would tell you, repetition is the key to great shooting. It is a natural, free-flowing, instinctive act. If the shooter's head participates in the process, the ritual is corrupted and the harmony that unifies the body, ball and net is disrupted.

Quentin's fourteenth consecutive free throw dropped through the net the very moment the cordless phone on the wall beneath the basket began to ring. Dropping the ball as he walked under the basket, Quentin took his time answering the phone. He couldn't pick up until after the second ring because the agents needed time to prepare their equipment to tape and trace the call.

"You got Quentin," he said expecting his best friend on the other end.

"And you got, Mike. What's up brother?"

"Shooting a few in the gym. I've been waiting for your call." The agents stopped taping the conversation when they knew it wasn't Ben Rooks. Quentin had an unlisted telephone number, but Ben Rooks had been able to kill a congressman, an athletic trainer and two FBI agents so McCaskill wasn't taking anything for granted. "You home now?" Quentin asked.

"Yeah," Mike replied wearily. "I've been at the hospital and the police station all night. I got home a little bit ago, but I've been on the phone with Diana. She's a great listener and a helluva sweet girl. Hey, I wanted to talk because I know you're worried about me, Q. You've got to trust me, man. I know what I'm doing."

"I trust you always, Red, but I am worried. What happened at the station?"

"Taylor flew in to see me. We had a three hour conference call with McCaskill in Washington."

"Why that long? What'd they want?" Quentin asked noticeably surprised.

"It's okay, Q, they're only doing their jobs. They wanted to know what I saw, how my dogs usually acted and what I knew about Hawthorne's kennel. I told them what happened, including my argument with Turner. They were understanding about the way I treated him—too fucking understanding. I wish someone would blow-up at me. God, I'm a prick. I treated him like a piece of shit and he died doing me a favor. Stan Turner deserved so much more. The agents at my house have been cool, but they've got to hate me. I'd be out of my freakin' mind if I lost a friend or player like that. I'm losing it, Quentin. I can't handle this shit anymore. I just want this to be over so I can have my life back."

"So you've decided to step down." It was more of a statement than a question.

Mike was quiet for a moment. Quentin's remark made him uneasy. After a lengthy silence he spoke in a strained voice. "I'm done this year. Maybe for good."

"I don't like what I'm hearing. Still—this is getting to be an impossible situation." Public sentiment had begun to change. A growing number of media personalities had criticized Mike Redding. Some members of the media believed he had a moral responsibility not to endanger his players, coaches and the thousands of fans attending UNI's games. A small, outspoken group of right-wing journalists demanded UNI or the NCAA put Mike on temporary sabbatical.

During the past few days, Quentin and Mike had discussed at great length the moral and social consequences arising from his decision to coach. After exploring all aspects of the issue and consulting the team's priest, both friends were satisfied Mike bore no responsibility for anyone's safety other than his own. He was not forcing people into a harmful situation. They could choose what was best for them—the decision being entirely their own. None of his players or coaches had expressed undue concern or fear. Apparently, the individuals involved with the tournament agreed. No referees, NCAA administrators or moderators, vendors or arena employees had chosen to sit out a game Mike Redding was coaching.

"How much time and thought have you put into this decision?" Quentin asked. "Is it the answer to your problems?"

"Shit, I don't know."

"That's the most depressed voice I've heard from you in twenty years of friendship, Mike."

"I just don't know. Stepping down can't make things worse than they are. A national title won't bring Allan or David back. Two agents have died trying to protect us, and I'm directly responsible for one of those deaths. I'm not a moron. No matter how you look at it, it's my fault Turner's dead. Do you know how that feels, Quentin? If I hadn't ridden him so hard, he'd be alive today. Do you know how that feels? Huh? He'd be drinking beer with his buddies right now if I wasn't such a goddamned Nazi prick."

"Yeah, and you'd be a damn corpse. Is that what you want? Wake up, Mike. You aren't to blame for Turner's death. Ben Rooks is. The FBI doesn't blame you because they know you're not responsible. It's their job to protect us. Those guys know when they join the FBI they'll be putting their life on the line every day they're in the field. Besides, you don't deserve this shit. You didn't ask Ben to go crazy, kill your friends and stalk us. You didn't choose it—he chose you. Nobody blames you for anything. You can't be expected to take care of and look after everyone's best interests. You're a basketball coach, Mike. The best damn coach I've ever seen. Your obligation is to your players, your staff, UNI and most of all—yourself.

"Guilt's eating you up inside because you were an asshole to Turner and he died doing you a favor. You feel like you should've been the one to die, not him. Well, it didn't happen that way. Yeah, Mike, you definitely were a giant prick. You treated a great guy like crap. Damn straight he didn't deserve the treatment you gave him, and he certainly didn't deserve to die, but neither do you. And you sure as hell don't deserve all the crap that's been thrown at you. Your friends have been murdered, your life's been threatened, and your privacy and sanity have been stripped away by the media and the FBI. Your dream of winning a national championship is at stake and people are questioning your integrity and morality. You didn't bring this on yourself Mike, but you've got to deal with it and get through it. It's the same as when your dad died. You blamed yourself for something that wasn't your fault. You can't do that again, man. You'll make yourself miserable. You're not responsible for everyone and everything that goes on around you. You didn't do anything wrong other than being a jerk to that agent. You didn't cause his death or get him killed. Ben did. Stop taking the blame for everything bad that happens. Just let go of the guilt and blame. It's not your fault. You've got to go on with your life and put this crap behind you."

Mike was silent for a good ten seconds after Quentin's impassioned plea. When he spoke, it was the voice of a confused man with no direction. "You're right Quentin. It isn't my fault Turner died, and I didn't ask for this or bring it on myself. What I'm having trouble with is the thought I could be putting other people in danger. It scares the hell out of me. All I have to do is step down and lives might be spared."

"Can you live with yourself if you quit and walk away?" Quentin asked.

"I don't think I could live with myself if I coach and innocent people die. How important is my dream of winning a national championship? Is it worth two people dying? Ten people? What if I win it all, but four fans die because I coached. I feel so selfish thinking about my dream when people's lives are at stake. Would I be able to enjoy the title knowing a family lost their father or youngest boy because I coached? What if we don't win the championship and five fans die at one of my games. What the hell would I do then? I'm not handling Allan's, David's or Turner's deaths well. What would I be like if a hundred people died and I could have prevented it? I don't have any answers, Quentin, and I need some before I can coach again."

"Only you can make this decision, Mike, but to be honest with you, I'm not sure there *are* answers to those questions. I don't think anyone understands how you feel because you're the only one going through this. I'm angry, frustrated and frightened to death too, but I don't have to make the decision you do. If you coach, I'll be there. If you don't, I'll stay away. I just think you have to remember where your responsibility lies: it's to yourself, your team and your university. Those 20,000 fans are not Mike Redding's responsibility. They look after their own interests; it's not your job to do it for them. Allan was the public servant. You're a basketball coach. Your job is to win games, teach your players how to succeed in life, and represent UNI as best you can."

"Those bastards in the press would love to see me step aside," Mike replied. "They'd take credit for it too. There'd be tons of articles on how I was forced to do the right thing by mounting media pressure. That's such horse-shit. The media couldn't make me do jack. They have no idea what I'm going through. None of those reporters' lives are in danger. Their friends weren't murdered and their jobs and dreams aren't being destroyed. How can they tell me what I should or shouldn't do? The media is so quick to sit in judgment, yet there's little risk in what they do. No one critiques or questions them, yet they have free reign to trash anybody.

"The worst thing about it is the number of people they influence. People read their crap and hear it on TV, and take it as the gospel truth. It's sick—people don't think for themselves anymore, the media tells them what to think. They hammer the public with so much news and information people buy into it. No one questions things anymore. We just believe what we're told. It used to be the damned government conditioning us, now it's the media. I guarantee people won't stop to think about my situation. They'll believe what the media is saying: that I only care about winning a championship and making endorsement money.

"I'm sick and tired of hearing I don't care about the people at my games. It's the media that doesn't give a shit. It's just a story to them. Another hot story that sells papers. Why do they point fingers and judge me? What good comes out of judging anyone? I already feel like it's my fault when it isn't. Why are they trying to bury me?"

Suddenly, Mike realized he had bitched about the media for over two minutes. "Quentin, I've lost control of everything in my life and now I'm railing on the press. Sorry, man. I needed to let off some steam."

"It's all right, Red. You have every right to feel that way. Besides, I agree with you. The press always wants to knock down the guy on top. It's human nature. Remember what Michael Jordan told you at that charity game last year.

"The media built me up quickly because I represented what was good and wholesome. After my popularity became threatening and they got tired of me, they trashed me and tried to destroy the clean, wholesome image they created." That's what he said.

"He was absolutely right. The media picks and chooses who they want to help or hurt. Just think how bad it'd be if you were a black coach—you'd really be hung out to dry. I don't blame you for feeling bitter. That's why I want you to reconsider your decision. Ask your players again if any of them want you to step down and practice the rest of the week like everything's normal. By Wednesday if you haven't changed your mind, fine. Don't coach Thursday night or the rest of the tourney. Just don't forget where your responsibility lies and don't let the media make up your mind for you."

"Thanks, Q, I needed a kick in the ass. I don't know what to do, but at least I have time to think about it. You're right about two things—even though I was a major prick, it's not my fault Turner died and I shouldn't rush my decision about resigning."

"I'm glad you're thinking sensibly again," Quentin said.

Mike had grown sleepy. It was close to eleven in Lafayette and the events of the day had taken their toll on him. "Listen, Q, I'm beat. I'm gonna have to let you go."

"Sure, coach. Get some sleep and call me tomorrow after practice. Let me know how they're playing. By the way, get the ball to Byron more. He needs more touches so he can get more looks. He's going to lead you to the promised land."

Mike laughed while stifling a yawn. "Good night, man.

Thanks for talking me through this. You know I love ya like a brother."

"No problem, Red. I'm just paying you back for all you've done for me."

Quentin hung up the phone. He picked up the basketball and went back to the free throw line. He hit his fifteenth shot in a row and decided to keep shooting until he missed. After nearly ten minutes of deep thought, Quentin left a shot short and it bounced off the front of the rim. By then he had formed a new strategy and was confident Mike would continue coaching.

He sat quietly in the dark room. He had not moved an inch while watching the late news. When the report on Agent Turner's death was over, he hit the remote and turned off the television. He couldn't believe Mike Redding had survived the attack. The plan had been brilliant. It was executed flawlessly yet UNI's coach was alive and well. Redding should have been dead by now. With the deadline fast approaching there was no time for any more cat and mouse games. He had to move quicker—time was running out. Venomous anger simmered within him. The plan would have worked, Redding would be dead if the do-good agent hadn't interfered.

"Goddamned boy scout," he yelled at the top of his lungs. "That stupid FBI fuck deserved to die." His forehead was red-hot, the veins in his temples bulged and his pulse raced. "Two agents have died because they got in my way. If they do it again, I'll kill all of them. I'll blow the whole academy into the sky. I'm in control and I won't fail again. And I'm taking as many people to hell with me as I can."

McCaskill raised the mug of scalding hot coffee to his lips. He didn't have an answer for Bailey. It was 1:20 in the morning; he had been on the clock for sixteen hours and the end of his day was some two hours away.

"I don't know how to find him, L.C. We've tried flushing him out, we've swept motels, boarding houses, pubs, grocery stores, drug stores, everything. Nobody's seen or heard anything. We've got no idea what he looks like or what name he's using. He's had five years to work on a new identity; obviously it's a good one. Somewhere in Chicago or northwest Indiana, he's doing manual labor or factory work and laying low. He's done a helluva job of not drawing attention to himself.

"We've hit the south side of Chicago hardest, and then the Region in Gary and Hammond. Our field agents have talked to dealers, pimps and hookers—every type of street vendor, but no one's heard from him in sixteen years. It's amazing how people on the street know what's going on. A lot of dealers remembered Rooks. He must have been a good customer. Taylor even went through Cook County's informant roster, but the narcs on the payroll had nothing. From the dates his letters were postmarked, the attempts on Conway and Redding and his history in the Midwest, he's got to be between Indianapolis and Chicago. I'd be willing to bet he's underground between Lafayette and Chicago. He's either kicked the heroin habit or got a new fix because he's stayed away from past suppliers and major players in Chicago and Indy. I don't know what else to do. We've questioned all our sources twice and we're tailing the people he used to deal with. He disappeared into thin air."

"Nobody disappears," the deputy director responded. "They either hide or die, but they don't disappear. Rooks isn't dead, which means we have to find where he's hiding. Maybe we're looking in the wrong places. Are you sure he's between Indianapolis and Chicago?"

"Yeah. No question about it. We'd have found him by now if he was in a metropolitan area. We've checked farmhouses, motels, hotels, trailer parks . . . you name it. He had five years to plan everything and it's working. He's got a new identity, and with the Forsey kid dead, no one can recognize him. That's a big reason I didn't want to go public about him. It wouldn't have helped with his new name and look."

Bailey reflected on McCaskill's last comment. "Well, we've got to find him before Thursday night. Agents are dropping like flies. To be honest Frank, I'm not sure we can protect 20,000 people, and we sure as hell can't have families dying at a basketball game. He could blow up the whole damn arena. We don't have a lot of options. We've got to turn up the heat and locate him before Thursday's and Saturday's games. He's a showboat. His ego wants to kill them on live television while the whole country watches. By the way, what'd you find out about UNI's chances Thursday?"

McCaskill didn't need to look through his notes to answer this question. "Everyone I talked to said UNI would win. I called Billy Packer, Dick Vitale and three coaches whose teams played both UNI and Marquette this season. Nobody picked Marquette. They all said it was a done deal, that we can expect UNI to play Saturday night. I had all six of them sign an affidavit prohibiting them from talking to the media so there won't be any leaks."

Bailey nodded his head as if to say "nice work." He had grown used to Frank McCaskill's professionalism years ago and often took it for granted. McCaskill didn't bother to tell L.C. Bailey how difficult it had been to persuade Dick Vitale to sign the agreement. The special agent had found Vitale deserving of his reputation as college basketball's biggest mouth.

L.C. Bailey leaned back in his chair, stretched his long wiry arms above his head and stood up. "This coffee's going right through me. I've gotta use the bathroom. I want your opinion when I get back. Will Rooks go after Redding and Conway before Thursday, at Thursday's game or at Saturday's game?"

Bailey ducked out of his office leaving McCaskill deep in thought. He had been wrestling with this issue for the last forty-eight hours. During the course of the investigation, McCaskill had grown to admire and despise Ben Rooks more than any criminal he had tracked. A strange, enigmatic bond had developed between the two. From the background research on Rooks' early years, the documentation on his stay in prison, and the volumes of psychiatric reports, McCaskill knew Ben Rooks as well as anyone did.

The neurotic loner had become the central focus of McCaskill's life. Every day he thought about Ben Rooks, wondered what he looked like and what he was doing. He tried to put himself in Rooks' shoes so he could understand why he wanted to kill his high school buddies. As the investigation progressed, McCaskill became more repulsed by Rooks' actions. He was so caught up in his obsession that the few hours he slept at night, he dreamed of Ben Rooks. McCaskill knew one of them would be dead when the investigation was over. Even though it was dangerous to be emotionally involved with a suspect, he couldn't control his emotional outrage. He wanted Ben Rooks in the worst way.

McCaskill considered Rooks the ideal killing machine. Fearless and unremorseful, he possessed the mental acuity of a genius and the attention to detail of a skilled craftsman. The sociopath's poise and patience scared Frank McCaskill the most. Deep inside in a place he didn't like to admit existed, McCaskill felt admiration and respect for Ben Rooks' immense talent. To apprehend a killer of such supreme skill and ability, McCaskill had to be willing to give up his life. He was, but he knew Ben Rooks was prepared to do the same. In the past ten days, McCaskill had come to know certain things about the March Madness Murderer that no one else knew. He felt close to his prey, so close he believed he knew what Rooks' next move would be.

McCaskill's thoughts were interrupted by Deputy Director Bailey's return from the bathroom. "If I know you, Frank, you've been thinking about this for days. What's Rooks gonna do?"

"He'll want to do them together so it'll be during a game. Killing them at the same time is practical and efficient—Rooks' way of operating, but is still challenging and exotic which fits his flair for the dramatic. He's running out of time. UNI could lose on Saturday and the tournament's over in two weeks. Conway and Redding won't be in the same place until Thursday's game, so that's his first option. I don't think he'll do it Thursday, though. He'll be at the game or nearby casing the stadium, but he won't make an attempt."

Before McCaskill could continue, Bailey fired another question. "How strong's your feeling?"

"He's not ready," McCaskill answered. "It's not enough time since his last attack on Redding. Even if he made a plan in advance, three days is too little time to prepare and execute it. Plus, he'd want to see what we're doing as far as logistics, strategy and personnel. Bottom line, though, three days isn't enough time to implement a plan that large. The plan will have to be brilliant, which it will be, but it also has to be performed flawlessly.

"That's the problem with Thursday. It doesn't allow the time needed to scout the site, survey our security, adjust the plan and prepare contingency plans. Rooks is a control freak. He'll want everything to be perfect. If it isn't, he knows he won't be successful. He'll check out the stadium Thursday and use the next two days to prepare. Saturday's game is for a berth in the Final Four; it's the biggest game of the year. His ego can't pass that up. Plus, all the analysts I spoke with said if UNI was to lose, it'd be Saturday against Duke or Kentucky. Rooks has to do it before UNI's out of the tournament. The game Saturday is perfect because millions of people will be watching. Recognition is what he's after. He wants to show the world how great he is."

Not able to sleep, he looked at the clock on the night stand—4:07 AM. He had been lying in bed for hours playing back the day's events in his mind. He was restless. Saturday was D-day. UNI would win Thursday and advance to the Elite Eight Saturday evening. There was no other possibility. It had to be Saturday. Pulling the covers off himself, he swung his feet around until they touched the cold hardwood floor. He walked across the bedroom to the small folding table in the corner. He hadn't sealed the enve-

lope yet. He waited so he could check the letter again before mailing it. Everything had to be perfect or he'd burn the letter and start
from scratch. After putting on surgical gloves, he removed the typing paper from the envelope. The room was so dark the letter would
have been unreadable for any normal person, but he was far from
normal.

He loved darkness. He had learned to live in it while in
prison. In solitary confinement the darkness became his friend, an
ally that hid the dreary, gray walls and menacing iron bars. In a place
overrun with misery and despair, the darkness enabled his mind to
escape the drab surroundings and plot his revenge. On one occa-
sion he went three weeks in solitary without seeing sunlight or light
from a lamp. He felt secure in the dark because there his weaknesses
were easily disguised and hidden. He was so adept at functioning in
the dark, he could read the letter without straining his eyes. It didn't
matter, though. He knew it by memory. He had selected the words
carefully. Each one was chosen for a specific reason. The words had
come to him in a dream. Holding the letter in front of his face, he
studied his masterful work.

Mike and Quentin,

Both of you have been lucky. I wonder if your good
fortune can continue?
You best be careful. I fear the end is near. There will
be nothing left.

Your Shadow

In each of the first four sentences a single word had been
circled in black crayon. In the first sentence it was the word lucky.
Fortune was circled in the second sentence, best in the third sentence, and the word near was circled in the fourth sentence. No word
was circled in the last sentence. As he peered at the letter through
the darkness, his eyes were drawn to the four words: lucky, fortune,
best and near. Each word described one of his high school friends.

Allan was lucky, Quentin had a fortune, Mike was the best coach, and David was always near Mike. The fifth sentence referred to the entire group of friends: there will be nothing left. No words needed to be circled in that sentence. After Mike and Quentin were killed, nothing would be left of the group's friendship.

He folded the letter neatly and slid it back into the envelope, being careful not to seal it. He wanted to examine it again before mailing it in the morning. He placed the white envelope on the folding table and pulled off the latex gloves. Reaching into the file cabinet next to the table, he took out two photo albums. One was marked Mike Redding across the top, the other Quentin Conway. He flipped through the albums for a few minutes. At the back of each album was an empty page. He stared at the blank pages. After Saturday's game, they would be filled in. Satisfied with his work and feeling a headache coming on, Ben Rooks put the photo albums back in the file cabinet and climbed into bed.

The man's voice haunted him. There was something familiar about it. He had dreamed this same flashback so many times he knew it by heart. Each time the flashback occurred, it lasted a bit longer, and he remembered slightly more than the previous time. The flashback was a scene from his past. In his mind's eye Ben Rooks saw himself enveloped in darkness. It was so dark he wasn't sure if he was standing, sitting, or lying down. He couldn't discern where he was, but Rooks knew he was the person in the dream. Two other people were in the room with him—he saw them in his mind's eye. More importantly, he felt their presence.

Three nights ago during the flashback, Ben Rooks realized one of them was a man. That night the man in the dream spoke. Since that night each time he had the flashback, the man's voice sounded clearer and hung a little longer in his memory. Last night the flashback showed more—the people in the dream laughed at him. It was a mocking, condescending laugh that terrified him. He woke up more frightened then ever. He vowed not to sleep the next night.

Ben Rooks was both scared and intrigued by the flashback. After the condescending laugh the previous night, he was desperate to know what it meant. What happened to him in prison? Who were these people and what had they done to him? Why was there a sexual undercurrent to the flashback? He couldn't stop the dreams. After being buried by layers of years, the horrible knowledge of a traumatic event could no longer be suppressed. Ben Rooks' subconscious mind was unraveling the trauma and weaving it into his dreams. Regardless of whether he wanted the truth exposed or not, his subconscious mind would reveal it.

On this night he had been asleep two hours when the flashback started. It was the same as always—he was suspended in darkness with nothing around him. He was confused and unsure of his surroundings. Suddenly, he heard two voices. Straining to hear them speak, he sensed they were men because one of them threatened his physical security. The distant voices grew silent only to be replaced by the sound of sinister laughter, a noise so gut-wrenching the flashback had become a nightmare. With the laughter echoing through his head, he woke from the dream soaked in sweat, petrified of what he remembered. A wall of denial and deceit had come crashing down. For the first time he was able to look on the other side. What he saw infuriated him. Ben Rooks was now more determined than ever to complete his mission.

Chapter Sixteen

Alec Taylor studied McCaskill's face as the higher-ranking special agent cradled the phone to his ear. He searched for a clue concerning the news McCaskill was receiving, but the stoic expression on his face gave nothing away.

"Thanks for getting the results to me so quick, Larry. Tell the other white coats they did good."

Frank McCaskill believed it was twice as important to praise people when they did good as it was to correct or discipline them when they screwed up. Unlike some agents in the Bureau, he made a concerted effort to compliment the scientists, doctors and technicians that worked in the Bureau's research laboratories. Larry Wiseman and his team of forensic experts had labored into the early hours of the morning performing autopsies and blood and tissue tests on the dogs. Because of their late night, McCaskill received test results hours earlier than expected. As usual, he would write a note in his report acknowledging the speed and efficiency of the forensic lab's work. Because of small yet important gestures like this, Larry Wiseman and his staff always worked a little harder and faster for Frank McCaskill.

McCaskill set the phone down and turned to Taylor. "They found injection marks in the dogs. Preliminary reports show Detracil in both dogs. They found traces of another substance, but don't know what it is yet. Final results should come back in two hours. It doesn't matter what the other drug was, the attack was planned. Detracil and a number of other drugs produce a chemical reaction that releases large amounts of hormones and adrenaline through the bloodstream. The effect lasts for a short time, but is obviously very powerful. At the end of this short cycle, the dogs' hearts blew up. Wiseman compared it to souping up a Volkswagen with special fuel. For a brief stretch the Volkswagen would go 200 mph and outrun a Porsche, but then its engine would overheat. Shortly thereafter, the engine would explode."

"No doubt it was Rooks. He was in Lafayette the day before," Taylor said.

"Yep, it was Rooks," McCaskill sighed wearily. It was only 8:50 in the morning and the day was already long.

"I can't believe this shit," Taylor said. "We've got ten agents in and around Redding's home and five state troopers surrounding his house at all times. Rooks mails a death threat here to taunt us, we know he's in the same city as Redding and what happens? He poisons the damn dogs right under our noses and they kill for him. How'd Rooks think of poisoning the dogs? What kind of a sick mind would come up with that?"

McCaskill had heard enough. He was frustrated and burnt out as well, but he didn't want Taylor's negativity to affect the other agents' morale. "Calm down, Alec. He poisoned the dogs at the kennel. That's the only way it could have been done. We've got to start thinking like him. His only objective is to kill Redding and Conway. He knows they're heavily guarded so he has to do everything in an unconventional manner. He's good at it, very good, but we'll catch him because we know what's most important to him."

Now calmer and more poised, Taylor interrupted McCaskill. "We hold the cards because we've got Redding and Conway."

"Exactly," McCaskill said. "Rooks has to come to us because we've got what he wants. We also know when he'll make the attempt. We need to put ourselves in his shoes. His situation calls for creativity so we should expect something unusual. That's what he did with the dogs. He didn't have much to work with, so he used what he had. From here on I want you to think like Rooks. He's driven by a compulsion to kill two well-protected people. The only time the targets will be in public and in the same place is at a basketball game with 20,000 people present. How will Rooks do it? I want you to focus on that."

"I'll change my approach," Taylor said. "Let me ask you about something else. We've turned Chicago and northwestern Indiana upside down. Bailey wants the field search to be more aggressive, so why don't we extend it farther to the east in Indiana and also south of Chicago in downstate Illinois. It might be a long shot, but Rooks is too clever and unpredictable to be in an obvious place. We should broaden the search and look in less obvious places."

"It can't hurt. Set it up ASAP. I've got to get to a meeting with the director about a scholarship fund honoring Stan Turner. First Eric Howard, now Turner. Let's put an end to this, Alec. I don't want to see any more scholarships started in memory of dead agents. We don't have a lot of time either. Rooks is planning his next move as we speak."

After placing his cordless phone back in the cradle, Quentin leaned back in his ergonomically designed executive's chair and put his feet up on his desk. Tilting his head back and stretching his arms out above him, he closed his eyes and indulged himself in the simple pleasure of a long, deep yawn. A soft knock on the door interrupted him.

"Come in," he called, before picking up where he left off.

"Here's the prospectus on the Dillard Steel merger," Jennifer Countryman said, setting the folder on his "in" tray.

A full three seconds elapsed before Quentin was done yawning and could respond. "Thanks Jen. I'll get to them later."

"I'm glad to see you so relaxed, Quentin. You haven't been like this in a while," the secretary commented, conscious of the FBI agents milling around her office and the outer sanctum of QuinWay Inc. headquarters.

"I just had the best conversation one can have with a woman, considering she told me she liked my best friend, not me."

"Ms. Fleming actually said that?" the secretary exclaimed, immediately regretting the use of Diana's name. Jennifer Country-man knew how much Quentin treasured his privacy. Besides her machine-like work ethic, six, fifteen-hour-a-day work weeks were common, and gaunt, physically unattractive appearance, the administrative assistant had endeared herself to Quentin by revering his desire for privacy and never gossiping about her boss.

"Mr. Conway, I am so sorry," she said earnestly. "It's none of my concern who you . . ."

"Forget it, Jen," Quentin replied, waving it away with his hand. "There's nothing to hide. Diana and Mike are compatible—she and I aren't. If a woman doesn't respond to me right away, it's usually a sign we'll just be friends. We never had the chemistry it takes, but from what she said that connection is there between Mike and her."

"If you don't mind me saying, Mr. Conway, for a man who never finishes second, you're taking this well."

"I don't plan on making a habit of it, Jennifer," Quentin said chuckling. "But if it has to happen once a year, I can live with it being my best friend. Especially since Diana Fleming is so impressive and he hasn't been on a date in months. Come to think of it, Jen, why don't you Fed Ex a friendship bouquet to Diana's apartment in Chicago. Make it twenty purple lilac sprays. She'll like those, won't she?"

"She'll love them," Jennifer said, admiring his knowledge of what women like. "I'll have them delivered tonight."

Mike tried to ignore the chaos that waited for him and his team at the top of the players' ramp. The reporters and journalists gathered at the entrance to the tunnel acted as if Elvis was about to appear with his son-in-law Michael Jackson. The NCAA had allowed UNI to work out first so the session could be closed to the public. The subsequent practice sessions for Marquette, Duke and Kentucky would then be opened to the public after Mike had left the building.

The NCAA's executive committee wanted to protect one of college basketball's best young coaches, so they allowed the practice to be closed. Since they also wanted to generate greater interest in the tournament and put more money in the NCAA's coffers, the committee permitted fifty members of the national media to witness UNI's practice. Mike was livid when he found out about the decision, but there was nothing he or UNI's athletic director could do to reverse it; he and his players were simply puppets in the grand scheme of things.

Mike was sure he wouldn't coach the rest of the tournament. Since the press conference two days earlier when the threat against him was revealed, the print and television media had focused on no other topic. Beginning the morning of the FBI press conference, an average of fourteen talk shows per day discussed the murder investigation and Mike Redding's plight. *Good Morning America*, the *Today Show* and other respected media vehicles analyzed the story in the morning while hard-hitting news shows such as *Dateline*, *Now*, *The McNeil-Lehrer Hour*, and *Larry King Live* debated the story at night.

Each evening CBS, NBC and ABC devoted five to ten minutes of their nightly news broadcast to the story. The two questions on Americans' minds: should Mike Redding continue to coach and would he be assassinated on live television while millions of viewers watched? Opinions ran the gamut. Many people felt Mike should be barred from coaching while a greater number believed it was within his rights to coach. Churches, political organizations and activist groups had also joined the debate. With the possibility of an assassination looming, some staunch conservatives thought CBS should not broadcast UNI's games because millions of children and younger viewers would be watching.

Despite the massive media attention, one angle of the story had not been reported, and it left the public and the national media in a frenzied state of curiosity. No one knew what Mike Redding thought because he had steadfastly refused to speak to the press. This absence of information only fanned the fires of intrigue. Human nature being what it is, Americans were frightened yet fascinated by the March Madness Murderer's reign of terror.

Finally, the security guards at the top of the ramp were able to clear a path through the press corps and signaled for Mike and his players to proceed up the ramp. Five minutes later, he stood at the ten-second line on the gorgeous home court of the Detroit Pistons. His players had already stretched in the locker room, so they warmed up by throwing overhand baseball passes in pairs of two. After a few minutes of light passing, they performed an intricate passing drill Mike called "the box." At any given moment four players in four corners of the human box were simultaneously running and passing four balls. In order to be performed the proper way, the drill required great concentration. He used the drill not just to warm up his players, but to get them mentally focused as well. A mistake or slow reaction by a player resulted in an oncoming pass nailing them in the face.

While his team ran through the drill, Mike stood at half court urging them to throw crisper passes. The photographers snapped picture after picture from their court side seats, yet the players had no idea what took place around them. They focused on passing, running, and catching. Mike called this intense type of focus "tunnel concentration."

At specific times during a game he wanted his players to zero in on only one task. Everything else had to be shut out. The classic example he preached to his team was free throw shooting at the end of a close game. When a player steps to the line with the game hanging in the balance, a colorful sea of opposing fans behind the basket tries to distract the player any way they can. Tunnel concentration allows the shooter to disregard the magnitude of the shot, overcome the mental pressure of the situation and block out the visual and audial distraction of the fans.

Once the drill reached a frenetic pace, Mike blew his whistle. He was pleased. His players looked extremely sharp for the beginning of practice. For the next forty minutes, Mike put his team through a variety of drills that emphasized defensive positioning, offensive spacing and transition offense and defense. When the players became slightly winded, he had them shoot free throws and jumpers. The team split up according to positions and spent twenty minutes on shooting drills. The guards fired long range jump shots, the forwards practiced medium range jumpers, and the two centers worked on interior and low post moves.

When Mike felt they had practiced shooting long enough, he blew his whistle and called his players down to the end of the court that was farthest from the media. For five minutes he talked about the keys to winning the next evening. Then he did something unusual for a college coach, something no one in the assembled media gathering noticed. He spent twenty-five minutes during a half-court scrimmage preparing his starting five players for Kentucky, not Marquette. UNI's second team played Kentucky's defense and ran the Wildcat's offense when they had the ball.

After scrimmaging his starters against Kentucky's simulated offense and defense, Mike had his second team players switch to Duke's offense and defense. By scrimmaging this way, he was gaining extra preparation time for Saturday's game. He knew his team was ready for Marquette and that UNI's talent and experience would enable them to win. The real test would be Saturday against the winner of the Duke-Kentucky contest. That game was a toss-up, either team could win, but he felt Kentucky had jelled at the right time and would be victorious. To cover all bases, he had been practicing his starters the last three days against both Duke's and Kentucky's offense and defense. He didn't want to overlook Marquette, but he felt certain UNI would beat them. It was Saturday's final eight game that concerned him. The team that survived that game would have an easy road to the championship game and would be the heavy favorite to win the national title.

Mike watched intently as his starting five scrimmaged against the simulated Duke defense. He was so engrossed in what he was doing, his passion for coaching so strong, he temporarily forgot he had decided not to coach the rest of the tournament. The myriad of negative feelings that troubled him, uncontrollable anger, self-doubt and sadness, were not able to harm him when he was on the court. He was lost in basketball. His lone thought was preparing his team to beat Marquette and the winner of the Kentucky-Duke clash.

Leaning over to LaMont DuPree, his top assistant and right-hand man, Mike whispered, "If those dumb ass reporters knew anything they'd realize I've spent forty five minutes preparing for Kentucky and Duke instead of Marquette. I'm giving them great material. If they put that in their papers Marquette would be pissed off. But check in the morning, I bet there's not one damned word about it."

LaMont DuPree laughed because he knew his boss was right. Mike Redding knew how to play the public relations game as well as anyone in college basketball. He always had the right answers to the questions asked by journalists. He was on record as saying every regular season game was important and each tournament game crucial. He told reporters all games were tough, that as a coach he couldn't look past any team, and that he prepared for every game the same way. To Mike it was complete lip-service. He fed reporters clichés that sounded good and did what he was supposed to. He knew not to rock the boat. Pissing off the NCAA and other coaches only meant trouble.

During the 1980s, sports commentary had become dominated by trite, overused clichés. Formerly uncommon labels such as "legend," "superstar," and "one for the ages," had become far too common, yet fans across the country bought into the clichés and the stereotypical images they created. Fans based their opinions of sports figures as much on what they said and did as their accomplishments. Mike thought it was ridiculous for athletes to be judged this way. The primary objective of a sporting competition was to win; the secondary objective was to perform individually at the highest level of excellence possible. The fact that an athlete wasn't good looking, articulate or family-oriented was of no consequence to Mike; championships and titles were.

His opinion was different concerning off-the-court behavior. He felt strongly that athletes and especially coaches should conduct themselves in a manner that did not tarnish the sport they participated in. He didn't believe, however, that athletes should be expected to behave any better or worse than the rest of society. The whole notion of their being role models amused Mike. Athletes were no better equipped to be role models than anyone else. If anything, they were less equipped than the average citizen because of the adoration and pampering they received. But because of the boundless wealth and fame many athletes enjoy, they were measured against a different set of rules. Off the playing court Mike did not agree with this practice. On the court, however, he judged athletes by one major criteria, the stiffest one of all: championships.

With the advent of lucrative commercial endorsements and the comprehensive media coverage of sports during the 1980s, athletes started being judged not just by their achievements on the court, but on what they said, how they looked and what they did off the court. It made no sense to Mike that certain athletes who didn't excel at their particular sport were immensely popular because they said and did the right things. He wasn't paid by the University of Northern Indiana to make friends, look good or contribute to society—those were personal choices for him to make on his own—he was paid to win conference titles and gain Final Four berths. Mike told reporters what sounded good, but he coached his players to accomplish two objectives when they stepped on the court: to play as well as they could, and to beat their opponent so decisively basketball wasn't fun for them.

UNI's practice session ended with ten minutes of free throw shooting. Whenever UNI played in a new arena, Mike made sure his players got in extra shooting practice. Since every stadium possesses a unique backdrop behind the baskets, a player's shot can be thrown off by the dimensions and lighting of a new arena. Depth perception is the biggest problem with shooting in a large, open stadium such as the Palace. Professional players acclimate more quickly than college players to the different rims, backdrops and lighting of the immense arenas, so Mike had his team take plenty of practice shots.

Satisfied with his team's shooting, Mike blew his whistle three times and his players jogged over to huddle around him at midcourt. First, he talked about the team's agenda. UNI had a mandatory press conference at 2:30 which the coaches and players had to attend. The NCAA's executive committee had approved Mike's absence and would not levy a fine against UNI. Publicly the NCAA's stance was one of concern, caution and sympathy, but privately, some of the senior officials on the governing board couldn't have been happier about the attention being drawn to the tournament. March Madness had been catapulted into international notoriety. It would easily be the sporting event of the year, resulting in a monetary windfall the NCAA would benefit from for years to come.

After complimenting his players' practice performance, Mike dismissed them so they could shower and eat lunch. While they ate and sat through the hour-long press conference, he would study film and go over his game plan for the fifth time that week. He wanted to make sure he wasn't missing anything. He might be taking Marquette lightly, but he wasn't overlooking them. As compulsive as he normally was about preparation, he had been worse than usual this week. The problems he was having caused him to throw himself into his work with such demonic compulsion even his assistants were concerned. Mike felt his game plan and practice preparation for Thursday's and Saturday's games had to be perfect because he wouldn't be on the bench supervising his team's effort. Once the ball was thrown up, his players would be on their own. Walking off the gleaming wood floor of the Palace, he worried about his team's chances against Kentucky or Duke. He wasn't sure they could triumph without him. It would take a near perfect game for UNI to win. Unfortunately, Saturday's Elite Eight showdown wasn't Mike's only concern. An equally formidable task lay ahead. He still had to figure out how he'd tell his players he wouldn't be coaching UNI's most important game of the year.

     Once again the instant he saw the envelope, Frank McCaskill knew who it was from. After putting on latex gloves, he went to his desk, pulled out a tape recorder and pressed "record." The Bureau recorded every conversation its agents had while working on a level one or two case. This investigation was a level one, the highest priority case the Bureau could be assigned. Administrative agents and inference readers pored over the mountains of paperwork field agents collected and played back the recorded audio tapes in an effort to find obscure data missed during the course of an investigation. McCaskill picked up a twelve-inch-long, razor sharp, silver-tipped letter opener given to him by Henry Kissinger, and cut open the envelope. He collected letter openers as a hobby, but this one from Kissinger was his favorite because it was a Chinese relic once owned by Mao Tse-Tung. Holding the envelope upside down, he shook it and let the folded letter fall onto his desk.

     Before reading the letter, McCaskill instructed his secretary to page Alec Taylor. Even though Taylor was flying to Detroit in an hour to join the army of agents preparing for Thursday's game, he wanted the special agent to review the letter. McCaskill carefully unfolded the sheet of typing paper and read the short message. When he finished reading it, he was perplexed. Why was Rooks sending the death threats? Why was he taking so many chances? The purpose of this threat eluded Frank McCaskill, but one thing was clear. Rooks was daring the FBI to stop him—he was playing a game. Suddenly, a light bulb went off in McCaskill's head and his mood improved instantaneously. He was so excited he felt like doing an Irish jig around his office. The letter represented the first real break since Jeremiah Forsey's anonymous phone call. Seconds later

McCaskill's train of thought was broken by Taylor's entrance.

"What is it?" Taylor asked, barely in the office.

"Another letter from Rooks. Read it," McCaskill said sinking into his chair.

Taylor quickly read the letter, not looking up until he was finished. "I know what you're thinking."

"What?" McCaskill asked.

"This letter confirms your theory Rooks will try to kill them at the same time."

"That's exactly what I'm thinking," said McCaskill. "Agree or disagree?"

Taylor thought for a moment before replying. "I agree and I'll point something else out. The other two times Rooks sent letters he tried to kill Redding and Conway shortly thereafter, within two or three days. If you're right, and I know you are, we not only know where Rooks will try to kill them, we know when. He'll definitely do it in the next few days which means . . ."

Before Taylor could finish his sentence, McCaskill cut him off. "Thursday or Saturday at the Palace."

Chapter Seventeen

Sitting cross-legged on the floor of her bedroom, Diana Fleming hummed to herself while she cut frayed edges of fabric from a garment. Her thoughts had been on Mike for the last two days. She was driving home from Marshall Fields two nights before when she turned on the radio and caught the tail end of a news broadcast about the FBI's press conference. Diana nearly slammed into the car in front of her when the disc jockey reported the threat against Mike. She drove home in a daze and spent the rest of the evening curled up in the fetal position on her living room couch, hugging herself tightly in an attempt to hold on to the last remnants of security and stability in her life.

The ordeal with Mike was almost more than she could take. Diana had lost her mother at a time she desperately needed the wisdom, compassion and love a mother provides. After finally coming to terms with the tragic death, she went on with her life by moving away from her family and friends to pursue her dream of designing clothing. Her stay in Chicago had been challenging and difficult during the best moments, and lonely and depressing during the worst. But in the last six months the tide had seemed to turn in her favor. Diana was happy with herself, her designing, and her job as a flight attendant. Meeting Quentin Conway and getting to know him had been exciting, but Mike Redding was a completely different story. Few people had touched her emotionally and spiritually in such a personal way and he had managed to do it in a short period of time. Just when things had started to go her way and a special man had entered her life, Diana feared she might once again be forced to deal with the worst adversity a person faces: the death of a dear friend or family member.

When Diana got home after hearing the news about Mike, she was a wreck. Sick with worry and emotionally numb from uncertainty, she was unable to do anything but think of him. She ached so bad her insides hurt. Rolled up on her couch like a ball of yarn about to unwind, she had fought back tears at the thought of losing someone so important before getting a chance to know him deeply. The following morning she awoke determined not to dwell on Mike's predicament. Scheduled to work a double shift, Diana threw herself into her work. She flew out of O'Hare at 9:05 AM. After flying to Miami and Pittsburgh, her plane touched down again in Chicago at 3:35 PM. She quickly boarded another jet, and following stops in Phoenix and Salt Lake City, she arrived in Los Angeles at 8:10 PM. As soon as the passengers had safely departed, the Boeing 727 flew back to Chicago and set down at 2:15 AM. Diana had gone to bed physically and mentally drained, but with her thoughts occupied by work, she had been able to keep her mind off Mike most of the day.

From the moment she had awakened the following morning, she had started drawing designs and cutting fabric for a new line of fall clothes. Once again, the idea was to keep herself busy so she wouldn't go crazy thinking about the danger Mike was in.

"It's really strange," she said to herself, "During times of personal or romantic crisis women become so productive. Whatever it is: cleaning, cooking, or in my case, designing—women direct their attention away from what's bothering them and channel it somewhere else. If women went through a crisis every day and could harness their energy and strength, watch out world. Instead of cooking and cleaning to distract ourselves, we'd run the country."

The mental image of millions of broken-hearted women

running the United States made her smile whimsically. It felt good; she hadn't done it in two days.

The sound of the phone ringing caught her off guard. "Hello," she said, after stretching across the floor to pick up the receiver.

"Diana, it's Mike. How are you?"

"Pretty good. And you?" She was surprised and delighted to hear his voice.

"Okay. I'm calling from Detroit. Actually we're in Auburn Hills, right outside Detroit. I've been holed up in a hotel most of the day, and I wanted to take a break from watching film. Do you have a few minutes to talk?"

Are you serious? Diana wondered to herself. *I've got all the time in the world.* "Sure, as much time as you need. I'm just sitting here doing nothing. It's good to hear your voice, Mike."

He noticed the affection in Diana's voice and it pleased him. The conversation was off to a good start, but Mike was still apprehensive. He had called to see if he could talk to Diana about the decision he needed to make. While she seemed receptive to listening to him, he was afraid he might be reading her wrong. Worse yet, he could be reading her accurately, but she could be turned off by his neediness and be scared away.

As he had many times in the past seven years, Mike faced the self-imposed dilemma of sharing his true feelings and possibly driving a woman away, or keeping those feelings bottled up inside and further damaging his self-image. At the point of no return, where he mistakenly believed the next minute would determine the entire future of the relationship, Mike allowed his bruised, lonely heart to get the best of him. He decided to confide in her.

"I'm all right considering what's happened the last few days. I've had a lot on my mind, the main thing being whether or not I should coach. After my huskies killed the FBI agent, I decided not to coach anymore. I don't want more people to die because of me. My mind was completely made up a few days ago, but now I'm having second thoughts. I've talked to Quentin several times and he thinks I should coach. I feel like I'm on a see-saw, I've gone back and forth so much. The public wants one thing, my athletic director wants another, the media's trashing me, my assistants are begging me to coach and I'm going stir crazy. I'm being yanked in so many directions I'm gonna be ripped apart."

"I understand Mike. I'd like to help you get through this. What can I do?" Diana asked.

Mike's chest heaved in and out as he exhaled and then inhaled deeply. He hadn't realized he was holding his breath since finishing his last statement. Cascades of soothing relief poured from his head, rolled through his nervous system and rippled outward to the most remote nerve centers in his body. Every pleasure center in his body experienced the delicious sweet rush of relief. The tenderness and understanding in her voice told him what he needed to know. Diana Fleming could be trusted. She wanted to help, and she wasn't scared away.

Mike felt as if he was straddling a fence, teetering one way and then the other. This was the biggest decision he had ever made. His life and many other lives depended on this decision, and he was about to ask for help from a woman he had known two and a half weeks. It was crazy for him to seek her help, insane, yet he wanted to anyway. Deep down he knew he was testing her, challenging her on many levels to see what she would do. Unfair as it was, he wanted to know what she was about, and he had to know soon.

Mike took a deep breath and prepared to ask one question, a question that had been on his mind all day. To a large extent the answer she gave would determine whether or not he would coach and if he would pursue her. Although he didn't know why—maybe because he was worn down and had no strength, because he couldn't decide himself, or because he dared to hope she was the woman who would make him right, he was basing the biggest decision of his life on the response of a woman he couldn't bear opening up to.

"Before you met me and Quentin, knowing what you did about me, would you have guessed I'd coach in this situation or step down?"

Diana didn't need to think about her answer. She remained

quiet a few seconds because it hurt her deeply to tell the truth. When she spoke, her voice was nothing but a whisper.

"You'd coach. Before I met you guys, you struck me as an intensely loyal man, a person of conviction who did what was best for yourself and the people most important to you. You'd tell the media to go to hell and then try to win a national championship for yourself, your players, the school and all those you care about. You'd let nothing stand in the way of a principle."

"Now that you know me, Diana, what do you think I should do?"

"Now doesn't matter, Mike. I just told you what I thought you'd do when I wasn't biased. You've got to stop listening to everyone else and start listening to yourself. You've got all the answers inside you. Look inward and you'll know what to do. I'm not trying to take the easy way out. I can tell you what my head thinks and what my heart thinks; they're two different things. I know what I'd like you to do, but honestly Mike, I don't think you'd be happy if you stepped aside. It all comes down to this: you've got to do what makes you happy. Think about what's best for you and follow your instincts and your heart."

The whole tone of their conversation had changed in the last minute. The depth of their relationship had also changed. After putting her on the spot and asking more of her than he rightfully should have, Diana had exceeded Mike's loftiest expectations. For the first time since his mother passed away, he felt he would be able to get past his fear of losing someone wonderful. He had tested her and she had passed with flying colors. An enormous weight was lifted from his back when he heard her answer. The proverbial monkey was gone; he was his own man again.

"I wish I had more time to talk, Diana. Hell, I wish I had more time to spend with you. Please be patient and let me get through all this. I don't want to bring someone into the mix when my life is so complicated. You deserve better and I want to give this every chance to work. I can't thank you enough for helping me with my decision. With all the crap that's happened the last two weeks, I'd lost track of who I am. What you said hit home. I do have the answers. After the tourney's over and this mess is behind me, I'd like to properly thank you. You've helped me much more than you realize, probably more than even I realize. Before I called you I was already feeling better, but now I really believe I'm regaining control of my life. I don't want the obsessive, domineering kind, but a purposeful, focused, going-in-the-right direction sort of control. I don't know how you have all this experience and life wisdom at your age, but I'm glad you do. Damn it, I hate to say this, Diana, but I have to go. My assistants are ready to watch film, and I can't keep them waiting any longer. I'll talk to you soon, okay? Take care of you."

Diana didn't bother saying goodbye. Mike was already gone. Instead, she answered his statement.

"My mom. She taught me about life at an early age." As she hung up the phone, Diana wondered if she would be able to help him with the problems that made him so vulnerable, or if like her mother, he would be taken from her just when she needed him most.

Quentin was sitting behind a huge mahogany desk in his den studying franchisee contracts in the Orient when the phone rang. He guessed it was Mike, no one else would call him on his private line at this hour. As he waited for the third ring, he heard agents scurrying to set up their equipment. Finally, Quentin picked up the telephone and spoke into the mouthpiece.

"Is Mike there?" Quentin answered. It was a joke he loved to play on his friends, Mike in particular, because it always tripped him up. Mike Redding constantly seemed to be in the middle of two or three activities when he called, so Quentin occasionally answered the phone as if he was the caller to poke fun at his friend.

"This is.., aah. Damnit, Quentin." Mike was in good spirits so he laughed at his blunder. "You're still pulling that stupid shit and I'm still falling for it. You'd think I'd be used to it."

"If you won't give me your full attention, I'm gonna mess with you. You're probably working on two things right now and thinking about a third."

"Oh, that's good," Mike said laughing. "You're dogging me for being efficient and you've got a couple thousand people doing your work. Excuse me, your majesty. Criticism from an emperor who hasn't had an original idea in five years is a hard pill to swallow."

"I don't need to come up with original ideas," Quentin drawled. "I pay peasants and indentured servants to do it for me."

"Well, I've got paid assistants, but I'll be up much later than them tonight studying film."

"Long night ahead?"

"Afraid so. I finished Duke a few minutes ago. I found a viable weakness we can exploit, but Kentucky's another story. They have few chinks in their armor, and Pitino hides them well. By 8:00 tomorrow morning I will have found their achilles heel or made one up."

"If any coach in America can break down Kentucky's strengths and weaknesses, it's you. Sounds like you're crushed for time so I won't keep you. Have you made your decision about tomorrow and Saturday?"

"That's why I called your highness at such a late hour. I hope you don't mind coming down from your throne to hob-nob with the little people. Even worse, co-cheese, you'll have to endure a bullet-proof vest and scores of sweaty, overbearing FBI agents for the next week and a half. I'm gonna coach UNI to the national championship and then get the hell out of Dodge while McCaskill plays pin the tail on that asshole, Ben. We'll see if he can follow me around the South Pacific. I'll sail to so many islands this summer he'll never live up to that nickname of yours. Will you come with me?"

Quentin was silent only for a moment. "Holy Toledo, Batman—that was close. It looked like the end. Glad you're back Red Dog. Hell, yes, I'll go. First things first. You've got to beat a good Marquette team tomorrow. Any predictions?"

"UNI by twenty," Mike said without hesitation. "Byron will

feast on their zone like Rush Limbaugh at a Flag Day pie-eating contest. Tip-off's at 8:05 so I'll see you around 7:00 PM. Bring Diana with you, all right." It was a command, not a request and there was only one way Quentin could answer.

"You got it, brother. Nothing in the world could make me miss it."

He knew the amateur actor was never home until after midnight so he didn't try the number until 12:15 AM. The voice that answered at the other end was deep and scratchy, but the manner in which the name was delivered was smooth and polished. "This is Derrick Jensen."

"I have work for you. I need you Saturday night. Maybe Friday night also."

Derrick Jensen could scarcely contain his excitement. He had done four jobs for this man in the last two and a half weeks. The work had been easy, all that was required of him was to look and act like someone else, and the compensation had been exceptional. The money was good, but the cocaine and heroin were out of this world—the highest quality, and plenty of it. For a struggling, out-of-work actor carrying an $800 a week heroin habit, the work had been a godsend.

"Cool. Yeah, I can help you Saturday night; Friday, too, if you need it. What's your heart's desire?" Jensen asked.

"Same as before. Just like last time. Only difference is, I'll pay double the horse and candy. Saturday is the Oscar and Emmy performance so it has to be perfect."

Derrick Jensen was elated. He would be doing the same easy job, but he'd get twice the heroin and coke. He decided to push a little to see if he could get more.

"What's happening Saturday? If it's such a big night, I think my work is worth double the money and the sweets."

The voice that answered was unlike any Derrick Jensen had ever heard. "Don't ever ask me what I'm doing. If you do I'll cut you open like a stuck pig and remove your organs with my bare hands. You'll be paid the same amount as before. After Saturday's job, I'll reward you with the extra product. If you have a problem with this, I'll hire someone else. Then when I'm done Saturday, I'll hunt you down and kill you. Before cutting you into little pieces, I'll shit in every hole of your body so flies eat your remains. Now that we understand each other, are you in?"

"Yes," the horror-struck actor meekly responded. He had no choice. He was far more scared of this madman than of the consequences of breaking into an office or being an accessory to a crime. Jensen was terrified not just by his mysterious employer's words, but also by the low, steady voice that crackled with fury and controlled rage.

"You're a smart man, Jensen. You made the right decision. I'll call tomorrow night with details." Before Derrick Jensen could think of a response, the line went dead.

Leaning back in his chair, the March Madness Murderer rocked slowly while thinking about Saturday night. Everything was falling into place. Derrick Jensen was his ace in the hole—the perfect fall guy.

"That stupid fucking actor won't know what hit him," he told himself aloud. "When I'm done Saturday night, the sorry bastard will just be starting. What he doesn't know is that he'll be impersonating the greatest serial killer of the twentieth century. I can see the headlines now: Druggie Actor is March Madness Murderer. All my shithead high school friends will be dead, and my work will be talked about and studied for years."

The letters had thrown the FBI off his trail. McCaskill and the rest of the Bureau believed he craved attention, that he sought the spotlight. The truth was he wanted no attention. He had to kill his friends and then he would quietly slip away. He didn't need to be told how good he was, he already knew. His high school friends were no match for him. Neither was McCaskill or the FBI. No one was. He was invincible.

He had known before he fell asleep this would be the night he'd learn the man's identity. He was right. As soon as his head hit the pillow, he fell into a deep slumber. It was as if his subconscious mind was tired of holding onto the secret and wanted to share it with his conscious mind. After reaching REM, he began to dream. The flashback began the usual way, but it was markedly different this night. The activity in the flashback progressed at a faster pace and the images and sounds were of greater clarity than they usually were.

At the crucial point of no return, instead of blacking out or shutting down, his subconscious psyche played out the rest of the scene. His conscious mind was overwhelmed by the manifestation and struggled to absorb and process the information it now possessed. No longer sleeping, he realized his thoughts were conscious and real, that his fear of the truth was unequivocally justified. After weeks of abbreviated and incomplete flashbacks, his mind would not let go of the image he had seen. The flashback was indeed a nightmare—the scene he had recalled truly horrific. Sitting rigidly upright in bed, he couldn't shake from his mind's eye the awful image nor comprehend the ramifications of his discovery. The implications of the flashback were staggering, the consequences catastrophic. If what he saw in the dream was any indication of the evil inside this man, many people were yet to die.

Chapter Eighteen

Frank McCaskill stood in the west parking lot of the Palace and supervised construction of the retaining wall. The idea came to him two nights earlier while he lay in bed unable to sleep. McCaskill mentioned the idea to L.C. Bailey only as a suggestion, but to his surprise, the Deputy Director liked the idea and implemented it. The purpose of the perimeter was to minimize the number of people in and around the stadium. The barricade enabled the FBI, state police and stadium security to monitor the flow of traffic in and out of the arena and provided a check point to search the people entering the Palace.

Since McCaskill wanted all security arrangements kept from the media as long as possible, construction of the barricade did not begin until 5:00 that morning. Repp Brothers Construction out of Detroit sold the materials to the Bureau at a discounted price and donated the services of ten employees to help build the makeshift wall. Industrial size buckets placed eight feet apart surrounded the arena. Each bucket held nine-foot-high wooden posts which were secured in cement. Sheets of plywood were nailed between the wooden posts.

Inside the perimeter, sawed off two-by-fours ran from the ground to the basin of the cement buckets and served to reinforce the temporary retaining wall. Sandbags were placed every four feet along the inside as additional buttresses of support. The giant wooden wall encircling the stadium was a rudimentary architectural structure. Certainly it would win no awards for design or beauty, but it was extremely effective. No one could get inside the arena without first passing through the FBI-manned checkpoints in the perimeter.

Three hours and ten minutes into the construction of the wall, McCaskill had grown more confident about the FBI's chances of catching Ben Rooks. Construction workers, Detroit policemen and FBI trainees nailed panels of plywood between the wooden posts while McCaskill mentally reviewed his plan to knock down the wall in the event an explosion or fire required a quick evacuation.

Pulling a walkie talkie out of his back pocket, McCaskill addressed his right hand man. "Taylor, come in."

Less than three seconds later he responded. "Taylor, here. Over."

"Alec, what's the shortest distance from the wall to an entrance? Also, break down all access routes for me. Over."

"In the rear lot it's 190 feet from the wall to the east entrance. It's a service driveway. The area back there is so small 190 is the furthest point we could build without cutting off access. Most of the wall is 500 feet from the stadium as you specified. There are two areas on the west side of the building where the distance dips to 380 and 420 because of the parking garages. Other than that, the wall's been erected 500 feet away in all areas. The public will enter through two check points, one at the north end of the stadium and another at the south end. Over."

"Absolutely no one gets inside the wall without a ticket, picture ID and a full body search. Make sure everyone knows that. Over," said McCaskill emphatically.

"No problem, Frank. We'll pat them down at the check points and again when they enter the building. We've got First Aid stations set up outside the wall at both check points. Large personal items like purses, coolers, and umbrellas will be held at the stations until the game is over. Metal detectors have been installed at the stadium entrances and two more will go up at the check points. The media will have to enter through the west check point. Same drill there. Only media members with proper ID and credentials will gain access inside the wall, and only after a thorough frisk. Players, coaches, officials and stadium employees will enter through the east check point using the service driveway. Everyone inside the wall will have been searched. At noon the local television and radio stations will begin airing spots notifying fans of the photo ID requirements. I don't want Rooks to have a lot of time to prepare. Over."

"Roger that, Alec. Remember what I told you. Rooks could disguise himself as a stadium employee, an NCAA official, press member, anybody. Whatever it is you can bet it'll be a great disguise. He'll probably only be casing the stadium tonight so now's the time to apprehend him. Spread the word among the division heads. If we stand any chance of grabbing Rooks, we've got to be critical of every person who passes through the check points. The most unsuspecting people are the ones we need to hone in on, especially women, obese individuals and senior citizens. He can make himself look like anyone he wants. The electronic sweeps of the stadium, garages and lots are finished. There's no bomb within a mile of the arena. Either he's not planted one yet, or he'll have to get inside the perimeter to kill Redding and Conway. The snipers along the wall and stadium roof will take him out if he tries to kamikaze the arena with a car bomb. We need to keep Rooks outside the wall. I don't want him near the fans or it's a blood bath. Over."

"Roger that," Taylor replied. "Why don't you get some doughnuts or bagels, Frank? You've been running on fumes the last few days. We've got a marathon day ahead of us and you'll need to be fresh tonight. Over."

"I'll grab something later. I'm late for a logistics and tactical review meeting with the national guard and the local vice-squad. I'll call you in an hour. Over and out."

McCaskill placed the walkie back in his rear pocket. He didn't like the end of the conversation. Taylor was beginning to pick up on his obsession with Ben Rooks. McCaskill's wife had gone to stay with friends five days ago because of her husband's workaholic schedule and obsessive behavior. Now, Taylor was noticing the long hours, his poor physical appearance and lack of eating and sleeping. It was amazing more people around him hadn't noticed his intense personal involvement with the case.

Putting Taylor's and his wife's concerns out of his mind, McCaskill gazed over the retaining wall at the spacious stadium. That evening Ben Rooks would look at the same sight. McCaskill wondered if the March Madness Murderer would see something different. Where were the soft spots in the FBI's security net? What weakness could be exploited? Without warning, McCaskill felt chills run down his spine. He couldn't think of a single weakness in his strategy. What should have pleased him, instead frightened him. So far Rooks had been two steps ahead of the Bureau. If McCaskill couldn't find any weak spots, but Rooks could, the FBI would be caught with their pants down and Mike Redding and Quentin Conway would stand little chance of surviving.

He was neither afraid nor too vain to ask for help. In fact, Ben Rooks enjoyed having people help him. He had kept the reference staff at Chicago's downtown library busy all morning. He got there thirty minutes after the public library opened so he wouldn't draw attention to himself. He was careful to talk to a different librarian each time he needed help locating materials so he wouldn't make a lasting impression. Augmenting his cautious behavior, he altered his physical appearance, so if the library personnel remembered him, they would remember the wrong person.

Rooks enjoyed changing appearances and transforming himself into someone else. He learned the craft years before while in prison at Michigan City. One of his few acquaintances in prison was Art Woods, a homosexual hair stylist and cosmetologist. During his two years at Michigan City, Art Woods taught Ben everything he knew about hair, skin care, makeup and clothing. By the time

Woods was released from Michigan City, the student was more skilled than the teacher.

Ben Rooks' doubt faded with each additional page he read. Everything was right in front of him in black and white. When he finished poring over the reference information about Mike and Quentin, he decided there was only one way the job could be done. He was struck by the bitter-sweet realization that the group's friendship was about to come to a violent end. Rising from the table, Rooks headed to the computer lab on the third floor. Seated in front of a computer, he tapped a few key strokes on the keyboard and accessed the file he needed. The computer enabled him to quickly research back issues of newspaper and magazine articles. It also gave him access to current and past newspapers and periodicals from cities such as Washington, D.C., Indianapolis, Indiana, and Auburn Hills, Michigan. For forty minutes Rooks scanned back issues of *The Indianapolis Star* and *The Los Angeles Times*. Finally, he found what he needed. The moment he pulled the contract onto the screen, he had the necessary verification. His suspicions had been confirmed— the entire plan had to be revamped.

After walking down to the second floor, Rooks holed up in a cubicle for two hours. He spent the first hour and a half developing a plan, figuring out exactly what needed to be done. During the next thirty minutes he went over every aspect of the newly-devised plan in an attempt to find flaws in it. He found only two problems which he corrected with another thirty minute brainstorming session. During the final twenty minutes, he rehashed the plan from start to finish by writing it down on legal pages. Writing it out made it easier to remember.

After putting the plan on paper, he thought up possible obstacles that might hinder him and memorized various options to overcome these hurdles. Finally, when he was done revising and memorizing the plan, he put away the books strewn across the cubicle and went to the bathroom. Confident no one was in the restroom with him, he burnt the legal pages filled with notes and flushed them down the toilet. When the final charred remains swirled majestically down the ceramic hole, Rooks checked his Swiss

Army watch. It was 1:50 PM. He needed to get home. He had a few final arrangements to make before he made the afternoon drive to Michigan.

As Mike knelt on one knee with his head down and eyes closed, he racked his brain to find some detail of preparation he might have missed, yet listen to the team prayer at the same time. While Mike tried to concentrate on both his loves—God and basketball—the team chaplain, Father John Gallagher, stood at the front of the locker room and led the UNI basketball team in a pregame prayer. Mike was having trouble following the words. He had worked himself into a bundle of nervous energy, as he did before every big game. This contest was different from other big games though, and the players sensed it. There was more tension and electricity in the air than the first and second round games. This was the Sweet Sixteen. Only sixteen teams remained alive in the hunt for the national championship. From this point on, every game would be a war.

When Father Gallagher finished intoning the Lord's Prayer, Mike stood and walked to the middle of the locker room. The room was quiet. Headphones had been turned off, basketballs had been set aside and the playful bantering between players had stopped. Sizing up his players and assistants, he surmised every person including himself was nervous—except Byron Lewis. UNI's star forward sat on a bench in the corner of the room lounging against a locker. He chewed a wad of gum as carelessly as a ten year old would and wore a relaxed smile on his unassuming face. *He's having fun*, Mike thought. *This is pure entertainment for him.*

Mike knew the reason Byron was so calm and unaffected by the pressure of a Sweet Sixteen game. His father had abandoned his mother while Byron was a young boy growing up in Hammond,

Indiana. His mother worked two, sometimes three jobs a day to support her three children. Byron was the youngest and most gifted of the three. His mother dedicated her life, her complete existence, to raising the children. For her the struggle wasn't keeping them out of trouble, it was keeping them alive. Byron's older brother didn't make it—he died in a gang shootout at age eighteen, but Byron and his sister Senequa did.

One day after a particularly poor practice during his freshman year, Mike had called the precocious youngster into his office for a private meeting. After bitching and screaming at him for ten minutes, Mike asked what his excuse was for playing so badly the last two days. Byron offered no excuses, just a reason. His mother had fallen behind paying some bills, so her phone and electricity had been shut off. He explained to his coach how he had been homesick and had taken to calling his mother every day. Even when she couldn't afford it, she continued talking to her son because he needed her. He learned of his mother's problems only two days before when her utilities were cut off. That day in his office Byron said something Mike would never forget.

"Basketball is just a game to me, coach. I love the game and enjoy playing it, but it's nothing compared to my family being happy and healthy. There's no pressure in winning a big game or hitting the last shot in the Final Four. Pressure's putting food on the table when you're out of money or protecting your family from fifteen-year-old gang-bangers with guns." When Byron Lewis spoke those words, Mike knew his freshman phenom was something special. He also knew this young man had a Hall of Fame career ahead of him.

Mike had covered everything in his pre-game preparation. All he had to do now was send his team out on the court fired up. Motivating players, especially college athletes, is one of the more challenging and misunderstood functions of coaching. Most sports fans associate the process of motivating with fiery speeches and in-your-face challenges. Mike frequently used passionate speeches and volatile outbursts when he believed that technique was most appropriate or when he lost his temper, which was often. His techniques were rooted in education, history and common sense. He was an avid student of history, especially military history, and had studied great motivators from Niccolo Machiavelli to Napoleon Bonaparte to Vince Lombardi.

From his study of history and psychology, Mike reached the conclusion that all great motivators regardless of the field—sports, politics, child-rearing or business, shared two common qualities. They were feared and respected by the individuals they sought to motivate. Drawing from Machiavelli's views on leadership and power, Mike firmly believed if a player did not respect a coach, no amount of yelling or screaming would motivate the player to perform better. Conversely, all the respect in the world was useless if a player did not fear a coach's punishment when the player didn't perform well or do as he was told.

Depending on the player and the situation, Mike oscillated back and forth between positive and negative techniques. He challenged his players to perform at higher levels. He pushed them to be better than they imagined they could be and encouraged, supported and praised them while they pursued their goals. He was more than just an authority figure to his players; they craved his attention and approval the way a son would from a father. And when he gave it, nothing on the playing court satisfied them more. Other times he employed negative motivation techniques such as punishing players with less playing time during games, conducting two and three-a-day practices and subjecting players to grueling early morning workouts. At times he goaded players, teased them, even mocked them to get the result he desired.

His motivation techniques weren't questioned because his players graduated and he produced more wins and Final Four appearances than any other coach. Then too, his players swore by him. No other college coach enjoyed such unconditional loyalty from his players. His players never transferred to other schools. The motto on the team was: "UNI for life." Mike Redding was considered the premier motivator in college basketball, and the label was accurate because his players had equal amounts of fear and respect for him.

In his entire coaching career the only player Mike Redding had not been able to motivate was Byron Lewis. He was as fiercely competitive as his coach and didn't fear him. He had no reason to. He was the best player in the country, maybe college basketball's best in the last ten years. Because of his humble background, important life issues were the only things that worried Byron Lewis. Mike had not found a way to motivate him, and probably never would. The chances of his staying at UNI the full four years of his eligibility became slimmer and slimmer with each outstanding game he played. Before games Mike simply told the All-American what he expected and Byron motivated himself.

Bringing his attention back to the locker room and his players, Mike was ready to address his team. He had decided to keep the pre-game talk low key and upbeat. He was usually positive before a game; half-time was when he turned over tables and berated his players. Taking a deep breath, he wiped perspiration from his brow.

"I'm going to make this short because at this point in the year, not a lot needs to be said. Every person in this room knows what it took to get here. And everyone here knows this is not the goal we're aiming for. There are people in this building and a lot more watching at home that don't know shit about basketball. They have no idea what we've gone through to get to this point. Let's show them."

Mike paused for a few seconds. He was speaking from his heart, nothing rehearsed or planned, simply how he felt. He was at his best in moments like this. He had to be careful though. He didn't want to get his players overly excited and emotional. That often meant trouble at the beginning of a big game. All too frequently, Mike had seen good teams start games slowly because they were too fired up emotionally to concentrate and execute sharply.

"You have a unique opportunity tonight. Not only do you get to represent yourself, your family, your school, and take another step toward your dream of winning the national championship, you get to make a statement about the type of men you are. With all the bull shit going on around us, you can make a statement about who you are and what you believe in. Like me, you're going to be judged tonight. This game, and how you play, is your forum to show your grandparents, your friends back home, your old teachers, coaches—everyone—what type of men you are. You can back down from the pressure or threat of harm, and that'd be fine. There's absolutely no shame in that."

Mike looked directly at Reggie Avant. His boyish-looking guard was so uptight he appeared to be cemented to the wooden bench beneath him. "Or you can put all the pressure and hype out of your mind. Ignore the assholes in the media, block out the danger that might or might not happen, and play the best forty minutes of your life. That'd be quite a statement. An unbelievably strong statement. I believe in each of you as individuals, and I believe in us as a team. Every single person in this room is family to me. Now let's go out there and make a statement Marquette and everyone watching will never forget."

The Palace was packed. Despite the risk of being harmed or killed, people attending the NCAA's Midwest Region semifinals had to get, and pay for, the hottest tickets in the country. Reports earlier in the day estimated scalpers were getting $3,000 a ticket for lower level mid-court seats and $1,500 to $2,000 for the rest of the arena. Tucked away on the bench between two FBI agents, Mike tried to shut out the crowd, and instead to concentrate on the starting lineups being announced over the PA system. It was hard not to notice the spectators. Twenty thousand basketball fanatics were making more noise than Mike thought was humanly possible.

From the moment UNI's players ran out of the tunnel the noise had been deafening. Normally, the noise at a basketball game comes in spurts according to the action on the court. An arena could erupt with thunderous applause at any time if an exciting play was made. On this night the noise in the Palace was different. It was a loud, steady humming whose generating elements were notoriety and excitement. The atmosphere was so charged with anticipation, the underlying questions on everyone's minds were nearly audible: was Mike Redding going to win or was he going to die? Was his best friend Quentin Conway present, and if so, would he live to see the end of the game?

Quentin was not in his customary position behind UNI's bench. Instead, he sat on the other side of the court opposite UNI's bench. He wore a Fila cap pulled down low, glasses and a bullet-proof vest and was surrounded by eight agents and two state police-men. Two other decoy groups were strategically placed around the court in lower level seats. Diana Fleming sat behind the basket at the south end of the court one row away from the floor. Mike had asked McCaskill to place her there so she could leave the arena quickly if the need arose. He also asked for an agent to stay with her during the game. McCaskill refused the request because she wasn't a target, but he did arrange to have two state troopers escort her to the game and sit on either side of her.

The game started well for UNI. After the ball was thrown into the air for the opening tipoff, a wild scramble ensued as players from both teams fought to gain control of the loose ball. Craig Coryell came out of the pile with the basketball and found Byron Lewis streaking up court ahead of the Marquette defenders. Coryell's long pass hit him dead in stride and 20,000 people were hushed into silence waiting for the highlight they knew would come. After catch-ing the ball with one hand and taking a quick power dribble, Byron exploded off the ground some eight feet from the basket. As he rose effortlessly through the air, he cocked his right arm behind his head. Just when it appeared he wouldn't reach the basket, he climbed a bit higher and unleashed his right arm in a rapid fire stroke. The motion of his arm, whipping forward like a tomahawk and crush-ing the ball through the rim, took place so quickly the crowd's re-action came a full second later. The roof of the Palace seemed to shake in the explosion of noise as Byron stylishly finished the dunk by grasping the rim with one hand, spreading his legs apart and rais-ing his knees toward his chest.

From that remarkable beginning, UNI got off to a strong start and controlled the first half. Marquette played well and stayed within ten points of UNI, but Mike felt the opposing team could not continue to perform at such a high level for twenty more minutes. He encouraged his players at half time and told them to turn up the defensive intensity and attack more offensively. The second half was an easy downhill ride for UNI. Mike's players remained sharp while Marquette wilted under the pressure of UNI's trapping, man- to-man defense. Byron Lewis finished with thirty- three points, fourteen rebounds and a career high, eight blocked shots as UNI won 81-60.

After shaking hands with Marquette's coach, Mike and his bodyguards rushed off the court. His pre-game prediction that UNI would win by twenty points had been gratifyingly prophetic. As he sprinted down the players' tunnel toward UNI's locker room, two thoughts ran through his head. The next game would be the game of the year. Kentucky had beaten Duke earlier in the evening and looked good doing it. And he had gone most of the game without thinking about Ben Rooks or an assassination attempt.

As he approached the locker room and heard his players carrying on inside, Mike's stomach was growing queasy, so he slowed to a walk and collected his thoughts for a moment. He was in no mood to celebrate. The team's biggest challenge would come in Saturday's Elite Eight match up against Kentucky, and his toughest challenge with Ben Rooks probably loomed ahead. If UNI beat Kentucky, Mike knew they would win the national title, and that presented the most dramatic opportunities for killing.

There was more on Mike Redding's mind than Kentucky. Coming down the tunnel, Mike had taken his mind off basketball for just a few seconds. It was long enough to feel something he hadn't noticed all evening and it made him sick to his stomach. He sensed Ben Rooks' presence in the building. The instinctual feeling that Ben was watching him—and Quentin—turned Mike's stomach inside out. When he walked through the locker room door and saw his players shouting and cutting up, Mike wasn't sure what he should be more concerned with. The challenge Kentucky presented his team or the danger Ben Rooks presented him and Quentin.

The ringing phone annoyed him more than it surprised him. Frank McCaskill was used to getting phone calls at all hours of the day and night, but tonight he was exhausted. During this investigation, going to bed completely drained had become the norm, but this particular evening was the worst. McCaskill was trying to sleep off the effects of a third straight eighteen-hour work day, so the piercing sound of the telephone was especially irritating. He grimaced at the sound of the incessant ringing as he rolled over onto his back and reached through the darkness for the phone beside his bed.

"Frank McCaskill," he said in a sleep-induced, groggy voice.

When the caller gave his name, McCaskill's eyes shot wide open. "Give me some information so I know it's you and not a prank," McCaskill demanded. He not only wanted to verify the caller's identity and turn on a tape recorder, he intended to make the conversation last as long as possible so the call could be traced. Within ten seconds of answering the phone, McCaskill was wide awake and alert.

"Why are you calling me?" he asked, both curious and put out by the intrusive contact.

"We need to talk about the assassination attempts," the caller said in a cold, measured voice that betrayed to emotion.

Sixty seconds later Frank McCaskill's temper was boiling over. After two minutes, an expression of shock had spread across his usually stern, stoic face. Just as quickly as McCaskill's solitary slumber had been shattered by the noisy telephone, the caller disconnected the line. McCaskill sat in his bed, the phone resting on his lap, trying to absorb what he had just heard. His face wore the look of a man hopelessly lost. Never in his life had he been so confused and unsure of himself. Frank McCaskill was stunned—he felt impotent. He needed to vomit. The room spun around in circles and his skin suddenly felt hot and sweaty. Morbid scenarios swirled through his mind as he contemplated the chilling information he now possessed. The man in charge of the Clancy-Butler murder investigation, the best the FBI had to offer, felt completely powerless to stop what he had just been told. He knew in all likelihood the bold prediction was accurate.

McCaskill pushed the phone off his lap and got out of bed. He had to start confirming facts from the phone call.

"You'd better be thorough, but quick—the clock's ticking," the agent told himself as he rewound the tape recorder so he could take notes of the conversation. He prayed he would have enough time to verify the information and still prepare for the assassination. If Ben Rooks meant what he had just said, all hell was about to break loose the next two days.

Chapter Nineteen

"How'd we look last night?" Mike asked, looking around the deserted restaurant while speaking to Quentin. Even though he was pleased with his team's performance, Mike wanted to hear Quentin's opinion. His friend usually played devil's advocate and pointed out flaws when Mike's team played well. Conversely, when UNI performed poorly, he was always able to find something positive in their play. After UNI's stellar performance the previous night, it was hard for even Quentin to find something to criticize.

"Awesome!" responded Quentin. "The younger guys, Watkins and Hardt, were sharp. They've grown up during the tournament. Your depth is unbelievable, Red. Subbing players in waves of three and four killed Marquette. Byron had one of his best games of the year. If it's possible, he seems to be getting better each week. Everybody knows their roles. Your boys are rallying around you, UNI's the team to beat. Speaking of that, have you read *USA Today* this morning? How do you feel about being underdogs?"

Mike chewed the bavarian cream doughnut in his mouth before taking a swig of orange juice. "We should be. Kentucky's as hot as we are. Derwin Griffith is the second best player in the country, Pitino's a great coach and their size and three-point shooting will burn your eyes out."

"I hear ya, Red, but you're awfully strong. Why's KY favored?"

"They're the defending champs and they returned nearly everyone from last year's team. Did you see the non-conference schedule they played at the beginning of the year? Unbelievable. And their SEC schedule was brutal. As far as I'm concerned, until they get beat, they're the best. Besides, their coach isn't being hunted by a fanatical high school buddy. Vegas has to prefer Pitino to me even if you discount the fact his extended family owns half the city."

Quentin laughed while swallowing a jumbled fork-full of scrambled eggs and hash browns, bacon and biscuits and gravy.

"It's a good thing you have a fat bank, Q, or you wouldn't be able to afford that crap."

"You know my motto, Red. We only live once. When I'm six feet in the ground, nutrition won't matter. Hell, Ben's trying to kill me. If I'm gonna die, I'm going out eating the best food, drinking the finest wines and kissing the prettiest girls."

While Quentin attacked his mountain of fried slop, Mike's thoughts shifted to Diana. Quentin's remark made Mike think of her and he felt a pang of loneliness. She was easily the sweetest, most beautiful woman he knew. The transformation she had stimulated in him was impressive. He wondered whether she would be patient enough to wait for him or if his ordeal would be too much. More than anything, he wondered if he would live long enough to not only tell Diana how he felt, but to show her as well. In a cruel twist of irony, just as Mike's fear of involvement and his inability to deal with the loss of loved ones seemed to be easing up a bit, his future happiness and well-being were threatened by an even larger obstacle.

The sound of Quentin's voice brought Mike back to the present. "What'd you say, Q?"

"You've cleaned up your language the last couple of days," Quentin repeated. "I can't remember when you've cussed this little. What's up?"

"Diana," Mike replied, not a bit embarrassed. "It bothers her. I won't stop completely, but she asked if I'd tone it down. It's weird, Q, I never had a reason to watch my language until now. After I bitched out Stan Turner and with Diana being so classy, I want to cut out the bad habits and garbage. Now that I have a reason, I'm doing a lot better. I'm also dealing with Allan's and David's deaths and this coaching nightmare. Talking about it with Diana and you has been great. I'm learning to release my frustrations instead of acting like a raving lunatic."

"Good deal. Sounds like she's a positive influence."

As he spoke, Quentin glanced over his shoulder and then to both sides of their table. FBI agents were all around them. There were twelve agents surrounding their table on the enclosed patio and eight more scattered throughout the hotel restaurant. At any time during the day or night there were a minimum of eight agents in the same room or perhaps one room away from Mike and Quentin.

Lowering his voice, Quentin leaned closer to his friend and whispered. "Have you been able to go through Allan's personal items yet?"

Mike looked up in surprise. "I haven't had time to get through any of it. No one has. His only relative left is that aunt in Terre Haute and she's nearly dead. Most of his stuff is in the apartment in D.C. I've picked up a few boxes from the house in Indy, but I haven't opened them. I'm too busy with the team, but it's the first thing I plan to do when the tourney's over."

Quentin pushed back his plate and nodded at his friend. Mike was quiet for a moment. A recurring thought of the last week came into his mind.

"Something's been bugging me, Q. I was shocked to find out Allan changed his will right before he died. Do you think it's odd Allan left his estate to me? It almost makes me look suspicious."

"You were closest to him," Quentin said, finishing off a glass of chocolate milk.

"We were all close to him," Mike replied. "You still don't seem surprised the new will left everything to me. Don't you think it's a bit strange?"

"Not really. I didn't need anything and David never cared about material possessions. Allan left a ton of money to environmental causes, but gave you control of the estate and left his belongings to you because he knew it'd mean a lot. It was a shrewd decision. His money will go exactly where he wanted and by giving you his art, antiques, memorabilia and souvenirs, he made sure they'd be taken care of. With you in control of his personal papers and records, he knew his name wouldn't be tarnished after he died. Let's face it, Allan did some serious drinking and whoring after Karen divorced him. As far as his dying thirty-six hours after he changed the will, it's an uncanny coincidence. I'm sure McCaskill checked it out; any agent in his first week of training would know to examine the will. Don't lose any sleep. McCaskill can't be too concerned. He hasn't arrested you yet."

Mike winced at Quentin's sarcastic remark. He was glad they were still whispering because the agents around them hadn't heard the last comment. "Let me ask you something else, Quentin. Remember me telling you Allan called the day before his death? He was acting strangely. You had a similar conversation with him. Allan told me his problems were about to be solved. I've already asked you this, Q, but I can't move past it. It makes no sense that Allan's more excited than ever one day and the next day he's dead. It's too damn weird, there's got to be a connection. Both of us agree whatever made Allan so excited is probably related to his murder. Well, what the hell does Ben have to do with Allan being excited and his problems being solved?"

"Mike, I'm as puzzled—angry even—as you. I don't know what to tell you. It's hard to say why Allan was so excited and if it's related to his death. Every little detail, no matter how irrelevant, of their last days is going to go through our heads now. We could spend the rest of our lives trying to find a connection, and we still might not have an answer. The only way we'd know for sure is if Ben's taken alive and he talks. I'm not going to waste my time wondering, though. I say we do what Allan and David would want."

"What's that?" Mike asked, seduced by Quentin's sly tone.

"You win the national championship, I make a few million dollars and we take a vacation. We can leave the morning after the final game. We'll go deep into the Pacific, drink barrels of rum and get lost sailing the islands. Maybe even jump off a bridge or two in their honor. Sound good?"

Mike didn't need time to think about it. He swallowed the last of his doughnut and smiled broadly. "Perfect!"

Frank McCaskill arrived at his office each morning before most of Washington, D.C.'s eight-to-fivers woke up, but this morning he had reached his office early even by his standards. After receiving Ben Rooks' late-night phone call, he had immediately begun poring over case files at his home. Since he was anxious to review the Clancy-Butler master file, McCaskill left his house at 4:30 AM and headed for the Bureau's downtown office. From the time he arrived in his office, McCaskill sat quietly at his desk and studied piles of documents accumulated during the investigation.

McCaskill didn't know what game Rooks was playing, but he was determined to find out. His head and his heart told him Rooks' claims could not be true, but in his gut he knew anything was possible. Common sense told him to discard Rooks' ridiculous prediction, it made no sense; but he had long ago become accustomed to motives and crimes that on the surface seemed puzzling, yet under close scrutiny made sense.

When Alec Taylor entered the office at 6:00 AM, McCaskill played the recording of his conversation with Rooks. The call stunned Taylor just as it had his superior. Like McCaskill, Taylor didn't believe Rooks' dire threat was possible. After re-reading case files for two hours and listening to the tape again, Taylor began calling law enforcement agencies, newspapers and FBI branch offices around the country. Beginning at 9:00 AM the FBI's Washington office was flooded with hundreds of faxes that confirmed Rooks' ominous prediction. Despite the plethora of corroborating information coming in, a troubling thought nagged at McCaskill's logical, computer-like mind. He still wasn't convinced Rooks' statements should be accepted as legitimate.

"Alec, I've spent the last couple hours persuading you to keep an open mind, yet I have doubts myself. The evidence is there, but it's so hard to believe. Why go to so much trouble? Rooks is a psycho, a certifiable looney-tune. We've got five staff doctors who swear he's mentally unbalanced. Two of them think he's got multiple personalities. And now this crazy prediction that's being verified from independent sources across the country."

Taylor didn't have a response. He too was shaken by Rooks.

"I'm not comfortable with the security detail we have covering Redding and Conway," McCaskill said out of the blue. "I'm going to put two more agents on each of them. I don't want anything to happen while we're gathering information."

While Taylor stepped over to the fax machine and pulled reports out of the machine's tray, McCaskill called the division head in Auburn Hills and assigned two more agents to Mike and Quentin, bringing the number of agents guarding them to ten each. As he hung up the phone a light bulb went off in his head. McCaskill's face lit up like a Christmas tree with triumph and relief. He had made the connection.

"Boom baby! I finally figured out what's been bugging me. I missed it twice in the written reports, but not this time."

The look on Taylor's face changed from curiosity, to surprise, and finally admiration as McCaskill explained the tiny nuance that had eluded him for more than a week. After confirming the hunch against data from the master file, McCaskill checked the security arrangements for the UNI-Kentucky showdown. He knew the assassination attempt would be made the next evening and he wanted to be ready.

Two hours later Alec Taylor received a phone call from a field agent in Chicago. The call was in response to research Taylor was doing on Ben Rooks' drug arrest in 1979. Upon hearing the first part of the agent's report, Taylor immediately transferred the call to McCaskill. Three minutes later McCaskill slammed the receiver down and jumped out of his chair.

"Bingo. We've got him cornered. Alec, call Bailey and tell him I need an emergency meeting with him and the director. I want Redding and Conway watched extra closely. We did it, Alec. We've nailed the son of a bitch!"

Chapter Twenty

Thirty-three minutes after Alec Taylor called to set up the emergency meeting, he and Frank McCaskill walked into Director Warren Jacobs' office. They had flown via helicopter from Washington to Quantico at the director's request. Warren Jacobs' wrinkled face was ashen gray and blank, so empty and devoid of expression that he resembled an old, weathered statue. From behind his immense cherry-wood desk, he solemnly motioned for McCaskill and Taylor to sit down. While the agents took seats and opened their files, Deputy Director Bailey flipped a tape recorder on and nodded toward the stenographer in the corner of the large office. When Bailey returned his attention to the agents, McCaskill wasted no time getting to the point. His first words were a bombshell.

"Ben Rooks is not the March Madness Murderer. Quentin Conway is."

Director Jacobs' face betrayed little emotion; he had forgotten more shocking news in the last year than most agents hear their entire careers.

While Jacobs remained stoic, L.C. Bailey could not hide his astonishment. "Goddamnit, Frank, that's quite an accusation. You know I always support your hunches, but you better have a damn good reason for saying that."

"It does sound ludicrous, L.C. I didn't believe it at first either. We're still gathering information and some of it's sketchy, but hear me out. I wouldn't be standing in front of the director without rock hard facts."

Up to this point Warren Jacobs had simply observed the dialogue between Bailey and McCaskill, but now he interceded. "Frank, your instincts got you where you are. I've taken a lot of heat from the media and the re-elects over this investigation. I stuck with you because your record is impeccable. You've got fifteen minutes to make your case against Conway and convince me he's our man. If you can't, not only will it be the last time this topic is discussed, this conversation never took place. Understand?"

McCaskill didn't bother answering, instead he plunged into his explanation. "I felt all along the motive was personal. I was right on that count, but I had the wrong person. We have a deep, long-time, hidden drug habit here. And Conway has the split personality, not Rooks. Conway had major motives for wanting Clancy dead. He's got secrets from the past he's trying to protect. Drug-related secrets involving millions of dollars and numerous murders. Clancy got wind of this damaging info and within forty-eight hours he turned up dead. A Hispanic prostitute is the link. The hooker, Carmen Jalomo, spent the night with Clancy two days before he died. Her pimp confirmed it. Three days after Clancy's body was found, Carmen Jalomo was murdered with Clancy's congressional watch in her possession.

"The hooker is the key to Conway's past. She was arrested in December, 1979, in a drug raid on Chicago's south side. Also arrested that day was Ben Rooks. This isn't just a coincidence. The apartment building was the property of SharpWay Investment Corporation, which was owned by Grant Sharp and Quentin Conway. The drug house was busted that day because the police received a tip from an anonymous man. Everyone arrested in the raid, including Carmen Jalomo, was released on the spot. Ben Rooks was taken downtown, booked, and incarcerated until his court date three weeks later. Seven years went by before Rooks got out of the state pen. Someone had it in for him and/or it was safer to have him locked up and kept quiet. Either way, I think it was Quentin Conway. Incidentally, Grant Sharp, Conway's business partner, disappeared in 1981 and his body was never found."

McCaskill glanced at his watch, looked down at his notes again and picked up the pace. "Late last night I received a phone call from Ben Rooks."

L.C. Bailey's eyebrows rose into his forehead at McCaskill's second bombshell. "Jesus H. Christ. Rooks called you at home?" Bailey asked in disbelief.

"That's right, our primary suspect called me. You won't believe the reason he gave me. He said he had information that would solve the case. Either he's the best actor I've ever seen, or he genuinely had no idea he's the prime suspect. He talked extremely fast, but sounded sincere as hell. He's been having dreams the last few weeks, flashbacks he called them, from his past. After weeks of seeing partial images, two nights ago he experienced a complete flashback in which he saw the faces of two men. He claimed the flashback was from 1979 and that Conway was one of the men in the drug house when he was arrested. I told him I thought he was full of it, but Rooks was adamant. He predicted Conway was going to kill Redding during a game. He said he researched Conway's past the day after seeing the complete flashback and that I should, too.

"I explained Bill Cooper had done that, but Rooks was persistent. He said to check the Cook County Assessor's office in Chicago, the Treasurer's and Recorder's offices and the back files of Cook County's police department from 1977 to 1981 when Conway was in college. Sure enough, Conway was everywhere. Tax problems, questionable loans, vendor's bids he won on municipal projects he should have never been involved in. Most importantly, there were four citations in '78 and '79 for possession of a controlled substance with intent to distribute, criminal recklessness, assault and battery and possession of unregistered firearms. There's a high probability he participated in and ordered a number of drug-related hits, but they would be impossible to prove fifteen years later. There are countless unsolved murder investigations that occurred in real estate he owned, and like Grant Sharp, of business associates of his."

"Why didn't Cooper find this when he did the background on Conway?" Bailey asked, infuriated by what he was hearing.

"He didn't look in the right places," McCaskill said. "He believed there was more than one killer and never suspected Conway, so he did a fluff check. He researched the obvious sources, did a superficial inquiry and merely scratched the surface of Conway's past. The information was effectively buried, but Cooper didn't take the search seriously."

"Ben Rooks found it. It couldn't have been buried that well," thundered Bailey.

"I agree," McCaskill said, aware of the trouble that lay ahead for Bill Cooper. "I'm upset too, L.C. I will say one thing on Cooper's behalf. It's no secret he and I have had our differences, but Rooks knew exactly where to look because of his past with Conway. He was in the drug house with Conway and had the flashbacks so he specifically knew about Conway's involvement with drugs. Cooper's search was a half-hearted, unprofessional attempt, but the information was hidden incredibly well by a few well-placed policemen and city employees. It was Chicago; L.C., Conway knew who to buy, and they did a great job burying his secret. As far as we can tell, almost all of these people are no longer living. Cooper didn't find the trail because it barely exists today, and he and Rooks were approaching the problem from different perspectives."

"They shouldn't have been," said Director Jacobs. "Cooper should have suspected Conway and everyone else from the outset."

Not wanting to defend Bill Cooper any longer, McCaskill found his place in his notes and plowed ahead. "The other reason Cooper didn't find Conway's record was because most of it had been wiped clean. Rooks went through literally hundreds and hundreds of pages of microfiche and discovered Conway had been cited by Chicago's police department on numerous occasions, not formally arrested and never convicted. Within days of these run-ins, the police department had mysteriously lost the information. Rooks found huge gaps of missing records in Cook County's files, but through sources in other departments, found corroborating information about encounters between Conway and the police.

"Steroids are a good example. Conway was busted twice in 1978 for selling steroids, but nothing ever came of it. Obviously, steroids weren't known to be a huge problem in the late seventies, but they were a controlled substance and only doctors could prescribe them. Conway was busted twice for distribution and three times for forging a doctor's signature. The first time he was caught distributing steroids, four officers confiscated the paraphernalia yet no arrest was made. The report the policemen filed was concealed in a different subject section in a completely different department. Instead of narcotics, it was filed under delinquent alimony payments in the domestic affairs department. The names and badge numbers of the four patrolmen weren't on the report.

"The second time he was busted for selling steroids, a homicide occurred during the transaction. Conway was never questioned about it. No statement was taken from him, even though he was the last person seen in the room where the homicide took place. This report was also misfiled. It turned up in missing persons records. Conway was as dirty as they got in Chicago in the late 70s and early 80s. He just had more smarts and connections than other convicts."

"I assume you verified all this. How'd you know where to find the data?" asked Bailey.

"Rooks told me last night what to look for and where to find it. I ended up finding much more than he told me about. None of this information about narcotics possession and distribution, weapons charges, assaults and so forth went on Conway's permanent record. Cooper didn't find it because he looked in the normal places and used proper bureaucratic channels. But it was those administrative and bureaucratic channels that protected Conway. The information was there to be found; someone just had to look specifically for it. And of course, Conway never gave anyone a reason to look for it."

"That's an understatement," Bailey added.

"He had everybody fooled. He got a lot of help seventeen years ago from the Chicago police force. The way they hid his garbage has continued to help. Out of curiosity I checked Conway's donations to the city of Chicago. Starting in 1977 when he was just a freshman in college, Conway has privately donated money every year to both the Cook County Policemen's Fund and a private municipal organization for retired policemen and firemen. From what I was able to trace in only three hours, he has discreetly donated over twelve million dollars to Chicago's police department, the policemen's union and the Democratic party. This takes on extra significance when you consider he's a registered Republican in Arizona: an active, staunch Republican, according to the party chairman there."

McCaskill paused a moment to gather some notes from the file on his lap. This time he didn't bother to look at his watch. He was nearing the fifteen minute time limit Director Jacobs had imposed, but he knew neither the director nor L.C. Bailey would stop him.

"At this point of the conversation with Rooks, I had begun to look at things differently, but still wasn't convinced Conway was our man. When I asked Rooks about the letters, he readily admitted writing them, yet said they were warning letters, not death threats. He claimed to be an ardent fan of all his friends. He admitted he always felt jealousy towards them and even animosity at times, but insists he's followed their entire careers out of pride and respect for their accomplishments. When he started having dreams and flashbacks, he felt they were somehow connected to Clancy's and Butler's deaths, so he wrote the letters to warn them. Rooks' contention is that the letters made him feel useful and less helpless. He urged me to read them again. He said nowhere in the letters does it state he will kill someone."

"Son of a bitch. Is this true?" Bailey asked shaking his head.

"Yes. He never said *he* was going to kill them." While McCaskill spoke, Alec Taylor pulled out copies of the three letters and passed them to L.C. Bailey and Warren Jacobs. "As you can see, they could be warning letters or death threats. From our vantage point, they read like threats. The code breaker from NSC agreed with us. Schwoman, the CIA's best decoder, said from the beginning the letters were asexual—meaning they could go either way—but his opinion drowned in anti-CIA prejudice."

"Damn political cluster fucking," L.C. Bailey muttered disgusted.

"They obviously read differently now. Rooks made a good point last night. He reminded me the letters were signed 'Your Shadow.' It seems a bit irrational to think someone would sign a death threat with their own nickname.

"During the investigation I wondered why Rooks was taking extra chances by sending threats. It didn't make sense. The letters only increased the odds of his identity being discovered. In hindsight it's easy to see he was actually trying to be found out. He did want attention, just not the kind we suspected. The bottom line is Rooks fit the stereotypical profile of the killer—Conway didn't. We were fooled by Conway just like everyone else."

Bailey seemed to be mulling over some troubling detail. Finally he was able to articulate it. "If Rooks' letters weren't death threats, why was he in Redding's hometown when he mailed the one letter?"

"I asked the same question," McCaskill said, nodding his head as if to acknowledge the deputy director's astute observation. "I wasn't a hundred percent sold on his answer and I'm sure you won't be either, but I do think it's genuine. Rooks said he's a huge fan of Redding's and follows UNI so closely that he frequently visits Lafayette, especially during the tournament. He wouldn't reveal where he lives, but admitted it was within one hour of Lafayette. Rooks said he was in the city when he mailed the letter because he was concerned about Redding and wanted to be close to him."

"You're right. It's difficult to swallow," Bailey said. "Too damn convenient."

"I agree it's far-fetched, L.C., but we know he's followed Redding's career religiously for years. If it was any other college basketball fan it wouldn't be unusual, but since he's our primary suspect, it's flimsy. After hearing Rooks' explanation about the letters, I opened my mind to the possibility he was telling the truth. I looked at the case from a different angle. For two weeks I've had a nagging thought in the back of my mind that there was a discrepancy between something Quentin Conway and Mike Redding told me."

"For Christ's sake, Frank. Don't tell me Redding's involved

in this, too," Bailey said growing more frustrated by the second.

"He's not. When I originally interviewed Conway about the first letter he told me he didn't recognize the name 'Shadow.' Later, while we were telling him about the suspect, he remembered 'Shadow' was the high school nickname for Rooks. I thought it strange Conway didn't recall the nickname when he initially received the letter, but remembered it later when we told him Rooks was the primary suspect. When I asked him about the discrepancy, he said he didn't call Rooks by that name, only Clancy and Redding did. Conway even went so far as to say Clancy came up with the name and he never used it himself.

"Re-analyzing Conway's statement today finally struck a chord. This morning I went through David Butler's personal effects. In his high school yearbook I found an obscure remark Conway had written. The remark made reference to him naming David Butler, 'Bull Dog,' and Ben Rooks, 'Shadow.' The following year he wrote another comment about bestowing nicknames and joked that he would take them back if his friends didn't live up to them.

"After discovering Conway's lie, I called him and talked around the topic of the letters. I didn't want to alert him so I tip-toed around the nickname. At any rate, I have the previous conversation on tape and Conway definitely lied. There's no way he forgot, or failed to remember who created the nickname—he's got a photographic memory! I think he recognized the nickname when he received the letter, but didn't say anything because he wanted to see what we'd do. Later, while we were telling him Rooks was our prime suspect, Conway saw the opportunity to use him as a scape goat. The letters were an unexpected gift. We concentrated on Rooks while Conway went completely unnoticed."

While he paused to catch his breath and start on new notes, McCaskill felt a surge of adrenaline flow through his body. He felt as if he were in a courtroom in front of a judge and jury. He was on a mission and nothing could stop him. McCaskill knew the truth behind Clancy's and Butler's slayings and like a prosecuting attorney in a capital murder case, his job was to show the judge and jury, the director and deputy director in this case, the truth.

"After my conversation with Conway this morning, red flags were everywhere. I started thinking about aspects of our investigation that were incriminating for Rooks. They were equally incriminating for Conway. One example is motive. Conway has more motive than Rooks. He's trying to conceal felonious activities with hundreds of millions of dollars at stake. His whole empire—his entire life—hangs in the balance. That's as strong a motive as revenge. The problem with all this is Conway's alibi for Clancy's and Butler's deaths, and the fact he was being guarded by our agents during the hooker's murder in Washington, the attack at Redding's home and the explosion of his limousine. None of it adds up unless you look deeper."

"He was nearly killed when it blew up. How do you explain that?" Bailey asked.

"It was a diversion to throw us off. I don't know how he planted the bomb under our men's noses, but remember, Conway escaped the blast because he spontaneously ran off to Nashville. I don't think it was a spur-of-the-moment decision. He planned it."

"Did he contract the work?" Bailey countered.

"No. He did it himself. I did some digging into Conway's alibi and revisited data from the murder sites. I can place him within two miles of Butler's murder site minutes before the time of death. If he lied about his whereabouts during Butler's murder, his alibi for Clancy's murder is bogus too."

"Holy shit, Frank. How can you place Conway in Lafayette?" asked Bailey, stunned by McCaskill's comment.

"Conway said he stayed the night at his office in Phoenix and his bodyguard and attorney confirmed it. But at 5:45 AM on March 3rd, a twin engine Cessna landed at a remote air strip in Monon, Indiana. The man piloting the plane registered as Thomas Kirbing."

"Kirbing. Why does that sound famil . . . Tony Kirby. Conway's bodyguard flew in?" Bailey asked puzzled.

"Not Conway's bodyguard. Conway. We ran the serial numbers the groundsman took off the plane. It was definitely Conway's Cessna. He used a variation of his bodyguard's name. Taylor talked to the groundsman today. He gave a physical description of the pilot that could pass as Conway's twin. He said the pilot had on dark glasses, a baseball hat and wore loose, baggy clothes. The height, weight and hair color all matched. Without any prompting, the groundsman mentioned the pilot's deep, husky voice—said it was the kind of voice that's hard to forget. When Taylor played a tape of Conway's voice, the groundsman swore it was the pilot's voice. He signed an affidavit two hours ago—he was that confident."

"Impressive stuff but it won't hold water in court," Bailey said matter of factly. "Conway has two credible witnesses supporting his alibi."

"Hold on, it gets better. The groundsman said the pilot seemed to be in a hurry. He got in a blue Ford Taurus rental he had arranged for in advance and drove off quickly. He returned to the air field at 7:50 AM. The groundsman is sure of the time because the Taurus's right front fender and headlight were badly damaged. The pilot told him he had hit a deer. The groundsman remembered the time because he couldn't call the rental company to report the damage until they opened at 8:30 AM. The pilot gave the groundsman $4,000 cash to cover the cost of the repairs without even asking his opinion of the damage. At 8:10 our mystery man flew out of Monon for Kansas City. The plane never arrived in Kansas City, though. He filed a fake flight plan and landed somewhere else."

L.C. Bailey stared intently at McCaskill, riveted to every word. Even Warren Jacobs seemed transfixed. McCaskill had been speaking for twenty minutes, but no one dared stop him. McCaskill could smell intensity in the room like sulfuric acid so he went for the jugular.

"The coroner's time of death for David Butler is between 7:00 and 7:10 AM. It's a forty minute drive from the murder site on State Road 43 to the airstrip in Monon; our field agents timed it this morning doing fifty-five the whole way. Conway could have made it there and back with no problem—he's familiar with the area. Scanning the files this morning, I found a notation that a West Lafayette couple questioned the day after Butler's death had casually mentioned a blue four door sedan on a bypass road just north of

State Road 43. They said the car was sitting in a parking lot and was empty. According to the husband's estimation, they saw this Taurus two to three minutes before 7:00 AM. When our men checked it out, the parking lot the couple described was less than two miles from the murder site.

"Conway was the pilot, there's no doubt in my mind. He was in the Taurus two miles from the murder site minutes before it happened, yet he says he was at his office in Phoenix the night before and that morning. His alibi for Butler's death is pure fiction which means, logistically, his alibi for Clancy's death can't be true. There's no such thing as a perfect murder, L.C., you taught me that. Conway came close, but he's not God or Superman. He left clues and we finally found them."

"You've won me over," L.C. Bailey said, his voice tinged with respect. "The groundsman's physical description, the serial numbers from the plane and Conway's lie about not using the nickname seal it."

"There's something else, L.C. It won't help convict Conway, but I think it's relevant. All along we believed we were dealing with a psycho head-case. We were right, but it's Conway, not Rooks. To be honest, Conway's worse than Rooks could ever hope to be. To pull off this monumental betrayal and deception against one's closest friends requires an extraordinarily evil character."

McCaskill paused for a moment while he flipped through his file. Upon finding a fresh page of notes, he continued. "Conway's younger brother died in an accident when he and Quentin were boys. Immediately after the accident Quentin's parents packed up and moved to Indianapolis for a fresh, new start. Rooks told me to look into it because it was the one thing Conway had always refused to discuss. At the age of nine, Cory Conway fell out of a tree-fort while playing with Quentin. He plunged thirty feet to his death. There were some unusual circumstances surrounding the accident, but the boys' parents failed to cooperate with the police, so a formal investigation was never conducted."

"What were the circumstances?" Warren Jacobs asked.

"Quentin said his brother stepped backward, lost his balance and fell out of the tree, yet Cory Conway's body hit the ground face first. Very unlikely if he fell backward. The body wasn't found under the tree like you'd expect either. It was farther out, away from the tree indicating . . ."

"He was pushed," Bailey said.

"Correct," McCaskill replied.

"How old was Conway?" Jacobs asked.

"Twelve. That's what's scary. Earlier today Haslett talked to a retired policeman in Eugene, Oregon. Nice old guy who said he hadn't forgotten the accident because it stank so bad. He was the first patrolman at the house that day. When he got there he saw Quentin by himself, looking very composed for a twelve-year-old who had just watched his kid brother die. Later, when he questioned Quentin, he said the boy was distraught and completely shaken up. A few minutes after that, he saw the poise and control of an adult again, as Quentin comforted his hysterical mother. The patrolman sensed Quentin was acting or putting up a front. He said it was common knowledge among family friends that there was an intense rivalry between the boys. Severe animosity was how he described their relationship. He wanted to investigate the accident, but as I said before, the parents wanted to put everything behind them, so an investigation was never conducted. Within days a 'For Sale' sign was in the yard and the family moved. To this day Conway is said to have a distant relationship with his parents, even though they live off him and he maintains their lifestyle."

"Do you think a twelve-year-old could pull that off?" asked Bailey, more than a little skeptical.

"We're not talking about a normal kid. He was making $200 a week and hardly working. He was lazy, but ambitious even at that age. What's interesting is Rooks' comments about Conway. They're ominously similar to our profile of the killer. I asked him how Conway could be so close to Redding, yet secretly plot to kill him. He said Conway could simply turn emotions on and off. In Rooks' words: 'Quentin is a chameleon. He wears many different masks, and always camouflages his real intentions.He can adapt and change his behavior at a moment's notice to serve whatever purpose he desires. He has no true colors—only varying shades of deception.'"

Looking up from his notes, McCaskill stared directly at Warren Jacobs and L.C. Bailey. "I believe Ben Rooks. All the information he gave me checks out. Conway has conned people his entire life. When Clancy found out about his past and blackmailed him, there was only one thing Conway could do to ensure he wouldn't lose his fortune. In his mind, killing a few life-long friends was probably a small price to pay to keep his past a secret and his empire intact."

Frank McCaskill had taken twenty-five minutes to build his case against Quentin Conway. He hoped he made his point because it would be the only chance he'd get to go after such big game.

After a few seconds of silence, Warren Jacobs spoke. "I'm not completely convinced Conway's our man, but he's a stronger bet than Rooks. What do you recommend, Frank?"

"We barely have enough evidence to get Conway indicted, let alone convicted. We need more concrete evidence before we talk about arresting him: the murder weapon used on Clancy, information on the Taurus, eyewitnesses, corroborating data. We also need to establish a definitive time line and bolster the motive. I say we continue investigating Conway and place him and the agents guarding him under surveillance, but don't question or arrest him yet."

L.C. Bailey couldn't believe what he had just heard. "You want to tail our own agents? Great idea, Frank, but we don't have the manpower. Everyone's in Michigan doing real FBI work like preparing for tomorrow's game. Why the hell do you want to stake out our own men?"

"Because Conway will try to get away from the agents guarding him. He *is* a chameleon—his colors change quickly. For the life of me, I don't know how in the world he does it, but he'll do it again. He can't plant a bomb or shoot Redding if he's surrounded by twenty agents. In four hours I'm pulling the field agents who've been searching for Rooks. We can use them to tail Conway and his agents."

L.C. Bailey nearly jumped out of his chair. "You're doing what? What the hell's gotten into you, Frank. We're not calling off the search for Rooks because he says someone else did it. Why in the name of God do you want to stop looking for Rooks?"

"Because he's coming to Washington tonight. I talked to him two hours ago and he agreed. Actually, he offered to come in. It was his idea. I'll detain him until after tomorrow night's game. I'm not proposing we stop investigating Rooks, I just think with him in our custody, we should focus on Conway and find something that will stick."

While L.C. Bailey was still reeling from the shock of McCaskill's last comment, Warren Jacobs took charge. "Start a full-scale investigation of Conway through special agents. I don't want the other agents to act funny and tip him off. We can't let him know he's a suspect. Frank, question Rooks yourself when he comes in. Get everything you can out of him. In light of what we now know and with Rooks coming in, Conway is our primary suspect and Rooks a material witness. Conway might be the killer, but I want to protect against giving Rooks the best alibi in history if he's the murderer and something goes down tomorrow. I'll make a decision within two hours whether or not to tell Mike Redding."

Taylor hastily wrote down notes while McCaskill listened to the director and mentally took in the information. The director continued firing instructions at them, pausing only to take a few breaths of air. McCaskill noticed the director had turned off the tape recorder on his desk and had not switched it back on. Warren Jacobs did not want recorded evidence of what was being discussed. A monstrous can of worms had been opened and none of them knew what would come crawling out. He cleared his throat.

"First things first. Get started assigning special agents to Conway's past. Let the division heads in Michigan know what's going on and notify the lead agents in Phoenix that they're no longer conducting protective custody, it's now mobile detention. Make sure it stays hushed. It's imperative he doesn't find out we're on to him. The guy's got senators, publishers and pro sports owners in his back pocket. Everyone and their brother will come to his aid so we've got to do this by the book. A billion dollars can buy the best legal defense in the world so we need shit-hot evidence and immutable facts. Nothing circumstantial or metamorphic that a defense team could pick apart. No procedural errors. Frank, now that we have a new suspect, do you still think Redding's in danger tomorrow?"

"More so than ever. Conway's reasons for wanting him dead must be compelling, or else he wouldn't be killing his circle of friends. The sooner he can get rid of Redding, the better off he'll be. The tournament's the best time to do it. A large, crowded place is the perfect locale for an assassination. There's so much activity and confusion, it's hard to keep track of what's happening. A crowded, public place gives Conway a greater chance of escaping. Can you imagine the pandemonium if shots were fired or if a bomb went off in the Palace? I'm not a betting man, but if I was, my money would be on tomorrow night's game. Any way you slice it, tomorrow's game is Armageddon."

"I agree," Jacobs replied. "I want Conway arrested by the time the game starts. Since we don't have enough to hold him, we're going to have to find conclusive evidence before tomorrow night."

"And if we don't?" Bailey asked his superior.

"Then we'll have to catch him in the act, and I'd rather not be faced with that," Jacobs responded. "You did a great job, Frank. You'll get sole credit for the arrest. Anything else?"

"One last thing, Warren," McCaskill said pulling a letter from the file and sliding it across the director's desk. "Here's my formal resignation. My retirement will begin immediately upon the completion of this investigation."

Before each game Mike Redding analyzed UNI's opponent and wrote down five things he thought would be the keys to winning the game. After picking five things, he isolated the two or three keys he believed to be most important. Sitting in his hotel room taking notes, Mike was so engrossed in breaking down Kentucky's offensive attack he didn't hear the knock on the door. A second later two agents ushered Byron Lewis into Mike's suite.

" 'sup, coach? Got a few?"

"Sure. Let me finish here," Mike said without looking up from his notes.

Byron walked over to a couch opposite Mike and sat down. His black and green metallic jogging suit hung loosely off his tall, lanky frame. Around his neck was a Sony walkman and on his head was a black baseball cap with the insignia THE REAL THING spelled in large white letters. When Mike got to a stopping point, he put his pen down and looked up at Byron, who was now leaning back on the couch with his eyes closed and the headphones stuck to his ears.

Mike studied his All-American sophomore closely. If Byron Lewis left college at the end of the school year to turn pro he would most likely be the first player chosen in the NBA draft and could reasonably expect a contract worth thirty million dollars. If he stayed in college another year to earn his degree, he might become one of the greatest college players ever, win a national title and command a contract of $30-$50 million, or he could have a disappointing year which might lower his stock. Worse still, he could suffer an injury that would cost him tens of millions of dollars.

Watching Byron sit on the couch jamming to music, Mike thought about how much college basketball had changed the last ten years. The game had become a fast-paced, high-flying, trash-talking Hollywood production. Young players, many of them still teenagers, were expected to make incredible plays, entertain fans, sell clothing, yet still win conference titles. That's too much to ask of nineteen-year-olds, Mike thought sadly. Byron opened his eyes, saw his coach looking at him and pulled the headphones off his ears.

"All set, Byron. Fire away."

No longer slumping over, the star forward sat up straight on the couch and looked his coach square in the eyes. Accustomed to Mike Redding's no-nonsense, business-like manner, Byron did not hesitate. "Outside of Mom, I wanted to tell you first. I've decided to go pro. I'm not gonna tell anyone else 'cause I don't want the media going ape shit. I'll announce it after the tourney. Thanks for everything you've done for me. You're the closest thing to a father I've had. Leaving you and the guys is the hardest part. All the stuff you're going through has shown me there's no guarantees in life. I know I'm doing the right thing, coach. I've accomplished just about everything there is in college ball. I'm ready for bigger challenges in the NBA.

"The money's cool, too. Mom'll never admit it, but she needs it. She's had it hard for a long time; I don't want her slaving anymore. It's always been my dream to play against the best and school 'em. I can't do that unless I'm in the bigs. I won't know how good I am or be able to perform at my highest level of excellence if I'm not playing against Jordan and them." Byron smiled as he finished speaking and Mike suddenly realized why. His star player was teasing him by using Mike's favorite injunction: "Perform at the highest level of excellence."

"Congratulations, Byron. I know you've given this a lot of thought. You're doing the absolute right thing. I'd never say that publicly because it'd piss everyone off, but there's nothing left for you here other than your degree and enjoying campus life. You've outgrown the college game, and the media and fans have put you in a fish bowl. You might as well get paid for the crap you have to endure. Hell, the money is too good to pass up!"

Rising, he began pacing the room. "All the righteous, armchair critics who preach athletes should stay in school and get a degree won't like your decision, but they've never had an opportunity to make thirty million dollars. Would they defer their winnings if they won a giant lottery? Hell no. One of the biggest reasons you go to college is to get a high paying job—to put off making millions of dollars whether you're a doctor, lawyer or athlete is ridiculous. You'll be the first player taken in the draft and you'll probably end up in some sunny city with a huge house on the water. I'm happy for you, Byron. I just hope you come back during the off-season to finish your degree." He turned suddenly to face the young man. "What'd your mom say?"

Byron reached into his pocket and removed a folded piece of paper. "It's cool with her, but she made me promise I'd get my degree. I had to sign this contract saying I'll get my diploma within three years of the draft. I want you to sign it so I'm accountable to both of you."

Mike took the paper from Byron and glanced over it. "What happens if you don't finish in three years?"

"I'll have to donate $50,000 to any charity of yours and mom's choice. It's down there at the bottom."

"This is great. Your mom's a smart woman," Mike said as he signed his name to the bottom of the contract. "I know you'll get your degree, Byron. This just gives you more incentive."

"You ain't lying, coach. You won't believe what she'll do."

"What? Who gets the donation if you don't graduate?"

"Some Aryian power group and The Nazi Party of America. Can you believe that noise? You know my mom, coach. She'll make me do it. There's no way in hell I'm giving $100,000 to any skin heads. But I am gonna give 'em nightmares. I'm their worst fear: an educated young black man with extremely large bank." To emphasize the point, Byron spread his arms wide, using his considerable wing-span and enormous hands to show how much money he would soon have.

Mike couldn't help but laugh. Byron's mother was even smarter than Mike guessed. The kid's degree was as good as finished. "Now I finally know how to motivate you," Mike said still laughing. "Listen, Byron, you're gonna get your diploma and $30 million. How about a national championship too?"

The smile on Byron Lewis' face instantly disappeared. "You've been through a lot for us, coach. Every time you go out there, you risk your life. I've got helly talent, but you prepared me for the next level. I won't let you down. We're going to win tomorrow and next weekend. I want the title for myself, my mom and you. We've come too far and been through too much. I won't let us lose."

During the ride back from Quantico to Washington, McCaskill tried to figure out how Conway would kill Mike Redding.

By the time the helicopter landed at Washington's National Airport, he was sure he would act alone.

"It's Conway's nature to do it himself," McCaskill told Taylor as they entered the senior agent's office. "He doesn't trust anyone, and he can't risk someone rolling over on him if they got caught. No delegating here. He'll do it himself."

"How's he gonna do it?" Taylor asked, plopping down in a seat. "We have ten agents on him at all times, those agents are tailed by five more, and the whole damn stadium will be crawling with feds, national guardsmen, state police and arena security."

"I don't know, Alec, but he'll find a way. The guy's a genius and he's got billions of dollars. We can't underestimate him. He got away from us in Knoxville and faked his own limo explosion. There's no partner. It's not his style. We need to figure out how he planted the bomb in his limo and poisoned Redding's dogs. That would tell us what we need for tomorrow night."

"What about Redding? When do you think the director will tell him?" Taylor asked.

"Not for awhile. Maybe after tomorrow's game. It depends on how fast we can build a case against Conway. Jacobs doesn't want to tip our hand and Redding couldn't keep quiet. We don't have enough evidence to convict Conway of jaywalking, so the director will wait. Redding won't believe us anyway. He's gonna go nuts, absolutely ballistic, when we tell him. He'll probably beat the tar out of the agent that tells him and then run straight to Conway and spill everything."

"That's what I was thinking on the ride back," said Taylor. "I wouldn't want the job of telling Redding his best friend killed Clancy and Butler and is after him. I still can't believe it's Conway. What kind of person stalks his closest friend? While he was acting like a great friend—loyal, supportive, encouraging—he was trying to kill Redding. Those guys seemed like brothers. You studied psychology, Frank. How could Conway pull off such a charade?"

McCaskill had given this question a great deal of thought since early that morning. "Conway's got to be mentally sick or have zero conscience. My guess is he has no conscience and is morally bankrupt. He could have split personalities. Either way, he's been this way a long time, probably his whole life, but had everybody snowed. This is light years beyond the cruel pranks and gamesmanship we knew he loved. Remember the stories we heard at the beginning of the investigation about how ruthless he was. This really shouldn't be that big of a surprise considering his reputation. He's always been about money and power. Turns out he's also into drugs and murder. Unfortunately, he's a master at stroking egos, making people feel warm and fuzzy inside, and disguising his true intentions. He's a master manipulator. Conway is twice as dangerous as we thought Rooks was."

Looking far off into the distance, McCaskill suddenly seemed distracted and his clear, booming voice wavered. Just as Alec Taylor started to speak, more from discomfort than desire, Frank McCaskill opened his vault of emotions and shared a side of himself Alec Taylor had previously not seen.

"My stubborn old man, God bless his soul, told me when I was a young boy how to win a fight. He said the man who always wins a scuffle, regardless of size or strength, is the man who's fighting for the more personal reason. All I had to do to win every time, he assured me, was never get into a scuffle unless my reason for fighting was more personal than the other guy's. In the forty some years since he told me that, I've never seen that theory proven wrong and I've never lost a fight. Now, for the first time in my life, I don't know if I'll win. Conway scares me—his reasons are as personal as mine, maybe more. And unlike the guy at the bottom who will do almost anything to be on top, Conway has no limits. He's already on top—has been for a long time—and will do anything to stay there."

"Including wasting his best friends," Taylor said ruefully, not sure how to respond to his superior's candid observations.

"Especially that. Permanently silencing them was the best way to protect himself. It probably wasn't hard for him to kill Clancy and Butler. Just a simple rational decision. He owns everything under the stars and moon and one of his best friends threatens to take it away. Think about it. For years he killed people over money and drugs. Why stop now when he stands to lose the treasure at the end of the rainbow? If one of his high school friends blew the whistle, how would that look? Come to think of it, Alec. There could be more to this then we know."

"Like what? He killed JFK and he's friends with the aliens from Roswell," Taylor replied. "What more is there then drug trafficking, laundering and murder. He'd get at least five life sentences from what we know now."

"I don't mean other crimes, I mean other players. Powerful players. For Conway to go to so much trouble to wipe out his whole group of friends, there'd have to be major stakes involved."

"What? Six billion dollars and freedom isn't big enough?" Taylor asked in disbelief.

"Usually it'd be more than enough, but maybe not in this case. He'd likely be ruined if his past ever saw the light of day, but the way our judicial system works now days for the rich and famous, he could walk almost as easily as fry. His desperate actions tell me there're higher stakes involved. Look at all the dope he's brought into the country for years. No one even knew he was trafficking and he's been at it forever. I find it too incredible to believe someone could do that without getting special assistance. He had to get help from someone or some people. My guess is those are some very important and powerful people. If someone goes down, it'd be Conway. That must be why he's killing everyone in sight. I'm sure he didn't think twice about killing his friends and he won't hesitate snuffing out Redding. The man's sick—money and power are the gods he worships."

"You're right, he is a sick bastard. How sick, I'm afraid to guess. Listen, Frank, I didn't get much accomplished in the chopper. I've got to bust ass to catch up. Promise me you'll eat something other than that crap in the vending machines."

"Who are you, Taylor? My wife or my mother? Why are you looking out for me all of a sudden?" asked McCaskill, cynicism crowding into his voice.

"I'm not. I'm looking out for me. Your ass has smelled like toxic waste since your wife stopped cooking and you started eating that junk food."

"I'll ignore that comment," McCaskill replied suppressing a tiny smile, "until I fill out your performance review report. Let me ask you something, Alec. You know the idea I told you about in the chopper, the long shot."

"The desperation, if-all-else-fails plan?" responded Taylor, still grinning from the previous exchange. "I'm trying to forget it. Why?"

"I want to be prepared for every eventuality. If we don't get enough evidence by game time, we're gonna have to catch Conway in the act. The director doesn't want to endanger the fans, but it's going to be hard to find indisputable evidence in twenty-four hours. I want to have a plan ready in case we need to catch Conway red-handed. What'd you think of that plan?"

"Well, it's risky and definitely off the wall, but in theory I suppose it'd work," Taylor replied. "It's awfully radical for us. I could see the DEA or CIA doing it, but not us. It doesn't sound like something we'd do."

"That's why I like it. It isn't something we'd do. Conway would never expect it. It's too dangerous."

"Are you seriously considering pitching it to Jacobs?" Taylor asked incredulously.

"Affirmative. If we can't arrest Conway before tip-off, we'll have to stop him during the game. I'm not about to let college basketball's best coach die and 20,000 fans get hurt. Granted, the plan is very dangerous and agents could die, but if all else fails, it might be our best hope of catching Conway and preventing a blood bath."

"There is another option. Nobody wants to talk about it after Deputy Director Bailey squashed it, but we have to consider canceling the tournament."

"I don't want to hear that, Alec. Do you realize what would happen on campuses and cities across the country?"

"Possibly riots, protests turning into mob scenes and general chaos and lawlessness. I admit it's a gamble Frank, but that gamble might end up being our best option."

"Let's hope not. If we cancel the tourney, we'll have hell to face."

Since it was unseasonably warm for late March even by Phoenix's standards, Derrick Jensen had worked up a dry sweat while scaling the two story landing of his apartment building. As the telephone continued ringing inside his unit, he fumbled around for keys in his right pocket and balanced a bag of groceries on his left arm. After unlocking the dead bolt and slamming the door behind him, he dropped the groceries on a love seat in the living room and grabbed the receiver on the seventh ring.

"Speak," he said, annoyed at whoever was on the other end.

"I need you tonight at 8:00."

Derrick Jensen had mixed feelings as soon as he heard the voice. He could use the money and his stash of dope had nearly run out, but he wasn't expecting the call tonight. He had planned on spending the evening with his new friend Janis. Jensen had told the sexy young waitress she could smoke a couple bowls with him and shoot some horse. After opening her veins he wanted to open her legs and have her chase his dragon.

"I wasn't counting on working tonight," Jensen began confidently. "I made plans to . . ."

"Cancel them. I'll triple your pay. It's another real estate transaction. Exact same job as last time. It's money for nothing and your drugs for free." The words came rapidly and were spit at Derrick Jensen. They weren't statements; they were commands.

"What I meant to say was, I'd love the work," retorted Jensen, playing the game. "What do I need to bring?"

"Same pair of Levi's and Nike running shoes. Bring the Lakers cap, white oxford, and the Raybans in the duffel bag I gave you. Don't forget the makeup and hairpiece. Make sure your goatee is trimmed and the same color as mine. Be at the office dressed and ready at precisely 7:55 PM. Leave the car in the parking garage and come up the service stairs. The key and clearance code haven't changed. Wait in the private suite until I get there.

"The meeting starts at 8:15 PM. My attorney will do all the talking; just read the dummy files and sign my name wherever he tells you to. The meeting is with some builders and developers. Very informal—builders act like pigs in a fucking trough. They're scared to death of me, so don't hesitate to be a prick. Remember to use my accent and talk as little as possible. My attorney thinks I have the flu and I bitched him out this afternoon so he'll stay away from you. Don't worry about the Feds. There'll only be one in my private office and he's a newer agent. The other G-men will be waiting next door in the conference area. Be on time. I've got an important function tonight, so there can be no mistakes in the exchange. Your money and medicine will be delivered tomorrow. Any questions?"

"Hell yes," Derrick Jensen said after he'd hung up. "Why do you want me to impersonate you and what will you be doing this time?"

Later that evening Frank McCaskill was studying blueprints of the Palace when Alec Taylor burst into his office. One look at the agent's face and McCaskill knew something terrible had happened. "Out with it," McCaskill ordered.

"Conway's gone."

"He's what?" McCaskill yelled.

"We lost him. He's AWOL," repeated Taylor timidly.

McCaskill's forehead was suddenly hot and his head felt as if it would explode from the twenty different thoughts racing through it, each more dreadful than the previous one.

"Talk to me, Alec. How did ten agents lose our primary suspect?"

" No one knows. He just fucking vanished. Ted McGraw's the lead and he doesn't have a clue. Conway and his attorney had an 8:15 PM meeting in his office with a group of real estate developers. At 8:20 Conway went into his bedroom suite to use the bathroom and get a file from his safe. He never came out. By 8:30 the attorney was worried and began knocking on the door. A few minutes later he gave McGraw permission to take the door off. Conway was gone. It's a second floor office so he could have gone out a window. McGraw . . ."

"Goddamnit. How the fuck did I miss it?" McCaskill screamed. The senior agent was so upset, his face so red, he looked like a ripe tomato ready to burst. Taylor was stunned by McCaskill's profane comments. Long before he met him, Taylor had heard McCaskill rarely cursed. The younger agent didn't know how to respond, so he didn't. He waited to see what his superior would say.

Emotionally rocked by the news of Conway's escape, McCaskill was more surprised by his demonstrative outburst than Taylor was. The seasoned federal agent quickly collected himself and organized his thoughts.

"He didn't use a window," McCaskill said, rubbing his temples and forehead to relieve the mounting stress behind his eyebrows. "There's a hidden room in his office. In the bedroom suite there's a private room or passageway leading outside. That's got to be it. I should've known his office had a hidden chamber. They're common in Japanese corporate culture and Conway deals with Tokyo regularly."

"That explains how he poisoned Redding's dogs and killed the hooker," said Taylor.

"Correct. A tunnel or exit gets him out of the office. Think back on the number of times he's stayed overnight in his suite the last three weeks. I don't know how he gets back so quickly, but at least we can prove his alibi is bogus. Have you or McGraw notified any outside law enforcement agencies?" asked McCaskill.

"No. McGraw found the nest empty less than five minutes ago and I came straight to you."

"Good," McCaskill said already deep in thought. Reaching into the bottom drawer of his desk he pulled out a large map and spread it across his desk.

"Tell McGraw to find the hidden chamber and secure it. Put out an APB. Have your men contact every police and sheriff station in Phoenix, Scottsdale and Tempe. Go ahead and include Glendale and Tucson, even Flagstaff. Give them Conway's description and if they've been in a cave, a brief bio. Have them call the airports, bus terminals and train stations and post the description. I want road blocks and check points set up at every county line throughout Arizona and at fifteen mile intervals in the cities I named. Call CNN first, then the AP wire and the networks. Inform them of the manhunt and give Conway's description."

"Do you think I should be the person to tell them Conway is the March Madness Murderer?" Taylor asked.

"No, I am. That comes later though. Just tell them Conway's missing. I don't care what you say: the pressure got to him, he snapped and ran from us, he fled and is hiding on his own. Give them anything. Just don't alert them to the fact he's our suspect. I want Conway's face, description, background, everything we have on him, splashed across every television set and newspaper in America. Get the entire country hunting him. I want him found before tomorrow's game. He fled federal protective custody so we've got our reason to question him and detain him overnight."

"Do you think he'll flee the country or go after Redding?" Taylor asked.

McCaskill swiveled back and forth in his chair as he always did when he was analyzing a complicated situation. After ten seconds of silence, McCaskill had made his mind up. "He'll go after his buddy. He's been trying to kill Redding for three weeks—he won't stop now. Conway needs him dead. There's a helluva big reason he's after Redding. He's trying to keep his past a secret so he won't lose paradise. Fleeing the country means surrendering the empire and the lifestyle. That's what he's trying to avoid. Redding is the last link to his past. He'll definitely go after Redding. If we don't find strong evidence that holds up in court, he could kill Redding and not have to leave the country. He'd proclaim his innocence, hire the best lawyers money can buy and skate right back to easy street."

"How would he explain running?" asked Taylor.

"Any number of ways. He could say he felt safer on his own or use depression as an excuse. Or he had to escape the incredible intrusion of the FBI and media. The point is, without irrefutable evidence like a weapon or eyewitness, we can't touch Quentin Conway. Okay, enough philosophizing. Get to work on your problem, and I'll tackle my two."

"I'll check back when I'm done notifying the media and setting up. Besides coming up with a plan to catch Conway in the act, what's your other problem?"

"Figuring out how to break the news. With Conway running, I have no choice but to tell Mike Redding his best friend will try to kill him tomorrow."

Chapter Twenty-one

Lost in thought preparing for the game that evening, McCaskill sat in the back of a blue Crown Victoria as it sped toward the arena. In the front seat of the vehicle Alec Taylor went down the Palace's employee roster. Over the course of the last eighteen hours, Taylor had personally met with eighty percent of the stadium's parking attendants, concession vendors, ticket-takers and custodians. Each of them wore a badge with his or her name, picture ID, social security number and signature. The FBI had matching badges of all the employees. Taylor would interview the rest of the arena's staff in the next two hours. If Conway tried to disguise himself as a stadium employee, the badges would enable McCaskill to immediately check the photo and signature.

Pictures of Quentin Conway were being distributed to NCAA officials and employees and would be posted throughout the arena. Canine search teams had scoured the Palace twice in the last twenty-four hours and had found no bombs, explosives or plastic detonation devices. Two more electronic sweeps and canine searches were scheduled during the preceding eight hours before tip-off. Comprehensive background checks had been run on every NCAA official who would be in attendance. When the report came back that two NCAA administrators were close to bankruptcy, McCaskill secretly ordered one man surveillance teams to tail them.

He didn't want to chance Conway buying a NCAA official in an attempt to get close to Mike Redding during the game.

As Taylor reviewed the positioning of the FBI's sharpshooters, McCaskill concentrated on developing alternate plans to stop Conway. L.C. Bailey held out little hope the field units in Phoenix, Los Angeles, Washington and Chicago would be able to find Conway prior to the start of the game. Bailey had not yet conceded defeat, but realistically he believed the Bureau's chances of locating him were slim to none. Instead, he instructed McCaskill to devise three plans to catch Conway during the assassination attempt. Cancelling the tournament had been ruled out by Director Jacobs.

McCaskill went over the second plan in his mind. It wasn't very strong, and he knew it. His first plan was exceptional, but it was dependent upon Conway's actions. The third alternative was extremely proactive and incredibly dangerous. It would be used only in an extreme emergency or if the first two plans failed. As the motorcade approached the stadium, McCaskill thought back to his conversation the night before with Mike Redding. It had been terrible, one of the worst experiences McCaskill had been through at the Bureau. He had called the coach late in the evening and asked to speak to him in person. Both the FBI and UNI's basketball team were staying at the Hyatt Regency, so Mike arrived at McCaskill's room a short five minutes after they had hung up. Knowing there was no good way to deliver the news about his friend, McCaskill had been blunt and to the point.

At first Redding had not believed McCaskill. Thinking the agent was putting him through a perverse test, he became angry and belligerent. When McCaskill did not back down, but continued outlining a case against Quentin, Mike realized the agent was serious. He became enraged, livid to the point he had to restrain himself from striking McCaskill. The two went round and round, each unwavering in his belief. Mike steadfastly refused to consider the possibility Quentin was involved in the murders.

More than once during the argument, McCaskill feared for his safety. He wasn't sure if Mike's profanity-laced-tirade was simply the infamous temper erupting, or if the coach would actually inflict bodily harm on him. After vehemently defending his best friend for ten minutes, Mike was stunned when McCaskill told him Quentin had deceived the FBI and escaped earlier that evening. Only the news that Quentin had fled the FBI's protection and was nowhere to be found convinced Mike the horrible story McCaskill told was the truth.

McCaskill vividly remembered the look of devastation on the coach's face. He had never seen a grown man so empty and lost. Moments before an obstinate Mike Redding had stormed around the hotel room, shouting obscenities, overturning chairs and throwing lamps and threatening McCaskill. When the realization of the truth finally hit him, that Quentin had not only murdered Allan Clancy and David Butler, but was trying to kill him as well, Mike had collapsed in tears, a broken man defeated by an evil leviathan larger and more grotesque than he could comprehend.

As the Crown Vic slowed to a stop outside the east checkpoint of the FBI barricade, McCaskill tried to shake from his memory Mike Redding's foreboding prediction. "You won't catch him," the coach had warned. "What Quentin wants—Quentin gets. He never loses."

Upon hearing this prediction, McCaskill asked Mike if he would consider not coaching the rest of the tournament. The heated response did not surprise the agent.

"It's all I have. Everything I cared about is dead. My life is worth jack shit, but I won't let him take away my coaching."

As he stepped from the Crown Vic's back seat, McCaskill's thoughts drifted to his third plan. He didn't want to use it. It was risky, unpredictable and life threatening. Unfortunately, it was quite possibly the only way to end Quentin Conway's March Madness mayhem.

I'll keep him around as long as I need him, thought Quentin as he waited in the parking lot at 7-Eleven. *Then I'll kill the worthless piece of shit and McCaskill will never get a shot at him. Corpses don't talk so they won't be able to touch me.* While Quentin sat in Derrick Jensen's beat-up old Blazer and plotted the man's death, the drugged-out actor paid for gas, food and cigarettes inside. During the cross country trip Quentin had kept his traveling companion quiet and out of his way with an endless supply of cocaine and hash. Quentin needed time to review his new plan, and the drugs were an excellent way of keeping Jensen at arm's length.

"Son of a bitch," Quentin said aloud. "He'd make a perfect diversion. I'll have Jensen create a disturbance and when the Feds grab him, I'll ring Mike's bell and then bolt. Jensen'll roll over, but my alibi is rock solid."

Quentin's thoughts shifted to the other person he was paying to impersonate him in Los Angeles. For five years he had paid a middle level employee of his company to attend meetings, seminars and title closings in his place. The employee bore a striking resemblance to Quentin, had mastered his tiny, slanted signature and had been granted private access to Quentin's office. With the employee's help, Quentin had managed to improve his efficiency, increase his profitability and maximize his time by being in two places at the same time. Since he had always kept himself distant and removed from even high level managers and assistants and demanded complete privacy, Quentin's executives were also fooled by the double who appeared at closings and final settlements. After enjoying so much success with a double in business transactions, Quentin had discreetly carried the practice over to his darker, more sinister activities. It worked perfectly. The assistant doubled for him at private meetings, luncheons and real estate closings, and unknowingly provided Quentin an indisputable alibi for his illegal activities.

Still waiting for Jensen to return to the Blazer, Quentin basked in the pleasure of his own brilliance as he pictured the alibi he had set up for that evening. It was a beautiful plan. Ten minutes before Redding would be gunned down by sniper fire, Quentin's employee/body double would cause a scene while entering an exclusive restaurant in Los Angeles. So as not to arouse the close scrutiny of the restaurant's staff or patrons, the double would stay only five minutes. The brief yet impressionable appearance occurring minutes before Mike Redding was slain on the other side of the country would produce an iron-clad alibi.

After he had killed his best friend, Quentin would flee by car to another state and then fly himself to Los Angeles and hole up in the motel the double had checked into the night before. Jensen would be arrested by the FBI and spill his guts, but Quentin would have an airtight alibi. He'd simply say he had fled FBI protection and driven straight to Los Angeles because he felt safer on his own and the intrusion of privacy was too great a burden. Upon arriving in LA, he had checked into a motel and hid from the media. With his double planted in the motel Friday night and then spotted at the restaurant minutes before the assassination, McCaskill wouldn't be able to place him within thousands of miles of the murder site.

Quentin's thoughts were interrupted when he saw Jensen come out the door of the convenience store. Jumping inside the Blazer, the burnt-out actor didn't waste any time negotiating.

"I'm well beyond the call of duty, boss man. You're all over the TV and newspapers in there. You've got to pay if you want me to play."

"Shit, you've got me over a barrel," Quentin said solemnly. "Looks like I've got no choice. One condition though. You stay with me when we get there. My best friend Mike Redding might be in grave danger. I won't insult you by asking if you care. I'll just leave the decision up to you. You'll get $50,000 for driving me across the country. For staying with me and doing the job, I'll pay you $250,000 and a year's supply of dope. I don't like it one bit, but like you said, everyone's looking for me. I'm in a helluva bind and my buddy needs my help. How much time do you need?"

Jensen could barely hide his euphoria. For nearly three weeks he had been waiting for a big payday and here it was. "Are you kidding? For $250,000 and a year of medicine, I'm yours."

"Good decision. You won't regret it. My attorney's could learn a thing or two about negotiating from you. Now, if you don't mind, I need to make some plans, so let's not talk for two hours or so. I'll drive this shift. Help yourself to more of the feel-goods."

"You're the boss," the actor said happily as he began day-dreaming about the $250,000 he would never see. Derrick Jensen was on top of the world. In his simple mind, he had gone toe-to-toe with one of America's most powerful men and trampled him.

Quentin immediately went to work modifying, then polishing, his rough plan. On their way out of Phoenix, he had stopped at one of his warehouses and picked up cash, clothes, dope, two hand-guns and the AK-47 assault rifle that would make Mike Redding stop breathing. Using his photographic memory, Quentin envisioned in his mind's eye that evening's setting. After analyzing shooting angles, he narrowed the locations he could shoot from to two places. No one, not even Mike, knew how adept Quentin was with a gun. He was an excellent marksman. Whenever he and Mike went hunting or skeet shooting, he shot well enough to beat his friend but never showed his true skill. Like many things in his past, Quentin had effectively hidden his talent, so the FBI's research had not uncovered his outstanding prowess as a marksman.

While Jensen consumed large quantities of cocaine and heroin, and floated in and out of a stoned stupor, Quentin drove across the flat plains of the Midwest and planned the final chapter of his gruesome horror story. As long as he wasn't caught in the act of shooting Mike, he knew the FBI and the Attorney General wouldn't be able to convict him. He'd buy the souls of the world's best attorneys and never spend a night in jail. His Dream Team of lawyers would make O. J. Simpson's look like a high school debate team. By the time the media had reported the story to every household in the country, a prospective jury pool would be so contaminated no twelve citizens in America would be able to sit in a jury box and give him a fair trial. *I almost wish I'd get caught so I could beat them in court at the real trial of the century. God, I'd get a lot of pussy. It'd be like those women on* Hard Copy *who fall in love with guys on death row. I'd get all the freaky pussy out there.*

Quentin was confident his close associations with numerous senators and congressmen would make it easy to beat a murder rap. But with many high ranking officials of the CIA and NSC heavily involved in his trafficking business in the early 80s, he would not make it through a wide-scale congressional investigation. Even with his money and connections, the top brass of those federal agencies involved would go unscathed while he would be hung out to dry and publicly crucified. Clearly, he had to finish the task of silencing all his friends. He would skate through any murder trial, but if the truth came out and congressional hearings were held, the heads of the CIA and NSC would protect themselves and make Quentin the fall guy just as they did with Charles Keating during the Savings and Loan scandal.

Checking his watch, Quentin noticed it was past noon. He accelerated a bit, but was careful not to exceed the speed limit. He wasn't about to risk everything by getting pulled over for speeding. As the rusty old Blazer bounced down the interstate in the bright, mid-day sun, he wondered what expression would be on his best friend's face when the bullet ripped through him. Killing Mike was far different from killing Allan and David. Allan had been fun, extremely gratifying, while David's murder was simply a mistake.

Mike was different. Quentin cared deeply for him. His feelings for Mike had never been a ruse. Even with Mike becoming softer and weaker because of his budding romance with Diana Fleming, Quentin genuinely respected and loved him as his best friend. *It's a shame Red was going to find out about my past*, Quentin thought. *One of our heads has to roll and it's not going to be mine. This will be the first time I don't enjoy it.*

As Mike waited for the hotel operator to connect him to Diana's room, he tried to figure out the best way to tell her about Quentin. Before he found the right words, she came onto the line.

"Mike, how are you? God, it's good to hear from you. Where's Quentin? I heard he's missing. What happened? Is he okay?" She spoke so fast he could hardly understand her.

"I'm fine. Quentin's another story. Listen, Diana, we need to talk. I don't like telling you this over the phone, but McCaskill won't let me see anyone or go anywhere. The reason for all this cloak and dagger precaution is Quentin. He's not missing—he's running from the FBI."

"What do you mean he's running? He's got no reason to run," Diana said as waves of shock resonated through her voice.

"He killed Allan and David. The FBI is sure *he's* the murderer."

"He's what?" Diana shrieked. "Tell me you're kidding, Mike. It can't be him."

"I wish I were kidding. I didn't believe it either, but it's true. McCaskill's got the facts to back it up. When Quentin suspected McCaskill was on to him, he jumped ship. Now the FBI is trying to find him before tonight's . . .."

"Oh my God. He's trying to kill you," Diana exclaimed, completely stunned. It had taken her a few moments, just as it had Mike when McCaskill told him, to fully comprehend the news. Figuratively punched in the stomach, her breathing became labored and tears streamed down her face as she tried to imagine the unfathomable. "Why does he want you dead? Why's he killing all his friends?"

"The FBI only knows part of the story, but it has to do with drug money and drug murders. Years ago Quentin made his fortune selling drugs. Nobody knew about his past until three weeks ago when Allan found out. We all thought—well, you know the Horatio Alger story. McCaskill thinks Allan tried to blackmail Quentin and he started killing the rest of us to protect his secret. If it came out, he'd be screwed."

"I can't believe it," Diana said, the fog of fear and uncertainty growing deeper. "All this time he's been acting so cool and playing the supportive friend, he's been trying to kill you. It makes my skin crawl. What a snake. I remember what the pilot told me the day I met Quentin. Ninety-five percent of Quentin Conway is pure gold....the other five percent is what you need to guard against. He's instinctive, aggressive and unremorseful. He always finds people's weaknesses and is relentless and merciless in exploiting them. A lot more than five damned percent is bad," Diana said vehemently as she switched the phone from one ear to the other.

"Does Agent McCaskill still think things will happen tonight?"

"More than ever. He thinks Quentin needs me dead soon, that there's some sort of deadline hanging over his head. Son of a bitch, I don't believe what I'm saying. Quentin wants me dead. What the hell happened to my life?"

"Are you coaching?" Diana asked quietly, afraid of the answer she expected.

"I don't give a shit anymore," Mike growled. "Probably. It doesn't make a fucking difference either way," he snapped angrily.

"Yes, it does," she said tenderly.

Immediately, Mike regretted lashing out at Diana. He sensed the affection in her voice and yearned toward it.

After taking a deep breath and calming himself, he said, "I'm sorry for attacking you, Diana. None of this is your fault. But what's the difference between my team winning and losing when I don't believe in anything? Everything that was important to me—my parents and family, my friends, working to be the best—all those things and the person I believed in most are gone. Basketball is still important, but I have no family or friends to share it with. Without the people I love, being successful doesn't matter."

"I'm so sorry, Mike. I know it doesn't help one bit to hear that, but I am truly sorry. If I could take your place, or somehow shield you from this pain for just one hour, I would. I don't know what you're going through, nobody does, but I don't want you to give up on yourself or basketball. Those two things have never let you down or hurt you."

"Thanks for listening to all my shit the last few days," Mike said wearily. "I don't mean to unload on you, Diana, but you've been there for me when no one else was. I just called to tell you about Quentin and to say I'm sorry. I don't know when we'll talk next. Diana, if something was to happen tonight . . . I'm so sorry for getting you involved when something terrible . . . ."

Diana hesitated, obviously struggling for composure. "Don't apologize, Mike. You've been nothing short of wonderful. I've treasured the time we've shared. Go out and coach a great game. Forget about Allan and David and Quentin—just coach your butt off. We'll worry about our relationship and everything else later. Go do what you do best. But don't forget that I believe in you and what's inside you. You're more alive than anyone I've ever met, so full of passion and fire it's amazing. It makes you who you are. Most importantly, please remember that I believe in you: as a coach and a friend, but especially as a God-fearing man."

The sweet, gentle words of encouragement soothed his burning heart. Still boiling with rage, bitterness and embarrassment from Quentin's monumental betrayal, Diana's words of consolation and support filled Mike with the two emotions that had been missing from his life: hope and faith. In her reassuring words, he found hope that he might once again live a happy and fulfilling life, and the faith to trust and believe in someone he cared for.

There were so many things Mike wanted to tell her, but he couldn't. He wanted to express his true feelings, describe how she had changed his perspective in three short weeks, even confess that he was falling in love with her, yet he couldn't. He had come a long way recently, but not far enough to take that leap of faith.

"Diana," the name, said with raw hunger and desire, hung in the air. "In case something happens tonight, I want you to know you are . . .."

Mike's voice became crackly and choked, then trailed off as he searched in vain for the words to express the emotion he felt. *Try again*, he thought. *She's worth it.* Digging deep inside, he found a reservoir of courage he didn't know he had, which had not existed until literally that moment. He never wanted to be without Diana's friendship and affection. This time, after years of holding himself back and holding everything in, the emotion flowed from deep within.

"Diana, darling, I want you to know you are the warmest, sweetest, kindest, most beautiful woman I've ever known. No one has touched me the way you have. You are so unbelievably precious.

I've never had feelings so strong and pure about anything or any-body. You'll always be inside me—in my thoughts and prayers and especially my heart. No matter what happens or what the future holds, I'll never forget how we feel about each other. You're an angel from God, a dream come true. Despite losing my friends and all the shit that's happened with Quentin, I feel more awake and alive than ever before. You've made me this way."

After she hung up the phone minutes later, Diana laid down on her hotel bed and sobbed uncontrollably. If she continued to stand by him through his ordeal, Diana knew she would be madly in love with him. That meant the very real possibility of indescrib-able heartache and pain in her immediate future. If she wanted to avoid a misery unlike any she had experienced, Diana needed to distance herself from Mike as soon as possible. At that moment she hated Quentin Conway so much she would do anything to keep Mike out of harm's way.

The Palace was filled to capacity for the biggest college bas-ketball game in the last ten years. 20,500 fans made as much noise as they possibly could. An estimated 120 million Americans were expected to watch the game on television. In addition, 750 million viewers from around the world would tune in to see if Mike Redding would live long enough to lead UNI to the Final Four three con-secutive years. Auburn Hills, a quiet, serene hamlet not far from Detroit, had been transformed into the communications capital of America for the Elite Eight showdown. Dual epicenters of the mas-sive media contingency were the Hyatt Regency Hotel, a modern day architectural wonder which housed the UNI and Kentucky basketball teams as well as all FBI personnel, and the Palace, a state-of-the-art basketball facility which was the home court of the De-troit Pistons. For the last thirty-six hours, the media had focused on the Hyatt Regency, Mike Redding's newest temporary home during his tragic quest to win the national championship.

News of Quentin Conway's disappearance had spread like wildfire through the media ranks late Friday and early Saturday morning. Saturday at noon CNN's Vince Cellini went on the air with a story that had been leaked from within the FBI. Cellini's report, that the FBI was guarding against an assassination attempt during the UNI-Kentucky game, set off another feeding frenzy in the media. Now thirty minutes prior to tip-off, the firestorm Cellini started at noon had not subsided.

While the electricity throughout the stadium kept the crowd of twenty thousand buzzing with anxious excitement, below the court in UNI's locker room the mood was subdued and eerily quiet. Mike's players and coaching staff had sensed something different about him in the last two hours. His behavior was markedly different than it had been the last ten days and when Byron Lewis had asked him what was wrong, Mike had not responded. Now, as he stood in front of his team ready to send them up the tunnel to take the floor against Kentucky, they knew something was terribly wrong.

"I want to take a few minutes to talk to you guys. You've all done a tremendous job handling the pressure and hype the last couple of weeks. I know it hasn't been easy. You've made sacrifices, worked your asses off and done what I've asked. I wish things didn't have to be this way, but it's out of my control. We all have to do what we can to make this work. That's why I've decided not to coach tonight."

A few mumbled groans could be heard around the locker room, but for the most part there was stunned silence. Even the assistant coaches were shocked. They had no idea Mike planned to watch the game from the locker room.

"I don't know if that's an unpopular decision, or even if it's a wise one, but it's what I've decided. My head's not where it should be. I can't coach this type of a game—one of this magnitude—with my mind not one hundred percent on basketball. I can't explain everything going on inside me, but understand one thing. My decision is in the best interests of myself, this team and the University of Northern Indiana. I want the best for all of you and this program. If I coached tonight feeling the way I do, in the frame of mind I'm in—our chances of winning would be greatly diminished.

"I've always sworn to myself that when I put a team on the floor, I'd prepare them as well as I could and give them every opportunity to win. I've never broken that promise and I don't intend to now. Coach DuPree will run the show tonight. I'll be watching the game down here on TV. Give him everything you have, just like you would for me, and leave it all on the court. No one ever remembers who finishes second, so play like there's no tomorrow."

Later twelve shaken and confused UNI players walked up the ramp toward the deafening noise created by twenty thousand delirious basketball fanatics. In the locker room, Mike settled uncomfortably in front of a television in the coach's office and waited for the opening tip. *This is too weird,* he thought. *It's so damn hard watching from down here instead of being there.* Even though the game was being played on the court above, he felt as if he were a thousand miles from the action. As the referee prepared to toss the ball into the air to start the game, Mike sat glued to the television wondering if he was doing the right thing. After all, he made the decision not to coach only twenty minutes before when he realized Diana was the woman with whom he could spend the rest of his life.

Chapter Twenty-two

If during the first half Kentucky was a model of how basketball should be played, UNI was the polar opposite. While Kentucky's players performed flawlessly, executed with precision and discipline and excelled in all facets of the game, UNI's players were tentative, sloppy and out of sync. Kentucky's aggressive, man-to-man defense stifled UNI's attack, while Mike Redding's team played lackadaisical defense and was continually beaten by dribble penetration and back door cuts. Offensively, Kentucky's players set jarring screens, made crisp ball-reversal passes, kept proper spacing on the court and moved without the ball, making it difficult for the defense to guard them. UNI's players, on the other hand, missed routine assignments, failed to run appropriate plays, exercised poor shot selection and stood around, making it easier for the defenders to guard them.

By half-time the capacity crowd had been treated to a classic example of how hard work, unselfishness and talent can be meshed together. Unfortunately for Mike, UNI was on the receiving end of the lesson. The half-time score of 47-24 was not reflective of Kentucky's true dominance over the bewildered UNI squad. If not for Byron Lewis's occasional flashes of brilliance, the sell-out crowd would have witnessed an even more one-sided Great Eight match-up. Kentucky was administering such a methodical beating, the only real excitement came when a UNI cheerleader was thrown high in the air during a stunt and was dropped by the spotter below. The cries of pain she let out paled in comparison to the hysterical shrieks which ensued as hundreds of fans feared the March Madness Murderer had struck. It took ten minutes for the FBI to calm the crowd and restore order.

In the visiting team's locker room, Mike waited impatiently for his players to come down the tunnel. As his team and coaches entered the locker room, he quickly closed the door behind them shutting out the trainers, team managers, reporters and cameramen. The major topic of discussion during the first half of CBS's telecast had been his absence from the bench. As the rumors and speculation swirled around court level, Mike faced his players in the locker room below.

"You have nothing to be upset about. None of you should be ashamed of your performance. We're down twenty-three points and you guys probably feel like it's the end of the world, right? This is the biggest game of the season, maybe the biggest game you'll ever play and we're behind twenty-three points. Do you think you screwed up, that everything's gone to shit? Well, let me tell you something. You guys have already won tonight simply by playing. You didn't screw up—I did. You haven't lost anything. I'm the one who's lost."

Mike's voice had slowly risen from an even monotone to a booming, angry shout. Everyone in the room knew it would get louder. "I made a mistake by not coaching. A big mistake. I let you guys down, I let myself down and I disappointed our loyal fans. With all the shit going on around me, I lost sight of something very important. No matter what happens to me, regardless of what is happening in my personal life, I have to coach basketball. It's my passion. Being a coach is what I am. I let someone scare me into giving that up, and in the process I lost myself and abandoned my team when you needed me most.

"The issue isn't twenty-three points or winning and losing the game. It's following your dreams and living your passion. Twenty-three points isn't shit. I know we're better than Kentucky— you know we're better than Kentucky. Hell, Pitino's in the other locker room telling his players twenty-three points isn't enough."

Mike was yelling now, not out of anger or fury, rather out of hunger and desire. Unbeknownst to his players, he was repeating the number of their deficit again and again so they wouldn't be overwhelmed by it. In saying "twenty-three" over and over, he was subconsciously making the number more familiar and less intimidating. Most of his players had never been down twenty-three points at half-time, and Mike didn't want them feeling hopeless or to think Kentucky's lead was insurmountable. He knew he had to be positive—ripping his players in their already fragile state of mind would be completely counter-productive. He believed performance followed attitude and execution followed concentration, so he wanted to reprogram their attitudes. In essence, UNI's second half comeback had begun while they were still in the locker room.

"I'm coaching this half. No one can keep me from realizing my dream of winning a national championship. You guys have done everything I've asked of you all year long. Now, I want you to do one more thing. Think of nothing but basketball for the next hour. Commit yourselves and all your energy to playing the best twenty minutes of your lives. I've committed myself to the same goal. If you give everything you have and hold nothing back, I promise we will win. Those players in the other locker room have no idea what we've been through. No one does. Let me tell you one last thing. Twenty-three points isn't enough—it's a shit lead. We'll get those points back one bucket at a time, and we'll win this game. I didn't come this far to lose. We will win this game!"

As he walked along the upper level of the stadium, Frank McCaskill wiped perspiration from his forehead and glanced at the huge scoreboard that hung high above center court. Two minutes and thirteen seconds remained on the clock, Kentucky led by seven and UNI had the ball. McCaskill didn't care much who won the game. He wanted to see UNI do well because the team and coaching staff had been through so much the last three weeks. Inwardly, he hoped UNI lost so the FBI would not have to protect Mike Redding at the Final Four. The outcome of the game really didn't mean a lot to him. What he was concerned with was finding Quentin Conway and keeping Redding alive.

McCaskill had noticed a dramatic change in the crowd since half-time, and not being a fan of basketball, he thought it was extremely odd. In the first half when Mike Redding had been tucked safely away in the UNI locker room, the crowd had been noticeably nervous and antsy, almost fearful. Yet during the second half when Redding was running up and down UNI's sideline screaming instructions, berating the officials and exhorting his players, the spectators became wholly engrossed in the game and forgot the threat against the coach and the potential danger to themselves.

McCaskill hadn't forgotten, though. In fact, as the second half wore on he became increasingly agitated. He anticipated Conway would try to kill Redding during the second half, toward the end of the game. With less than two minutes left, it appeared Conway would either not strike that evening, or the attempt would come at any moment. Holding his walkie-talkie close to his mouth so he could be heard over the thunderous crowd noise, McCaskill shouted instructions to agents stationed throughout the arena.

"This is McCaskill. Agents, be on your toes. It's going to happen soon. Be ready for anything. Take him alive if you can. Out."

Frank McCaskill was nervous. Extremely nervous. He was in a building with 20,000 people and a killing-machine was running loose. Going through a checklist of items, he went over for the umpteenth time the locations of all doors, ventilation ducts and unloading docks that led outside. Were they all covered? Were the sharpshooters in place on the catwalks high atop the arena ceiling? Were the parking garages still sealed off? As he paced the Palace's upper level aisle and scanned the mass of humanity below, McCaskill knew it was pointless to worry about security preparations now. He could sense something was about to happen; there was an ominous, palpable evil in the air. Any last minute security arrangements would be futile.

The long, slow road back from a twenty-three point deficit

had started in the locker room and continued the entire second half. With twenty-one seconds left to play, UNI trailed Kentucky by a single point. A twenty-five-foot three-pointer by Byron Lewis cut Kentucky's lead to 84-83, and put UNI on the brink of coming all the way back from a supposed death. The moment Byron's trey swished cleanly through the net, the All-American forward had signaled for a time-out per his coach's instructions.

In the UNI huddle Mike yelled as loud as he could, so his players could hear him over the roar of the deliriously excited crowd. "Here's what I want. Coryell, foul their point guard within two to three seconds of getting the ball in. Everyone else stick to your men no matter where they go. Lay off your man a little, Coryell, so he can get the ball and then go after him. Go for the steal first, but the second you know you can't get the ball, foul him. He's gonna miss the free throws—he's scared shitless. He's one of four from the line tonight and he's not a money player." Mike's players nodded their heads in agreement. If their coach said it, it was true.

"Okay, after he misses the second free throw, I want to own the rebound. Block out everyone, no second chances. We have no time-outs left. I'll repeat that: we have no more time-outs! After we get the rebound or take the ball out of bounds, push the ball up court quickly. Don't let 'em set up. I want to run the high/low with Byron and Keith. We want a shot with six seconds on the clock. Take the shot, Byron, unless they swarm you, then kick it down to Keith. Everyone else crash the boards for the put back. Any questions?"

"I got one, coach," said Craig Coryell. "If he hits the second free throw and we take the ball out under our basket, where should I push the ball?"

"Go up the middle but once you get past half court, get the ball to the corners. Byron, make yourself available in the far corner and then run the high/low with Keith. Remember, we have no time-outs, foul within three to four seconds, push the ball up, get a shot with six seconds left and then go strong to the glass. Let's go guys, this is what you've dreamed of your entire lives. Who wants it more? Effort and execution are the difference between national champs and final eight chumps. I guarantee you'll remember these twenty-one seconds the rest of your lives. Make it a good memory."

The moment Kentucky in-bounded the ball to their cat-quick point guard, Craig Coryell sprung at the guard and hawked him. He had watched the guard's dribbling pattern the whole game and had picked up on his rhythm. When the Kentucky player put the ball on the ground, Coryell deftly lunged toward the bouncing ball. Stopping his momentum on a dime, the guard expertly shifted his weight, reversed his dribble and used his tiny body to shield Coryell from the ball. With nothing left to do but stab at the ball, Craig Coryell got more arm then ball and was whistled for a foul.

The UNI cheering section let out a collective groan at the near steal, while the Kentucky fans clapped with anxious relief. Sportswriters sitting in the press section scribbled notes and pondered both coaches strategies. UNI had no choice but to foul to stop the clock. The question on the sportswriters' minds was if Kentucky converted one of two free throws to push the lead to two points, would UNI attempt a two point shot to tie the game and send it into overtime or would they go for the win in regulation with a three-pointer?

As the diminutive Kentucky guard set himself on the free throw line and prepared to shoot the first foul shot, the UNI faithful wildly waved their arms in an attempt to distract the shooter. Frank McCaskill was the person most distracted by the noise, however. On the upper level walkway, ninety rows above the court, McCaskill desperately tried to hear Alec Taylor's frantic warning. The tiny wire plug McCaskill wore in his ear to hear the walkie-talkie was no match for the deafening noise that shook the walls of the Palace.

While McCaskill helplessly struggled to hear Taylor's message, the Kentucky shooter rose out of his half-crouch and released the ball. Arching high over the rim, it hit the back of the iron and bounded hard to the floor. The UNI contingency erupted in excitement. During the few seconds between the errant first shot and the preparation for the second free throw attempt, the noise level dropped just enough for McCaskill to hear Taylor's panic-stricken voice.

"There's a gun in section B, row eight, seat three. Conway's in the UNI student section. He's got a gun in the front right pocket of his coat. Brown trench and black hat in row eight, three seats from the aisle. All agents proceed immediately to section B, row eight, seat three!"

McCaskill was running at a dead sprint by the time Taylor's voice cut out. As he raced across the upper level walkway toward the aisle above section B, he heard the UNI crowd erupt again, but didn't know it was because the Kentucky guard had missed the second free throw. It wasn't until McCaskill got to the top row of section B that he saw Taylor and six agents closing in from various directions. As he ran down the stadium steps two at a time, still some forty rows above row eight, the noise around him had reached a fever pitch. The game clock was down to twelve seconds. 20,500 rabid fans stood in unison as UNI prepared to take the last shot.

Oh, Jesus God, please help, McCaskill's mind screamed when the tall, lean man wearing a trenchcoat in row eight put his hand in the right front pocket of the coat. Only thirty-five feet away and completely unaware of the drama unfolding behind him, Mike stood on UNI's sideline watching the climactic final play that would determine which team advanced to the Final Four. A horrible realization flashed into McCaskill's head as he leapt down the steps. *He's going to shoot him as the game ends and then get lost in the melee,* the special agent thought.

With nine seconds on the game clock, Byron Lewis was twenty-five feet from the basket on the left side of the court. After glancing at the clock above the basket and stutter-stepping to his right, he exploded hard back to his left. After three successive rapid-fire dribbles, the clock was down to six seconds and Byron was six feet from the baseline, still fifteen feet from the rim, apparently trapped by two Kentucky defenders. With one final machine-gun dribble, he pulled the ball in tight to his body and elevated powerfully off the floor.

The two Kentucky players guarding him were surprised by the sudden shot, but a third defender in the vicinity reacted quickly and jumped horizontally to block it. As the third defensive player flew past him and the first and second defenders reached the apex of their leaps, Byron Lewis continued to ascend. The Kentucky players raised their outstretched arms while he hung in mid-air, waited a split-second, then softly released the ball an inch above the defenders' descending fingertips. At the same moment Byron Lewis's high arcing jumper swished cleanly through the net, the scorer's buzzer went off and Frank McCaskill tackled the suspect and sent him sprawling into the people in row seven.

All around McCaskill the UNI fans were going crazy. There was so much hugging, hand-slapping and dancing, he nearly lost hold of the suspect. Finally, with the help of Taylor and another agent, he was able to spin him over onto his back. While McCaskill ripped the hat and glasses from the man's head, Taylor reached into the front pocket and pulled out a rolled up game program. The scare was nothing more than a false alarm. Instantly, McCaskill was on his feet, his eyes combing the mob scene down on the court. As crazy as it was in the UNI student section, it was bedlam on the playing court.

UNI's players, coaches, cheerleaders and managers, as well as the numerous television reporters and cameramen who flooded the court, were all congregated in front of the scorer's table at the ten second line. The celebration was wild, unrestrained and euphoric. McCaskill's discerning eye found Byron Lewis at the bottom of a massive pile of players and cheerleaders near half court. He wasn't looking for Byron Lewis, though. The person he searched for was nowhere to be found. Running his eyes from one end of the court to the other, McCaskill grew panicky as the seconds passed and Mike Redding could not be located.

Finally, he spotted the coach. Redding was surrounded by fifteen agents who formed a human shield around him as they darted off the court toward the players' tunnel. His worst fear now alleviated, McCaskill sifted through the jubilant students and found his walkie-talkie on the ground in the sixth row. After giving orders to his division heads to put the third plan into effect, he apologized to the graduate student he had tackled and made sure he was not injured.

McCaskill checked his watch. It was 9:20 PM. Mike Redding would be taken to a different hotel and guarded while his players attended a mandatory press conference. Everything had gone well. The evening appeared to be a huge success for both UNI and the FBI. For the first time in two days Frank McCaskill saw light at the end of the tunnel. *Redding will arrive in Indianapolis at 12:30 AM and everything should go off without a hitch from there*, he thought as he made his way toward UNI's locker room.

Chapter Twenty-three

When the buzzer sounded signaling the end of the game, Quentin turned off the television set. "Congratulations, Red. UNI's going to the Big Dance a third year in a row. It's a shame you won't be going to Seattle with your team. Your road to the Final Four ends tonight in Indianapolis."

Quentin lay back on the motel bed. He was a bit tired from not sleeping the previous night. Although he regularly slept only three to four hours a night, the events of the last three days were beginning to wear on him. He yawned lazily and stretched his lean, muscular body across the tiny motel bed. The roar of a commercial jet overhead reminded him why he had picked this motel: the location. It was seven miles from Indianapolis's International Airport. More importantly, it provided him quick and easy access to I-465, Indianapolis's major interstate that circled the city. I-465 connected to 74 East, the interstate that led from Indianapolis to Cincinnati, Ohio.

Under an alias that was known only to him, Quentin had stored a four-seater, twin engine Bonanza Vector in a grain warehouse in Dylon, Ohio, a quiet agricultural town just across the Ohio state line. Figuring Frank McCaskill anticipated he would flee west to Arizona or California, even south to Mexico or South America, Quentin planned on traveling east by car to Dylon, which was a short hour and a half drive from the Indianapolis airport. From Dylon he would make his way by air to the private airstrip outside Los Angeles that he used for incoming drug shipments. His double would be waiting at the airstrip to rendezvous with him. Quentin would kill him, dispose of the body, and head for the motel the double had checked into, the perfect alibi in place.

As Quentin reclined on the grungy twin bed, he glanced next to him at the bathroom door. Derrick Jensen had been in the bathroom ten minutes and both water faucets had been running the entire time. Quentin knew he was snorting coke again, but didn't care. As long as Jensen did what he was told, Quentin didn't care if he drank rubbing alcohol and sniffed glue to maintain his high. So far everything was going smoothly. UNI had won the showdown with Kentucky in dramatic fashion, setting off a massive celebration that would make Quentin's task easier.

Earlier in the day, when a semi-sober Derrick Jensen had grown suspicious and questioned why he had fled the FBI's protection, Quentin's response that the FBI couldn't adequately protect him and that he didn't trust McCaskill and was safer on his own satisfied the actor. By giving him additional cocaine and hash, stroking his ego and lying about their activities at the airport, he kept Jensen in the dark about his true intentions.

I bet McCaskill thinks he beat me, thought Quentin as he mentally pictured the brutal execution that would take place in a few hours. It was ironic he had used visualization so extensively in formulating the plan to kill his best friend. Mike was the person who had turned Quentin on to the power and effectiveness of visualization—now it was being used to kill him. Still hearing the water running in the bathroom, Quentin relaxed and reveled in the illicit pleasure his masterful work gave him.

"McCaskill thought I was going to do it during the game," he said out loud, yet not loud enough that Jensen could hear. "Fuck that. I would've never escaped. McCaskill doesn't know shit about college basketball. If he did, he'd know the two craziest moments are at the end of the game when the clock hits zero and when the winning team arrives home and is greeted by their fans. Those fucking FBI robots will go hog wild when they hear Jensen's shots.

The way Feds shoot first and ask questions later, they'll probably kill the stupid fuck. Ruby Ridge revisited. I wonder how many innocent civilians they'll murder tonight. It'll take just one shot. They'll be so busy with Jensen they won't know where my shot came from. One shot and Mike and my past will be dead."

Quentin heard the faucet in the bathroom shut off, so he stopped talking and waited for Jensen to come out of the bathroom. Twenty seconds later Jensen emerged from the bathroom barely able to walk, groggy and spaced out, his eyes glassy and blood shot. He was so whacked out he didn't bother to stop the blood that dripped from his cocaine-ravished nose and spilled down his shirt. Quentin didn't mind the actor using drugs because they kept him out of the way and inhibited his cognitive reasoning abilities which prevented him from growing suspicious. But Quentin was obsessive-compulsive, a control freak. After hundreds of hours of tireless preparation, careful planning, and numerous murders, he was so close to eradicating his problem, the successful containment of his secret so close at hand, Quentin could taste victory. He would allow nothing to get in his way, especially at this late stage of the game. No one would take from him or deny him what was his. Not Allan Clancy, David Butler, Frank McCaskill, not even the person most dear to him, Mike Redding. There was no way Derrick Jensen would ruin his final plan.

Thirty minutes after Quentin had broken his nose, submerged him until he nearly drowned in a bathtub of freezing-cold water, and promised him half a million dollars, Derrick Jensen was alert, coherent and scared out of his mind. Most importantly, he was ready to do exactly what The Chameleon asked of him.

The joyous celebration had not stopped since the buzzer had gone off. The multitude of hugs, handshakes, laughter and tears that started when the final horn sounded did not cease when UNI's players, coaches, and managers boarded the commercial Boeing 727 jet for the flight home. Now, as the players recounted the incredible ending and the coaches kicked back for the first time in a week, the wild celebration seemed destined to continue long into the night. While the camaraderie and partying went on around him, Mike got up from his seat and walked to the front of the airplane in search of McCaskill. He found him in the first row, deep in conversation with Alec Taylor.

"Sorry to interrupt, McCaskill. I need to make a call. The flight attendant told me you had the second phone from the cockpit. Can I use it?"

"Sure," McCaskill said and reached under his seat for his briefcase. After pulling out a large, portable phone, he unlocked it by punching in a code the first officer had given him. "Here you go. Use the bathroom in the rear, it's quieter and more private. Just plug this cord into the wall outlet and press "send" after you dial."

"Thanks," Mike said absently, his mind far away. He turned, started back down the plane's middle aisle, then suddenly stopped. Swinging around to face McCaskill again, he addressed the agent with a hopeful look on his face. "Let me ask you something. You thought Quentin would come after me tonight, but the game's over and there's been no sign of him. Could it be he's not involved, and Ben really is the killer?"

McCaskill could hear the optimism in Mike's voice. He knew he had to make him understand the truth without being insensitive. "I'm sorry, Mr. Redding. As much as I'd like to tell you that, I can't. Quentin is the killer. I was wrong about him coming after you at the game, but that doesn't change the facts. He's lied about a number of important things, he was minutes from David Butler's murder site at the approximate time the murder took place, he's lived a secret life for seventeen years that none of his closest friends knew about and now he's on the run from federal agents. I wish it hadn't turned out this way. I'm sorry."

Amidst the noise of music, laughter and spirited conversation, McCaskill's comments hit Mike like a hard slap in the face. On what should have been one of the happiest nights of his life, he was despondent. Racked by loneliness, disappointment and bitterness, Mike felt empty inside. At the most exciting time in his professional life when he was closer than ever to reaching his loftiest dream, he had no family or close friends to share his success with. UNI's amazing Great Eight victory, his personal accomplishment of coaching teams to three consecutive Final Four tournaments, the chance to become one of the youngest coaches in history to win the national championship, were hollow, unsatisfying achievements because his best friend and confidante was living a lie.

Mike wanted to talk to Diana and then go to bed for a day or two. The only person that didn't hurt him or cause him pain, Diana Fleming had become the one thing in his life with meaning, a refuge of understanding and compassion that shielded him from the cold, deceptive, unforgiving world. With Kentucky behind them, Mike knew UNI would win the national championship, but he had grown tired wondering whether he would be alive or dead for the title game. He was exhausted from the ordeal, more so mentally and emotionally than physically.

Looking down at his watch, he was surprised at how late it was. "Why are we going to Indianapolis?" he asked.

"It's safer than Lafayette," replied McCaskill. "We're flying into Indiana Beechcraft instead of the main airport because it's smaller, more restricted and we can control the public and keep them contained. We have security personnel stationed all over Beechcraft. It's just a precautionary measure. Everything's gone well tonight, and I don't want to take a chance now. We'll take you off the plane first so you can get out of there quickly. After you've left the airfield, we'll get your team and coaches off the plane. You'll be escorted home by state troopers as will the bus carrying your players and coaching staff."

"Whatever you say," replied Mike.

"Mr. Redding, one more thing." Mike turned around wondering what else the agent wanted. There was nothing McCaskill had failed to do. "I didn't see the game, of course, but one of my men overheard the TV announcers saying your win was the greatest comeback in NCAA history. They're really praising the coaching job you did in the second half. Congratulations. I'm not a basketball junkie, but I have tremendous respect for anyone who's that good at what they do. Obviously you're the best at what you do. I think you deserve it more than anyone—the championship, that is."

Mike didn't know what to say. For what seemed like an eternity but was actually only a second or two, he stood in the center aisle of the plane staring awkwardly at McCaskill. He was slightly embarrassed by the heart-felt compliment, yet was surprised at how proud he felt. He couldn't believe the pride and satisfaction that swelled in his chest. It felt great to once again receive uplifting and fulfilling emotions from coaching.

"Thanks, McCaskill. That means a lot coming from you." Turning away, Mike walked down the aisle to the bathroom in the rear of the aircraft. For the first time since he found out about Quentin's dark secret, he felt good about something other than Diana. After knocking on the door to make sure no one was using it, he entered the bathroom anxious to speak to Diana, his disposition and mood not great, but certainly not dejected or angry anymore. When he shut the bathroom door behind him, Mike failed to notice the person sitting in the corner seat of the flight attendant's compartment. The obscure stranger, hidden from view by the shadows cast from the luggage rack, did not take part in UNI's festive celebration, but definitely noticed Mike Redding.

Quentin lay flat on his stomach in damp grass. The long prickly blades tickled his anterior frame, but he paid no attention to the distraction. The field was pitch black and eerily quiet. Since his motionless body was covered in dark clothing and his face with paint, he easily blended into the backdrop of an expansive, black sky. More than a hundred and fifty yards in front of him, Indiana

Beechcraft's two narrow runways came together, forming a broad tarmac where incoming planes taxied before unloading passengers. Quentin hit the display button on his watch and the digital time glowed in the dark; 1:22 AM. The plane would land in ten to fifteen minutes.

From his present vantage point, Quentin would have a clear, unobstructed line of fire when Mike stepped off the plane. He was approximately 210 yards east of the tarmac so he would be aiming at the left side of Mike's body. He hadn't decided whether to hit him in the neck or the head. His target would be wearing a bullet-proof vest so he had to be hit above the chest area. At the distance he was firing from, Mike would scarcely be bruised if a bullet struck the vest. *I need to hit him in the throat or neck,* Quentin thought, his mind shifting to James Brady's survival of a bullet to the head that was intended for Ronald Reagan.

Quentin's attention returned to the airstrip in front of him when he saw three ground technicians walking across the concrete tarmac. Picking up the butt of his rifle and balancing it on both his shoulder and the six-inch tripod mounted on the thin layer of grass, he studied the technicians through the high-powered scope. He didn't recognize any of the groundsmen and none of them moved with the familiar, business-like gait of a federal agent. They appeared to be what they looked like, Indiana Beechcraft employees. Almost two football fields away, the technicians stood no chance of notic-ing Quentin. Lying prone on the ground in the immense field, dressed entirely in black, his lithe, dark figure was engulfed by the monolithic sea of darkness behind him.

After Derrick Jensen had dropped him off at a car rental agency across the street from Indianapolis's International Airport, Quentin had switched disguises and stashed a rental car in a tree-lined ditch half a mile from the rental office. While Quentin jogged the remaining fourth of a mile to Indiana Beechcraft's airfield, Jensen drove to Beechcraft's public parking lot which was directly west of the runway and tarmac. Once there, he would wait in his Blazer for UNI's plane to land. When Jensen saw Mike Redding and his en-tourage exiting the plane, he was to fire three or four rifle shots high into the air away from the airfield and then drive as fast as possible out of the parking lot.

Had Jensen known Quentin's simultaneous shot wouldn't be fired into the air, rather it would be targeted at Mike's neck, the actor would not have agreed to the plan. Earlier in the evening while they were going over the plan, he had asked why they were firing shots into the air with scores of fans, FBI agents and state police present. Quentin had answered that Mike Redding was in danger of being killed by their old acquaintance Ben Rooks. His intention was to open his friend's eyes to the predicament he was in. He explained that the FBI couldn't protect him and Mike sufficiently. Getting close to Mike and firing a few harmless shots into the air would prove that the FBI's protection was woefully inadequate.

Quentin had reassured Jensen he would cover the actor's legal expenses if he was caught and arrested for firing the shots. When he feigned breaking down into tears and confessed Mike was so stubborn and bull-headed he wouldn't listen to anyone, Jensen became convinced exploiting the FBI's poor protection was the only way the coach would listen to his best friend. Jensen found himself wanting to help Mike Redding. He also found himself more terrified than ever of Quentin Conway. It made him feel important that Redding and Conway needed him. Like the rest of the country, he had followed the March Madness Murders story when it first broke. Now, the central players in the drama needed his help. To Derrick Jensen, this feeling of power was more intoxicating than the rush from cocaine or heroin.

In the end, the excessive, day-long drug binge and the story about a mock attack were only contributing factors in Jensen's decision to take part in the plan. The truth was he was afraid of Quentin Conway and wanted to believe his story. Just like the friends, colleagues and associates that surrounded Conway, Jensen was hypnotized and intimidated by the chameleon's charisma, confidence and aura. Quentin had made it easy for the actor to accept the tale. The drugs and money, the appeal of having a celebrity seek his help—Jensen couldn't say no. He didn't want to say no. Ultimately, he was too frightened to say no. As he had thousands of times before with people in all stations of life, Quentin Conway had figured out what Jensen wanted most. Then he made it impossible to say no. It was that simple. He was the master of a game in which anyone could be made to do what he wanted. And what he wanted most was for Mike Redding to stop living.

As he lay under the stars and calculated the effect the wind would have on the angle of the shot, Quentin visualized his friend stepping out of the plane and walking down the portable stairway surrounded by ten agents. He hoped McCaskill was one of them. More specifically, he hoped the special agent was beside the target, so the bullet could pass through Mike and hit the agent on the other side. Killing McCaskill was not Quentin's objective; nevertheless, it would give him special gratification to end his honorable, pathetic existence.

"Lucky for Byron and his buddies Mike is tall," Quentin said softly, a wry smile creeping from the corners of his mouth. "If Red were three inches shorter, I would've had to blow up the whole fucking plane."

After trying the Marriot's switchboard twice with no luck, Mike finally got an operator on the line. Now that he was speaking to a human voice and not a recording, it was hard for him to hear because of the boisterous party goers in the background. A tiny smile escaped from his lips when he heard the chant "UNI-three in a row, way to go!" being sung in the lobby. After nearly sixty seconds went by with Mike now feeling as if he'd lose his mind if he had to wait any longer, he was connected to room 724.

"Hello," Diana said hoping the call was from Mike.

"Diana. It's me, hon."

"Mike, it's so good to hear your voice. God, I'm thrilled for you and your team. The game was incredible, the best I've ever seen. You were incredible. Congratulations."

"Thanks, darling. Nice to hear your voice, too. I wish I could see the gorgeous face that goes with it. Listen, I can't talk long. I'm still on the plane. We'll be landing in Indy soon. I couldn't wait until later to talk to you though."

"What is it? Is everything okay?"

"Yeah, everything's fine. It's about tonight. After the game I was really happy for my players and relieved for my assistants, but I wasn't pleased or satisfied myself. I've never felt that way after a win, especially a big tournament win. At first I thought it was the whole ordeal with Quentin trying to kill me. I had this numb, empty feeling inside that wouldn't go away. It was like something huge was missing, something so important I couldn't enjoy the biggest win of my life. Coming home on the plane I realized it wasn't Quentin making me feel like this—it's you."

Diana felt the air going out of her. What did he mean it was her? Before her mind could conjure up any traumatic thoughts, Mike continued speaking.

"I was wrong to try to wait until after the tournament to be with you. I felt so lonely and unfulfilled after the game because you weren't with me. I didn't have you by my side to share my success and that's what caused the emptiness. You were what's missing. Before the game when I thought I might not make it, the person I couldn't get out of my mind wasn't Quentin. It was you. When I was risking my life coaching, I wasn't thinking about his betrayal, I was thinking about not ever getting the chance to be with you. I don't want to wait until the Final Four ends to be with you, Diana. I want to see you tomorrow and the day after, and the day after that. What I'm trying to say is that I've fallen in love with you."

"Oh, thank God you said it," Diana whispered. "I've wanted to hear that so badly. I feel the same—I love you too."

"Damn it, Diana, I hate this. I hate that we're apart and I have to do this over the phone, but I can't wait. I've missed out on too much already. I know what I need and it's you. Your strength and purity and beauty humble me. I want to take care of you, be your best friend and make sure nothing bad ever happens to you. I want to make you happy, Diana. After the tournament is too long.

My feelings for you will not change, they'll only grow stronger. No matter what happens, I'll love and adore you. I want to walk through life with you and I want it to start now . . .."

Neither the noisy partying on the plane nor the rough landing on the narrow runway distracted Mike Redding. He was preoccupied with thoughts of the woman he hoped to spend the rest of his life with. Even though their relationship had developed quickly under extremely intense circumstances, he knew he had done the right thing by opening up to her. He had never felt so calm and relaxed. Strangely enough, the conversation with Diana had done the opposite of what he expected. Mike always imagined the moment he found his soul mate would be the most exciting, exhilarating experience of his life. Instead, a sense of security and comfort had come over him. He felt as if all the doubt and uncertainty he had been saddled with was suddenly gone. Even Quentin's colossal deception had become a less bitter pill to swallow. The potent pain and anger caused by the monumental betrayal had lost much of its sting. It was a magical event, a man at the brink of despair, brought back from the edge by the love and support of a woman.

Worn out by the evening's excitement and drama, the light slumber Mike had fallen into prevented him from hearing the sound of McCaskill's voice on the intercom as the aircraft taxied down the tarmac.

"Please remain in your seats. When we are finished taxiing, you can gather your carry-on luggage. You'll exit the plane in about ten minutes. Thank you."

As the players, coaches and team managers put away their magazines, walkmans and other valuables in preparation for departing the plane, dark-suited agents carrying walkie-talkies and handguns moved hurriedly up and down the center aisle and sealed off the front and rear hatches. At the front of the aircraft, McCaskill, Taylor and ten of the Bureau's top agents formed a two-deep circle around Mike and waited in silence. Thirty seconds later the hydraulic lock on the massive front hatch popped open as the portable walkway was wheeled up to the belly of the plane.

When Quentin saw the ground technicians and FBI agents begin rolling the portable walkway across the tarmac, he positioned the rifle in the tripod, located the proper angle in the scope and gingerly wrapped his finger around the trigger. Focusing on the step at the top of the stairway, he followed it in the scope as it made the slow trek toward the aircraft. Gauging the distance between himself and the plane at 200-225 yards, roughly 625 feet, Quentin's computer-quick mind recalculated the speed and direction of the wind currents. With steely cold precision he slightly shifted his center of gravity upward, which lowered the angle of the rifle's barrel a sixteenth of an inch. The minute shift threw nothing else off—the top stair of the walkway was still dead center in his scope. Now that he had assumed shooting position, Quentin was locked into the stance. He would not move again. The next time he did, it would be his palm and trigger finger.

Settled in place, his mind relaxed and devoid of all thoughts, he became aware of the incredible noise the assembled UNI fans were making in the parking lot west of the runway. Unbeknownst to Quentin, who had been deep in concentration, they had been chanting for more than fifteen minutes. When the plane had landed and taxied near the chain link fence that held them back, the fans exploded with excitement. Like Quentin, over six hundred of UNI's faithful had correctly guessed that their team would fly into Indiana Beechcraft.

As the groundsmen approached the aircraft with the portable stairway, the crowd cut loose with still louder cheers. Hysteria reigned in the parking area. It appeared as if Mardi Gras had come to Indianapolis and Fat Tuesday had been moved to the last Saturday in March. The fans knew they were witnessing history in the making. Not only had UNI earned a berth in a third straight Final Four, Mike Redding had survived an assassination attempt and coached the greatest comeback in NCAA tournament history. The game, the team, the coach and especially the circumstances surrounding the tournament would never be forgotten by college basketball fans. The crowd understood what had happened that evening, and they let Mike Redding know they appreciated him. Their cheers reflected not just their happiness that he had engineered the unbelievable comeback, but that he was alive and well.

The instant the plane door began to lift upward, the congregation of UNI fans erupted in a tumultuous roar. Seconds later two agents leaned out the hatch and fastened two hooks from the top of the stairway's platform to the side of the jet. The circle in the middle of Quentin's scope had not moved from the stairway's top step for more than four minutes. When the entourage of FBI personnel stepped onto the platform, Quentin knew it was the real thing. As the twelve agents rushed down the steep stairway, he began rhythmically counting backwards from ten. He had studied the number of steps on the walkway as it was rolled across the tarmac and had calculated when he would get the best shot.

Upon seeing the UNI cap bobbing up and down in the middle of the FBI's human shield, the crowd outside the fence went nuts. They clapped, yelled and whistled, showering their beloved coach with unbridled adulation. Oblivious to everything except for the numbers in his head, Quentin reached five and ever-so-gently tightened his grip on the AK-47's trigger. He had estimated the shot would come at either three or two, when Redding was at the bottom of the stairway. As usual, Quentin was right. The hulking agents leading the entourage hit the last step as Quentin whispered the number three. Before he said two, he squeezed the trigger softly, his eyes never leaving the head in the middle of the procession.

The moment the lead agents jumped from the bottom step down to the tarmac, Quentin could see his friend's upper torso and head were clearly exposed. Watching through the scope, he saw the bullet enter the left side of Redding's neck with such great force it ripped a golf-ball size hole below his ear. At the point of impact, the bullet exploded outward. The right side of his throat was blown wide open by the velocity of the projectile, while debris of wet flesh and blood splattered all over the agents behind him. Alec Taylor reared back in astonishment and pain when he was simultaneously struck in the left triceps by the ricocheting bullet, and cartilage and muscle from the disintegrated windpipe and larynx soaked the side of his face. In cruel irony, Mike Redding's favorite UNI cap remained securely attached to the pitiful cerebral remains as the limp body slumped to the ground. In a matter of seconds the black cap had turned murky red.

Springing to his feet, Quentin ran at a dead sprint across the dark field toward the hole he had cut in the airfield's chain link fence. Not more than a second or two after he had fired his lone shot, a battery of rifle shots rang out from the parking lot on the other side of the tarmac. Quentin couldn't help but smile while he ran through the darkness. Jensen had come through after all. By firing the shots into the air, he had provided Quentin the necessary diversion that would enable him to escape. As he bolted for the hole in the security fence Quentin heard his other distraction, the petrified crowd of UNI fans, screaming in terror in the parking area. His plan was working to perfection, better than he had anticipated.

The first bullet tore into his leg and lodged in his hamstring. It nearly knocked him off his feet. He had never been shot before and it felt nothing like he imagined. Falling to one knee in the grass, Quentin used his hand to balance himself. As he struggled to right himself and make a final dash for the fence, a second bullet punctured his kneecap, shattering the bone and socket and all the ligaments, tendons and cartilage which held the knee together. Unable to walk and writhing in pain, Quentin dragged himself face down through the grass. The hole in the security fence was eight feet away.

Moments later two agents disguised as ground technicians reached him as he floundered in pain on the ground. Coming up behind him, the agents ordered Quentin to put his hands over his head and lie motionless on the ground. When he ignored the command, one of the agents stepped solidly on Quentin's back, aimed his gun at his head and held him down while the other agent pulled his arms behind his back and snapped handcuffs on his wrists. Not until the agents had turned him over onto his back and begun reading his Miranda rights did they discover the gaping slash across his throat.

While the agents searched the grassy field for the razor blade Quentin had used to kill himself, Frank McCaskill radioed the approaching EMS units from the tarmac and informed them no emergency care was needed. The stiff, lifeless body of a heroic man lay at his feet. The white sheet that covered the corpse was stained blood red. By the time the ambulances reached the airstrip, McCaskill had stopped crying and was in enough control of his emotions to remove the soggy UNI cap and diamond-studded Final Four watch.

Chapter Twenty-four

7:28 AM
Quantico, Virginia
March 26, 1995

Frank McCaskill walked slowly down the long, dark corridor. He was both emotionally and physically drained. In less than an hour the most grueling case of his career would be over, as would his career in law enforcement. Earlier that morning Deputy Director L.C. Bailey had tried unsuccessfully to persuade him to stay on at the Bureau, if not full-time, then as a consultant in an advisory capacity. McCaskill had graciously rejected his old friend's proposal. He was tired of fighting crime. He no longer wanted any part of it. The Clancy-Butler murder investigation had changed his view of people and human nature so much, Quentin Conway had put such a vile, repugnant taste in his mouth, that McCaskill couldn't stomach the law enforcement process any more. He needed to be as far away from the Bureau and organized crime as possible. McCaskill didn't want a lot—just to spend time with his wife, play some golf and fish, and visit his grandchildren.

At the end of the long corridor, he took a right turn and walked down another empty hallway. It was Sunday morning, most of the Bureau's agents were either training at the outdoor facility, or weren't working at all. Halfway down the hall, McCaskill stopped in front of a large, stainless steel door. After punching in his personal code and swiping his card key through the number pad, the steel door swung open and he walked into the large conference room. Four people were seated around a long, rectangular table while a stenographer sat in the corner of the room. McCaskill hardly noticed Director Warren Jacobs or Deputy Director L.C. Bailey sitting at the table. Glancing past his two superiors, his focus rested on the sleep-deprived eyes of Diana Fleming and Mike Redding.

"I thought you'd never get here, McCaskill. Mr. Bailey said we couldn't start until you arrived. Will you please tell me what the hell happened last night?" Mike demanded.

"Before I tell you, I want to remind you both that you've signed affidavits swearing the information you hear today will never be repeated. If anything leaves this room, you both will be subject to the most severe penalties the FBI can enforce, and will be prosecuted for divulging confidential information in a federal capital murder investigation. Do you understand? Nothing leaves this room."

"Damn it, McCaskill, we already signed the affidavit," Mike retorted, nearly rising out of his seat. When Diana reached her hand out and placed it on Mike's arm, he calmed down, leaned back in his chair and tried to relax. "We're not gonna blab anything to the press. I hate those bastards—you know that. I just want to know what happened last night and how this whole mess got started."

"I'll begin with last night and then go through everything. We drugged you on the plane before we touched down. We put a sedative in your drink. I did it because I didn't think you'd go along with our plan."

"What plan was that?" Mike asked, already angry by what he was told.

"The plan to use Ben Rooks as your decoy. Unbeknownst to you and your team, he was on the plane. After you passed out, he took your place. While exiting the plane, he was shot and killed by Quentin. Ben Rooks came up with the idea of using a decoy two days ago, and he volunteered to do it himself. At first I wouldn't consider the idea, but eventually I gave in. I thought you'd fight the idea and we were running out of options. I knew Quentin was going to make an attempt last night. When he didn't try at the game, we went to our third plan which was use a decoy to catch him during the assassination attempt. We could have used an agent or policeman as the decoy, but Rooks convinced us to use him. We hoped and believed if shots were fired, they'd go astray. But we knew the risk was high."

"I don't know which is harder to believe," Mike said looking over at Diana. "Ben gave up his life for me or Quentin was trying to take it. You're right, McCaskill. I would've never agreed to the plan. Ben went through enough. He shouldn't have had to sacrifice his life. One of your men should have done it. Why the hell 'd you listen to him?"

"If you could please be patient, Mr. Redding, I'll get to it in a minute. I'd like to explain everything from the beginning. I think you'll have an easier time following what happened and why it happened," McCaskill said. *Starting from the beginning might make it easier to understand, but it won't make it easier to accept,* he thought.

After sitting quietly next to Mike without saying anything, Diana finally spoke. "Mr. McCaskill, I'm sure you realize how hard this is for Mike. Whatever you think is the best way to go through this is fine. All I ask is that you remember how difficult this is for him."

"I will, Ms. Fleming," McCaskill said and he meant it. "Quentin was a drug baron. A big-time drug lord. He made his fortune selling drugs. While he was amassing this fortune, he maimed and killed a lot of people. When he was enrolled at Saint Thomas, he got involved with people from Chicago who manufactured and distributed heroin and cocaine. He used the dirty money he made in drugs to finance a number of legitimate businesses: medical equipment, real estate investments, health care agencies and so forth. He was a complete fraud; everything he owned came from drug money. His entire financial empire was built on it. He used the legitimate businesses to launder the money. Conway cleaned the money long enough and well enough and had so many legitimate investments, no one would've ever discovered the truth."

"Except Allan, right?" Mike said.

"No, not Allan Clancy," McCaskill replied. "Carmen Jalomo and Ben Rooks. They uncovered Quentin's secret."

"Who the hell is Carmen Jalomo?" Mike asked bewildered. "And how'd Ben figure it out?"

"Carmen Jalomo was a Washington, D.C., prostitute who told Congressman Clancy about Quentin's past. We're not positive how she knew about Quentin, but we do know two days after she and the congressman spent the night together, Clancy was murdered. Thirty-six hours after his death, she was murdered as well. We believe the connection is Chicago. She lived in Chicago back when Quentin started selling drugs in college. She must have met him while they were working the streets. Somehow she remembered him and told Clancy. Thirty-six hours after he tried to blackmail Quentin, Clancy was dead."

"God, this is all about money," Mike said in disbelief. In an attempt to fully grasp the information he had been told, Mike talked his way through the scenario. "Quentin lied, cheated and stole his whole life to get money—then Allan did the same thing. He was blackmailing Quentin, so Quentin killed him to keep his money and protect his secret. I can't believe they did all that for money. Wait a second, why did Quentin kill David? What'd he have to do with the blackmailing?"

"Nothing. He was in the wrong place at the right time. Quentin was trying to kill you. Butler was running where you usually jogged. Quentin believed he was killing you, but hit Butler instead. I'm sorry."

"That's what I don't understand," Mike said exasperated. "Why was Quentin trying to kill me?"

"There were two reasons. He knew Congressman Clancy called you the day before he died. He didn't know what Clancy told you or how much you knew, and he didn't want to take a chance. He was willing to do whatever was necessary to protect his fortune. That's the reason for attempting the hit and run. The second reason was equally pressing. When Congressman Clancy blackmailed Quentin, he protected himself and made Quentin aware of it. He left sealed documents outlining Quentin's illegal activities and named him as his murderer should something happen. Clancy left the documents in a private letter attached to his will, in two separate safety deposit boxes and among his personal belongings. He warned Quentin that if anything happened to him, everything he owned—his belongings, his valuables, the safety deposit boxes— all would go to you.

"By making you sole executor and leaving everything he owned to you, Clancy protected himself against retribution from Quentin. But in the process, he involved you. That's why Quentin wanted you dead. If you were alive, you'd find out about his past and know he was responsible for Clancy's death. Allan Clancy was smart enough to anticipate Quentin might kill him, but he never imagined he'd kill *all* his friends to protect the secret. If Clancy would have known how dirty Quentin really was, he probably would have protected himself differently. Quentin tried to kill you during the tournament because he didn't have a lot of time. He knew there was a thirty-day waiting period after Clancy's death before the will could be reviewed. The waiting period is up the following Tuesday, so Quentin had to prevent you from opening the will and finding the documents that incriminated him."

"So many little things he said and did make sense now," Mike said, holding Diana's hand in his. "The questions about my last conversation with Allan, wanting to know if I'd gone through the boxes Allan left for me, sneaking off to Nashville while he faked the attempt on his life. At the time I thought he was encouraging me to continue coaching because he believed it was the right thing to do. Now, I see it was to keep me going to the games so I'd be an easier target. Oh, shit. He asked me to go on vacation with him after the tourney. He would have killed me and made it look like an accident. I can't believe he could act so loyal to my face, but behind my back be trying to kill me.

"Many times I wondered why he wasn't more frightened about being stalked. For Christ's sake, we were being hunted by a deranged killer, and he was barely worried. I should have seen it. He was my best friend. I talked to him every day. I guess I just wanted to believe that since he was Quentin, he didn't get scared. The whole time he was supporting and comforting me, he was really fattening me for the kill."

Worried that Mike blamed himself for not seeing through Quentin's deceptive ways, Diana rubbed his arm and shoulder and said what everyone in the room knew was the truth. "Mike, you couldn't have known. Nobody knew. Not you, Allan, David, myself or the entire FBI. It's not your fault Quentin hurt so many people. He was a pro at exploiting people's weaknesses. Please believe me when I say there's no way you could have known what he was really like. He tricked half the country. Everyone loved him because he gave people what they wanted. You shouldn't feel embarrassed because you didn't see him for what he was."

"I'll try not to," Mike said, feeling exactly that way. "I've got a question, McCaskill. What's going to happen to Quentin's friends in Washington when it comes out his money was dirty. He donated a ton of money to political campaigns the last ten years. Won't that be damaging to a lot of people?"

"Yes, it would, but it's not going to happen," McCaskill replied. "In the early 80s Quentin received a lot of help bringing drugs into this country. Some very powerful people made a lot of money with Quentin. DEA agents and Coast Guard deputies died trying to thwart these shipments. Since the assistance came from high places within certain key government agencies, only a partial account of this investigation will be made public. As we speak, agents are going through Quentin's records at his office and in his home. We've found secret files on senators, businessmen and pro athletes. Apparently, Quentin had a personal investigator who gathered information on everyone around him. He used the information to blackmail people, gain leverage on adversaries, or just manipulate situations. I'm told a great deal of the information in these files is of a highly sensitive and controversial nature. That's why you signed affidavits. Quentin's dead and his secret is going to die with him. A written report of this investigation will be presented to a congressional ethics committee. That report will contain seventy percent of what you're hearing today. For the sake of many people—you, Congressman Clancy's family, the politicians who unknowingly accepted his blood money, and the countless people whose life stories are in those files, Quentin's history is going to remain just that—history."

McCaskill did not bother mentioning the phone call he and Director Jacobs received early that morning. He had seen executive power used broadly in his many years at the Bureau, but in no other instance could he recall the umbrella of national security being opened so broadly.

"Is that your decision or someone else's?" Mike queried.

"It was my decision, Mr. Redding," Warren Jacobs interjected. The Director had sat in stony silence until now. Diana got the impression from watching the Director's face he did not like divulging this much information. "Had Agent McCaskill gotten his way, the entire story would have been on the front page of this morning's *New York Times*. I agree with Frank. Unfortunately, my job is influenced by politics out of my control, so I have decided to close the can of worms Mr. Conway left us."

Mike knew the only politics that could influence the Director of the FBI had to come from above, which meant the White House. The ramifications of what might happen if Quentin's past was exposed made Mike shudder. What if some elite power brokers in Washington knowingly accepted dirty money or were intimately involved with Quentin? Suppose certain individuals in the White House had known about his illegal activities all along? The possibilities were too mind-boggling for Mike to consider. He wanted to put the whole ordeal behind him and go on with his life.

After Warren Jacobs finished speaking, there was a tense moment of silence. Everyone in the room knew they were privy to information that might possibly topple the current White House administration, bankrupt powerful international corporations and ruin the personal lives of some of America's most aristocratic families. If Warren Jacobs was overwhelmed by the information he possessed, he certainly didn't show it. The expression on his face had become so indifferent, it appeared he received information of this nature twice a day. Finally, McCaskill broke the uncomfortable silence.

"Do you have any questions, Mr. Redding?"

"Yeah. You told me two days ago that Quentin used a double to get away from your men. Was the double involved in the murders?"

"No. The double had nothing to do with the murders. Actually, there were two doubles. The first one was a former assistant of Quentin's. He used the man as a decoy when he killed Clancy and Butler. He was also going to use this man as an alibi for your murder. We've been interrogating the assistant since early this morning. So far we've found nothing to indicate he was involved in the murders and I don't think we will. The guy simply impersonated Quentin Conway and got paid well to do it. He didn't know what Conway was doing, didn't bother asking and probably didn't care."

"Who's the other guy?" Mike asked.

"An out-of-work actor with a major-league drug habit. Like the assistant, he bears a strong resemblance to Conway. He has a goatee similar to Quentin's. We think Quentin grew it to hide some facial differences between them. The assistant was already a dead-ringer. This actor, Derrick Jensen's his name, doubled for Conway five times in the past two weeks. We've got Jensen in custody and he's singing. We can't shut him up—he's scared to death. He was with Conway last night at the airport and fired a couple shots into the air. His story is that he was helping Quentin Conway show you how much danger you were in and didn't know Conway was trying to murder you. I believe him. He was just a decoy. Conway wouldn't have trusted him to do anything important. He used Jensen as a double to establish alibis so he could poison your dogs, kill the prostitute, plant the car bomb on his limo and run from us when we found out about him."

"It's pathetic to think how much trouble Quentin went to protecting his fortune: the decoys, sneaking around, planting bombs—all that for money and power," Mike said.

"And pride," McCaskill added. "He couldn't stand to lose. His ego proved to be his fatal flaw. It got him in trouble sixteen years ago with Ben Rooks and it got him in trouble last night."

"How does Ben figure into all this? I don't understand how he went from being your number one suspect to devising the plan to catch Quentin and dying for me."

"You might have a hard time believing this," replied McCaskill. "He solved the investigation."

"Come again?" Mike said in astonishment.

"Ben Rooks is the reason you're sitting here today. He saved your life twice. You already know he traded his life for yours last night, but what you don't know is he's the person that figured out Quentin Conway was the March Madness Murderer. Without his help, we would never have been able to solve the investigation."

"How'd he do it?" Mike asked.

"You know about his arrest in 1979 in the drug house in Chicago. The building Rooks was arrested in was owned by Conway. When he saw Rooks in the house, he toyed with him awhile then called the police and had the place busted. His friends on the force made sure Rooks got the special treatment, and he ended up doing seven years hard time. Due to the combination of a heroin addiction and the beatings and rapes that occurred in prison, Rooks forgot the whole experience.

"From the day of his arrest in the drug house until the end of his prison term, everything traumatic and painful was blacked out. It's called Post Traumatic Stress Disorder. The arrest triggered the blackout, apparently because his psyche couldn't deal with the horrors he experienced in jail. As a defense mechanism, he repressed that part of his life from his memory. A few nights ago the involuntary repressions ended and he remembered being arrested. Ben Rooks didn't have multiple personalities or schizophrenia. He just suffered from a severe inferiority complex which led to his drug problem. It's a shame. He was a good guy with a lot of problems. The only thing he was guilty of was being a bit weird."

"What made him stop blocking out the memory of the arrest?" Mike asked.

"Clancy's and Butler's deaths. He had followed your careers religiously. He was proud of your successes and considered himself a failure. When Clancy and Butler were killed, he began to have nightmares while he slept. After a few nights, he realized the dreams weren't nightmares, but painful flashbacks from earlier in his life. In Rooks' own words, his 'gut told him' the flashbacks were connected to Clancy's and Butler's deaths, so he wrote the letters to warn you and Quentin. He wanted to tell you to be careful, but he was embarrassed at how his life had turned out, so he kept his identity hidden. Personally, I think deep down he wanted you to know it was him and that's why he signed the letters with his high school nickname. He had become a hermit and changed his name long before any of this happened, five years to be exact, so none of his old friends would be able to find him.

"Late Thursday night he contacted me. The entire flashback had come to him the night before. He remembered Conway had been in the drug house the day of his arrest, so he did a ton of research and called me. After receiving Rooks' phone call, I dug deeper into Conway's past and found Ben Rooks' claims were accurate. Not only did Rooks solve the case, he told me Conway would try to kill you Saturday night. He was right about everything."

"How'd Ben know last night would be the night?" Diana asked.

"Conway's ego. Rooks told me that was the one thing that always tripped him up—even back in his childhood. Last night's game was the biggest of the year. Conway wanted to steal the show. Plus, it was an ideal time all things considered."

"Why did you let Ben take my place last night," Mike said, frustration written all over his face. "You knew Quentin would try something."

"That's why I let him do it. Ben Rooks wanted to be reunited with you one way or the other. If he survived he would have accomplished his goal. If he died it would be for you and he could accept that."

"Still, how could the FBI put an innocent person at risk?

Aren't there rules or laws preventing you from endangering civilians?" Mike countered.

L.C. Bailey quickly entered the discussion, coming to McCaskill's defense. "We're the FBI, Mr. Redding. We can do whatever we want. In this situation, unconventional law enforcement procedures were justified. Quentin Conway wasn't an ordinary suspect and his methods were far from ordinary, so we had to be unorthodox ourselves."

"I understand you had to use unorthodox tactics to stop Quentin, but Ben's death just seems so unnecessary," Mike said stubbornly.

"Please believe me when I say this," McCaskill said in a solemn voice. "Mr. Rooks truly wanted to face death so you could live. He begged and pleaded with me. He told me the decoy was his idea and that he had figured out Conway was the killer—so he should be the double. He was adamant about doing it. In the end, I realized he didn't have a lot to live for. He didn't want someone with a family to die. We have agents without families, but Rooks argued he had nothing to lose and everything to gain. As much as it was done for you, Mr. Redding, he did it more for himself. It healed a lot of scars from his past. He was happy to do it. I think it restored his self-respect and pride. He died a satisfied man at peace with himself. His selfless act saved three lives—yours, an agent who would have died, and his own."

Without notice Director Warren Jacobs rose from his seat and extended his hand toward Mike. "Mr. Redding, I'm sorry we didn't meet under more pleasant circumstances. Nevertheless, it's been an honor and a pleasure."

"Thank you, Mr. Jacobs."

After shaking hands with Diana Fleming, Warren Jacobs and L.C. Bailey turned and walked out of the conference room leaving Mike and Diana alone with McCaskill. Not knowing exactly what to say to the agent, Mike tried to express himself as best he could.

"I'm not quite sure how to thank you, McCaskill. If it wasn't for you I might not be—"

The agent cut him off in midsentence. "That's not necessary. I was just doing my job. There is one final detail before you leave. Ben Rooks left this for you. Take all the time you need. When you're done in here, I'll see you out." Reaching into his breast pocket, McCaskill pulled out a white envelope and slid it across the table. After shaking hands with Mike and Diana, he turned and exited the room. With Diana peering over his shoulder, Mike opened the envelope and removed the letter. The note was written in handwriting he hadn't seen in seventeen years.

> Mike,
> By the time you read this Quentin will be in jail
> and I may be dead.
> If so, that's how it should be. I've
> followed your career since college. I'm very proud of you.
> I haven't done well for myself, but in the
> end, I feel good knowing I did something worthwhile.
> We were a special group in high school. I know that's
> changed, but you haven't. You're the only
> one in the group that stayed true to yourself. Thanks for
> always treating me as an equal. You're all that's
> left of the group now. Keep the memories alive. Take
> care of yourself, Mike, and congratulations on your
> soon-to-be-won national championship.
> Forever your friend and Shadow,
>> Ben

Taped to the bottom of the letter was a picture of five teenage boys standing on a dock overlooking a lake. The picture was old and greatly worn, but it nearly glowed from the spirit and camaraderie radiating from the boys' faces. The five friends stood bunched in a group. It was a casual picture, three of the boys wore ridiculous expressions on their faces, while a fourth held his fingers over another's head in the shape of rabbit ears. In the middle of the circle, where he usually never was, but deserved to be more than any of his friends, Ben Rooks wore the group's lone smile.

Mike brushed a final tear from his cheek as he and Diana stepped out the front door of the FBI's offices. It was a beautiful, sunny March day; signs of spring were all around them.

"You know that vacation I've been promising? How about taking one this week and another one after the Final Four?" Mike asked as he slipped his arm around Diana's slender hips.

"That'd be great honey, but you have to prepare for Saturday's game. Where would we go?"

Mike was ready with his answer. "How about Monticello, Indiana for three or four days. My grandparents have a wonderful home on a lake. It's only thirty minutes from campus so I wouldn't miss any practices. It's the perfect place for deep wounds to heal and for people to fall deeper in love. I can prepare for the Final Four, you can plan our vacation to Tahiti and both of us can start figuring out ways to spend the money."

"What money?" Diana asked, surprised by Mike's remark.

"The money from Quentin."

"What are you talking about, Mike? What money did Quentin give you?"

"He didn't give it to me, he left it for me in his will."

Diana was shocked. She couldn't believe Quentin had left Mike money when he was trying to kill him. "Quentin left you money. That doesn't make sense. Why would he do that?"

"Well, he didn't exactly do it. Yesterday morning I called his attorney and disguising my voice, I pretended to be Quentin. I told the attorney I was on the run, confessed that I was the killer and asked for his help. I knew Quentin kept different wills in his private safe. Years ago when we were shit-faced drunk he confided to me that he had four or five confidential wills, any of which could be used as an original, if need be. No one other than his attorney knew about the separate wills. I never understood why he had so many drawn up, but when I learned the truth about him and his past, it made sense. Gambling that one of the wills left me a lot, I told the attorney that I was going to kill Mike Redding and that I needed to cast suspicion away from me. I instructed him to save the will that left Mike Redding the most and burn the other ones, so there wouldn't be any incriminating evidence."

"I can't believe you did that, Mike. That's not you at all. What if someone contests it?"

"Who'll challenge me after what I've been through? Besides, everyone with a claim to the money is dead and I covered my tracks perfectly. I guess I'm a bit different after what I've been through," Mike said unashamedly. "My survival instincts are at an all time high. Plus, I've got more than myself to take care of now. Hopefully I'll have many college trust funds to set up soon. And I plan on establishing scholarships and charitable trusts in David, Allan and Ben's names for inner-city kids and for students interested in going to college. I want to help families, like Byron's, get by a little easier. Through scholarships, clinics, and camps, I hope to teach less fortunate kids how to read and write and play basketball."

"What does it all mean?" Diana asked, suddenly finding it hard to breath.

"It means I guessed right. The separate wills were drawn up so Quentin could change his will for emergency purposes. His attorney bought it all—hook, line and sinker. He called this morning to tell me about Quentin's will. In it, Quentin named me the executor of his estate as well as primary beneficiary."

"Primary beneficiary? What does that mean?" Diana demanded, her head starting to spin with anxious thoughts of having six or seven of Mike's children.

"I'm not the chameleon Quentin was, but disguising my voice was one of my stronger abilities. Primary beneficiary means you'd better start planning your new spring and summer lines of clothing. After Uncle Sam fleeces me with inheritance and income taxes, the phone call was worth at least 450 million dollars."